PENGUIN BOOKS

P9-CZV-568

THE MAGICIAN'S LAND

LEV GROSSMAN is the book critic for *Time* magazine and the author of five novels, including the international bestseller *Codex* and the #1 *New York Times* bestselling Magicians trilogy. He lives in Brooklyn with his wife and three children.

**A #1 *New York Times* Bestseller and
A *New York Times* Notable Book of the Year**

Named one of the Best Books of the Year by:
The San Francisco Chronicle • *Salon* • *The Christian Science
Monitor* • *AV Club* • *BuzzFeed* • *Kirkus Reviews* • *NY1* •
Bustle • *The Globe and Mail*

Praise for *The Magician's Land*

"Richly imagined and continually surprising . . . The strongest book in Grossman's series. It not only offers a satisfying conclusion to Quentin Coldwater's quests, earthly and otherwise, but also considers complex questions about identity and selfhood as profound as they are entertaining. . . . *The Magician's Land*, more than any other book in the trilogy, wrestles with the question of humanity. . . . This is a gifted writer, and his gifts are at their apex in *The Magician's Land*."
—Edan Lepucki, *The New York Times Book Review*

"The strength of the trilogy lies . . . in the characters, whose inner lives and frailties Grossman renders with care and empathy. . . . Quentin['s] . . . magical journey is deeply human."
—*The New Yorker*

"[A] wonderful trilogy . . . If the Narnia books were like catnip for a certain kind of kid, these books are like crack for a certain kind of adult. . . . Brakebills graduates can have a hard time adjusting to life outside, though some distract themselves by lazily meddling in world affairs (e.g., the election of 2000). Readers of Mr. Grossman's mesmerizing trilogy might experience the same kind of withdrawal upon finishing *The Magician's Land*. Short of wishing that a fourth book could suddenly appear by magic, there's not much we can do about it."
—Sarah Lyall, *The New York Times*

"Grossman makes it clear in the deepening complexity and widening scope of each volume that he understands the pleasures and perils of stories and believing in them. . . . *The Magician's Land* triumphantly answers the essential questions at the heart of the series, about whether magic belongs to childhood alone, whether reality trumps fantasy, even whether we have the power to shape our own lives in an indifferent universe."
—Gwenda Bond, *Los Angeles Times*

"A wholly satisfying and stirring conclusion to this weird and wonderful tale. . . . Relentlessly subversive and inventive . . . Grossman can . . . write like a magician. . . . [He] reminds us that good writing can beguile the senses, imagination, and intellect. The door at the back of the book is still there, and we can go back to those magical lands, older and wiser, eager for the re-enchantment."

—Keith Donohue, *The Washington Post*

"A huge part of the pleasure of this trilogy in general and this volume in particular is that, even as we consume the story just to find out what happens to Quentin, we know that we are collaborating in our own versions of its creation, its animation. The reader gets to be a magician, too."   —Nancy Klingener, *The Miami Herald*

"[A] stirring finale to Grossman's acclaimed trilogy."   —*People*

"*The Magician's Land* . . . does all the things you want in a third book: winding up everyone's stories, tying up the loose ends—and giving you a bit more than you bargained for. . . . Starting very early in *Magician's Land*, Grossman kicks off a series of escalating magical battles, each more fantastic, taut, and brutal than the last, which comes to a head in the final chapters with a world-shattering Götterdämmerung scene that stands with great war at the climax of *The Return of the King*. At the same time, Grossman never loses sight of the idea of magic as unknowable and unsystematized, a thread of Borgesian Big Weird that culminates in a beautiful tribute to Borges himself. It's this welding together of adventure-fiction plotstuff and introspective, moody characterization that makes this book, and the trilogy it concludes, so worthy of your reading time, and your rereading time."   —Cory Doctorow, *Boing Boing*

"The world of Grossman's Magicians series is arrestingly original, joyful, and messy. It's so vividly rendered that it's almost disappointing to remember that it doesn't, after all, exist. The overall effect is—well, there's really only one word for it: It's magical."   —*Chicago Tribune*

"[A] satisfying ending to the series . . . Saying goodbye to Quentin is bittersweet, but saying goodbye to a Quentin who achieves some peace at last fills the farewell with a reassuring optimism for his future."   —*The Boston Globe*

"An enchanting conclusion . . . to a series that references C. S. Lewis and J. K. Rowling while remaining refreshingly original. . . . *The Magician's Land* is that rare novel that looks at what happens after the child prodigy grows up and has to get a job. . . . [It] features the return of a character sorely missed by both Quentin and readers alike, as well as Grossman's trademark witty dialogue."

—*The Christian Science Monitor*

"The last (and IOHO, best) book in the hit Magicians trilogy. Savor every word."

—*Cosmopolitan*

"An explosive conclusion to Quentin Coldwater's adventures."
—*Entertainment Weekly*

"A satisfying finale to the series, while adding depth and shading to the world. . . .
Grossman tells exciting fantasy adventures, but at the same time deconstructs the
fantasy, as his characters discover that even magical wish-fulfillment is no guarantee of happiness, and even a job casting spells in a magical land is still work."
—*A.V. Club* (A–)

"When read straight through, the Magicians trilogy reveals its lovely shape. The
world of the books wraps around itself, exposing most everything necessary by its
conclusion, but occluding operations that we'll never need to see. There's still a series
of mysteries and untold tales left unknown deep inside the books."
—Choire Sicha, *The Slate Book Review*

"All lovers of Lev Grossman's first two books of the Magicians trilogy: This is the
end, beautiful friend. . . . One of the lovely things about this series is watching
Quentin evolve from depressed teen to clear-eyed man. If Grossman raises his
kids with the same sympathy with which he parents his literary teen, he'll be a
smashing success. . . . Battle scenes are laid out with vivid, near-storyboard detail.
There's so much excitement as to make the temptation to race ahead a serious
danger. . . . Grossman brings the story home on a very satisfying chord. The
chorus: We are all magicians. Life, like magic, gives back only as much as you put
into it. It takes hard work, it hurts, and you have to be ready to fail. But deep
within us all lies the power to enchant the world."
—Cindy Bagwell, *Dallas Morning News*

"So you've torn through all the volumes of A Song of Ice and Fire (aka *Game of
Thrones*), and you're a little over the whole dystopian young-adult thing. What's an
adventure-minded reader to do for a fat beach book this August? Look no further
than Lev Grossman's Magicians trilogy." —Sara Stewart, *The New York Post*

"The very satisfying final book in [Grossman's] trilogy . . . This third book, at
turns a heist story, a meditation on the act of creation, and an apocalyptic disaster
tale, continues the adventures of main character Quentin Coldwater. It mixes
genre deconstruction with psychological realism, full of self-aware figures who
are cognizant of all the tropes of fantasy fiction, while at the same time working
to fulfill those tropes or push against them. There are great swaths of high imagination in *The Magician's Land*, evocative passages that contain entire worlds.
Writing, like magic, is a craft, and Grossman performs it oh so well."
—Gilbert Cruz, *NY1*

"In the smash trilogy's thrilling end, Quentin is cast out of Fillory, the enchanted
realm he once ruled. But he'll risk his life (and make dangerous allies) to save the
threatened world."
—*US Weekly*

"[A] deeply satisfying finale . . . [Grossman's] characters' magical battles have a bravura all their own. . . . The essence of being a magician, as Quentin learns to define it, could easily serve as a thumbnail description of Grossman's art: 'the power to enchant the world.'" —*Kirkus Reviews* (starred review)

"An absolutely brilliant fantasy filled with memorable characters—old and new—and prodigious feats of imagination . . . Endlessly fascinating . . . Fantasy fans will rejoice at its publication." —*Booklist* (starred review)

"[The Magicians] series taken as a whole brings new life and energy to the fantasy genre. The final volume will please fans looking for action, emotion, and, ultimately, closure." —*Library Journal*

"An elegantly written third act to Quentin's bildungsroman . . . Fans of the trilogy will be pleased." —*Publishers Weekly*

"If you haven't read the first two books in Grossman's Magicians trilogy, buy them immediately and set aside a weekend to read them straight through before you turn to *The Magician's Land*. The series, which follows a group of—you guessed it—magicians through the emotional foibles of young adulthood has been called 'Harry Potter for adults.' But it's way more complex than that. Grossman hones in on the particularly brutal business of being young, and then adds layer upon layer of literary allusion, creating works that are both homages to fantasy's past and glimpses at its future." —*The New Republic*

"Sink your mobile devices into the nearest wishing well and duct-tape your front door against gnomes, pollsters, and other distractions. *The Magician's Land* is beckoning, and demands your full attention. Lev Grossman proves again that the costs and consolations of creation—both of Fillory and of this conclusion to his trilogy—are mighty forces. Quentin Coldwater, Grossman's Orpheus and his Abraham, his Yahweh and his Puck, enchants as few other magicians can, or dare." —Gregory Maguire, author of *Wicked* and *Egg & Spoon*

"Lev Grossman has conjured a rare creature: a trilogy that simply gets better and better as it goes along. *The Magician's Land* is sumptuous and surprising yet deliciously familiar, a glass of rich red wine left out for a hungry ghost. Literary perfection for those of us who grew up testing the structural integrity of the backs of wardrobes." —Erin Morgenstern, author of *The Night Circus*

"*The Magician's Land* is a triumphant climax to the best fantasy trilogy of the decade." —Charles Stross, author of *Accelerando* and *The Rhesus Chart*

"Poignant and messy, fearsome and beautiful—like a good magic spell, the final book in this trilogy is more than the sum of its parts. Also, damn. Just some of the best magic I have read, ever." —Maggie Stiefvater, author of *Shiver*

Praise for *The Magician King*, Book Two of the Magicians Trilogy

"[A] serious, heartfelt novel [that] turns the machinery of fantasy inside out."
—*The New York Times* (Editor's Choice)

"A spellbinding stereograph, a literary adventure novel that is also about privilege, power, and the limits of being human. *The Magician King* is a triumphant sequel."
—NPR.org

"[*The Magician King*] is *The Catcher in the Rye* for devotees of alternative universes. It's dazzling and devil-may-care. . . . Grossman has created a rare, strange, and scintillating novel."
—*Chicago Tribune*

"*The Magician King* is a rare achievement, a book that simultaneously criticizes and celebrates our deep desire for fantasy."
—*The Boston Globe*

"Grossman has devised an enchanted milieu brimming with possibility, and his sly authorial voice gives it a literary lift that positions *The Magician King* well above the standard fantasy fare."
—*San Francisco Chronicle*

"Grossman expands his magical world into a boundless enchanted universe, and his lively characters navigate it with aplomb."
—*The New Yorker*

"Grossman is brilliant at creating brainy, distinct, flawed, complex characters, and nearly as good at running them through narrative gauntlets that inventively tweak the stories that generations have grown up on."
—*The Portland Oregonian*

"*The Magician King*, the immensely entertaining new novel by Lev Grossman, manages to be both deep and deeply enjoyable."
—*The Chicago Sun-Times*

"Readers who have already enjoyed *The Magicians* should lose no time in picking up *The Magician King*. For those who haven't, read both books: Grossman's work is solid, smart, and engaging adult fantasy."
—*The Miami Herald*

"Now that Harry Potter is through in books and films, grown-up fans of the boy wizard might want to give this nimble fantasy series a try."
—*New York Post*

"*The Magician King* is Grossman's sequel to *The Magicians*, and while it is every bit as delightful and smart as the first one, it's a very different kind of book. . . . *The Magician King* is at once an existential exercise that angrily shakes escapism by its shoulders and demands that life have a purpose, and a story about extraordinary deeds, heroism, magic, and love—all the stuff that makes escapism go. It's a fantastic trick that makes this into a book that entertains and disturbs at the same time."
—*Boing Boing*

"Lev Grossman's *The Magician King* is a fresh take on the fantasy-quest novel—dark, austere, featuring characters with considerable psychological complexity, a collection of idiosyncratic talking animals (a sloth who knows the path to the underworld, a dragon in the Grand Canal), and splendid set pieces in Venice, Provence, Cornwall, and Brooklyn."   —*The Daily Beast*

"In this page-turning follow-up to his best-selling 2009 novel *The Magicians*, Grossman takes another dark, sarcastically sinister stab at fantasy, set in the Narnia-esque realm of Fillory."   —*Entertainment Weekly*

Praise for *The Magicians*, Book One of the Magicians Trilogy

"Fresh and compelling . . . *The Magicians* is a great fairy tale, written for grown-ups but appealing to our most basic desires for stories to bring about some re-enchantment with the world, where monsters lurk but where a young man with a little magic may prevail."   —*The Washington Post*

"Grossman is a bewitchingly gifted writer. . . . *The Magicians* blooms with grace and wit and imaginative brio."   —*Chicago Tribune*

"This gripping novel draws on the conventions of contemporary and classic fantasy novels in order to upend them and tell a darkly cunning story about the power of imagination itself. [*The Magicians* is] an unexpectedly moving coming-of-age story."   —*The New Yorker*

"*The Magicians* is to Harry Potter as a shot of Irish whiskey is to a glass of weak tea. Solidly rooted in the traditions of both fantasy and mainstream literary fiction, the novel tips its hat to Oz and Narnia as well to Harry, but don't mistake this for a children's book. Grossman's sensibilities are thoroughly adult, his narrative dark and dangerous and full of twists. Hogwarts was never like this."
—George R. R. Martin, bestselling author of *A Game of Thrones*

"Sly and lyrical, [*The Magicians*] captures the magic of childhood and the sobering years beyond."   —*Entertainment Weekly*

"Grossman's triumph is that he treats these magical worlds of childhood seriously. . . . *The Magicians* is the best urban fantasy in years, a sad dream of what it means to want something badly and never fully reach it."   —*A.V. Club* (A)

THE
MAGICIAN'S LAND

A Novel

LEV GROSSMAN

PENGUIN BOOKS

PENGUIN BOOKS
An imprint of Penguin Random House LLC
375 Hudson Street
New York, New York 10014
penguin.com

First published in the United States of America by Viking,
an imprint of Penguin Random House LLC, 2014
Published by Plume, an imprint of Penguin Random House LLC, 2015
Published in Penguin Books 2016

THE LIBRARY OF CONGRESS HAS CATALOGED THE HARDCOVER EDITION AS FOLLOWS:
Grossman, Lev.
The magician's land : a novel / Lev Grossman.
pages cm
ISBN 978-0-670-01567-2 (hc.)
ISBN 978-0-14-751614-5 (pbk.)
1. Magic—Fiction.   2. College students—Fiction.   3. Fantasy fiction.   I. Title.
PS3557.R6725M37 2014
813'.54—dc23   2014010097

Printed in the United States of America
10

Map by Roland Chambers

For Halcyon

Further up and further in!

—C. S. Lewis, *The Last Battle*

CHAPTER 1

The letter had said to meet in a bookstore.

It wasn't much of a night for it: early March, drizzling and cold but not quite cold enough for snow. It wasn't much of a bookstore either. Quentin spent fifteen minutes watching it from a bus shelter at the edge of the empty parking lot, rain drumming on the plastic roof and making the asphalt shine in the streetlights. Not one of your charming, quirky bookstores, with a ginger cat on the windowsill and a shelf of rare signed first editions and an eccentric, bewhiskered proprietor behind the counter. This was just another strip-mall outpost of a struggling chain, squeezed in between a nail salon and a Party City, twenty minutes outside Hackensack off the New Jersey Turnpike.

Satisfied, Quentin crossed the parking lot. The enormous bearded cashier didn't look up from his phone when the door jingled. Inside you could still hear the noise of cars on the wet road, like long strips of paper tearing, one after another. The only unexpected touch was a wire birdcage in one corner, but where you would have expected a parrot or a cockatoo inside there was a fat blue-black bird instead. That's how un-charming this store was: it had a crow in a cage.

Quentin didn't care. It was a bookstore, and he felt at home in bookstores, and he hadn't had that feeling much lately. He was going to enjoy it. He pushed his way back through the racks of greeting cards and cat calendars, back to where the actual books were, his glasses steaming up and his coat dripping on the thin carpet. It didn't matter where you were, if you were in a room full of books you were at least halfway home.

The store should have been empty, coming up on nine o'clock on a cold rainy Thursday night, but instead it was full of people. They browsed the shelves silently, each one on his or her own, slowly wandering the aisles like sleepwalkers. A jewel-faced girl with a pixie cut was reading Dante in Italian. A tall boy with large curious eyes who couldn't have been older than sixteen was absorbed in a Tom Stoppard play. A middle-aged black man with elfin cheekbones stood staring at the biographies through thick, iridescent glasses. You would almost have thought they'd come there to buy books. But Quentin knew better.

He wondered if it would be obvious, if he would know right away, or if there would be a trick to it. If they'd make him guess. He was getting to be a pretty old dog—he'd be thirty this year—but this particular game was new to him.

At least it was warm inside. He took off his glasses and wiped them with a cloth. He'd just gotten them a couple of months ago, the price of a lifetime of reading fine print, and they were still an unfamiliar presence on his face: a windshield between him and the world, always slipping down his nose and getting smudged when he pushed them up again. When he put them back on he noticed a sharp-featured young woman, girl-next-door pretty, if you happened to live next door to a grad student in astrophysics. She was standing in a corner paging through a big, expensive architectural-looking volume. Piranesi drawings: vast shadowy vaults and cellars and prisons, haunted by great wooden engines.

Quentin knew her. Her name was Plum. She felt him watching her and looked up, raising her eyebrows in mild surprise, as if to say *you're kidding—you're in on this thing too?*

He shook his head once, very slightly, and looked away, keeping his face carefully blank. Not to say *no, I'm not in on this, I just come here for the novelty coffee mugs and their trenchant commentary on the little ironies of everyday life.* What he meant was: *let's pretend we don't know each other.*

It was looking like he had some time to kill so he joined the browsers, scanning the spines for something to read. The Fillory books were there, of course, shelved in the young adult section, repackaged and rebranded with slick new covers that made them look like supernatural romance novels. But Quentin couldn't face them right now. Not tonight, not here. He took down a copy of *The Spy Who Came in from the Cold* instead and spent ten contented minutes at a checkpoint in gray 1950s Berlin.

"Attention, Bookbumblers patrons!" the cashier said over the PA, though the store was small enough that Quentin could hear his unamplified voice perfectly clearly. "Attention! Bookbumblers will be closing in five minutes! Please make your final selections!"

He put the book back. An old woman in a beret that looked like she'd knitted it herself bought a copy of *The Prime of Miss Jean Brodie* and let herself out into the night. So not her. The skinny kid who'd been camped out cross-legged in the graphic novels section, reading them to rags, left without buying anything. So not him either. A tall, bluff-looking guy with Cro-Magnon hair and a face like a stump who'd been furiously studying the greeting cards, pretty clearly overthinking his decision, finally bought one. But he didn't leave.

At nine o'clock exactly the big cashier closed the door and locked it with a final, fateful jingle, and suddenly Quentin was all nerves. He was on a carnival ride, and the safety bar had dropped, and now it was too late to get off. He took a deep breath and frowned at himself, but the nerves didn't go away. The bird shuffled its feet in the seeds and droppings on the bottom of its cage and squawked once. It was a lonely kind of squawk, the kind you'd hear if you were out by yourself on a rainy moor, lost, with darkness closing in fast.

The cashier walked to the back of the store—he had to excuse himself past the guy with the cheekbones—and opened a gray metal door marked STAFF ONLY.

"Through here."

He sounded bored, like he did this every night, which for all Quentin knew he did. Now that he was standing up Quentin could see that he really was huge—six foot four or five and deep-chested. Not pumped, but with broad shoulders and that aura of slow inexorability that naturally enormous men have. His face was noticeably asymmetrical: it bulged out on one side as if he'd been slightly overinflated. He looked like a gourd.

Quentin took the last spot in line. He counted eight others, all of them looking around cautiously and taking exaggerated care not to jostle one another, as if they might explode on contact. He worked a tiny revelation charm to make sure there was nothing weird about the door—he made an OK sign with his thumb and forefinger and held it up to one eye like a monocle.

"No magic," the cashier said. He snapped his fingers at Quentin. "Guy. Hey. No spells. No magic."

Heads turned.

"Sorry?"

Quentin played dumb. Nobody called him Your Majesty anymore, but he didn't think he was ready to answer to *guy* yet. He finished his inspection. It was a door and nothing more.

"Cut it out. No magic."

Pushing his luck, Quentin turned and studied the clerk. Through the lens he could see something small shining in his pocket, a talisman that might have been related to sexual performance. The rest of him shone too, as if he were covered in phosphorescent algae. Weird.

"Sure." He dropped his hands and the lens vanished. "No problem."

Someone rapped on the windowpane. A face appeared, indistinct through the wet glass. The cashier shook his head, but whoever it was rapped again, harder.

He sighed.

"What the shit."

He unlocked the front door and after a whispered argument let in a man in his twenties, dripping wet, red-faced but otherwise sportscaster-handsome, wearing a windbreaker that was way too light for the weather. Quentin wondered where he'd managed to get a sunburn in March.

They all filed into the back room. It was darker than Quentin expected, and bigger too; real estate must come cheap out here on the turnpike. There were steel shelves crammed full of books flagged with fluorescent-colored stickies; a couple of desks in one corner, the walls in front of them shingled with shift schedules and taped-up *New Yorker* cartoons; stacks of cardboard shipping boxes; a busted couch; a busted armchair; a mini-fridge—it must have doubled as the break room. Half of it was just wasted space. The back wall was a steel shutter that opened onto a loading dock.

A handful of other people were coming in through another door in the left-hand wall, looking just as wary. Quentin could see another bookstore behind them, a nicer one, with old lamps and oriental rugs. Probably a ginger cat too. He didn't need magic to know that it wasn't a door at all but a portal to somewhere else, some arbitrary distance away. There—he caught a telltale hairline seam of green light along one edge. The only thing behind that wall in reality was Party City.

Who were they all? Quentin had heard rumors about dog-and-pony shows like this before, gray-market cattle calls, work for hire, but he'd never seen one himself. He definitely never thought he'd go to one, not in a million years. He never thought it would come to that. Stuff like this was for people on the fringes of the magical world, people scrabbling to get in, or who'd lost their footing somehow and slipped out of the bright warm center of things, all the way out to the cold margins of the real world. All the way out to a strip mall in Hackensack in the rain. Things like this weren't for people like him.

Except now they were. It had come to that. He was one of them, these were his people. Six months ago he'd been a king in a magic land, another world, but that was all over. He'd been kicked out of Fillory, and he'd been kicked around a fair bit since then, and now he was just another striver, trying to scramble back in, up the slippery slope, back toward the light and the warmth.

Plum and the man with the iridescent glasses sat on the couch. Red Face took the busted armchair. Pixie Cut and the teenage Stoppard reader sat on boxes. The rest of them stood—there were twelve, thirteen, fourteen in all. The cashier shut the gray door behind them, cutting off the last of the noise from the outside world, and snuffed out the portal.

He'd brought the birdcage with him; now he placed it on top of a cardboard box and opened it to let the crow out. It looked around, shaking first one foot then the other the way birds do.

"Thank you all for coming," it said. "I will be brief."

That was unexpected. Judging from the ripple of surprise that ran through the room, he wasn't the only one. You didn't see a lot of talking birds on Earth, that was more of a Fillorian thing.

"I'm looking for an object," the bird said. "I will need help taking it from its present owners."

The bird's glossy feathers shone darkly in the glow of the hanging lights. Its voice echoed in the half-empty stockroom. It was a soft, mild-mannered voice, not hoarse at all like you'd expect from a crow. It sounded incongruously human—however it was producing speech, it had nothing to do with its actual vocal apparatus. But that was magic for you.

"So stealing," an Indian guy said. Not like it bothered him, he just wanted clarification. He was older than Quentin, forty maybe, balding and wearing an unbelievably bad multicolored wool sweater.

"Theft," the bird said. "Yes."

"Stealing back, or stealing?"

"What is the difference?"

"I would merely like to know whether we are the bad guys or the good guys. Which of you has a rightful claim on the object?"

The bird cocked its head thoughtfully.

"Neither party has an entirely valid claim," it said. "But if it makes a difference our claim is superior to theirs."

That seemed to satisfy the Indian guy, though Quentin wondered if he would have had a problem either way.

"Who are you?" somebody called out. The bird ignored that.

"What is the object?" Plum asked.

"You'll be told after you've accepted the job."

"Where is it?" Quentin asked.

The bird shifted its weight back and forth.

"It is in the northeastern United States of America." It half spread its wings in what might have been a bird-shrug.

"So you don't know," Quentin said. "So finding it is part of the job."

The bird didn't deny it. Pixie Cut scooched forward, which wasn't easy on the broken-backed couch, especially in a skirt that short. Her hair was black with purple highlights, and Quentin noticed a couple of blue star tattoos peeking out of her sleeves, the kind you got in a safe house. He wondered how many more she had underneath. He wondered what she'd done to end up here.

"So we're finding and we're stealing and I'm guessing probably doing some fighting in between. What kind of resistance are you expecting?"

"Can you be more specific?"

"Security, how many people, who are they, how scary. Is that specific enough?"

"Yes. We are expecting two."

"Two magicians?"

"Two magicians, plus some civilian staff. Nothing out of the ordinary, as far as I know."

"As far as you know!" The red-faced man guffawed loudly. He seemed on further examination to be a little insane.

"I do know that they have been able to place an incorporate bond on the object. The bond will have to be broken, obviously."

A stunned silence followed this statement, then somebody made an exasperated noise. The tall man who'd been shopping for greeting cards snorted as if to say *can you believe this shit?*

"Those are supposed to be unbreakable," Plum said coolly.

"You're wasting our time!" Iridescent Glasses said.

"An incorporate bond has never been broken," the bird said, not at all bothered—or were its feathers just slightly ruffled? "But we believe that it is theoretically possible, with the right skills and the right resources. We have all the skills we need in this room."

"What about the resources?" Pixie Cut asked.

"The resources can be obtained."

"So that's also part of the job," Quentin said. He ticked them off on his fingers. "Obtaining the resources, finding the object, breaking the bond, taking the object, dealing with the current owners. Correct?"

"Yes. Payment is two million dollars each, cash or gold. A hundred thousand tonight, the rest once we have the object. Make your decisions now. Bear in mind that if you say no you will find yourself unable to discuss tonight's meeting with anyone else."

Satisfied that it had made its case, the bird fluttered up to perch on top of its cage.

It was more than Quentin had expected. There were probably easier and safer ways in this world for a magician to earn two million dollars, but there weren't many that were this quick, or that were right in front of him. Even magicians needed money sometimes, and this was one of those times. He had to get back into the swim of things. He had work to do.

"If you're not interested, please leave now," the cashier said. Evidently he was the bird's lieutenant. He might have been in his mid-twenties. His black beard covered his chin and neck like brambles.

The Cro-Magnon guy stood up.

"Good luck." He turned out to have a thick German accent. "You gonna need this, huh?"

He skimmed the greeting card into the middle of the room and left. It landed face up: GET WELL SOON. Nobody picked it up.

About a third of the room shuffled out with him, off in search of other pitches and better offers. Maybe this wasn't the only show in town tonight. But it was the only one Quentin knew about, and he didn't leave. He watched Plum, and Plum watched him. She didn't leave either. They were in the same boat—she must be scrabbling too.

The red-faced guy stood against the wall by the door.

"See ya!" he said to each person as they passed him. "Buh-bye!"

When everybody who was going to leave had left the cashier closed the door again. They were down to eight: Quentin, Plum, Pixie, Red Face, Iridescent Glasses, the teenager, the Indian guy, and a long-faced woman in a flowing dress with a lock of white hair over her forehead; the last two had come in through the other door. The room felt even quieter than it had before, and strangely empty.

"Are you from Fillory?" Quentin asked the bird.

That got some appreciative laughter, though he wasn't joking, and the bird didn't laugh. It didn't answer him either. Quentin couldn't read its face; like all birds, it had only one expression.

"Before we go any further each of you must pass a simple test of magical strength and skill," the bird said. "Lionel here"—it meant the cashier—"is an expert in probability magic. Each of you will play a hand of cards with him. If you beat him you will have passed the test."

There were some disgruntled noises at this new revelation, followed by another round of discreet mutual scoping-out. From the reaction Quentin gathered that this wasn't standard practice.

"What's the game?" Plum asked.

"The game is Push."

"You must be joking," Iridescent Glasses said, disgustedly. "You really don't know anything, do you?"

Lionel had produced a pack of cards and was shuffling and bridging it fluently, without looking, his face blank.

"I know what I require," the bird said stiffly. "I know that I am offering a great deal of money for it."

"Well, I didn't come here to play games."

The man stood up.

"Well why the fuck did you come here?" Pixie asked brightly.

"You may leave at any time," the bird said.

"Maybe I will."

He walked to the door, pausing with his hand on the knob, as if he were expecting somebody to stop him. Nobody did. The door shut after him.

Quentin watched Lionel shuffle. The man obviously knew how to handle a deck; the cards leapt around obligingly in his large hands, neatly and cleanly, the way they did for a pro. He thought about the entrance exam he'd taken to get into Brakebills, what was it, thirteen years ago now? He hadn't been too proud to take a test then. He sure as hell wasn't now.

And he used to be a bit of a pro at this himself. Cards were stage magic, close-up magic. This was where he started out.

"All right," Quentin said. He got up, flexing his fingers. "Let's do it."

He dragged a desk chair over noisily and sat down opposite Lionel. As a courtesy Lionel offered him the deck. Quentin took it.

He stuck to a basic shuffle, trying not to look too slick. The cards were stiff but not brand new. They had the usual industry-standard anti-manipulation charms on them, nothing he hadn't seen before. It felt good to have them in his hands. He was back on familiar ground. Without being obvious about it, he got a look at a few face cards and put them where they wouldn't go to waste. It had been a while, a long while, but this was a game he knew something about. Back in the day Push had been a major pastime among the Physical Kids.

It was a childishly simple game. Push was a lot like War—high card wins—with some silly added twists to break ties (toss cards into a hat; once you get five in, score it like a poker hand; etc.). But the rules weren't the point; the point of Push was to cheat. There was a lot of strange magic in cards: a shuffled deck wasn't a fixed thing, it was a roiling cloud of possibilities, and nothing was ever certain till the cards were actually played. It was like a box with a whole herd of Schrödinger's cats in it. With a little magical know-how you could alter the order in which your cards came out; with a little more you could guess what your opponent was going to play before she played it; with a bit more you could play cards that by all the laws of probability rightfully belonged to your opponent, or in the discard pile, or in some other deck entirely.

Quentin handed back the cards, and the game began.

They started slow, trading off low cards, easy tricks, both holding serve. Quentin counted cards automatically, though there was a limit to how much good it could do—when magicians played the cards had a way of changing sides, and cards you thought were safely deceased and out of play had a way of coming back to life. He'd been curious what caliber of talent got involved in these kinds of operations, and he was revising his estimates sharply upward. It was obvious he wasn't going to overwhelm Lionel with brute force.

Quentin wondered where he'd trained. Brakebills, probably, same as he had; there was a precise, formal quality to his magic that you didn't see coming out of the safe houses. Though there was something else too: it had a cold, sour, alien tang to it—Quentin could almost taste it. He wondered if Lionel was quite as human as he looked.

There were twenty-six tricks in a hand of Push, and halfway through neither side had established an advantage. But on the fourteenth trick Quentin overreached—he burned some of his strength to force a king to the top of his deck, only to waste it on a deuce from Lionel. The mismatch left him off balance, and he lost the next three tricks in a row. He clawed back two more by stealing cards from the discard pile, but the preliminaries were over. From here on out it was going to be a dogfight.

The room narrowed to just the table. It had been a while since Quentin had seen his competitive spirit, but it was rousing itself from its long slumber. He wasn't going to lose this thing. That wasn't going to happen. He bore down. He could feel Lionel probing, trying to shove cards around within the unplayed deck, and he shoved back. They blew all four aces in as many tricks, all-out, hammer and tongs. For kicks Quentin split his concentration and used a simple spell to twitch the sex amulet out of Lionel's pocket and onto the floor. But if that distracted Lionel he didn't show it.

Probability fields began to fluctuate crazily around them—invisible, but you could see secondary effects from them in the form of minor but very unlikely chance occurrences. Their hair and clothes stirred in impalpable breezes. A card tossed to one side might land on its edge and balance there, or spin in place on one corner. A mist formed above the table, and a single flake of snow sifted down out of it. The onlookers backed away a few steps. Quentin beat a jack of hearts with the king, then lost the next trick with the exact same cards reversed. He played a deuce—and Lionel swore under his breath when he realized he was somehow holding the extra card with the rules of poker on it.

Reality was softening and melting in the heat of the game. On the second-to-last trick Lionel played the queen of spades, and Quentin frowned—did her face look the slightest bit like Julia's? Either way there was no such thing as a one-eyed queen, let alone one with a bird on her shoulder. He spent his last king against it, or he thought he did: when he laid it down it had become a jack, a suicide jack at that, which again there was no such card, especially not one with white hair like his own.

Even Lionel looked surprised. Something must be twisting the cards—it was like there was some invisible third player at the table who was toying with both of them. With his next and last card it became clear that Lionel had lost all control over his hand because he turned over a queen of no known suit, a Queen of Glass. Her face was translucent cellophane, sapphire-blue. It was Alice, to the life.

"What the shit," Lionel said, shaking his head.

What the shit was right. Quentin clung to his nerve. The sight of Alice's face shook him, it froze his gut, but it also stiffened his resolve. It reminded him what he was doing here. He was not going to panic. In fact he was going to take advantage of this—Alice was going to help him. The essence of close-up magic is misdirection, and with Lionel distracted Quentin pulled a king of clubs out of his boot with numb fingers and slapped it down. He tried to ignore the gray suit the king wore, and the branch that was sprouting in front of his face.

It was over. Game and match. Quentin sat back and took a deep, shaky breath.

"Good," the bird said simply. "Next."

Lionel didn't look happy, but he didn't say anything either, just crouched down and collected his amulet from under the table. Quentin got up and went to stand against the wall with others, his knees weak, his heart still racing, revving past the red line.

He was happy to get out of the game with a win, but he'd thought he would. He hadn't thought he'd see his long-lost ex-girlfriend appear on a face card. What just happened? Maybe someone here knew more about him than they should. Maybe they were trying to throw him off his game. But who? Who would bother? Nobody cared if he won or lost, not anymore. As far as he knew the only person who cared right now was Quentin.

Maybe he was doing it himself—maybe his own subconscious was reaching up from below and warping his spellwork. Or was it Alice herself, wherever she was, whatever she was, watching him and having a little fun? Well, let her have it. He was focused on the present, that was what mattered. He had work to do. He was getting his life back together. The past had no jurisdiction here. Not even Alice.

The red-faced guy won his game with no signs of anything out of the ordinary. So did the Indian guy. The woman with the shock of white hair went out early, biting her lip as she laid down a blatantly impossible five deuces in a row, followed by a joker, then a *Go Directly to Jail!* card from Monopoly. The kid got a bye for some reason—the bird didn't make him play at all. Plum got a bye too. Pixie passed faster than any of them, either because she was that strong or because Lionel was getting tired.

When it was all over Lionel handed the woman who'd lost a brick of hundred-dollar bills for her trouble. He handed another one to the red-faced man.

"Thank you for your time," the bird said.

"Me?" The man stared down at the money in his hand. "But I passed!"

"Yes," Lionel said. "But you got here late. And you seem like kind of an asshole."

The man's face got even redder than it already was.

"Go ahead," Lionel said. He spread his arms. "Make a move."

The man's face twitched, but he wasn't so angry or so crazy that he couldn't read the odds.

"Fuck you!" he said.

That was his move. He slammed the door behind him.

Quentin dropped into the armchair the man had just vacated, even though it was damp from his wet windbreaker. He felt limp and wrung out. He hoped the testing was over with, he wouldn't have trusted himself to cast anything right now. Counting him there were only five left: Quentin, Plum, Pixie, the Indian guy, and the kid.

This all seemed a hell of a lot more real than it had half an hour ago. It wasn't too late, he could still walk away. He hadn't seen any deal-breakers yet, but he hadn't seen a lot to inspire confidence either. This could be his way back in, or it could be the road to somewhere even worse. He'd spent enough time already on things that went nowhere and left him with nothing. He could walk out, back into the rainy night, back into the cold and the wet.

But he didn't. It was time to turn things around. He was going to make this work. It wasn't like he had a lot of better offers.

"You think this is going to be enough?" Quentin asked the bird. "Just five of us?"

"Six, with Lionel. And yes. In fact I would say that it is exactly right."

"Well, don't keep us in suspense," Pixie said. "What's the target?"

The bird didn't keep them in suspense.

"The object we are looking for is a suitcase. Brown leather, average size, manufactured 1937, monogrammed *RCJ*. The make is Louis Vuitton."

It actually had a pretty credible French accent.

"Fancy," she said. "What's in it?"

"I do not know."

"You don't know?" It was the first time the teenage boy had spoken. "Why the hell do you want it then?"

"In order to find out."

"Huh. What do the initials stand for?"

"Rupert John Chatwin," the bird said crisply.

The kid looked confused. His lips moved.

"I don't get it," he said. "Wouldn't the *C* come last?"

"It's a monogram, dumbass," Pixie said. "The last name goes in the middle."

The Indian guy was rubbing his chin.

"Chatwin." He was trying to place the name. "Chatwin. But isn't that—?"

It sure is, Quentin thought, though he didn't say anything. He didn't move a muscle. It sure as hell is.

Chatwin: that name chilled him even more than the night and the rain and the bird and the cards had. By rights he should have gone the rest of his life without hearing it again. It had no claim on him anymore, and vice versa. He and the Chatwins were through.

Except it seemed that they weren't. He'd said good-bye and buried them and mourned them—the Chatwins, Fillory, Plover, Whitespire— but there must still be some last invisible unbroken strand connecting them to him. Something deeper than mourning. The wound had healed, but the scar wouldn't fade, not quite. Quentin felt like an addict who'd just caught the faintest whiff of his drug of choice, the pure stuff, after a long time sober, and he felt his imminent relapse coming on with a mixture of despair and anticipation.

That name was a message—a hot signal flare shot up into the night, sent specifically for him, across time and space and darkness and rain, all the way from the bright warm center of the world.

CHAPTER 2

It wasn't supposed to happen that way. Quentin had tried to go straight.

It started in the Neitherlands, the silent city of Italianate fountains and locked libraries that lies somehow behind and between everywhere else. The fountains were really doorways to other worlds, and Quentin stood leaning against the one that led to Fillory. He had just been forcibly ejected from it.

He stood there for a long time, feeling the cool roughness of the stone rim. It was reassuringly solid. The fountain was his last connection to his old life, the one where he'd been a king in a magical land. He didn't want it to be over; it wouldn't really be over till he let go and walked away. He could still have it for a little longer.

But no, he couldn't. It was done. He patted the fountain one more time and set off through the empty dream-city. He felt weightless and empty. He'd stopped being who he was, but he wasn't sure yet who he was going to be next. His head was still full of the End of the World: the setting sun, the endless thin curving beach, the two mismatched wooden chairs, the ringing crescent moon, the sputtering comets. The last sight of Julia, diving off the edge of Fillory, straight down to the Far Side of the World, down into her future.

It was a new beginning for her, but he'd hit a dead end. No more Fillory. No further.

Though he wasn't so far gone that he didn't notice how much the Neitherlands had changed. Before this it had always been quiet and serene, trapped under a bell jar of stillness and silence beneath a cloudy twilight sky. But something had happened: the gods had come back to fix the flaw in the universe that was magic, and in the crisis that followed the bell jar broke, and time and weather had come flooding in. Now the air smelled like mist. Ripped, ragged clouds streamed by overhead, and patches of blue sky were mirrored in shivering pools of snowmelt. The sound of trickling water was everywhere. Reluctantly, resentfully, the Neitherlands was having its first spring.

It was a season of wreckage and ruin. All around Quentin roofless buildings lay open to the elements, the toppled bookshelves inside lying in domino rows, exposed like the ribs of rotting carcasses. Stray pages torn from the libraries of the Neitherlands floated and tumbled high in the troubled air overhead. Crossing a bridge over a canal Quentin saw that the water was almost level with the banks on either side. He wondered what would happen if it overflowed.

Probably nothing. Probably he'd get wet.

The fountain that led to Earth had changed too. The sculpture at its center was of a great brass lotus, but in the struggle over magic a swarm of dragons had used it to enter the Neitherlands, and when they came surging up through it, the flower had ripped open at the seams. Quentin thought maybe somebody would have come by and repaired it by now, but instead the fountain was repairing itself. The old flower had withered and flopped over to one side, and a new brass lotus was budding open in its place.

Quentin was studying the bud fountain, wondering if even his narrow, bony hips were narrow and bony enough to fit through it, when something brushed his shoulder. By reflex he snatched it out of the air: it was a piece of paper, a page ripped from a book. The page was dense with writing and diagrams on both sides. He was about to let it go again, to give it back to the wind, but then he didn't. He folded it in quarters and shoved it in his back pocket instead.

Then he fell to Earth.

It was raining on Earth, or at least it was in Chesterton: bucketing down, hard and freezing cold, a November New England monsoon. For reasons best known to itself the magic button had chosen to place him in the lush Massachusetts suburb where his parents lived, on the wide flat lawn in front of their too-large house. Rain hammered on the roof and streamed down the windows and vomited out of a drainpipe in a rooster tail. It soaked through his clothes almost immediately—in the Neitherlands he'd still been able to smell the sea salt of Fillory on his clothes, but now the rain dissolved it and washed it away forever. Instead he smelled the smells of autumn rain in the suburbs: mulch rotting, wooden decks swelling, wet dogs, hedges breathing.

He took the silver watch out of his pocket, the one Eliot had given him before he left Fillory. He'd hardly glanced at it before—he'd been too shocked and angry when they told him he had to leave—but now that he did he saw that its face was studded with a really glorious profusion of detail: two extra dials, a moving star chart, the phases of the moon. It was a beautiful watch. He thought about how Eliot had harvested it himself, from a clock-sapling in the Queenswood, and then carried it and kept it safe for him during all his months at sea. It was a great gift. He wished he'd appreciated it more at the time.

Though it had stopped ticking. Being on Earth didn't seem to agree with it. Maybe it was the weather.

Quentin stared at his parents' darkened house for a long time, waiting to feel an urge to go inside, but the urge never came. As dark and massive as it was the house exerted no gravitational pull on him. When he thought of his parents it was almost like they were old lovers, so distant now that he couldn't even remember why his link to them had once seemed so real and urgent. They'd managed the neat trick of bringing up a child with whom they had absolutely nothing in common, or if there was something none of them had ever risen to the challenge of finding it.

Now they'd drifted so far apart that the silver thread connecting them had simply snapped. If he had a home anywhere, it wasn't here.

He took a deep breath, closed his eyes, and chanted four long, low syllables under his breath while at the same time making a big circle with his left hand. The rain began sheeting off an invisible lens over his head, and he felt, if not dryer, then at least that he had taken the first step on the long and arduous path to dryness.

Then he walked away down the wide wet suburban sidewalk. He was out of Fillory, and he wasn't a king anymore. It was time to start living his damn life like everybody else. Better late than never. Quentin walked half an hour to the center of Chesterton, caught a bus from there to Alewife, took a subway to South Station, and got on a Greyhound bus bound for Newburgh, New York, north of Manhattan on the Hudson River, which was the closest you could get to Brakebills via public transportation.

Coming back was easier this time. Last time he'd been with Julia, and he'd been panicked and desperate. This time he was in no particular hurry, and he knew exactly what he needed: to be somewhere safe and familiar, where he had something to do, where people knew magic and knew him. What he needed was a job.

He stayed at the same motel as last time, then took a taxi to the same bend in the road and picked his way in through the damp forest from there. It had rained here too, and every twig and branch he brushed soaked him all over again with cold water. He didn't bother with any fancy visualization spells this time. He figured they would see him, and that when they did they would know him for what he was.

He was right. Quentin spotted it a long way off through the trees: just a stray patch of sunlight on an otherwise overcast day. As he got closer it resolved itself into an oval of lighter, brighter air hanging there among the wet branches. The oval framed a woman's disembodied head and shoulders, like a cameo in a locket. She was fortyish, with almond-shaped eyes, and though he didn't recognize her she had the unmistakably alert air of a fellow practitioner.

"Hi," Quentin said, when he was close enough that he didn't have to shout. "I'm Quentin."

"I know," she said. "You coming in?"

"Thanks."

She did something, made a small gesture somewhere out of view, and the portrait went full-length. She was standing in an archway of summer light and grass carved out of the gloomy autumn forest. She stood aside to let him pass.

"Thanks," he said again. When the summer air hit him, tears of relief prickled unexpectedly at the corners of his eyes. He blinked and turned away, but the woman caught it.

"It never gets old, does it?"

"No," he said. "It really doesn't."

Quentin went the long way around, bypassing the Maze—it would have been redrawn ten times over since the last time he knew it—and walked up to the House. The halls were quiet: it was August here, and there were no students to speak of, though if they hadn't filled the incoming class yet they might still be holding entrance exams. Early afternoon sunlight fell undisturbed on the much-abused carpets in the common rooms. The whole building felt like it was resting and recovering after the catastrophe of the school year.

He didn't know what to expect from Fogg: the last time they spoke they hadn't parted on the best possible terms. But Quentin was here, and he was going to make his case. He found the dean in his office going through admissions files.

"Well!" Still groomed and goateed, the older man made a show of surprise. "Come in. I didn't expect to see you back so soon."

Fogg smiled, though he didn't get up. Quentin sat down, cautiously.

"I wasn't expecting it either," he said. "But it's good to be here."

"That's always nice to hear. Last time I saw you I believe you had a hedge witch in tow. Tell me, did she get wherever it was she was going?"

She had, though by a long and circuitous route, and Quentin didn't want to go into detail about it. Instead he inquired after the fortunes of the Brakebills welters team, and Fogg filled him in on that in all the detail he could have wanted and more. Quentin asked after the little metal bird that used to inhabit his office, and Fogg explained that someone had made it their doctoral project to turn it back into flesh and feathers. Fogg took out a cigar and offered one to Quentin; Quentin accepted it; they smoked.

It was all going more smoothly than he'd expected. He'd formed an idea of Fogg as a petty, spiteful tyrant, but now he began to wonder if the dean had changed, or if he'd gotten it wrong in the first place. Maybe Fogg wasn't as bad as all that. Maybe he, Quentin, had always been a bit too sensitive and defensive around him. When Fogg asked Quentin how he could help him, Quentin told him.

And just like that, Fogg helped him. As luck would have it there was a vacancy in the faculty at the most junior level—a week earlier an incoming adjunct had had to be dismissed after it came out that he'd plagiarized most of his master's thesis from Francis Bacon. Quentin could pick up his teaching load, if he liked. Really, he'd be doing Fogg a favor. If there was any Schadenfreude there, if Fogg took any pleasure from the sight of a newly chastened and humbled Quentin, the high-flying, adventure-having, mischief-managing prodigal son, coming crawling back begging for a handout, he hid it well.

"Don't look so surprised, Quentin!" he said. "You were always one of the clever ones. Everyone saw it but you. If you hadn't been so busy trying to convince yourself you didn't belong here, you would have seen it too."

Just as it had years ago Brakebills opened its doors to him, took him into itself, and offered him a place in its little secret hideaway world. From a pegboard Fogg gave him the keys to a room so small and with a ceiling so high that it was not unlike living at the bottom of an airshaft. It had a desk and a window and a bathroom and a bed, a narrow twin bed that had lost its twin. Its sheets had the unmistakable scent of Brakebills laundry, and the smell immediately sent Quentin dropping like a stone down a well of memory, back to the years he'd spent sleeping snugly wrapped up in Brakebills bedclothes, dreaming of a future very different from the one he now inhabited.

It wasn't nostalgia exactly; Quentin didn't miss the old days. But he did miss Fillory. It was only when he was finally alone in his room—not a king's room, a teacher's room, a very junior teacher's room—with the door shut that Quentin allowed himself to really truly long for it. He yearned for it. He felt the full force of what he'd lost. He lay down and stared up at the faraway ceiling and thought of everything that was happening there without him, the journeys and adventures and feasts and all the various magical wonders, all across the length and breadth of Fillory, the rivers and oceans and trees and meadows, and he wanted to be there so badly that it felt like his desire should be enough to physically pull him out of his flat hard bed, out of this world, and into the one he belonged in. But it wasn't, and it didn't.

They gave him a teaching schedule. They gave him a seat in the dining room, and the authority to discipline students. They also gave him something he should have gotten long ago, something he'd almost forgotten he didn't have: a discipline.

Every magician had a natural predisposition to a certain specific kind of magic. Sometimes it was something trivial, sometimes it was genuinely useful, but everyone had one: it was a kind of sorcerous fingerprint. But they'd never been able to find Quentin's. As part of his induction into the Brakebills faculty Quentin was required to state his discipline, at which point it occurred to him that he still didn't know what it was.

Just as they had a dozen years ago they sent him to Professor Sunderland, a woman with whom he'd been seethingly, volcanically infatuated when he was an undergraduate. She met him in the same long sunlit lab she'd worked in back then; it was weird to think that she'd been here this whole time while he'd been off careening disastrously around the multiverse, and that they were now, for most practical purposes, peers.

If anything she was even more beautiful than she had been at twenty-five. Her face had ripened and softened. She looked more like herself, though what he'd thought of at the time as her serene, otherworldly quality now felt a bit more like a slight lack of affect—he hadn't noticed how withdrawn and shut-down she was.

He'd felt so far below her then, he wasn't sure she'd even remember him. But she did.

"Of course I do. You weren't quite as invisible as you thought you were."

Had he thought that? Probably he had.

"Does that mean my secret crush on you wasn't as secret as I thought it was?"

She smiled, but not unkindly.

"The concealment of crushes probably isn't your discipline," she said. "Roll up your sleeves, above your elbows. Let me see the backs of your hands."

He showed her. She gave them a brisk rub with fine powder and an irregular pattern of tiny cold sparks appeared on his skin, like a sparsely populated countryside seen from above by night. He thought he felt a web of icy prickles too, though that could have been his imagination.

"Mmmmm."

She chewed her lip, studying him, then she tapped his hands, one, two, like a child playing a game, and the sparks went out. There was nothing there that interested Professor Sunderland. Or Pearl—now that they were colleagues he should get in the habit of calling her by her first name.

She snipped a lock of his hair and burned it in a brazier. It smelled like burning hair. She scrutinized the smoke.

"Nope."

Now that the pleasantries were out of the way she was all business. He could have been a tricky flower arrangement that she couldn't get quite right. She studied him through a graduated series of smoked lenses while he walked backward around the room.

"Why do you think this is so difficult?" Quentin asked, trying not to run into anything.

"Mm? Don't look over your shoulder."

"My discipline? Why do you think it's so hard to figure out?"

"Could be a few things." She smoothed her straight blond hair back behind her ears and switched lenses. "It could be occluded. Some disciplines just by their natures don't want to be found. Some are just really minor, pointless really, and it's hard to pick them out of the background noise."

"Right. Though could it also be"—he stumbled over a stool—"because it's something interesting? That no one's ever seen before?"

"Sure. Why not."

He'd always envied Penny his fancy and apparently unique discipline, which was interdimensional travel. But from her tone he suspected she could have listed a few reasons why not.

"Remember when I made those sparks, that one time?"

"I remember. Aha. I can't believe I didn't think of this before. Stand still."

He stopped, and Pearl rummaged in a drawer and took out a heavy, brass-edged ruler marked in irregular units that Quentin didn't recognize.

"Close your eyes."

He did, and immediately an electric bar of pain flashed across the back of his right hand. He clamped it between his knees; it was ten seconds before he even recovered enough to say *ow*. When he opened his eyes he half expected to see his fingers sheared right off at the second knuckle.

They were still there, though they were turning red. She'd whacked them with the sharp edge of the ruler.

"Sorry," she said. "The pain response is often very revealing."

"Listen, if that doesn't do it I think I'm all right with not knowing."

"No, that did it. You're very sensitive, I must say."

Quentin didn't think that not wanting to get smacked across the knuckles with a ruler made him unusually sensitive, but he didn't say anything, and Pearl was already paging through a huge old reference book printed all in jewel type. Quentin had a sudden crazy urge to stop her. He'd been living with this for so long, it was part of who he was—he was the Man Without a Discipline. Was he ready to give that up? If she told him he'd be like everybody else . . .

But he didn't stop her.

"I had a pet theory about you." Pearl ran her finger down a column. "Which was that I couldn't find your discipline last time because you didn't have one yet. I always thought you were a bit young for your age. Personality is a factor—maturity. You were old enough to have a discipline, but emotionally you weren't there yet. You hadn't come into focus."

That was kind of embarrassing. And like his crush, it had probably been obvious to more people than he realized.

"I guess I'm a late bloomer," Quentin said.

"There you are." She tapped the page. "Repair of small objects, that's you."

"Repair of small objects."

"Uh-huh!"

He couldn't honestly say that it was everything he'd hoped for.

"Small like a chair?"

"Think smaller," she said. "Like, I don't know, a coffee cup." She shaped her hands around an invisible mug. "Have you had any special luck with that? Lesser bindings, reconstitutions, that kind of thing?"

"Maybe. I don't know." He couldn't actually say that he'd ever noticed. Maybe he just hadn't been paying attention.

It was a bit of an anticlimax. You couldn't call it sexy, exactly. Not breaking new ground, so much. He wouldn't be striding between dimensions, or calling down thunderbolts, or manifesting patroni, not on the strength of *repair of small objects*. Life was briskly and efficiently stripping Quentin of his last delusions about himself, one by one, shucking them off in firm hard jerks like wet clothes, leaving him naked and shivering.

But it wasn't going to kill him. It wasn't sexy, but it was real, and that was what mattered now. No more fantasies—that was life after Fillory. Maybe when you give up your dreams, you find out that there's more to life than dreaming. He was going to live in the real world from now on, and he was going to learn to appreciate its rough, mundane solidity. He'd been learning a lot about himself lately, and he'd thought it would be painful, and it was, but it was a relief too. These were things he'd been scared to face his whole life, and now that he was looking them in the eye they weren't quite as scary as he thought.

Or maybe he was tougher than he thought. At any rate he wouldn't have to be retroactively expelled from the Physical Kids. Repair of small objects would have made the cut.

"Off you go," Pearl said. "Fogg will probably have you take over the First Year class on Minor Mendings."

"I expect he will," Quentin said.

And he did.

CHAPTER 3

Quentin thought he'd find teaching satisfying, but he didn't actually expect to enjoy it. That seemed like too much to hope for. But as it turned out he did enjoy it.

Five mornings a week at nine A.M. he stood up in front of Minor Mendings, chalk in hand, scribbled lecture notes in front of him, and looked out at the students—his students now—and they looked back at him. Mostly their faces were blank—blank with terror, blank with total confusion, blank with boredom, but blank. Quentin realized now that that must be how he used to look. When you were just one of the class you tended to forget the professor could see you.

His first lecture was not a success. He stuttered; he repeated himself; he lost his train of thought and stopped cold, dead air, while he tried to figure out where he'd been going with this a second ago. He'd prepared ten points he wanted to cover, but he was so afraid that he'd run out of material that he dragged out the first point for half an hour and then had to rush through the other nine at top speed to fit them all in. It turned out that teaching was a skill you had to learn, like everything else.

But gradually it dawned on him that he at least knew what he was talking about. His track record in life and love wasn't exactly flawless, but he did possess a large amount of practical information about the care and feeding of supernatural forces, and teaching was just a matter of getting that information out of his head and into the clever, receptive heads of his students in orderly installments. It was a long way from running a secret magical kingdom, but then again Fillory had never really needed him that badly, had it. Fillory pretty much ran itself. Whereas these kids, floundering as they were in the choppy, frigid waters of introductory gramarye, would have been lost without him. They needed him, and it felt good to be needed.

Knowing his discipline helped too. He'd always considered himself decent at magic, but he'd never had a strong sense of exactly who he was as a magician. Now he did: he was someone who fixed things. He saw that now. Give Quentin a broken object and in his hands it woke up, as if from an unhappy dream, and remembered that it had once been whole. A smashed coffee cup, so utterly hopeless and without power, bestirred itself and regained some of its old gumption. It hadn't always been this way. No—it had once had a convenient handle. It had once had the power to hang on to a liquid instead of letting it gush through its shattered innards onto the floor.

And with a little encouragement from Quentin, it would again. God, but he loved doing magic. He'd almost forgotten how satisfying it was, even the little things. Doing magic was like finally finding the words you'd been groping for your whole life. You'd always known what you wanted to say, it was on the tip of your tongue, you almost had it, you knew it a moment ago but somehow forgot it—and then there it was. Casting the spell was like finally finding the words: there, that's what I meant, that's what I've been trying to say all along.

All he had to do was explain this to his students. As a faculty member he was also expected to conduct independent research, but until he could come up with a problem that was worth researching, teaching was what he did. He did it five days a week, a lecture at nine and then Practical Applications at two.

At the same time he settled back into the rhythm of life at Brakebills, which wasn't so different as a professor than it had been as a student. He didn't have homework anymore, but he had to spend his nights preparing lectures, which was fine because he didn't have much else to do anyway. He held himself appropriately aloof from his students, and so far the other faculty, appropriately or not, left the new fish to his own devices.

Little things had changed. Rumor had it that Brakebills had

acquired a ghost, and though Fogg hadn't seen it himself—it wasn't clear who had—he was bursting with pride about it. Apparently all the old European institutions had them, and in those circles a magic school hadn't really arrived till it was haunted. The library was still giving trouble: a few books in some of the more obscure corners of the stacks retained some autonomy, dating back to an infamous early experiment with flying books, and lately they'd begun to breed. Shocked undergraduates had stumbled on books in the very act.

Which sounded interesting, but so far the resulting offspring had been either predictably derivative (in fiction) or stunningly boring (nonfiction); hybrid pairings between fiction and nonfiction were the most vital. The librarian thought the problem was just that the right books weren't breeding with each other and proposed a forced mating program. The library committee had an epic secret meeting about the ethics of literary eugenics which ended in a furious deadlock.

Quentin could feel himself slipping back into the thick, rich, comforting atmosphere of Brakebills, like a bee drowning in honey. Sometimes he caught himself thinking about what it would be like to stay there forever. And he might have done that if something hadn't interrupted him: his father died.

It caught Quentin off guard. It had been a long time since he'd felt close to his father. He didn't think about him much, or his mother. It had never even occurred to him that his father could die.

Quentin's dad had lived an unspectacular life, and he slipped out of the world at sixty-seven with the unshowiness that was his trademark: he died in his sleep of a stroke. He even managed to spare Quentin's mom the shock of waking up next to a slowly cooling corpse: she was doing an artist's residency in Provincetown, and his body was discovered by the woman who did the cleaning instead, a stolid, rigorously Catholic Ukrainian who was in every way more spiritually prepared for the experience than Quentin's mom would have been.

It happened in mid-October, about six weeks after Quentin came back to Brakebills. Dean Fogg brought him the news, which had been transmitted to him via the school's one ancient rotary telephone. When Quentin understood what Fogg was telling him he went very cold and very still. It was impossible. It made no sense. It was as if his father had announced that he was going to take up mariachi drumming and march in the Cinco de Mayo parade. His father couldn't be dead—he wouldn't be. It just wasn't *like* him.

Fogg seemed nonplussed by his reaction, almost disappointed, as if he were hoping to get a little more drama out of it. Quentin would have given him drama if he knew how, but it wouldn't come. He didn't sob or tear his hair or curse the Norns who had snipped his father's thread too soon. He wanted to but he couldn't, and he didn't understand why he couldn't. The feelings were missing; it was like they'd been lost in transit from whatever country feelings come from. Only after Fogg had offered him a week of compassionate leave and then tactfully withdrawn did Quentin begin to thaw out and feel something besides shock and confusion, and when he did what he felt wasn't grief, it was anger.

That made even less sense. He didn't even know who he was angry at or why. What, was he angry at his dad for being dead? At Fogg for telling him? At himself for not grieving like he should?

When he thought about it Quentin couldn't remember ever having felt very close to his father, even as a little kid. He'd seen photographs from his childhood that showed boy-Quentin in scenes of ordinary family happiness with his parents, that could have been convincingly presented in family court as evidence that the Coldwater home was a warm and loving one. But Quentin didn't recognize the child who looked back at him out of those snapshots. He couldn't remember ever having been that person. He felt like a changeling.

Quentin took Fogg up on that week of compassionate leave, not so much because he felt like he needed it but because he thought that his mom might need the help. As he packed for the trip to Chesterton, Quentin realized he was gritting his teeth against actual panic. He was worried he wouldn't be able to feel the emotions people wanted him to feel. He made himself a promise that whatever happened, whatever anybody asked of him, he wouldn't pretend to feel anything he didn't really feel. If he could stick to that things couldn't get too bad.

And as soon as he saw her Quentin remembered that even if he and his mom weren't especially close they got along fine. He found her standing by the kitchen island, one hand on the granite countertop, a ballpoint pen next to it—she looked like her mind had wandered off in the middle of making a list. She'd been crying, but her eyes were dry now.

He put his bag down and they embraced. She'd put on weight; she made a significant armful now. Quentin had the sense that she hadn't talked to very many people since it happened. He sat down next to her on a stool.

"The tennis girls will be here in a minute," she said.

"That's good. Good to see them."

The tennis girls—Kitsy, Mollie, Roslyn—were his mother's best friends. It had been a long time since any of them had played tennis, if they ever had, but Quentin knew his mom could count on them.

"I wasn't done with the wall treatment in the bathroom." She sighed. A heavy chunk of ice like a giant tooth hung from the eave outside the kitchen window—it was January in the real world. "I knew he was going to hate it. I keep thinking that if he hadn't died the wall would have killed him."

"Mom. The wall would not have killed him."

"I was doing mini–palm trees. I hid it behind that old Japanese screen. I didn't want him to see till it was too late to do anything about it." She took off her oversized glasses and rubbed her face with both hands, like a diver taking off her mask after a deep descent. "And now it's all too late! I don't know any of his passwords. Can you believe it? I can't even find his keys! I can't even get into the basement!"

He made a mental note to locate those keys later with a spell. He might even be able to come up with the passwords too, though that would be trickier.

Part of the trouble between Quentin and his parents, he knew, was that they had no idea who he really was, which wasn't their fault because he'd never told them. Quentin's mom thought her son was a comfortably but not spectacularly successful investment banker specializing in real estate transactions. She didn't know that magic was real. Quentin's father hadn't known either.

Quentin could have told them—the information was tightly

controlled by magicians, and transgressions were punished sharply, but exceptions could be obtained for parents and spouses (and children over fourteen). But he never had, because it seemed like such a terrible idea. He couldn't imagine the two worlds touching: his parents' sedate, orderly marital idyll and the wild, messy, arcane world of magic. It was impossible. They would explode on contact, like matter and antimatter.

Or he always assumed they would. Now he wondered if that secret, the absence of that confidence, was what had come between them. Maybe he'd underestimated them.

Quentin and his mother spent his week of leave rattling around the Chesterton McMansion like two dice in a plastic cup—it was a huge house for a middling-successful painter and a textbook editor, bought with money from a Brooklyn brownstone they'd cashed out of at just the right time. There was a lot to do. Death was an existential catastrophe, a rip in the soft upholstery with which humanity padded over a hard uncaring universe, but it turned out there were an amazing number of people whose job it was to deal with it for you, and all they asked in return were huge quantities of time and money.

Quentin spent a whole day on the phone with his mother's credit cards fanned out on the cold kitchen counter in front of him. She watched him with wary surprise. They'd seen so little of each other these past few years that she still thought of him as the shoe-gazing teenager he'd been when he left for Brakebills. She was baffled by this tall, firm, no-longer-teenaged man who presented her with lists of urns to choose from, menus of hors d'oeuvres for the reception, times when town cars would pick her up and drop her off.

At night they ordered take-out and played Scrabble and watched movies on the couch, drinking the melony Sonoma Chardonnay that she ordered by the case. At the back of his mind Quentin kept cuing up and replaying scenes from his childhood. His father teaching him to sail on a sandy-bottomed, brown-water lake in New Hampshire. His father picking him up from school after he got sick in gym class. When he was twelve they'd had a full-scale blowout shouting match when his father refused to sign the permission slip for Quentin to go to a chess tournament; it was the first time he'd qualified in the under-fifteens, and he was desperate to make the trip to Tarrytown. It was strange: his father had never seemed comfortable with Quentin's efforts to stand out academically. You'd think he would've been proud.

That first night, after his mom went to bed, Quentin went and sat in his father's study. It was a boxy, white-walled room that still smelled like new construction. The parquet looked brand new except for the matte circle where the wheels of his father's desk chair had worn away the finish. He was half drunk on Chardonnay.

He knew what he was looking for: he was looking for a way to stop feeling angry. He was still carrying the anger around and he wanted somewhere he could safely put it down. He sat in his father's chair and rotated slowly in place, like a lighthouse. He looked at the books, the files, the window, the dead computer screen. Books, files, window, screen. Particles of faint sodium-orange light from the streetlights outside lay on everything like dust.

That was when it occurred to Quentin for the first time that maybe his father hadn't been his real father. Maybe he wasn't who he appeared to be. Maybe Quentin's father had been a magician.

The next morning, after his mother left to do a big shop at Whole Foods, Quentin went back to his father's study. He resumed his post in his father's chair.

Quentin knew he was a little old to be wrestling with questions like this—probably he should have had them wrapped up by around puberty—but he'd always paid more attention to magical problems than to the personal kind. Maybe that had been a mistake. Your father was supposed to love you, to pass on his power to you, to show you what it was to be a man, and his father hadn't. He'd been a good person, or good enough, but mostly what he'd showed Quentin was how to move through the universe while disturbing it as little as possible, and how to compile and maintain the world's most complete collection of Jeff Goldblum movies on Blu-ray, apart, presumably, from Jeff Goldblum's.

Quentin hadn't had much luck with father figures. Not Dean Fogg, not Mayakovsky, not Ember the ram god. They hadn't dispensed a whole lot of paternal wisdom to him over the years. Whatever power and wisdom they had, they hadn't been eager to share it with him. Maybe they didn't want to be his father figures. Maybe he hadn't made an especially appealing son figure.

Quentin tried to imagine what his father should have been like, the father he wished his father had been. Brilliant. Funny. Intense. A bit of a rogue—at times even eccentric—but steady in a crisis. A man of grit and energy, a man who faced the world around him and brought it to heel on his own terms. A magician's father. A father who would have seen what Quentin had made of himself and been proud.

But Quentin's father seemed not to have had any power at all, let alone any to share. Quentin's actual father had had one wife, one son, no hobbies, and probably a case of mild clinical depression which he self-medicated with work. Not everybody led a double life, but Quentin's father had barely led a single one. How could somebody who seemed so determined to be powerless have a magician for a son?

Unless he hadn't been powerless, Quentin thought. Unless that wasn't the whole story. It was starting to sound like a cover story—exactly the kind of cover story a magician would use.

Methodically Quentin examined the study for evidence that his father wasn't what he seemed to be—that he'd left some legacy for his son that for whatever reason he couldn't share with him while he was alive. He went through his father's filing cabinets—there were charms for searching paper documents for keywords, the same way computers searched digital files. He checked for codes or hidden scripts. He got back no results of any significance.

He hadn't expected any. That was merely due diligence. Now the hunt could begin in earnest.

He examined the light fixtures. He squeezed the couch cushions and pulled up the rugs. He used a spell to peer into the walls and under the floorboards. He looked behind the pictures. He scoured the room to the studs for any trace of hidden magic, but all he found was an old library book with a weak anti-theft charm put on it by somebody else, which in any case didn't appear to have worked. At least the missing keys turned up in the couch.

He checked the furniture for hollow legs. He riffled through every book on the shelves in case one was underlined or hollowed out. Once in a while he thought he was picking up on something, a secret pattern or a code, but every time he did it dissolved again like fairy gold, back into random noise. What dark magicks could his father have been trafficking in, that he would have kept them this well hidden? That he would have leaned on his son, tried to stop him from drawing attention to himself? What sinister fate had Quentin avoided in Tarrytown? What did it mean that his father kept an old unstrung banjo in one corner? What was with his weird obsession with Jeff Goldblum?

The longer he worked with no result, the more clearly he felt the ghostly presence of his father, his real father, his true father, as if he were in the room with him even now. Quentin booted up the computer and after a half hour of sweaty-palmed cryptomancy and educated guesswork he cracked the password *(thelostworld*—starring Jeff Goldblum!) and began casing file directories, one after the other.

They were almost eerily clean. No diary, no poetry, no mistresses, no Ponzi schemes, nothing that wasn't what it appeared to be. Not even any porn. Well, not much porn.

Quentin was no hacker—he'd spent way too much time in the technological black hole of Brakebills to have any serious chops with computers—but he knew some electromagnetic sorcery. He cracked the case and went directly after the silicon, feeling with magical fingertips for anything weird, any walled-off caches of hidden electrons pregnant with meaning. All he could think was, this can't be it. This cannot be everything. He must have left me something.

Come on. Help me, Daddy. It was a word he hadn't said or even thought in twenty years.

He stopped and sat for a minute, his hands trembling, in the empty house, in the deep cold suburban winter silence. Where is it, Dad? It must be here. I can't be alone. You must have left me something. This was always how it worked: the distant, withholding father was always guarding a terrible secret, always keeping his son safe from it, able to pass on his legacy of power only in death.

And then he found it. It was at the back of a closet: a nubbly red plastic carton of index cards scribbled on in pencil, shoved behind a box of obsolete electronics and mysterious cables that were too important-looking to throw away. He set the carton on the desk and flipped through the cards, one by one. Strange names, columns of numbers, pluses and minuses. It went on and on. It was a lot of data. A cipher like this could contain whole worlds of power, if he could break it. And he would. It was left here for him.

He stared at the cards for it must have been ten minutes before the pattern solved itself all at once. It wasn't a cipher at all. These were stats from his father's old fantasy golf league. Quentin pushed the plastic box away from him violently, convulsively. The cards spilled out all over the rug. He left them there.

There was no mystery to solve. What had come between him and his father wasn't magic. The terrible truth about Quentin's father was that he was exactly the person he seemed to be. He wasn't a magician. He wasn't even a good person. He was an ordinary man who hadn't even loved his only son. The hard truth was that Quentin had never really had a father.

And now he never would. Quentin put his head down on his father's old desk and pounded his fist until his father's crap old plastic keyboard jumped.

"Daddy!" he sobbed, in a voice he barely recognized. "Daddy, Daddy, Daddy!"

Quentin went back to Brakebills the day after the funeral. He didn't like to leave his mother, but she was more comfortable with her friends than she was with him, and it was time for them to take over. He'd done his part.

She drove him to the airport; he waited till she was out of sight before he walked away from the departure area to a parking garage that was still under construction. He took the elevator to the empty top floor. At the stroke of noon, under a flat white sky, a portal opened for him, a ring of white dots connected by white lines that sizzled and sparked in the cold dry air, and he stepped through it and back onto the Brakebills campus. Back home.

Climbing the stairs to his room, he felt strange. It was like he'd had a week of high fever that had finally crested and broken, leaving him empty and cold and shaky but also washed clean, the toxins sweated out, the impurities burned away. His father's death had changed him, and it was the kind of change that you didn't change back from. Daddy was gone. He was never coming home. It was time to move on.

When he walked into his room Quentin performed a small incendiary charm to light a candle, a spell he'd done a thousand times, but this time the sudden flare startled him. It was brighter and hotter than he remembered.

Quentin snuffed out the candle and lit it again. There was no question: his magic was different. The light that played around his hands as he worked was more intense than it had been a week ago. In the darkness the colors were shifted a bit toward the violent violet end of the spectrum. The power came more easily, and it buzzed harder and louder in his fingers.

He studied his hands. Something had broken loose in him. He was truly alone in the world now, no one was coming to help him. He would have to help himself. Somewhere deep in his unconscious he'd been waiting, holding back some last fraction of power. But not anymore.

Late that night something woke Quentin up out of a deep, dreamless sleep. A dry, scrabbling noise—it sounded like a small rodent was trapped in his room. He lit a lamp. It was coming from his desk.

It wasn't a rodent, it was a piece of paper. He'd all but forgotten about it: it was the page he'd snatched out of the air as he left the Netherlands and stuffed into his pocket and then shoved to the back of a desk drawer. Something had woken it up, and it was uncrumpling itself.

When he opened the drawer it made a wild bid for freedom. The page had folded itself in three sections like a business letter and now it unfolded all at once, launching itself a couple of feet in the air. Having gotten that far it hastily refolded itself the long way and began flapping frantically in circles in the dim light, around and around his head, like a moth around a lamp. Or like a memory of another life, another world, that wouldn't stay buried.

CHAPTER 4

Quentin didn't look at the page from the Neitherlands that night. That night he put a paperweight on it, locked the desk drawer, and propped a chair against it to make sure it stayed closed. He had to teach in the morning. He went back to bed and put a pillow over his head.

It wasn't till late the next afternoon, after P.A., that he unpropped the chair and unlocked the drawer. Slowly he eased it open. The page had gone still—but evidently it had been psyching itself up for this moment because as soon as he took away the paperweight it took off again.

Quentin watched it thrash along in the air, feeling a little sorry for it. He wondered where it was trying to get to. Back to the Neitherlands, probably. Back home.

He plucked it gently out of the air and took it over to the window seat so he could look at it in the sunlight. Holding it flat with his palm, he weighed it down at its four corners with a candlestick, an alarm clock, an empty wineglass, and a fossilized ammonite that he kept on his desk. The page knew when it was beaten. It gave up and went still.

Now he could see what he was dealing with. The text was handwritten, both sides, closely and minutely lettered in black ink with an occasional important word in red. It was a serious sort of page, dense with information. The paper was old, not modern paper—which gradually ate itself because of the acid in its own wood pulp—but rag paper, made from cotton scraps, which would last practically forever. It was torn along one edge where it had been roughly ripped from its host book. A few letters had been left behind in the process, but only a few.

The regular, urgent forward tilt of the black script gave the words a purposeful look, like they were trails of gunpowder leading toward some explosive revelation. Whoever wrote it had had something to say. In places the text blocks were broken up to make room for charts and diagrams: a table of numbers with a lot of decimal points; a small but precise botanical sketch of a flowerless plant, with neat rows of leaves and a hollow seedpod; an elegant diagram of concentric and overlapping circles and ellipses that could equally easily have been an atom or a solar system.

The page began in the middle of one sentence. It ended in the middle of another.

When he looked closer he saw that the leaves of the plant were wavering very slightly in the breeze, and the planets (or electrons) in the diagrams were very slowly progressing in their orbits, which themselves precessed in an orderly dance around one another. The values in the table changed in sync with them.

At first Quentin thought he couldn't read the script at all, and he sighed out loud with relief when he began to recognize a word here and there. It was a late, rather corrupt form of Old High German, written in some eccentric variation of black-letter Gothic. He could hum the tune even if he didn't quite get every single lyric.

That, however, was the last break he caught. The contents were highly theoretical and abstract—seriously high-altitude stuff, up there where the conceptual oxygen was dangerously thin. There was a lot of business about magic and matter and high-level exchanges between the two under extreme conditions, at the quantum level. Sometimes it was hard to tell how much of it was literal and how much of it was metaphor: when it talked about a rooster, was that some kind of symbolic alchemical rooster? Or was it an actual rooster, with feathers, cock-a-doodle-do? There wasn't much context to go on.

And that plant. He was going to have to take this over to Professor Bax in the greenhouse (or as the students referred to it, inevitably, Botany Bay). After staring at the page for three hours, during which he didn't even make it to the other side, Quentin sat back and pressed the heels of his hands against his aching eyes.

He'd missed dinner, but he could still eat with the kitchen staff. One thing was clear: this was a fragment chipped off the great arcane magical database of the adepts of the Neitherlands themselves, Penny's gang. It was like an ultradense meteorite from some extrasolar intellectual realm, and it had come crashing to Earth, and there was no telling what exotic, unearthly elements it might contain.

He'd found a topic for his independent research project, anyway, Dean Fogg could stop noodging him about that. And in a small way he'd found a new adventure. It was a different kind of adventure from what they had in Fillory, a small and kind of nerdy adventure, but there was no question that's what this was.

"Thank you," he said to the page. "Thank you for being here. Whatever it is you've got inside you, I'll take good care of it. I promise."

Was it his imagination? Did the page unfold itself slightly—did it preen itself a little, basking in the praise of its reader? He took the heavy candlestick off one corner. Then, carefully, the wineglass and the clock. As soon as he moved the ammonite the page shot sideways, making for the crack under the window.

"Not yet." He slapped his hand down on it and replaced the candlestick with a clunk. "I'm sorry, I really am. But not yet."

There was one aspect of Quentin's life at Brakebills that was still less than ideal, and that was his social life. He didn't have one.

Even though he was almost thirty he was a lot younger than most of the faculty, and he was having a hard time connecting with them. Maybe it was the age thing, or that he hadn't properly paid his dues yet, which was true. Maybe they figured he wouldn't be here that long, so what was the point. The politics of the senior common room were byzantine and involved a lot of power struggles to which he, as low man on the totem pole, just wasn't very relevant.

Also it was possible that they just didn't like him very much. It had been known to happen.

Whatever the reason, he drew a lot of undesirable solo duties, like refereeing cold, wet welters matches and patching the dull but finicky network of spells that was supposed to bust students breaking curfew. (Now that he got a close look at it, he couldn't believe how much they used to worry about getting caught. The spells were so rickety and put out so many false alarms that the faculty mostly ignored them.)

The next day after P.A., Quentin walked over to Botany Bay. His expectations weren't high. He'd never spoken to the department chair, Hamish Bax, and he didn't know what to make of him. On the plus side he was youngish, at least by Brakebills standards, mid-thirties maybe. On the minus side he was unbelievably affected: he was black and from Cleveland but dressed in Scottish tweeds and smoked a fat Turk's-head pipe. He was the first person Quentin had ever seen in real life wearing plus fours. The whole business made him hard to read. Though maybe that was the point.

At least Quentin had an excuse to visit the greenhouse, which was a lovely bit of Victorian iron and glass tracery that looked too delicate to withstand an upstate winter. Inside it was a green bubble of warm, humid air full of tables of potted plants of all imaginable shapes and sizes. The cement floor was wet. Short and solidly built, Professor Bax greeted him with the same lack of interest as the rest of the faculty. He didn't seem particularly pleased to be interrupted doing whatever he was doing with his arms up to the elbows in a giant ceramic pot full of black earth. But he brightened up when Quentin zipped open a velvet-lined portfolio and the page immediately shook itself and wriggled free, like a silvery fish escaping a net.

"That's a live one," he said, teeth clenched around his pipe.

He wiped his hands on a rag. Using a quick spell that completely eluded Quentin's comprehension he trapped the page flat in the air in front of him, as if between two panes of glass. It was the kind of fluent, rather technical magic you didn't expect from a botanist.

"Mmmmm. You're a long way from home." Then he addressed Quentin. "Where'd you get this?"

"I could tell you but you wouldn't believe me. Do you recognize the plant?"

"I don't. Think it's a real plant? Drawn from life?"

"I have no idea," Quentin admitted. "Do you?"

Professor Bax studied the page for five minutes, first from so close his face almost touched the paper, then from a yard away, then—he had to shift a table crammed with seedlings in egg cartons—from across the room.

He took his pipe out of his mouth.

"I'm going to say a word you don't know."

"OK," Quentin said.

"Phyllotaxis."

"Don't know it."

"It's the way leaves are arranged around a central stalk," Professor Bax said. "It looks chaotic but it's not, it follows a mathematical sequence. Usually Fibonacci, sometimes Lucas. But the leaves on this plant don't follow either of those. Which suggests that its origin is exceptionally exotic."

"Or that it's just a made-up drawing."

"Right. And Occam's razor says it probably is. And yet." Hamish frowned. "It's got something. Plants have a certain integrity to them, you know? Hard to fake that. You're sure you can't tell me where it's from?"

"I shouldn't."

"Don't then." He gestured at the text. "Can you read that shit?"

"I'm working on it."

Professor Bax released the page from its trap. He plucked it out of the air before it could fall. It was limp and pliant in his hands—it seemed more submissive to his authority than to Quentin's.

"Grand," he said. "Drink?"

Yes was the only possible answer. Bax retrieved a fifth of rye from in among the flowerpots, where he'd apparently hastily concealed it right before Quentin came in.

Just like that Quentin had shattered whatever invisible barrier stood between him and the rest of the faculty, or at least one member of the faculty—it emerged over the course of the afternoon that Hamish wasn't much more popular with the other professors than Quentin was. Whatever nameless sin Quentin had committed, Hamish had committed it too. They were the same kind of radioactive. Quentin started coming by

the greenhouse regularly after Practical Applications, and he and
Hamish would have a couple of whiskeys before dinner.

Hamish initiated him into some of the deeper mysteries of the Brakebills campus. What was really surprising was how much of the stuff that
the undergraduates whispered about after hours was actually true. That
blank stretch of wall, for example, where there ought to have been a room,
and the plaster was a shade lighter—that really wasn't an air shaft. Back
in the 1950s some students had set up a cubic thermal field in their room,
possibly to keep beer cold, but having already consumed some of the beer
they inverted a couple of glyphs, which had the unexpected effect of driv-
ing the temperature inside down very close to absolute zero. The resulting
field was so stable that nobody could figure out a way to dispel it.

It was perfectly harmless unless you walked into it, in which case you'd
be dead before you knew it. One of the kids who cast it lost a hand that
way, or so it was said. Eventually the faculty just shrugged their shoulders
and walled it off. Supposedly the lost, frozen hand was still in there.

Likewise, it was true: the clock was powered by a gear made of metal
reclaimed from the body of the Silver Golem of Białystok. It was also true
that there was a childishly humorous anagram for Brakebills, that it was
Biker Balls, and that the chalkboards would squeak painfully if you tried to
write it on them. It was true that ivy wouldn't grow on that one bare patch
of wall behind the kitchens because one of the stones had been violently
cursed in a really ugly incident involving a student who'd slipped through
the admissions protocols meant to screen out sociopaths and other people
mentally unfit to handle magic. On humid days it sweated acid.

There was also a secret seventh fountain, underground, accessible
through a door set in the dusty plank floor of a gardening shed; it was
kept cordoned off because the water teemed with hungry, sharp-toothed
fish. And Quentin had never known how the Maze was redrawn over
the summer, but apparently every year in June the groundskeeper
goaded the topiary animals into such a feeding frenzy that they fell
upon and devoured each other in a kind of ghastly slow-motion vegetar-
ian holocaust. The Maze was built up again out of cuttings from the
survivors. Only the strongest made it through. They must have been
some of the most highly evolved topiary animals on Earth.

This was Quentin's world now, and it was amazing to him how quickly he came to accept it, even embrace it. He'd gone from king to schoolteacher, been forcibly transplanted from the grand magical cosmos of Fillory to this hole in the wall that he thought he'd escaped forever, and lo and behold he was adjusting. It turns out you can go home again, if you have to. His future was here; the years he'd spent in Fillory were gone now as if they'd never happened. He mourned them alone, the only person on Earth who knew that once upon a time he used to wear a crown and sit on a throne. But you couldn't mourn forever. Or you could, but as it turned out there were better things to do.

Pacing the aisles of a silent classroom, surveying the exposed napes of rows and rows of students bent over their fall exams, he realized he'd lost his old double vision, the one that was always looking for something more, somewhere else, the world behind the world. It was his oldest possession, and he'd let it slip away without even noticing it was gone. He was becoming someone else, someone new.

It was crazy to think that the others were still over there, riding out on hunts, receiving people in their receiving rooms, meeting every afternoon in the tallest tower of Castle Whitespire. And Julia was on the Far Side of the World doing God knew what. But that had nothing to do with him now. After all that it turned out that wasn't his story. It had all been a temporary aberration, and in due time it had corrected itself.

Though he did still look up at the moon once in a while, expecting to find the clean, crisp crescent of Fillory. By comparison Earth's moon looked as pale and shabby and worn as an old dime.

They were only a hundred miles north of Manhattan, but the winters at Brakebills had a different quality from winter in the city: deeper, heavier, firmer, more decisive. It was as if, because it came three months late, Brakebills winter was determined to sock you in for good and all. It was February on the outside, and the birds and plants were beginning to show glimmers of cautious optimism, but Brakebills was still wallowing in a foot and a half of deep silent November snow.

Now that he was teaching Quentin could see why the faculty didn't bother trying to improve the climate. It kept people amazingly focused. You saw the undergrads try to jog their way through the snow, kicking up puffs of powder, then give up and just slog. You could actually watch as the determination to seize the moment and live life to the fullest ebbed right out of them, and they resigned themselves to lonely, silent, indoor study instead. There was a perennial proposal on the table, never quite adopted, to keep it winter at Brakebills all year round.

Quentin was doing quite a bit of studying himself. He'd transcribed the whole page, 402 words arranged in twenty sentences, plus an incomplete one at the beginning and another at the end, and papered his walls with it. Each word got its own separate sheet, which he filled up with annotations and connected to other words with long curvy chalk lines to indicate related concepts. He was literally living inside the page.

He kept up with his teaching, but other than that decrypting the page was his full-time occupation. As he got deeper into it he began to run into a lot of mathematics, which he had to work out with a pencil and paper—you couldn't do magical equations with computers, they just spat out inconsistent answers before hanging completely. Magical math had to be thought through with a brain.

But the page was beginning to open up—like tightly furled buds the words began to bloom and reveal the ideas locked inside them. The concepts unfolded for him, displaying hidden dimensions and interacting with one another in unexpected ways. As they took shape they also gave up clues as to the much larger, more shadowy whole of which they were just a tiny fragment: the book that the page came from. It appeared to be a treatise on the interactions between magic and matter.

On Earth, magic and matter were distinct things: you could cast a spell on an object, and it became enchanted, but the object and the spell remained separate entities—the object was like a piece of metal on which you'd put a magnetic charge. But in Fillory, Quentin knew, or at least strongly suspected, magic and thing were somehow one and the same. Magic existed on Earth, sure, but Fillory *was* magic. It was a fundamental difference.

This was all very theoretical, and Quentin wasn't that into theory. He was still a Physical Kid at heart, and he was more into practice. Under the right conditions, with enough energy, could you make something on Earth magic? Infuse it with magic, melt them together till the seams were gone, like they were in Fillory? It felt like a forbidden idea, a boundary you weren't supposed to cross, but it was too delicious not to at least try.

He requisitioned an empty basement lab, but even with his newly enhanced magical abilities it was difficult to force the delicate abstractions of the page into the crude actual world. Either he came up with nothing, or one of the spells would release a huge wad of energy that lit up the room with icy blue light and practically blew out the wards he'd set up to keep himself from being vaporized. As a precaution he worked the enchantments inside increasingly large, heavy, gluey globes of force, like bubbles blown from a thick viscous translucent liquid, which made it hard to tell what exactly was going on.

And what would he do with it anyway, even if it did work? What good was something magic? This was a powerful enchantment, but it needed a purpose. It was an answer in search of a question. He was getting older, and it was time he thought about making something, building something that would last. But what? He couldn't see how this was getting him any closer.

One evening, standing alone in the senior common room, drinking his first glass of wine for the night and sketching diagrams in his head, he reached into his jacket pocket for his Fillorian watch—which still didn't work, but he liked having it with him anyway—and found an envelope there along with it. Inside was a letter typed on a manual typewriter inviting him politely, even decorously, to show up at such and such a bookstore on such and such a night in March if he was interested in a job. The signature was illegible—bird scratchings.

Huh. It was intriguing, and Quentin felt a little of the old restlessness. Here it was, another mystery to be solved. Your classic passport to adventure, just like back in the old days.

But that was the thing about the old days: they were old. This was his life now. He was content, and if not happy then happier than he ever thought he'd be again. He had work to do. He crumpled up the letter and winged it into the fire. It caught, and a heavy log shifted, sending up sparks. The past was what it was, his home was here, and anything else was a fantasy.

CHAPTER 5

Eliot frowned. The Lorian champion was a squat fellow, practically as wide as he was tall and of some slightly different ethnic background from most of his compatriots. The Lorians were Vikings, basically, Thor types: tall, long blond hair, big chins, big chests, big beards. But this character came in at about five foot six, with a shaved head and a fat round Buddha face like a soup dumpling and a significant admixture of some Asiatic DNA. He was stripped to the waist even though it was about 40 degrees out, and his latte-colored skin was oiled all over. Or maybe he was just really sweaty.

The champion's heavy round gut hung down over his waistband, but he was still a pretty scary-looking bastard. He had a huge saddle of muscle across his upper back, and his biceps were like thighs, and there must have been some muscle in there, just by volume, even if they did look kind of chubby. His weapon was weird-looking enough—a pole arm with a big curvy cross of sharp metal on the end—that you just knew he could do something really outstandingly dangerous with it.

When he stepped forward the Lorian army went nuts for him. They bashed their swords and shields together and looked at each other as if to say: yes, he may look a little funny, but our fellow is definitely going to kill the other fellows' fellow, so three cheers for him, by Crom or whoever it is we worship! It almost made you like them, the Lorians. They were more multicultural than you would have thought.

Though there was no chance that their champion was actually going to kill the Fillorian champion, Eliot's champion. Because Eliot's champion was Eliot.

There had been some debate, when the idea was first mooted, about whether it made sense to send the High King of Fillory into single combat with the handpicked designated hitter of the invading Lorian army. But it rapidly became clear that Eliot was set on it, though his reasons were as much personal as they were tactical. He had begun his stint as High King in a rather decadent vein—louche, you might even say. But as his reign lengthened he had grown into the role, and become more serious about it, and it was time he showed everybody—himself included—how serious he was. Kingship was not an affectation, it was who he was. Very publicly, very literally, he was going to put some skin in the game.

He stepped forward from the front rank of his army, who, predictably but gratifyingly, also went nuts. Eliot smiled—his smile was twisted by his uneven jaw, but his happiness was the real stuff. His heart was in it.

The sound of the king's regiment of the Fillorian army cheering was unlike anything else in the known universe. You had men and women shouting and banging their weapons together, good enough, but then you had a whole orchestra of nonhuman sounds going on around it. At the top end you had some fairies squeeing at supersonic pitches; fairies thought all this military stuff was pretty silly, but they went along with it for the same reason that fairies ever did anything, namely, for the lulz. Then you had bats squeaking, birds squawking, bears roaring, wolves howling, and anything with a horse-head whinnying: pegasi, unicorns, regular talking horses.

Griffins and hippogriffs squawked too, but lower—baritone squawking, a horrible noise. Minotaurs bellowed. Stuff with humans heads yelled. Of all the mythical creatures of Fillory, they were the only ones who still creeped Eliot out. The satyrs and dryads and such were cool, but there were a couple of manticores and sphinxes who were just uncanny as hell.

And so on down the line till you got to the bass notes, which were provided by the giants grunting and stomping their feet. It was silly really: he could have picked a giant as his champion, and then this thing would have been over in about ten seconds flat, pun intended. But that wouldn't have sent the same message.

When Eliot first got the news that the Lorians were invading it had been grimly exciting. Rally the banners, Fillory's at war! Antique formulas and protocols were invoked. A lot of serious-looking non-ceremonial armor and weapons and flags and tack had come up out of storage and been polished and sharpened and oiled. They brought up with them a lot of dust too, and a thrilling smell of great deeds and legendary times. An epic smell. Eliot breathed it in deep.

The invasion wasn't a complete surprise. The Lorians were always up to some kind of bad behavior in the books: kidnapping princes, forcing talking horses to plow fields, trying to get everybody to believe in their slate of quasi-Norse gods. But it had been centuries since they actually crossed the border in force. They were usually too busy fighting among themselves to get that organized.

More to the point, the peaks of the Northern Barrier Range were supposed to be enchanted to keep the Lorians out. That was the Barrier part. Eliot wasn't sure what had happened there. When this was all over he'd have to remember to figure out exactly why those spells had crapped out.

Eliot moved rapidly to expel the Lorians, though he found himself reluctant to be the direct cause of any actual killing. This wasn't Tolkien—these weren't orcs and trolls and giant spiders and whatever else, evil creatures that you were free to commit genocide on without any complicated moral ramifications. Orcs didn't have wives and kids and backstories. But he was pretty sure the Lorians were human, and killing them would be basically murder, and that wasn't going to happen. Some of them were even kind of hot. And anyway those Tolkien books *were fiction,* and Eliot, as High King of Fillory, didn't deal in fiction. He was in the messy business of writing facts.

It was a tricky, ticklish business. There was nothing—in Eliot's admittedly limited experience—more tedious than virtue.

Fortunately the Fillorians had an advantage, which was that they had every possible advantage. They outmatched the Lorians in every stat you could name. The Lorians were a bunch of guys with swords. The Fillorians were every beast in the *Monster Manual,* led by a clique of wizard kings and queens, and Eliot was very sorry but you knew that when you invaded us.

Still, there were a lot of them, and they knew how to do damage—doing damage was pretty much these guys' skill set. It was late spring when the Lorians came pouring through Grudge Gap and onto Fillorian soil. They wore steel caps and mail shirts, and carried notched old swords and war axes. Some rode big shaggy horses. They were met by a nightmare.

See, the Lorians had made a mistake. On their way down from the Northern Barrier Range they set some trees on fire, and an outlying farm, and they killed a hermit.

Even Janet was surprised by Eliot's anger. I mean, she was furious, but she was Janet. She was pissed off all the time. Poppy and Josh looked grim, which was how they got angry. But Eliot's rage was crazy, over the top. They burned trees? His trees? They killed a *hermit*? They *killed* a *hermit*? Where Fillory and the Fillorians were concerned Eliot no longer had any irony. His heart went out to that weird, solitary man in his uncomfortable hut. He'd never met him. They wouldn't have had much to say to each other if they had. But whoever that hermit was, he obviously despised his fellow man, and that meant he was OK in Eliot's book, and now he was dead. Eliot was going to destroy the Lorians, he would annihilate them, he would murder them!

Not murder-murder. But he was going to mess them up good.

He was tempted to let them try to cross the Great Northern Marsh, where the sunken horrors that dwelt there would deal with them, with extreme prejudice, but he didn't want to give them even another day's march on his grass. Besides, there were a couple more farms in the way. Instead he let the Lorians march part of one day, till noon, till they were hot and dusty and ready to knock off for lunch. Probably it was blowing their minds how easy it was all turning out to be. They were going to do it, lads, they were the ones, they were going to take fucking Fillory, dudes! He let them ford the Great Salt River. He met them on the other side.

Eliot went alone, disguised as a peasant. He waited in the middle of the road. He didn't move. He let them notice him gradually. First the guys in front, who when they realized he wasn't going to get out of the way called a halt. He waited while the guys behind those guys got crowded into them, soccer-stadium-style, and they called a halt, and all the way back down the line in a ripple effect. There must have been, he didn't know, maybe a thousand of them.

The man leading the front line stepped out to invite him—not very politely—to kindly get out of the way or one thousand Lorian linebackers would pull his guts out and strangle him with them.

Eliot smiled, shuffled his feet humbly for a second and then punched the guy in the face. It took the man by surprise.

"Get the fuck out of my country, asshole," Eliot said.

That one was on the level, no magic. He'd been taking boxing lessons, and he got the drop on the guy with an off-hand jab. Probably the Lorian wasn't expecting what amounted to a suicide attack from some random peasant. Eliot knew he hadn't done much damage, and that he wouldn't get another shot, so he held up his left hand and force-pushed the man back so hard he brought six ranks of Lorians down with him.

It felt good. Eliot had no children, but this must be what protecting your child felt like. He just wished Quentin could have seen it.

He dropped the cloak and stood up straight in his royal raiment, so it was clear that he was a king and not a peasant. A couple of eager-beaver arrows came arcing over from back in the ranks, and he burned them up in flight: puff, puff, puff. It was easy when you were this angry, and this good, and God he was angry. And good. He tapped the butt of his staff once on the ground: earthquake. All thousand Lorians fell down on their stupid violent asses, in magnificent synchrony.

He couldn't just do that at will, he'd been out here all last night setting up the spells, but it was a great effect, especially since the Lorians didn't know that. Eliot allowed it to sink in.

Then he undid a spell: he made the army behind him visible, or most of it. Take a good look, gentlemen. Those ones with the horse bodies are the hippogriffs. The griffins have the lion bodies. It's easy to mix them up.

Then—and he indulged himself here—he made the giants visible. You do not appreciate at all from fairy tales how unbelievably terrifying a giant is. These players were seven-story giants, and they did not mess around. In real life humans didn't slay giants, because it was impossible. It would be like killing an apartment building with your bare hands.

They were even stronger than they looked—had to be, to beat the square-cube law that made land organisms that big physically impossible in the real world—and their skin was half a foot thick. There were only a couple dozen giants in all of Fillory, because even Fillory's hyperabundant ecosystem couldn't have fed more of them. Six of them had come out for the battle.

Nobody moved. Instead the Great Salt River moved.

It was right behind them, they'd just crossed it, and the nymphs took it out of its banks and straight into the mass of the Lorian army like an aimable tsunami. A lot of the soldiers got washed away; he'd made the nymphs promise to drown as few of them as possible, though they were free to abuse them in any other way they chose.

Some of the ones who weren't swept away wanted to fight anyway, because they were *just that valiant.* Eliot supposed they must have had difficult childhoods or something like that. Join the club, he thought, it's not that exclusive. He and his friends gave them a difficult adulthood to go with it.

It took them four days to harry the Lorians back to Grudge Gap—you could only kick their asses along so fast and no faster. That was where Eliot stopped and called out their champion. Now it was dawn, and the pass made a suitably desolate backdrop, with dizzyingly steep mountainsides ascending on either side, striped with spills of loose rock and runnels of meltwater. Above them loomed icebound peaks that had as far as he knew never been climbed, except by the dawn rays that were right now kissing them pink.

Single combat, man to man. If Eliot won, the Lorians would go home and never come back. That was the deal. If the Lorian champion won—his name for some reason was Vile Father—well, whatever. It wasn't like he was going to win.

The lines were about fifty yards apart, and it was marvelously quiet out there between them. The pass could have been designed for this; the walls made a natural amphitheater. The ground was perfectly level—firm packed coarse gray sand, from which any rocks larger than a pebble had been removed overnight. Eliot kicked it around a little, like a batter settling into the batter's box.

Vile Father didn't look like somebody waiting to begin the biggest fight of his life. He looked like somebody waiting for a bus. He hadn't adopted anything like a fighting stance. He just stood there, with his soft shoulders sloping and his gut sticking out. Weird. His hands were huge, like two king crabs.

Though Eliot supposed he didn't look much less weird. He wasn't wearing armor either, just a floppy white silk shirt and leather pants. For weapons he carried a long knife in his right hand and a short metal fighting stick in his left. He supposed it was pretty clear that he had no idea how to use either of them, apart from the obvious. He nodded to Vile Father. No response.

Time passed. It was actually a teensy bit socially awkward. A soft cold wind blew. Vile Father's brown nipples, on the ends of his pendulous man-cans, were like dried figs. He had no scars at all on his smooth skin, which somehow was scarier than if he were all messed up.

Then Vile Father wasn't there anymore. It wasn't magic, he had some kind of crazy movement style that was like speed-skating over solid ground. Just like that he was halfway across the distance between them and thrusting his blade, whatever it was, straight at Eliot's Adam's apple at full extension. Eliot barely got out of the way in time.

He shouldn't have been able to get out of the way at all. Like an idiot he'd figured V.F. was going to swing the blade at him like a sword, on the end of that long pole, thereby giving him plenty of time to see it coming. Which would have been stupid, but all right, I get it already, it's a thrusting weapon. By rights it should have been sticking out of the nape of Eliot's neck by now, slick and shiny with clear fluid from his spine.

But it wasn't, because Eliot was sporting a huge amount of invisible magical protection in the form of Fergus's Spectral Armory, which by itself would have saved his life even if the blade had hit home, but in addition to that he was sporting Fergus's A Whole Lot of Other Really Useful Combat Spells, which had amped his strength up a few times over, and most important had cranked his reflexes up by a factor of ten, and his perception of time down by that same factor.

What? Look, Vile Father spent his whole life learning to kill people with a knife on a stick. Was that cheating? Well, while he was doing his squats and whatever else, Eliot had spent his whole life learning magic.

When he and Janet had first finished up the casting, a couple of hours earlier, in the chilly predawn, he'd been so covered in spellcraft that he glowed like a life-size neon sign of himself. But they'd managed to tamp that down so that the armor was only occasionally visible, maybe once every couple of minutes and only for a moment at a time, a flash of something translucent and mother-of-pearly.

The trigger for the time/reflexes part of the enchantment system was Eliot twitching his nose. He did it now, and everything in the world abruptly slowed down. He leaned back and away from the slowly, gracefully thrusting blade, lost his balance and put a hand down on the sand, rolled away, then got back on his feet while V.F. was still completing the motion.

Though you didn't get to be as big and fat as Vile Father was without learning a thing or two along the way. He didn't look impressed or even surprised, just converted his momentum into a spin move meant to catch Eliot in the stomach with the butt of the pole. I guess it doesn't pay to stand around looking all impressed on the battlefield.

Though Eliot was impressed. Watching it slowed down like this, you had to admire the man's athleticism. It was balletic, was what it was. Eliot watched the wooden staff slowly approaching his midriff, set himself and, all in good time, hammered down on it as hard as he could with his metal baton. The wood snapped cleanly about three feet from the end. Fergus, whoever you were, I heart you.

V.F. course-corrected once again, reaching out with a free hand to snag the snapped-off bit while it spun in midair. Eliot batted it away before he could get to it, and he watched it drift off out of V.F.'s reach, moving at a stately lunar velocity. Then, seeing as how he had some time to kill, he dropped the baton and slapped Vile Father's face with his open hand.

Personal violence did not come naturally to Eliot; in fact he found it distasteful. What could he say, he was a sensitive individual, fate had blessed and cursed him with a tender heart; plus V.F.'s cheek was really oily/sweaty. He wished he'd worn gloves, or gauntlets even. He thought of that dead hermit, and those burned trees, but even so he pulled the punch. With his strength and his speed all jacked up like this he had no idea how to calibrate the blow. For all he knew he was going to take the guy's face off.

He didn't, thank God, but Vile Father definitely felt it. In slow motion you could see his jowls wrap halfway around his face. That would leave a mark. Emboldened, Eliot dropped the knife too, moved in closer and delivered a couple of quick body blows to Vile Father's ribcage—the hook, his instructor had told him, was his punch. Vile Father absorbed them and danced away to a safe distance to do some heavy breathing and reconsider his life choices.

Eliot followed, jabbing and slapping, both ways, left-right. My sister, my daughter, my sister, my daughter. His blood was up now. This was in every way his fight. He hadn't come looking for it, but by God he was going to finish it.

It was awfully calming, being sped up like this. It gave you time to think about things, to consider your own life choices. Mostly Eliot was satisfied with the ones he'd made. He was in the right place. He was living his best life. How many other people in the multiverse could say that? He woke up every morning knowing what he wanted to do, and then he went and did it, and when he was done he felt proud. He believed himself to be a good High King, and he had a lot of evidence to back it up. The people were happy. When it wasn't falling apart Fillory was a good place, a great place. It took a substantial amount of malicious mismanagement to make Fillory a lousy place to live in, and nobody was going to get away with that on Eliot's watch, ever again. Least of all the Lorians.

If he had a major unfulfilled ambition, currently, it related to Quentin. It had been a year since Quentin was dethroned and expelled from Fillory and Julia had gone over to the Far Side. That had come as a shock to everybody, but to Eliot most of all, or second after Quentin anyway.

The year since then had been peaceful and prosperous, and in some ways the mood was lighter in the castle with Josh and Poppy installed as King and Queen in place of Quentin and Julia, Fillory's brooders-in-chief. But Eliot missed Quentin. He wanted Quentin by his side.

For all his faults Quentin had been his best friend here, and really he'd just been coming into his own. That last adventure had been good for him. It had worn away the last of his adolescent self-consciousness, letting his better nature—his curiosity, his intelligence, his fanatical loyalty, his wounded heart—show through.

Fillory wasn't the same without him. Nobody loved Fillory the way Quentin did, not even its High King. Nobody understood it like he did. Nobody enjoyed it like he did, and nobody could troubleshoot it like him when things went south.

And Quentin was missing out on *so much*. The passing of Martin Chatwin and the subsequent crisis of magic had given way to a glorious period in Fillory's history, a new Golden Age unlike anything since the time of the Chatwins. It was an age of legends, of noble deeds and great wonders and high adventure, unfolding in a golden summer that went on and on and on. Already this year Eliot and the others had ousted a great barbed dragon from a box canyon out in the Cock's Teeth and recovered two Named Blades from its hoard. They'd hunted a pair of fifty-headed trolls through the Darkling Woods, and forced them into the open and held them down and heard the sputtering crackle, like ice cracking in a nice vodka tonic, as they turned to stone in the morning sun. Eliot had brought back a bristling, spitting black troll-cat for a pet. Quentin would have loved that!

Frankly Eliot worried about him. Quentin was perfectly capable of taking care of himself, except when he wasn't. He was fine when he was on an even keel, but last time Eliot saw him his keel was looking distinctly wobbly. Eliot had been scheming a way to get Quentin back to Fillory ever since the day he was banished, but he hadn't gotten very far. It was in the back of his mind that maybe if he defeated Vile Father, thereby saving the realm, Ember might give him a reward. He would ask Ember to pardon Quentin. It was half the reason he'd set up this duel in the first place.

Speaking of whom, Vile Father was moving in again, still without much expression on his stolid, hoggy face. Eliot felt as though he ought to be inspiring a little more terror in his adversary, but whatever. He flipped time to normal speed for just a second, coming up for air; Vile

Father was whirling his abbreviated pole arm in a tricky cloverleaf pattern, much good may it do him. Eliot slo-moed again, ducking under it, working around it, pounding the man's body like a heavy bag, trying to knock the wind out of him.

He ought to have been more careful. Eliot had underestimated how much punishment Vile Father could take, or maybe he'd overestimated how much he was giving out. He'd definitely underestimated how quickly V.F. could move even relative to Eliot's massively accelerated time frame, and how completely V.F. had sized up his overconfident, inexperienced opponent. Even as he sucked up a hail of body shots, Vile Father barged into Eliot and managed to get his arms around him.

Never mind, Eliot would just slip out—hm. You'd think you could just—but no. It was harder than he thought. A moment's hesitation had cost him. Vile Father's smooth baby face and yellow teeth and beefy breath were right up next to him now, and those ham-hock arms were starting to squeeze and crush.

V.F. had evidently assessed the situation and decided that it didn't matter how fast your opponent could move when he couldn't move a muscle, so you took whatever damage you had to to get the other guy in a bear hug. He had, and now he was trying, slowly but strangely unstoppably, to crush the life out of Eliot, and also to get his teeth into Eliot's ear.

Enough. This guy was strong, and he had all the leverage, but he wasn't superhuman. Eliot felt like he was practically encased in Vile Father at this point, and he hadn't taken a proper breath in about thirty seconds. He began to pry himself free.

It was still a lot harder than you'd think—he had no leverage whatsoever—and Vile Father was not at all kidding about his personal vileness, but Eliot slither-wrenched his way out of Vile Father's arms and staggered a few feet away. He was still getting his balance when he felt something poke him painfully behind one shoulder. He arched his back away from that fiery hot point and shouted:

"Ah!"

Nothing the Lorian was carrying should have been able to get through Spectral Armor. He spun away, still ahead of Vile Father, but not nearly as far ahead as he expected; in real life both their movements must have been a blur. This guy was running magic weaponry; Eliot should have looked at the blade on that thing more closely.

It must be Fillorian metal. Magic metal. I bet he took it from that hermit, Eliot thought. I bet that thing's made from a Fillorian plow blade.

Oh, that is *it*. Eliot snapped.

On his feet again, he spun around the blade and grabbed what was left of the weapon's shaft and wrenched it out of Vile Father's hands. That took some skin with it, he thought. Good. He threw it as hard as he could, as hard as Fergus could. It was still rising when it disappeared into the low-hanging cloud around a mountain peak.

He skipped back and set himself the way his boxing instructor told him to, then he shuffled forward. The boxing thing was mostly just for the aerobics, plus it was an excuse to enjoy the company of the boxing instructor, whose amazing upper body was enough to make Eliot not miss Internet porn in the slightest, but it had some practical value too. Jab, jab, cross. Hook-hook. He was snapping it out crisp and firm. No more holding back.

He was rocking Vile Father back on his heels now. Eliot found he was baring his teeth and spitting words with each punch.

"You. Killed. A. Hermit. You. Weird. Sweaty. Bastard!"

Don't go down, cocksucker. Don't go down, I want to hit you some more. They were practically back against the Lorian front line when Eliot kicked Vile Father in the balls and then, indulging a personal fantasy, he swept the leg and watched Vile Father rotate clockwise in a stately fashion and simultaneously descend until he crashed, thunderously and with a lot of slow-motion blubbery rippling, onto the packed sand.

Even then he started to get up. Eliot kicked him in the face. He was through with these fucking people. My kingdom. My country. Mine.

He dropped all the magic at once. The strength, the speed, the armor, all of it.

"Go."

Well, not *all of it* all of it. His amplified voice echoed off the stone walls of the pass like thunder. He picked up the broken end of Vile Father's weapon and threw it into the sand. Fortunately for his sense of theater, it stuck there upright.

"Go. Let this shattered spear mark the border between our lands. If any man cross it, or woman, I make no guarantee of their safety. Fillory's mercy is great, but her memory is long, and her vengeance terrible."

Hm. Not exactly Shakespeare.

"You mess with the ram," he said, "you get the horns."

Better leave it at that.

Eliot scowled a terrible royal scowl at the Lorian host and turned and walked away, speaking a charm under his breath. He was rewarded with the soft rustle and creak of the little stub of wood growing into an ash tree behind his back. A bit of a cliché. But hey, they're clichés for a reason.

Eliot kept walking. His breathing was going back to normal. He'd done it, he'd shown the world that when it came right down to it the High King would put everything on the line. The pass ran north–south, and the sun was finally cracking its eastern rim, having already been busy lighting the rest of Fillory for at least an hour now. The ranks parted to let him go through.

God he loved being a king sometimes. There wasn't much better in life than having your own ranks part before you, especially after you'd just delivered a bona fide public ass-kicking to somebody who deserved it. He avoided eye contact with the rank and file, though he did point two fingers at the most senior of the giants, acknowledging that he'd done the High King a personal favor by showing up. I owe you, man.

The giant inclined his huge head toward Eliot, gravely. Their kind played a deep game.

It was a funny feeling, coming back to real time after having watched the world in slow motion for half an hour. Everything looked wildly accelerated: plants waving, clouds moving, people talking. It was a beautiful clear morning, the air an icy coolant washing across his overheated brain. He decided he would just keep on walking—he would walk the whole mile back to the Fillorian encampment by himself. Why the hell not? A lot of people tried to fuss at him about his punctured shoulder, which was probably still leaking some blood, and now that the excitement was wearing off it had started to sting pretty furiously.

But he didn't want to be fussed over. Not quite yet. All in good time. The war with Loria was over. Life was good. It was funny how just when you thought you knew yourself through and through, you stumbled on a new kind of strength, a fresh reserve of power inside you that you never knew you had, and all at once you found yourself burning a little brighter and hotter than you ever had before.

Eliot thought Quentin would have understood.

"Honey! I'm home!"

He threw open the tent flap.

"Keep saying that." Janet didn't look up. "One day it might grow up to be funny."

Janet was bent over a big trestle table covered with the enormous maps of Fillorian terrain that they'd used to keep track of their brief but glorious anti-Lorian campaign. They were littered with miniature figurines—Eliot had had them made up specially to represent both sides of the action. Not strictly necessary, since there were only two armies, and only one front— it wasn't exactly *Axis and Allies* here—but they'd had a lot of fun pushing them around the maps with long-handled wooden paddles.

The tent was full of pink light, strained through its red silk walls. Eliot dropped into an armchair. It was hot in the tent, even at this altitude: Fillorian seasons were irregular and unpredictable, and they'd been on a streak of summer months for he didn't know how long now. It had been rather splendid at first, but it was getting to be a bit much.

"Did you take care of our daddy issues?"

"I did," Eliot said.

"My hero." She came around the table and kissed him on the cheek. "Did you kill him?"

"I did not kill him. Knocked his ass out though."

"I would have killed him."

"Well, next time you can go."

"I will."

"But there won't be a next time."

"Sad face." Janet sat down in the other armchair. "In anticipation of your inevitable victory I summoned a couple of pegasi to take us back to Whitespire. They'll be here in a few minutes."

"Want to see my war wound?"

"Show."

Eliot swiveled around as far as he could without getting up, far enough that she could see the divot Vile Father had gouged out of his deltoid or trapezius or whatever that muscle was.

"Nice," she said. "It's ruining the upholstery on that chair."

"That's it? 'It's ruining the upholstery'?"

"I would ask if you wanted a medal but I already know you want a medal."

"And I shall have one." Eliot closed his eyes, suddenly weary even though it was only 9:30 in the morning. The rush was gone, and he was shaking a little. He kept having flashbacks to Vile Father pressed up in his grill, crushing his ribcage. "I'll give it to myself. Maybe I'll start an order, the Order of the Broken Spear. It will be for people who are exceptionally valiant. Like me."

"Congratulations. Are you OK to fly?"

"Yes. I'm OK to fly."

He and Janet talked like this all the time. The Fillorians didn't really get it, they thought High King Eliot and Queen Janet hated each other, but the truth was that in Quentin's absence Janet had become his principal confidante. Eliot supposed it was partly because they both found real romantic intimacy elusive and kind of uninteresting, so usually neither of them had a serious boyfriend, and they had to turn to each other for intelligent companionship. Eliot used to worry that his lack of a long-term life partner meant that he was psychologically unhealthy—emotionally arrested, maybe, or commitment-phobic, or something. But he worried about that less and less. He didn't feel arrested, or phobic. He just felt like being single.

Not like Josh and Poppy. Six weeks after they took the thrones they were a couple, and after six months they were engaged. No one saw it coming, but now looking back it was hard to remember that they'd ever been apart. Eliot wondered if it was the crowns themselves—if there was some kind of ancient magic at work, that caused any royals who weren't actually related to couple up and produce heirs to the thrones. Having exhausted itself trying and failing to shove Eliot and Janet together, the spell had turned its attention to Josh and Poppy and had more luck.

Maybe it was true. But Josh and Poppy really did seem to love each other. Eliot thought it spoke well of Poppy that she saw the point of Josh, which not everybody could. He wasn't handsome, and although he was as clever as any of them he didn't walk around making sure everybody knew it all the time. No, the point of Josh was that he had a big and noble heart. It had taken Eliot literally years to figure that out. Poppy was a quicker study.

Now the two of them were thoroughly nested, and a week ago they'd told him that Poppy was pregnant. It wasn't public yet, but she was starting to show. The people would love it. There hadn't been a prince or princess of Fillory in centuries. It made Eliot feel a little alone, and a little empty, but only a little. Life was long. Plenty of time for that stuff, if he ever found himself wanting it. He was High King in a Great Age. His business right now was logging some Great Deeds.

He heard the thump of hooves on the grass, and a stiff wingtip brushed the coarse silk wall by his head. The pegasi were here. He opened his eyes and heaved himself up; he was pretty sure the wound had stopped bleeding, though he could feel where his shirt was stuck to it. Quentin had been shot with an arrow there once. They'd fix him up back at Whitespire. He would have them leave a nice scar. Without waiting for Janet he put on his king-face and strolled outside.

The pegasi were trotting around on the cold grass, circling each other restlessly, their tremendous white eagle-wings still half extended. They hated to keep still, pegasi. Marvelous beasts they were, pure white and light as air, though they looked as solid as any regular horse, with thick muscles and squiggly blue veins standing out beneath the skin like power cords under a rug. Their silver—platinum? shiny anyway— hooves flashed in the morning sun.

They stopped pacing and stared at him expectantly. They could speak, but they hardly ever deigned to, not to humans, not even to the High King.

"Janet!" he called.

"Coming!"

"Just leave your stuff. They'll pack it for you."

"True."

She exited the tent a moment later, empty-handed; she'd changed into jodhpurs.

"You know, I had a thought," she said. "With the army all mobilized like this, why don't we take advantage of the momentum? Keep on pushing them back and take Loria?"

"Take Loria."

"Right. Then we bring the whole army to the Neitherlands and march it through the fountain and take Earth! Right? It would be so easy!"

"Sometimes," Eliot said, "I find it so hard to know when you're joking."

"I have the same problem."

The pegasi seemed even more reluctant than usual to remain earthbound. They barely stayed still long enough for Eliot and Janet to mount.

Pegasi wouldn't wear saddles, so you just hung on to their manes or necks or feathers or whatever you could get ahold of. Eliot felt thick muscles playing under skin as the beast pumped its way up into the air. They spiraled higher and higher, and his ears popped, and the camp shrank below them. He saw the pass where he'd fought Vile Father, the Fillorian host still formed up into crisp lines, the Lorians straggling away back home. When they were maybe a thousand feet up the pegasi leveled off and turned southeast for Whitespire.

Eliot loved Fillory at all times, but never more so than when he saw it from the air, when the land rolled out beneath you like a map in a beloved book that you'd spent your whole childhood gazing at, studying, wishing you could fall into it, *feeling* like you could. And Eliot had fallen.

From here he could see the old stone walls that crisscrossed Fillory, built by hands unknown, for no known reason. It made the green landscape look quilted. In some places the walls had been broken and scattered by weather or animals or people who needed the stones for more immediate and practical purposes. Dark green hedges followed the main roads for miles, neat double lines from here, but as thick and daunting as Norman hedgerows when you got up close to them. He made a couple of mental notes of where they were getting a bit unruly. He would notify the Master of Hedge.

They charged on and up into white cloud, and Fillory vanished. Clouds in Fillory weren't clammy and disappointing the way they were in the real world, they brushed past you all warm and soft and cottony, just solid enough to be comforting. Fuck love, fuck marriage, fuck children, fuck fucking itself: this was his romance, this fantasy land at whose helm he sat, steering it on and on into the future, world without end, until he died and tastefully idealized statues were made of him. It was all he needed. It was all he would ever need.

When they emerged from the clouds they were over the Great Northern Marsh. Bad shit down there, he knew. In fact there—the water was disturbed over a wide area as the mottled back of some vast living mass sank from view, into the black bogs. Maybe one day, if he ever got that bored, he would lead an expedition in there and see what was what.

Then again maybe he wouldn't. He stared down into the marsh for a long time, lost in thought, and when he looked up he found that they were no longer two, but three. Ember had joined them, in between him and Janet, flying in formation.

It had been some time since he'd had an audience with the god.

"High King," the ram said. "I would have words with you."

Ember's deep bass voice was clearly audible even over the rushing of the wind. He had no wings, and He didn't even bother to gallop, though occasionally the air ruffled His tight woolly curls. He just flew along in between them, stiff ram's legs tucked up under Him like He was sitting on an invisible flying carpet.

"Hi!" Eliot called out. "I'm listening!"

"You have won a great victory for Fillory today."

"I know! Thanks!"

Maybe this was the time to bring up Quentin. But Ember went on.

"But this was only one battle. A war is beginning, Eliot, a war we cannot win. The last war."

"What? Wait, I don't understand. What does that mean?"

This wasn't the speech Eliot was expecting. He was expecting the one where Ember praised him to the skies, showered him with fatherly approval, granted him a boon.

"What war are You watching?" Janet shouted. "We crushed those guys! Eliot crushed them! It's over!"

"Have you not wondered how it is that the Lorians could have crossed the Northern Barrier into Fillory?"

"Well, yeah," Eliot admitted. "A little."

"The old spells have weakened. This invasion was merely a portent, foretold long ago. The war we are losing is with time."

"Oh," Eliot said. "OK."

Was it? A war with time. He vaguely remembered something like this in the books, but it had been a long time since he read them. And even then he hadn't read them too closely. Once again he wished Quentin were here.

"The end is almost here, Eliot," Ember said.

"The end of what?"

"Of everything," Ember said. "Of this land. This world. Fillory is dying."

"What? Oh, come on!" That was ridiculous. A cheap shot, at best. Fillory wasn't dying. Fillory was kicking ass right now. Time of legends! World without end! "What are you talking about?"

Ember didn't reply. Instead the pegasus spoke for the first time. Eliot had never heard one speak before.

"Oh no," it said. It gave a horsey sigh. "Not again."

CHAPTER 6

They left the bookstore in two cars. A black Lexus SUV rolled up to the loading dock and Lionel loaded the birdcage carefully into the backseat, then put a seatbelt on it and climbed in the other side. Once they were gone a white stretch limousine pulled up.

It was still raining.

"If I'd've known it was prom night," Pixie said, "I would've worn a dress."

They piled in. The arrangement felt involuntarily intimate, like they were strangers who somehow wound up sharing a long cab ride from the airport. But they weren't strangers anymore, they were his comrades-in-arms now. Quentin wondered if their stories were as complicated as his was. He especially wondered about Plum. From what he knew of her story, it wasn't supposed to end up here.

The ceiling was mirrored, and the interior was black velvet trimmed with strips of LEDs. There was a moon roof in case anybody felt the urge to open it and stick their head out. It wasn't exactly dignified, but there was plenty of room, and the five of them spread out along the banquettes so as to put the maximum amount of distance between them. Nobody spoke as the limo slid smoothly out into the New Jersey night, through the parking lot and onto the turnpike, past a seemingly endless power plant lit up with a grid of pale orange lights.

For a second Quentin was reminded of nights in the *Muntjac:* gliding from island to island on oily blackness, far out in Fillory's Eastern

Ocean, seawater slapping wood, creamy wake streaming out behind. He was heading out into the unknown again.

Then the LEDs came on—the kid had found the controls. He'd chosen a disco rainbow pattern.

"What can I say," he said. "I love the nightlife."

"So," Plum said, to the group in general. "I'm Plum."

"I'm Betsy," said the Pixie.

"Quentin."

"My name is Pushkar," the older Indian man said. He had a salt-and-pepper goatee and looked way too placid and suburban to be involved in something like this. Everybody turned to the kid. Quentin put him at around fifteen.

"You're joking, right?" the boy said. "You're all gonna use your real names?"

"No," Quentin said, "we're not joking. And yes."

"Well, I'm not. You can call me the Artful Dodger."

The Pixie—Betsy—cackled.

"Try again."

"What's wrong with the Artful Dodger? Like in *Oliver!*"

"I know where it's from, I'm just not calling you that."

"Well I'm not going to be Fagin."

"Maybe we should call you Stoppard," Quentin said.

The boy looked confused.

"I don't get it," he said. "Is that from *Oliver!*?"

"That is the name of the man who wrote the book that you were reading earlier," Pushkar said. "At the bookstore. *Rosencrantz and Guildenstern Are Dead.*"

"Jeez, I thought that shit was Shakespeare."

"Well," Pushkar said pleasantly, "you thought wrong."

"Fine, OK. I'm Stoppard. Whatever."

"Stoppard, please set the lighting system to a neutral white."

Stoppard huffed loudly, but he did it.

In the white light Quentin could see better, and what he saw was five people who didn't look much like a team of world-beating master thieves. He felt more like he'd just joined the French Foreign Legion:

they were the sweepings of the magical world, the lost souls, here because nobody else would take them. When he leaned back Quentin caught a whiff of skunked beer and dead cigarette smoke, the ghosts of bachelor parties past.

"Anybody know where we're going?" Betsy said, studying her reflection in the ceiling.

"If I had to guess," Plum said, "I'd say Newark."

"You don't have to guess," Stoppard said. "We're going to the Newark Liberty International Airport Marriott."

"How do you know that?"

"I saw the guy put it into his GPS."

"Now that is some master magician shit," Betsy said. "Right there. Damn, I was hoping for at least a DoubleTree."

Of them all she was the only one who really fit the profile. Lots of attitude, lots of aggression. And something else. She kept the banter coming, but she had the air of somebody who'd survived some tough breaks along the way.

"So have you guys done stuff like this before?" Plum asked. She was showing a lot of persistence in keeping the conversation going.

"Like what?" Stoppard said. "Like stealing something?"

"Like stealing something."

"Torrenting porn doesn't count," Betsy said.

"I have," Quentin said.

"Really. You have." Betsy had dramatic eyebrows. She knitted them skeptically. "What have you stolen?"

"A crown. Some keys."

Betsy didn't look impressed, grudgingly or otherwise.

"Anybody else?"

"I've stolen things," Stoppard said.

"Like?"

"Like I'm going to tell you!" He opened the mini-bar, but it was empty. He slammed it shut. "Cheap crow."

"Like you're such a big drinker. What are you, twelve?"

"It's not a crow, it's a blackbird," Plum said. "Crows have black beaks. This one's was brown."

The mood in the limo was slightly hilarious—they might have been a bunch of tourists in the same gondola, passing a flask of schnapps around, and in another minute they'd get to the top of the mountain and ski off in separate directions forever. Except that they wouldn't. It was strange to think that he might have to trust these people with his life.

"Tell me," Pushkar said. "Who here went to Brakebills?"

"What's Brakebills?" Stoppard said brightly.

"Oh my God." Betsy looked like she was thinking about jumping out into traffic. "It's like a mobile fucking *Breakfast Club* in here!"

"I did." Quentin couldn't think of any reason to keep it a secret.

"I did." Plum shrugged. "Sort of."

The limo slowed down and went over a speed bump. They were almost at the airport already.

"So are we supposed to have specialties, or something?" Plum said. "Is that how this works? I got the impression we were all supposed to have special skills or something."

"You're saying you don't have any special skills," Betsy said.

"Is that what I said? Probably I'm here because they want somebody who does illusions."

"I specialize in transport," Pushkar said crisply. "And some precognition."

"Stoppard?"

"Devices," he said proudly. Quentin tentatively tagged him as some kind of prodigy, or precocious anyway. That would explain his youth, and the special treatment from the bird.

"All right," Betsy said. "I guess I'm offense. Penetration. Damage. What do you do, Quentin?"

She said it as if she were not completely convinced it was his real name.

"Not much," he said. "My discipline is mending."

"Mending?" Stoppard said. "The fuck do we need somebody who mends shit?"

"Beats me. You'd have to ask the bird that."

Quentin very much doubted that that was why he was here. He was doubting it more all the time.

Fortunately it was a short trip: the limo drew up under the lighted awning of the airport Marriott, and bellmen in cheap livery converged on it, probably hoping it contained drunk, heavy-tipping newlyweds. They were going to be disappointed.

"I cannot wait to get out of this thing," Betsy said.

"Speak for yourself," Plum said. "I never went to prom."

Lionel and the bird had reserved three suites. The five of them sat on a vast beige sectional couch in one of the living rooms, waiting to be briefed. Betsy paged through the room service menu. The bird pecked at some nuts from the mini-bar. A clutch of Heinekens stood on the coffee table, but only Stoppard was drinking. From his expression it seemed not impossible that this was a first for him.

"All right," Lionel said. "Here's what we know, here's what we don't know." He had the manner of a bored tech-support guy explaining something very, very basic. He was standing by the flat-screen TV, which he'd unplugged. He touched it and an image appeared—he was apparently able to project them straight from his mind, which was a trick Quentin hadn't seen before. "This is the case. Not the actual one, but same make and model."

It was a handsome but unassuming leather suitcase, pale brown, pleasantly battered, very English, with lots of nice straps and clasps on it. It looked ready for a weekend in the country.

"So we're looking for Bertie Wooster," Quentin said.

Nobody laughed.

"We're pretty sure it's on the eastern seaboard." A map appeared on the dead TV, showing the eastern states with possible sites pinpointed and annotated. "We're also pretty sure that the people who have it don't know what they have. As far as we know they haven't been able to open it."

"Why don't you just buy it off them?" Plum said. "If they don't know what it is. You obviously have plenty of money."

"We tried," Lionel said. "They don't know what they have, but they're pretty sure they have something big, and they don't want to give it up till they've figured out what. They acquired it as part of a cache of artifacts from a dealer, who we presume they killed. Unfortunately our attempts to purchase it from them have only confirmed their estimate of its value."

"Wait," Stoppard said. "They killed him?"

"Her. And yes."

Stoppard's eyes were wide. He looked more excited than appalled. He took another hasty swig.

"One thing you don't have to worry about with these guys is your conscience," Lionel said. "They're assholes, major league. They call themselves the Couple." Two photographs appeared, side by side, a man and a woman, both good-looking and in their early thirties, evidently taken from some distance away with a long-range lens. "They're manipulators. They work behind the scenes, messing around with the civilians. They get off on it; it's all a big game to them."

Quentin frowned. He'd heard about magicians who did that: competed with each other to move the stock market, throw elections, start wars, choose popes. The mundane world was a big chessboard to them. Supposedly the whole electoral debacle of 2000 was mostly a shoving match between two magicians who were trying to settle a bet.

"How are we going to find them?" he asked.

"Don't worry about it."

"I still don't understand why you want this thing," Plum said.

"You don't have to," the bird said. "We are not paying you to understand."

"Well, no. I guess not. It all seems kind of sketchy though."

Betsy cackled.

"Sketchy! I love that. You're talking to a bird in an airport Marriott."

Betsy had a point. Quentin badly wanted to get Plum alone and ask her why she was doing this and what she knew about it and if she was all right. He was worried about her, and what's more he needed an ally, and she was the likeliest candidate. Betsy picked up the phone and began whispering confidingly to room service.

"You're sure we don't need more people," he said. "What about a psychic? A healer?"

"I am sure."

"When do you expect this all to happen?" Pushkar asked. "How soon?" Of them all he looked the least like a master thief. He didn't look like a magician at all. Maybe it was camouflage; he certainly seemed to be the most comfortable with the whole situation.

"We don't know," Lionel said.

"Yes, but weeks? Months? I must notify my family." He was also the only one of them wearing a wedding ring.

"I am not living in Newark Airport Marriott for months." Betsy broke off her phone conversation. "FYI. Or weeks. Or one week singular. The only natural fibers in my room are the hairs in the bathtub."

"We'll tell you as soon as we know."

"So to recap," Quentin said. "Two bad people—known killers who are, with respect, much scarier than we are—have a suitcase somewhere on the eastern seaboard, precise location unknown, contents unknown, under an incorporate bond. And we are going to take it away from them."

"We have the numbers," the bird said. "And the element of surprise."

"If this works I for one will be very surprised," Pushkar said cheerfully. "Is there something you're not telling us?"

"What about that incorporate bond?" Plum said. "How are we going to break it? What with that being impossible and all."

"We will have to do the impossible," the bird said, "which is why I hired magicians and not accountants. I mentioned resources earlier. We will discuss each of your needs individually."

The meeting gradually disintegrated. Quentin stood up. They could talk about his needs later, whatever they were. For now he needed some air, and some food, and maybe a drink to celebrate the beginning of his new life of crime. Something soft brushed his ear and prickled his shoulder, and he had to resist the instinctive urge to slap at it. It was the bird.

"Christ!" he said. "Don't do that."

Maybe you got used to it. Julia had.

"Do you know why I asked you here?" it whispered, putting its beak right up against his ear.

"I could make a pretty good guess."

"It is not for your skill at mending."

"That wasn't going to be my guess."

The bird flew off again, back to Lionel's shoulder, which Quentin now noticed was worn and stained with use.

Plum agreed to meet him in the hotel bar.

The lights were too bright, and there were too many TVs, but it was a bar, and that was another place, like bookstores, where Quentin felt at home. Drinks were a lot like books, really: it didn't matter where you were, the contents of a vodka tonic were always more or less the same, and you could count on them to take you away to somewhere better or at least make your present arrangements seem more manageable. The other patrons appeared to be business travelers and tourists who'd been stranded by canceled flights; looking around Quentin was pretty sure there was not one single person in the bar who was actually there by choice.

It was no time for half measures. He took a seat next to Plum and ordered a gin martini, dry, with a twist.

"I thought you were a wine person," Plum said. She'd ordered mineral water.

"Lately I've had to up my dosage. I thought *you* were a wine person."

"I'm thinking right now I'd better try to keep my wits about me."

They watched TV for a minute, a soccer game. The green pitch looked cool and inviting; it was almost a shame it was covered with soccer players. She didn't seem eager to go first, so he did.

"So how'd they get to you?"

"A letter," she said. "When I got back to my room that night it was already on my bed. I'm still trying to figure out how they did that. So far it's the most impressive thing about this whole operation."

"Are you really sure you want to be here?"

"Of course I don't want to be here!" Plum snapped. "I want to be back in my damn dormitory, finishing my damn senior year like a normal person! But that's not going to happen. So."

"I'm just concerned about the risk."

"Well, me too. But I don't happen to have a lot of other choices right now. Don't worry about it. I'm not your responsibility anymore."

"I know that."

"And that's not your cue to hit on me."

"Jesus Christ," he said. "Give me some credit."

He was pretty sure that it wasn't really him she was upset with. He wanted to help her. His own transition from Brakebills to the real world hadn't exactly been graceful either. When he graduated he'd thought life was going to be like a novel, starring him on his own personal hero's journey, and that the world would provide him with an endless series of evils to triumph over and life lessons to learn. It took him a while to figure out that wasn't how it worked.

His martini came. A thick curl of gold lemon peel lay sunken in its silvery depths; it had spread a thin oily sheen across the surface. He drank quickly, before it had a chance to warm up.

"Look, I'm sorry," Plum said. "I didn't mean to snap at you. God knows this isn't your fault. It's just—I'm having trouble." She shook her head helplessly. "I don't know what I'm doing. I haven't told my parents what happened yet. I don't know how to do it. Brakebills was a big, big deal to them. I guess they're kind of overinvested in me. I'm an only child."

"Do you want me to talk to them?"

"Hmm." She sized him up. "No, I don't think that's going to help."

"I'm an only child too. Though my parents were more like underinvested in me."

"Right, see, but for me, it's going to mess them up."

"But it's good that they care," Quentin said. "I don't want to sound like a Pollyanna, but if they really love you they'll love you whatever happens."

"Oh, they'll love me." Plum's voice was rising again. "They'll love me, all right! They'll just spend the rest of their lives looking at me like a sick bird with a broken wing that will never get better!"

She sucked fiercely at her mineral water through a straw. Then she went on:

"I don't know. Anyway, this came along and I don't know what I'm doing, and I thought I'd take a look, and here I am taking it. It's different, anyway. What about you?"

"Similar," Quentin said. "I got a letter. I was going to ignore it, but then I found myself suddenly without employment. I was curious. And here we are."

"Don't get me wrong," she said, "I do feel some responsibility for that."

"Forget about it."

"I just—"

"Seriously, forget it. I made my own choices."

He said it without heat. It was the truth.

"So do you think we can pull this thing off?"

"I have no idea," Quentin said. "That bird is spending a lot of money. It has to be reasonably confident."

"Or reasonably desperate."

Quentin could feel the martini doing its wintery work, frosting over his mind, silvering over his frontal lobes, preparing the ground for a proper hard freeze. He hadn't eaten dinner, and it was coming on fast. He thought he might just order another one.

"Do you miss Brakebills?"

She didn't look at him. On TV, a headed ball pinged off the crossbar.

"Of course I do," he said. "All the time. But I'm getting used to it. It's not the worst feeling in the world. And there's a lot more to life than school. I'm trying to make the most of it."

"Now you do sound like a Pollyanna."

Quentin grinned. It was pretty clear that Plum was going to get through this—she was young and unworldly but she was also very tough. And very smart. Maybe they could help each other. He caught the bartender's eye and tapped his glass.

"I'll tell you what I'm wondering about," he said. "I'm wondering about how we're going to get that suitcase open, if the Couple can't."

"I have a theory about that. I don't think you'll like it though."

"Why not?"

"Because I don't like it," Plum said. "There's something about me you should probably—"

"*Chochachos!*" Somebody clapped them both on the shoulder at the same time. It was Stoppard. "What are we drinking?"

He looked happy the way only somebody who was inebriated for the first time in his life could be happy. It was incredible that they were even serving him here, considering that he was both underage and over-drunk. He frowned at them blearily.

"Wait," he said. "You two know each other or something? From before?"

"You could say that," Quentin said.

"It's not what you think," said Plum.

"Uh-huh." Stoppard leered knowingly.

"It really isn't."

"I just ruined his life, that's all," Plum said. "And mine. And I think maybe I'll have that drink now after all."

CHAPTER 7

You could say it all started out as an innocent prank, but that wouldn't strictly be true. Even Plum had to admit it wasn't all that innocent. And maybe, deep down, that was why she did it.

Plum was president of the League, unelected but undisputed, and also its founder. In enlisting the others she had presented the League as a glorious old Brakebills tradition, which it actually wasn't, though since Brakebills had been around for something like four hundred years it seemed very likely to Plum that there must have been another League at some point in the past, or at any rate something along the same general lines.

You couldn't rule out the possibility. Though in actual fact she got the idea from a P. G. Wodehouse story.

The thing was this: Wharton was behaving badly, and in the judgment of the League he would have to be pranked for it. Then maybe he would cut it out, or behave a little less badly, or at least the League would have the satisfaction of having caused Wharton to suffer for his crimes. You couldn't call it innocent, but you had to admit it was pretty understandable. And anyway, was there even any such thing as an innocent prank?

Plum loved Brakebills. It was November of her senior year and she still wasn't sick of it, not a bit. She loved its many and varied and intricate traditions and rituals and mythologies with an unironic and boosterish love that she refused to be embarrassed about. If anything she thought there should be more of them, which was one reason she started the League.

They met after hours in a funny little trapezoidal study off the West Tower that as far as Plum could tell had fallen off the faculty's magical security grid, so it was safe to break curfew there. She lay full length on her back on the floor, which was the position from which she usually conducted League business. The rest of the girls were scattered around the room on couches and chairs, limp and spent, like confetti from a successful but exhausting party that everybody was kind of relieved was now all but over.

Plum made the room go silent—it was a little spell that ate sound in about a ten-yard radius. When Plum did a magic trick, everybody noticed.

"Let's put it to a vote," she said gravely. "All those in favor of pranking Wharton, say aye."

The *ayes* came back in a range of tones: righteous zeal, ironic detachment, sleepy acquiescence. From Plum's vantage point on the floor, with her eyes closed, her long brown hair splayed out in a fan on the carpet, which had once been soft and woolly but which had been trodden down into a shiny hard-packed gray, it sounded more or less unanimous.

She dispensed with a show of *nays*. They were doing this. Wharton's crime was not a matter of life and death, but a stop would be put to it, this the League swore.

Darcy, sitting slumped down on the couch, studied her reflection in a long mirror with a scarred gilt frame. She had a big poufy 1970s afro; it even had an afro pick sticking out of it. She toyed with her image in the mirror—with both of her long, elegant brown hands she worked a spell that stretched it and then squished it, stretched then squished, stretch, squish. Her head blew up to the size of a beach ball; it stretched out like a sausage balloon. The technicalities were beyond Plum, but then mirror-magic was Darcy's discipline. It was a bit show-offy of her, but it's not like Darcy had a lot of opportunities to use it.

The facts of the Wharton case were as follows. At Brakebills most serving duties at dinner were carried out by First Years, who then ate separately afterward. But by tradition one favored Fourth Year was chosen every year to serve as wine steward, in charge of pairings and pourings and whatnot, and trusted with the key to the wine closet. Wharton had had this honor bestowed upon him, and not for no reason. He did know a lot about wine; or at any rate he could remember the names of a whole lot of different regions and appellations and whatever else.

But in the judgment of the League Wharton had sinned against the honor of his office, sinned most grievously, by systematically short-pouring the wine, especially for the Fifth Years (the *Finns,* in Brakebills parlance), who were allowed two glasses each with dinner.

Seriously, these were like two-thirds pours. Everybody agreed. Plum wasn't much of a drinker personally, but the League took any threat to its wine supply seriously. For such a crime there could be no forgiveness.

"What do you suppose he does with it all?" Emma said.

"Does with what?"

"All that extra wine. He must be skimming it off. I bet he ends up with an extra bottle every night, off the books."

There were eight girls in the League, of whom six were present. Emma was the only Second Year.

"I dunno," Plum said. "I guess he drinks it."

"He couldn't get through a bottle a night," Darcy said.

"He and his boyfriend then. What's his name, it's Greek."

"Epifanio." Darcy and Chelsea said it together.

Chelsea lay on the couch at the opposite end from Darcy, knees drawn up, lazily trying to mess up Darcy's mirror tricks. It was always easier to screw up somebody else's spell than it was to cast one yourself. That was one of the many small unfairnesses of magic.

Darcy frowned and concentrated harder, pushing back. The interference caused an audible buzz, and under the stress Darcy's reflection twisted and spiraled in on itself.

"Stop," she said. "You're going to break it."

"He's probably got some permanent spell running that eats it up," Emma said. "Has to feed it wine once a day. Like a virility thing."

"Wait," Plum said, "you're suggesting that Wharton has a wine-powered spell going twenty-four-seven on his penis?"

"Well." Emma flushed mauve. She'd overstepped herself in the presence of her elders and betters. "You know. He's so buff."

While everybody else was distracted by the question of Wharton's virility Chelsea caused Darcy's reflection to collapse in on itself, creepily, like it had gotten sucked into a black hole, and then to vanish altogether. In the mirror it looked like she wasn't even there, except that the couch cushion was slightly depressed.

"Ha," Chelsea said.

"Buff does *not* mean virile." That was Lucy, a pale and intensely philosophical Finn; her tone betrayed a touch of what might have been the bitterness of personal experience. "Anyway I bet he gives it to the ghost."

"There is no ghost," Darcy said.

Somebody was always saying that Brakebills had a ghost. It was a thing this year—there was practically a cult around it. Emma claimed to have seen it once, watching her through a window; Wharton said he had too.

Plum secretly wanted a ghost sighting of her own, but you could never find it when you were looking for it. She wasn't completely convinced it existed. It was like saying there used to be a League, no one could prove it either way.

"Come to that," Chelsea said, "what *does* virile mean?"

"Means he's got spunk in his junk," Darcy said.

"Girls, please!" Plum said. "Neither Wharton's spunk nor his junk is germane here. The question is what to do about the missing wine. Who's got a plan?"

"*You've* got a plan," Darcy and Chelsea said at the same time, again. The two of them were like stage twins.

It was true, Plum always had a plan. Her brain just seemed to secrete them naturally, leaving her no choice but to share them with the world around her. She had a bit of a manic streak.

Plum's plan was to take advantage of what she perceived to be Wharton's Achilles' heel, which was his pencils. He didn't use the school-issued ones, which as far as Plum was concerned were entirely functional and sufficient unto the day: deep Brakebills blue in color, with BRAKEBILLS in gold letters down the side. But Wharton didn't like them—he said they were too fat, he didn't like their "hand-feel." The lead was mushy. He brought his own from home instead, very expensive ones.

In truth Wharton's personal pencils were remarkable: olive green and made from some hard, oily, aromatic wood that released a waxy aroma reminiscent of distant exotic rainforest trees. The erasers were bound in rings of a dull-gray brushed steel that looked too industrial and high-carbon for the task of merely containing the erasers, which were, instead of the usual fleshy pink, a light-devouring black. He kept them in a flat silver case like a cigarette case, which also contained (in its own crushed-velvet nest) a little knife that he used to keep them sharpened to wicked points.

Plus he must have been into debate or academic decathlon or something in some earlier stage of his life, because he was always doing these pencil-tricks with them, of the kind generally used to intimidate rival mathletes. He did them constantly, unconsciously and apparently involuntarily. It was annoying.

Plum's plan was for the League to steal the pencils and hold them for ransom, the ransom being an explanation of what the hell Wharton did with all that wine, along with a pledge to stop doing same. By 11:30 that night the League was yawning, and Darcy and Chelsea had restored Darcy's reflection and then begun wrangling with it all over again, but the groundwork had been laid. The plan had been fully explained, fleshed out, approved, improved, and then made needlessly complex. Cruel, curly little barbs had been added to it, and all roles had been assigned.

It was rough justice, but someone had to enforce order at Brakebills, and if the faculty didn't then the League's many hands were forced. The administration might turn a blind eye, if it chose, but the League's many eyes were sharp and unblinking.

Darcy's image shivered and blurred, trapped between spell and counterspell like a teacup in a vise.

"Stop it," Darcy said, really annoyed now. "I told you—"

She had told her, and now it did: the mirror broke with a loud sharp *tick,* like one forward increment of a clock's works. A shatter-white star appeared in the lower right-hand corner of the glass, surrounded by concentric rings and spreading fracture-tendrils. For some reason it made Plum uncomfortable—for a moment she felt like the little room was a bathysphere that had reached crush depth, the windows were cracking, and the cold, heavy, mindless ocean was about to come pouring in . . .

"Oh, shit!" Chelsea said. Her hands flew to her mouth. "I hope that wasn't, like, super expensive!"

Plum got up at eight the next morning, late by her standards, but instead of rejuvenating her brain the extra sleep had just made it all muzzy. It had smeared all those clear thoughts she was supposed to be having all over the inside of her skull. Her depressive tendency, the flip side of her manic streak, was stirring. Why were they even doing this? it wanted to know. What a waste of time, of effort. Of pencils. Plum needed to get moving, but she was having trouble attaching meanings to things; the meanings kept peeling off like old stickers.

As a Finn who'd finished her required coursework Plum was taking all seminars that semester, and her first class was a colloquium on period magic, fifteenth-century Continental to be specific—lots of elemental stuff and weird divination techniques and Johannes Hartlieb. Holly—a fellow Leaguer, moon-faced and pretty, except for one ear which was covered in a port-wine birthmark—sat opposite her across the table, and such was Plum's smeary state that Holly had to touch her sharp little nose meaningfully, twice, before Plum remembered that that was the signal that Stages One and Two of the plan had been completed successfully.

Stage One: "Crude but Effective." A few hours earlier Chelsea's boyfriend would have smuggled her into the Boys' Tower under pretense of a predawn sex date. Nature having taken its course, Chelsea would have gone to Wharton's door, pressed her back against it, touched her fingers to her temples in a gesture so habitual that she no longer knew she did it, rolled her eyes back into her head and entered his room in a wispy, silvery, astral state. Chelsea did it all the time—astral projection was her discipline—but it was still one of the most flat-out beautiful pieces of magic Plum had ever seen. Chelsea tossed his room for the pencil case, found it and grasped it with both of her barely substantial hands. She couldn't get the pencil case out of the room that way, but she didn't have to. All she had to do was lift it up to where it could be seen in the window.

Wharton himself might or might not have been watching this, depending on whether or not he was asleep, but it mattered not. *Let him see.*

Because once Chelsea got the case over by the window, earnest Lucy had line of sight to it from a window in an empty lecture hall in the wing opposite Wharton's room, which meant she could teleport the pencil case in that direction, from inside Wharton's room to midair outside it. Three feet was about as far as she could jump it, but that was plenty. Thank God for people with actual useful disciplines.

The pencil case would then fall forty feet to where Emma waited shivering in the bushes in the cold November predawn to catch it in a blanket. No magic required.

Effective? Undeniably. Needlessly complex? Perhaps. But needless complexity was the League's signature. That was how the League rolled.

Then it was on to Stage Two: "Breakfast of Champions." Wharton would descend late, having spent the morning frantically searching his room. Through a fog of anxiety he would barely notice that his morning oatmeal had been plunked down in front of him not by some anonymous First Year but by the purple-eared Holly in guise of same. The first mouthful would not sit right with him. He would stop and examine his morning oatmeal more closely.

It would be garnished, not with the usual generous pinches of brown sugar, but with a light dusting of aromatic, olive-green pencil shavings. Compliments of the League.

As the day wore on Plum got into the spirit of the prank. She'd known she would. It was mostly just her mornings that were bad. It took a lot of energy to keep being Plum. Some days she just needed a few hours to get up to speed.

Her schedule ground forward: Accelerated Advanced Kinetics; Quantum Gramarye; Joined-Hands Tandem Magicks; Manipulation of

Ligneous Plants. Plum's course-load would have been daunting for a doctoral candidate, possibly several doctoral candidates, but Plum had arrived at Brakebills with a head full of more magical theory and practice than most people left with. She wasn't one of these standing-starters, the cold-openers, who reeled through their first year with aching hands and eyes full of stars. Plum was clever, and Plum had come to Brakebills prepared.

As the only accredited college for magic on the North American continent, Brakebills had a very large applicant pool to draw from, and it drank that pool dry. Technically nobody really applied there, Dean Fogg simply skimmed the cream of high school seniors off the top. The cream of the cream—the outliers, the extreme cases of precocious genius and obsessive motivation, the statistical freaks who had the brains and the high pain tolerance that the study of magic required. Fogg took them aside and made them an offer they couldn't refuse; or at any rate if they could refuse it, they wouldn't remember it.

Privately Plum thought they could put a tiny bit more emphasis in the selection process on emotional intelligence, along with the other kind. The Brakebills student body was a bit of a psychological menagerie. Carrying that much onboard cognitive processing power had a way of distorting your personality and to actually want to work that hard you had to be at least a little bit screwed up.

Plum's discipline was camouflage magic, the magic of concealment, and she was considered an illusionist, which she was perfectly happy about. Being an illusionist at Brakebills was, if Plum said it herself, a pretty sweet deal. You got to hang out in a tiny invisible folly castle on the edge of the forest that was quite difficult to find unless you had an illusionist-type discipline. The castle was delicate and gossamer and very Neuschwanstein, which was a nice way of saying—though Plum didn't say it—kind of Disney. To get up in one of the towers you climbed a ladder inside it, like you were negotiating a Jefferies tube, and there was just enough room for a little chair and a desk inside the round room at the top.

She didn't like to be partisan about it, but it was way better than that poky cottage the Physical Kids got stuck with. When they had parties the whole place could be made to twinkle and float up into the air a little ways, like a fairy castle, connected to the ground by only a rickety, railing-less staircase which people were always falling off of drunk onto the soft grass below. It reminded her of the floating castle at the end of *The Phantom Tollbooth*. Hell yes, it was Disney. Disney FTW!

Once in a while people would ask Plum what the hell kind of an adolescence she'd had that she arrived at Brakebills so cocked, locked and ready to rock. She told them the truth, which was that she'd grown up on an island near Seattle, in comfortable surroundings, the daughter of a mixed marriage: one magician, one non.

She was an only child, and they'd had high standards for Plum, Daddy especially—he was the magician of the couple. As the one basket they'd managed to weave, she had to hold all their eggs, so they'd home-schooled her, and once her talent for magic revealed itself they'd made damn sure she made good on it. Daddy sat with her and made her practice her languages and her exercises, and she'd made very good indeed. True, she'd never been to prom, or played a competitive sport that you couldn't play sitting down and in complete silence, but you don't make a magic omelet without breaking some magic eggs.

That was the truth. And if she liked and trusted the person who asked, she would add that yes, it was kind of a lot to deal with: her outward affect was bright and capable, and that was no illusion, but equally real was the yawning pit of exhaustion inside her. She just felt so *tired* sometimes. And because of everything her family asked of her, she was ashamed of being tired. She could not, would not let the pit swallow her up, as much as she sometimes wanted it to.

She could have gone on to say even more, which was that magic ran in her family, sort of, that it was something of a tradition, but she never did. People tended to be a bit funny about it, and actually Plum felt a bit funny about it too, so she kept it to herself. It wasn't hard, because she'd lived most of her life in America and had not even a trace of an English accent, and it was on her mother's side so Chatwin wasn't even her last name.

It was her mother's name though: she was the daughter of Rupert Chatwin's only son, and that made Plum, as far as she knew, the last living direct descendant of the famous Chatwins of the Fillory books. No one else in that generation had managed to reproduce, so she was the heir to whatever Chatwins were heir to (though as she was not slow to point out she wasn't a Chatwin at all but a Purchas, Plum Polson Purchas, Chatwin wasn't even her middle name). And as a matter of fact there had been a sum of money, royalties that Plover had graciously set aside for the children who'd made his fortune. (His second fortune; he'd been rich already when he started writing about Fillory.) Rupert had used his share to buy a big house in the countryside outside Penzance, which he barely ever left, until the army called him up to die in World War II.

Plum had seen pictures of it, one of those houses that always gets re-ferred to as a pile, a big Georgian pile. It had a name, but she'd forgotten it. Her mother had grown up there, but she didn't talk much about her childhood—a drafty, echoing place was how she described it. Not a place to be a kid in. The floor was littered with falls of plaster from the crumbling moldings, and Plum's mother spent winter afternoons hud-dled up on the stairs by a huge heating duct, big enough for her to have crawled into if the entrance hadn't been covered by a knotted-wrought-iron grate, and letting the lukewarm air wash weakly over her.

When she grew up Plum's mother left her heritage behind. Her Chat-win ancestors struck her as dangerously melancholy and fanciful, and she sold the house and its contents and moved to America to become a publicist for Microsoft. She met Plum's dad at a charity ball, and it wasn't till they were well into their courtship that he revealed to her what he really did in all his spare time. Once Mom got over the shock of a lifetime, they went ahead and got married anyway and had Plum, and they were a happy magical nuclear family.

You couldn't talk about the Fillory stuff at Brakebills. Everybody loved Fillory. It was their most precious childhood fantasy, they used to run around their backyards or basement rec rooms or whatever they ran around in pretending they were Martin Chatwin, boy-hero of a magical world of green fields and talking animals where they would attain total and complete self-actualization. And Plum got that, totally and com-pletely. It was their fantasy, and it was perfect and innocent and true, at least in the way that such things were true. She would never try to take that away from them.

And literally everybody at Brakebills grew up on Fillory. The place was one big five-year Fillory convention.

But Plum, through whose very veins the mighty blood of the Chatwins flowed, did not grow up on Fillory. They didn't even have the books; Plum had only read the first one, *The World in the Walls,* and that was on the sly, in snatches, at the public library. Plum's parents didn't smoke, didn't drink, and they didn't read Christopher Plover.

Plum didn't mind. Once you found out that magic was real, fictional wonderlands were pretty small change by comparison. So she quietly opted out of a public life as the last scion of the Chatwin line. She could do without the fuss: being the living incarnation of the most innocent, ardent childhood fantasies of pretty much everybody you met was not actually a gift from the gods.

But there was more to it than that, there always had been. Underneath her mother's scorn and indifference there was something else, and Plum wasn't completely sure but she thought it might be fear. Fillory had made the Chatwin family famous, but most people didn't know—or they knew but chose not to think about it—that it had ruined them too. Martin, Plum's great-uncle, high king and hero of the Fillory books, had disappeared when he was thirteen. He was never found. Jane, the youngest, the moppet, vanished when she was the same age. The others survived, more or less, but no one came out of it unscathed. Helen changed her name and ended her life as an evangelical Christian in Texas. Fiona Chatwin got along by never once mentioning Fillory as an adult; when pressed on the subject she exhibited faint surprise and claimed she'd never heard of it.

As for Rupert, Plum's great-grandfather, he was by all accounts a wreck of a man who spent his adult life in neurotic seclusion until Field Marshal Erwin Rommel came along to put him out of his misery.

Something had happened to that family. There was a curse on them, and its name was Fillory—Plum's mom talked about Fillory like it was almost real. Maybe it was the books, maybe it was Plover, maybe it was the parents, or the war, or fate, but when Fillory and Earth touched the collision was pure damage, and the Chatwins were the point of contact. They were right there at ground zero and they were blown to vapor, like the human shadows at Hiroshima. Plum was pretty sure that none of them had attained total or even partial self-actualization.

Plum's mother wanted no part of that. And a good thing too, as far as Plum was concerned, because deep down she felt the fear too. When Plum discovered magic it was the most magnificent kind of surprise, the kind that never got less surprising. The world was even more interesting than she thought it was! But it also made her uneasy. Because just speaking logically here, if magic was real then could you still be absolutely one-hundred-percent positive that Fillory wasn't? And if Fillory was real—which it almost certainly wasn't—then whatever it was that had torn through an entire generation of her family like a lion through a flock of loitering gazelle was real too, and it might still be out there. Plum dug into magic with both hands, but always at the back of her mind was the thought that she might go too far, dig too deep, and dig up something that she would wish had stayed buried.

She especially thought about that when those depressive, anhedonic chemicals were singing in her bloodstream, because then she kind of wanted to dig it up. She wanted to look it in the face. She could hear Fillory calling to her, or if not Fillory then something—somewhere beautiful and distant and sirenlike where she had never been but that was also somehow home. And she knew what side of the family her depressive streak came from. That was her Chatwin inheritance, right there.

So she kept her Chatwinity to herself. She didn't want people pushing at it, picking at it, lest its ragged, unstable edges start to unravel. Sometimes Plum wondered if there was a way to use her Discipline to hide not just things but words, facts, names, feelings, hide them so well that even she couldn't find them. What she wanted was to hide herself from herself.

But she couldn't. That was stupid. You were who you were. You lived your life. You didn't brood—ruminative thinking, that's what her shrink had called it. You got on with things. You founded the League. You pranked the hell out of Wharton.

Plum wound up having a pretty good day; at any rate it was a lot better than Wharton's. In first period he found more pencil shavings on the seat of his chair. Walking to lunch he found his pockets stuffed full of jet-black pencil eraser rubbings. It was like a horror movie—his precious pencils were being tortured to death, minute by minute, in an undisclosed location, and he was powerless to save them! He would rue his short-pouring ways, so he would.

Passing Wharton by chance in a courtyard, Plum let her eyes slide past his with a slow smile she felt only a little bit bad about. Was it her imagination, or did he look just the slightest bit haunted? Maybe Brakebills did have a ghost after all. Maybe it was Plum.

Finally—and this was Plum's touch, and she privately thought it was the deftest one—in his fourth-period class, a practicum on diagramming magical energies, Wharton found that the Brakebills pencil he was using, on top of its bad hand-feel and whatever else, wouldn't draw what he wanted it to. Whatever spell he tried to diagram, whatever points and rays and vectors he tried to sketch, they inevitably formed a series of letters.

The letters spelled out: *COMPLIMENTS OF THE LEAGUE.*

CHAPTER 8

Dinners at Brakebills had a nice formal pomp about them. When one was cornered by sad, nostalgic Brakebills graduates who had peaked in college and were back reliving their glory days, sooner or later they always got around to reminiscing about evenings in the ol' dining hall. It was long and narrow and shadowy and paneled in dark wood and lined with murky oil paintings of past deans in various states of period dress. Light came from hideous, lopsided silver candelabras placed along the table every ten feet, and the candle flames were always flaring up or snuffing out or changing color under the influence of some stray spell or other. Everybody wore identical Brakebills uniforms. Students' names were inscribed on the table at their assigned places, which changed nightly according to, apparently, the whims of the table.

That night Plum ate her first course as usual, two rather uninspired crab cakes, skipping the wine, as she usually did, then excused herself to go to the ladies'. As Plum passed behind her Darcy discreetly held out the silver pencil case behind her back, and Plum pocketed it. She wasn't going to the ladies', of course. Well, she was, but only because she had to. She wouldn't be going back after.

Plum walked briskly through the empty House to the Senior Common Room, which the faculty rarely bothered to lock, so confident were they that no student would dare to cross its threshold unchaperoned. But Plum dared.

The Senior Common Room was a cavernous, silent, L-shaped

chamber lined with bookcases and littered with shiny red-leather couches and chairs. It was empty, or almost. The only person there was Professor Coldwater, and she wasn't worried about him. She figured he might be there. Most of the faculty were at dinner, but according to the roster it was his turn to eat late, with the First Years.

He was an odd one, Professor Coldwater. Young for a professor. Kept to himself—you rarely saw him outside the classroom. He was new, and opinion about him was divided as to whether he was a genius or a bit insane or both. He had a cult following among the students: his lectures were peppered with exotic magicks and bravura demonstrations, or so the legends went. Plum had never seen one—she was way past Minor Mendings.

The other professors didn't seem that wild about him. He was constantly getting handed the crap jobs that nobody else wanted, like eating with the First Years. He didn't seem to mind, or maybe he just didn't notice. She got the impression he had something else going on, something that was part of a larger frame of reference than the changeless yet ephemeral world of Brakebills. He was always hurrying in and out of the library with thick books under his arms, mumbling to himself like he was doing math problems in his head.

That was one of the reasons she wasn't too worried about his catching her in the Senior Common Room. Even if he did notice her he probably wouldn't care enough to write her up; more likely he would just kick her out. Either way: totally worth it.

Right now Professor Coldwater was at the far end of the room with his back to her. He was tall and skinny and stood bolt upright, with his weird white hair, a wineglass forgotten in his hand, staring into the fire. Plum breathed a silent prayer to whatever saint it was who watched over absent-minded professors and made sure their minds stayed absent. She cut swiftly through the right angle of the L into its shorter arm where he couldn't see her.

Because it was time for the grand reveal. Toward the end of dinner, when Wharton was ready to bring out the dessert wines, he would retreat to the wine closet, which wasn't so much a closet as a room the size of a studio apartment. To his shock he would find Plum already in possession of same, having entered it on the sly through a secret back passage from the Senior Common Room. Fait accompli. Then she would present the League's demands, and he would capitulate to every single one of them.

It was the chanciest bit of the plan, because the existence of this secret back passage was a matter of speculation, but whatever, if it didn't work she'd find some normal, less dramatic way to corner him.

She looked quickly over her shoulder—Coldwater still out of view and/or otherwise engaged—then knelt by the wainscoting. She took a deep breath. Third panel from the left. Hmm—the one on the end was half a panel, not sure whether she should count it or not. Well, she'd try it both ways. She traced a word in Old English with her finger, spelling it out in a runic alphabet, the Elder Futhark, and meanwhile clearing her mind of everything but the taste of a really oaky chardonnay paired with a hot-buttered toast point.

Lemon squeezy. She felt the locking spell release even before it happened: the panel swung outward on a set of previously invisible hinges.

Annoyingly though, the passage had been sealed. Ten feet in it ended in a brick wall, and the bricks had been bricked in such a way as to form a design that Plum recognized as an absolutely brutal hardening charm—just a charm, yes, but a massively powerful one. Not undergraduate stuff. Some professor had bothered to put this here, and they'd spent some time on it too. Plum pursed her lips and snorted out through her nose.

Crouching down, she stepped into the passage and pulled the little door shut behind her. She snapped on a simple light spell, a friendly glowy will-o'-the-wisp. Then she stared at the brick wall for five minutes, in the dimness of the little passageway, lost to the world in an analytical trance. In her mind the pattern in the bricks floated free and hung before her all on its own, pure and abstract and shining. Mentally she entered the pattern, inhabited it, pushed at it from the inside with cognitive fingers, feeling for any sloppy joins or subtle imbalances.

There must be something. Come on, Plum: it's easier to break magic than to make it. You know this. Whoever drew this seal was smart. But was she smarter than Plum?

There was something odd about the angles. The essence of a glyph like this wasn't the angles, it was the underlying topology—you could deform it a good deal and not lose the power as long as its essential geometric properties remained intact. The angles of the joins were, up to a point, arbitrary.

But the funny thing about the angles of these joins was that they were funny. They were sharper than they needed to be. They were non-arbitrary. There was a pattern to them, a pattern within the pattern: 17 degrees, 3 degrees. Seventeen and three. Two of them here, two of them there, the only angles that appeared twice.

When she saw it she snorted again. It was a code. A moronically simple alphabetical code. Seventeen and three. *Q* and *C*. Quentin Cold-water.

It was a signature of sorts, a watermark. A Coldwatermark. Professor Coldwater had set this seal, and when she saw that, she saw it all. He'd wanted a weak spot, a back door in case he needed to undo it later. His vanity signature was the flaw in the pattern. She extracted the little knife from Wharton's pencil case and worked it into the crumbly mortar around one particular brick. She ran it all the way around the edge, then she knocked on the brick with her knuckles: *shave and a haircut*. Free and loose, it pushed out cleanly: clunk. Deprived of that one brick, and hence the integrity of its pattern, the rest of the wall gave up the ghost and fell apart.

Why would he have sealed it up? And why him in particular—everybody knew Coldwater was a wine lush. She could always ask him, he was standing about twenty yards away. Or she could get on with what she was here for. It was chilly in the passageway, much chillier than in the cozy Senior Common Room. The walls were unfinished boards over very old stone.

Dead reckoning, it was about one hundred yards from the Senior Common Room to the back of the wine closet, but she'd only gone half that distance before she came to a door, fortunately unlocked and un-sealed. More passage, then another door. Like she was going through a series of airlocks. Weird. You could never tell what you were going to find in this place, even after living here for four and a half years.

The fifth door opened onto open air. That was very odd. It was a pretty little square courtyard that she'd never seen before, maybe twenty yards on a side. Mostly grass, with one tree, a pear tree, espaliered against a high stone wall. She'd always found espaliers a little creepy. It was like somebody had crucified the poor thing.

Also she was almost positive that there shouldn't have been a moon tonight.

"Nutso," Plum said quietly. She frowned at it. The moon looked back at her blankly, pretending not to care. She hurried across the courtyard to the next door.

It opened directly onto one of the upper floors of the library. That definitely wasn't right; she was traversing some magically noncontiguous spaces here. The Brakebills library was arranged around the interior walls of a tower that narrowed toward the top, and this must have been one of the teensy tiny uppermost floors, which Plum had only ever glimpsed from far below, and which to be honest she'd always assumed were just there for show. She never thought there were any actual books up there.

In fact now she realized that these upper floors must be built to false perspective, to make the tower look taller than it was, because it was very tiny indeed, barely a balcony, like one of those tiny houses that mad kings built for their royal dwarfs. She had to navigate it on her hands and knees; she felt like Alice in Wonderland, grown too big. The books looked real enough though, their brown leather spines flaking like pastry, with letters stamped on them in gold. Some interminable many-volume reference work about ghosts.

The other weird thing was that they weren't quite inanimate: they poked themselves out at her from the shelves, butted her as she crawled past, as if they were inviting her to open them and read, or daring her to, or begging her. A couple of them actually jabbed her in the ribs pretty hard. They must not get a lot of visitors, she thought. Probably this is like when you visit the puppies at the shelter and they all jump up and want to be petted.

No, thank you. If she wished to consult them she would be in touch via the usual channels. It was a relief to crawl through the miniature door at the far end of the balcony—it was practically a cat-door—and back into a normal corridor. This was taking longer than she thought.

But it wasn't too late. The main course would be half over, but there was still dessert, and she thought there was cheese tonight too. She could still make it if she hurried.

This corridor was tight, almost a crawl space. In fact it was one—as near as she could tell she was *inside* one of the walls of Brakebills. On the other side was the dining hall: she could hear the warm hum of talk and the clank of heavy silverware, and she could look out through a couple of the paintings—there were peepholes in the eyes, like in old movies about haunted houses. In fact they were just serving the main, a nice rare lamb spiked with spears of rosemary, and the sight of it made her hungry. She felt like she was a million miles away from everyone and everything she knew. She was a ghost herself, the skeleton at the feast, the world in the walls. She already felt nostalgic, like one of those teary alums, for back when she was sitting at the table with her bland crab cakes, half an hour ago, back when she knew exactly where she was.

And there was Wharton, showily pouring his mingy glasses of red, totally unrepentant. The sight emboldened her. That was why she was here. She was going to get through this. For the League.

Though God, how long was it going to take? The next door opened out onto the roof. The night air was bone cold. She hadn't been up here since the time Professor Sunderland had turned them into geese and they'd flown down to Antarctica to study at Brakebills South. It was lonely and quiet after the dining hall—she was very high up, higher than the leafless tops of all but the tallest trees. The roof was so sharply raked she had to crawl again, and the shingles were gritty under her palms. She could see the Hudson River off in the distance, a long sinuous leaden squiggle. She shivered just looking at it.

And for the record: no moon. It was gone, back to its proper place.

Which way? She was losing the thread. After a long cold think, resulting in no definitive conclusions, Plum just jimmied the lock on the nearest dormer window and let herself in.

She was in a student's room. Actually if she had to she'd guess it was Wharton's room, though she'd never seen it.

"OMG," she said out loud. "The irony."

What were the odds? These spaces were beyond noncontiguous. Somebody at Brakebills, possibly Brakebills itself, was fucking with her.

The room was messy as hell, which was somehow endearing, since she thought of Wharton as a control freak. And it had a nice smell. She half suspected she had stumbled into a magical duel with Wharton himself, except no way could he pull off something like this. Maybe he had help—maybe he was part of a shadowy Anti-League, committed to frustrating the goals of the League! That would actually be kind of cool.

This would have been a reasonable moment to bail, exit the vehicle and slink back to the dining hall. But no: that would mean giving up, going back, and that wasn't Plum. She went forward, always forward, never look back. Eye of the tiger. She had a job to do, a mission for the League, of which she was the God damned chief executive officer.

So she wasn't going to fight against the dream-logic, she was going to steer into the skid and see where it took her. Onward and downward.

To leave by the front door, she knew instinctively, would have been to break the dream-spell, so instead she opened Wharton's closet door, somehow confident that—yes, look, there was a small door at the back of it. Turning to take a final look around she couldn't help but notice, by the by, on his desk, a fresh box of those pencils. He'd already got replacements. Why exactly had they thought those were the only ones? He probably had truckloads of them. She opened the door in the closet and stooped through.

From here on out her travels ran entirely on dream-rails. The door took her into another courtyard, but now it was daytime. The spaces were losing temporal, uh, contiguousness—contiguity?—as well as the spatial kind. In fact it was earlier today, because there she was, Plum herself, crossing the lightly frosted grass, and passing Wharton, and there was the eye-sliding. It was a strange sight. But Plum's tolerance for strange had been on the rise, lo this past half hour.

She watched herself leave the courtyard. She wondered whether, if she shouted and waved her arms, she would hear herself and turn around, and the timeline would be permanently busted and altered, or if this was more of a two-way mirror deal. Maybe she could tip herself off—have the shrimp *fra diavolo* instead of the crab cakes!

She frowned. The causality of it was tangled. Though this much at least was clear: those boots had had a good run but it was time for them to go. On the upside, if that's what her ass looked like from behind, well, not bad. She would take it.

The next door was even more temporally noncontiguous, because it put her in a different Brakebills entirely, though at first the difference was hard to put your finger on. It was a smaller and darker and somehow denser Brakebills. The ceilings were lower, the corridors were narrower, and the air smelled like wood smoke. The light was fire- and candlelight. She passed an open doorway and saw a group of girls huddled together on a huge four-poster bed. They wore white nightgowns and had long straight hair and bad teeth.

Plum understood what she was seeing. This was Brakebills of long ago, Revolutionary-era Brakebills. The Ghost of Brakebills Past. The girls looked up only briefly, incuriously, as she passed, then went back to talking. No question what they were up to.

"Another League," Plum said to herself. "I *knew* there must have been one."

She was still savoring the satisfaction of it when she opened the next door into a room she didn't recognize at all. Until she did.

She tried to back out, but the door had locked behind her. It wasn't even a room at all but a rough round rock-walled cave, where a group of strangers were playing out the bloody last act of some byzantine Renaissance tragedy. Two boys were on the ground, facedown, shivering as their precious blood turned the sand around them to dark muck.

"Oh, fuck," Plum whispered. "Fuck fuck fuck fuck fuck."

She plastered herself back against the wall. She had never seen real wounds before. Five more girls and boys were standing around in various states of shock and distress and anger. One girl had a gun; the others were focusing all their magical strength on a man in a gray suit. Crazy harsh enchanted energies streamed out of them and crackled through the air and assaulted the man, with hardly any effect other than to flap his lapels.

He looked vaguely familiar. And there was something wrong with his hands.

In the corner, in a heap, lay a huge woolly carcass with one thick curling knobby horn visible. Oh, God. The scene was starting to clarify itself to her, to take on a horrible meaning even over and above the obvious. That ram had to be Ember, one of the twin gods of Fillory. And the man in the suit, she did recognize him—she didn't, but she did. His round, pasty face had the unmistakable stamp of a Chatwin. This was some ancestor of hers, and she was in Fillory, and it was all real, all of it.

But it wasn't Fillory, not like in the books. It was a sick nightmare Fillory. The room flashed and flared with dangerous light. Rocks rained down on the man in the suit. The air smelled like cordite. She couldn't be here. She was going to go insane. Whatever it was that had chewed up her ancestors and spit them out had found her. It was here in this room with her. It was the room.

"No," she breathed. "Oh God, no! God no!"

She tried the door again just because it had to open, it had to, she couldn't be here! And now it did. It had mercy on her. Effortlessly, no resistance—it even opened out where before it had opened in. She half ran, half fell through it and slammed it behind her, and everything was quiet again. She was in a silent room, a safe room: the familiar homely little trapezoidal lounge where the League held its meetings.

Oh God. Oh, thank God. It was over.

She was breathing hard, and she sobbed once. A dry sob. It wasn't real. It wasn't real. None of it. Or it was real but it was over. She almost laughed. She didn't care either way as long as she was safe now. Maybe she'd fallen asleep here after the meeting last night and it was all a dream. Whatever, this whole fucked-up magical mystery tour was over. She wasn't going back, and she wasn't going forward either. She would stay in this stupid little windowless room with its crap carpet forever if necessary. She loved it. It was the most beautiful room she'd ever seen.

She had teetered on the edge of the rabbit hole, windmilling her arms for balance, but in the end she had not fallen. She had not. She had stayed in the safe sunlit world of grass and sky, and she would never leave it again. She had been so wrong ever to think about it. It had tried to take her, but she would not be taken.

Plum sank down on the couch. Her knees were two bags of water. She forced herself to think about what it meant. Someone had found out that she was a Chatwin, or something had found out, and they or it was trying to scare her. Or maybe it was one of those things where you automatically saw your greatest fear or something.

But what it felt like was, Fillory itself had reached out and tugged lightly on the invisible thread tied to the fishhook that was lodged firmly in her back, and it had whispered: Don't forget. You belong to me.

But she had learned her lesson. Or at any rate *a* lesson: she would never try to enter the wine closet in anything but a straightforward and conventional fashion. The couch was so saggy and brokeback that it almost swallowed her up. She stopped thinking. She looked at her reflection in the long mirror that Darcy and Chelsea had cracked last night.

But she wasn't in the mirror. There was another girl there instead of her. Or at least it was shaped like a girl. It was blue and naked and its skin gave off a soft unearthly light. Even its teeth were blue.

It smiled at her. Its eyes were the same color as its skin. It hung motionless in midair, a yard above the floor, slightly smaller than life size. The girl's outlines were strange: sometimes she was slightly blurry, other times crisp and clear.

Plum sat up. She got to her feet, but slowly, and after that she didn't move at all, because she understood that all moving was over with. She knew who this was.

It was the ghost of Brakebills. It had been the ghost all along. This wasn't a friendly ghost. It wasn't a mischievous poltergeist. This was a dead thing that hated the living. Once as a child, after a storm, Plum had seen a downed power line writhing like a lethal snake on a road, arcing over and over again on the wet asphalt, bright as a sun. This blue girl was like that. The insulation had come off the world, and Plum was facing the raw naked current.

The two girls stared at each other: the one who survived and the one who hadn't. It smiled wider, like they were having a tea party.

"No," Plum said. "It's not me. You don't want me."

But Plum was lying. She understood. The ghost did want her. It had always wanted her. She was a Chatwin, and Chatwins lived on borrowed time. Plum wondered if it would hurt.

Bump. The sound came from the wall to her left—something had run into it from the other side. A shower of plaster fell. A man's voice said something like "oof."

Plum looked; the ghost in the mirror didn't.

Boom! The wall exploded inward, throwing chunks of wood and plaster and stone in all directions, and Plum ducked, and a man came crashing through it covered with white dust. It was Professor Coldwater. He shook himself like a wet dog to get some of the dust off, though he still looked like he'd been hit with a sack of flour. White witchery sprayed out of both his hands like sparklers, so bright they made purple flares in her vision.

When he saw what was in the mirror he froze.

"Oh," he said quietly. "Oh my God. It's you."

Plum didn't think he was talking to her. Did he recognize this thing? It was almost like he knew it personally, which would be pretty weird even for him. He took a deep breath and pulled himself together.

"Don't move till I tell you," he said.

That was meant for Plum. She didn't move, but she didn't dare to believe that he could actually save her. All she'd done was drag him into the catastrophe too.

With an arm protecting his face Professor Coldwater reared back one of his long legs and kicked in the mirror. It took him three kicks—the first two times the glass just starred and sagged, but the third time his foot went right through it. It got a little stuck when he tried to pull it out. It was a measure of how shocked she was that Plum's first thought was, I must tell Chelsea that she won't have to pay for the mirror.

That didn't dispel the ghost, but it was definitely inconvenienced. It was still watching them, suspended in midair, but now it had to peer around the edge of the hole. Professor Coldwater turned his back on it—the ghost threw something at them, Plum couldn't see what, and he deflected it with one hand without looking. Then he placed his palms together.

"Get down," he said. "All the way. On the floor."

She got down. The air shimmered and rippled, and her hair crackled with so much static electricity it made her scalp hurt. The entire world was shot through with light. At the bottom of it was the dull bass pressure-beat of the door exploding outward out of its frame.

"Now get up and run," Professor Coldwater said. "Run! Go ahead, I'm right behind you."

Plum ran. She could have stayed and tried to help, but that would have been compounding her stupidity with more stupidity. She did the hard thing and trusted him: she hurdled the couch like a champion and felt a shockwave as Professor Coldwater detonated some final spell. The force of it lifted Plum off her feet for a second and made her stagger, but she found them again and kept on running.

Going back was faster than going forward had been. She was bounding ahead seven-league-boots-style, which at first she thought was adrenaline till she realized, nope, magic. One stride took her through the hell-room, another and she was in colonial Brakebills, then she was in Wharton's room, on the roof, in the dining room crawl space, the library, hard left turn at the creepy-pear-tree-courtyard, the passage. The sound of doors slamming shut behind her was like a string of firecrackers going off.

She didn't stop till she was back in the safety of the Senior Common Room, breathing hard. He was right behind her, just as he'd said. He'd done it, he'd gotten them out. Never had anything seemed so certain than that she was going to die in that room, but now it was over. The bad thing, the horror, had broken out of wherever it had been hiding all her life, but he'd shoved it back down. For now.

Without a word Professor Coldwater set about resealing the passageway behind them. She watched him work, her breath slowly going back to normal, dazed but not so dazed that she wasn't interested in the technical aspects: moving in fast-motion, his arms flying crazily like a time-lapse movie, he assembled an entire intricately patterned brick wall in about five seconds.

She wondered where he'd learned how to do that. Not here. This time he left out the fancy signature angles. Say that for him: he learned from his mistakes.

Then he climbed out and closed the door. They were alone. It could all have been a dream except for the plaster dust on the shoulders of Professor Coldwater's blazer.

"How did you know?" she said. "How did you know where I was? Where the ghost was?"

"Not a ghost. A niffin. Very bad news."

"What did it want?"

"She. She used to be human. And I don't know. Did she say anything to you?"

"No. Can they talk?"

"I don't know." One of his fingers was still crackling with a bit of white fire; he shook it and it went out. "Nobody knows much about them. I'm not even sure I did anything to her. I just distracted her and got out of there."

"But you looked surprised when you saw it. You looked like you recognized it. I mean her."

"I know." Professor Coldwater looked sadder and less triumphant than she would have thought. "I know I did. I wish she'd said something."

"I don't care if it recited the goddamn King James Bible."

Dean Fogg rounded the corner of the L at speed. He didn't look happy.

"Do you know how many alarms you two set off, blundering around in the subspaces like that?"

Professor Coldwater ticked off on his fingers, silently.

"Eleven?"

"Yes. Eleven." Fogg seemed perversely unhappy that Coldwater had got the right answer. "What the hell were you doing back there? Purchas?"

Plum flushed. The prank—she'd completely forgotten about it. She still had Wharton's stupid pencil case in her stupid pocket. It was so utterly pointless. Maybe that's what the ghost was trying to teach her: it's all pointless. Fate is coming whatever you do, so quit wriggling around, it's only making you look more ridiculous than you already do. We're all ghosts here, you just don't look like one yet.

But she wasn't having that. If that was true then what was the point of anything ever? She was going to wriggle a bit longer anyway. Who the hell cared how ridiculous she looked.

Plum squared her shoulders and lifted her chin.

"I was looking for a secret passage to the wine closet," she said, loud and clear, "so I could play a prank on Wharton."

"A prank." Fogg was unimpressed with her existential courage. "I see. Coldwater?"

"Dean Fogg."

"You didn't perform the incursion protocols, any of them."

"No," Coldwater said. "I didn't. There wasn't much time. The situation was pretty urgent."

"Did you at least try to terminate the damn thing? Or banish it?"

"I—" He bit something back. "No."

"Why not?"

A muscle moved in Professor Coldwater's jaw.

"I couldn't do that."

"Professor Coldwater saved my life," Plum put in.

"Thank you, Purchas," Fogg said, "and he also put the lives of everybody else at this school at risk. I took a chance on you, Quentin, and it was a mistake. You're fired. Be out of your rooms by end of day tomorrow. Professor Liu can pick up the rest of your teaching."

Coldwater didn't flinch, didn't even blink, but Plum flinched for him, the way you do when you see somebody else take a punch.

"All right. I understand."

"Do you?" Fogg was so angry he was spitting. "Do you? Well, you always were a quick one! I would think you of all people would have caught on a little quicker, given that you witnessed firsthand the reason why these protocols were created in the first place. Purchas?"

"Yes, sir."

"You can finish out the last three weeks of the semester. Then you're expelled."

Fogg glared at them both in turn, then walked out of the room.

Plum so wished she could be cool about it. She didn't think she was going to cry, she just had to sit down on one of the red leather couches and put her head between her knees for a minute while her vision grayed out around the edges. She really did love Brakebills. She loved it so much. She really did. She really had.

She felt the sofa squish as Professor Coldwater sat down at the other end. He blew out a long sigh.

"Well—"

"I'm so sorry, Professor Coldwater. I'm so sorry! I didn't mean to put you in danger! I didn't mean to get you fired!"

And now she did sob: once, twice, three times. They were going to turn her out into the cold, scary world. She wasn't ready. It wasn't safe. What was she going to do? How was she going to live now?

"I know. Please don't worry about it." He said it quietly. "I've been thrown out of better places than this. And you might as well call me Quentin."

"But what are you going to do? What am I going to do?"

"You'll find something. It's a big world. Probably bigger than you realize."

"But I'm a failure! I'm a freak! I got kicked out of Brakebills, for God's sake!"

The words barely had any meaning. They would soon, she knew, but right now it made her lips feel numb just to say them, as if the words were envenomed. *She was expelled.* She thought of having to say them to her parents and the gray came back.

"Something will come up, I promise you. Plenty of people have Brakebills degrees, but how many people can say they got kicked out? It's a pretty exclusive club."

She wasn't so far gone that she didn't snort at that.

"But if you don't mind my asking," he went on, "what exactly were you doing back there? I sealed that corridor off for a reason. Even I couldn't figure out where it went."

"Oh, I told Fogg the truth. I really was pranking Wharton."

"But why?"

"Well, he's been kind of stingy with the wine lately. Plus it just seemed to me like there should be more, I don't know, chicanery afoot around here. Generally. High jinks. It sounds silly now, but you know what I mean? To lighten the tone. Because basically who knows, we could all drop dead at any moment."

"That is true."

"Or get expelled."

Quentin appeared to accept her reasoning at face value. Old people: you never knew what you were going to get.

"Do you still want to know where the secret passage is? To the wine closet?"

"Sure," Plum said, though not unshakily. She managed a bitter little laugh. "Why the hell not?"

But she meant it. Fuck it. They could take Brakebills away from her—apparently—but at least the honor of the League would live on eternally. She would always have that.

"You want the next panel over," Quentin said. "You don't count the half-panel."

Aha. She drew the same rune-word she had before, and the door opened, and she peered inside. It was just what she thought: a cakewalk. Not even one hundred yards, more like seventy-five.

After all that the timing was pretty close to perfect. Plum had just closed the secret door to the wine closet behind her—it was concealed behind a trick wine rack—when Wharton came bustling in through the front door with the rumble and glow of the cheese course subsiding behind him. Her hair was a mess, but that was just part of the effect. It was all extremely "League."

Wharton froze, with a freshly recorked bottle in one hand and two inverted wineglasses dangling from the fingers of the other. Plum regarded him calmly. Some of the charm of Wharton's face came from its asymmetry: he'd had a harelip corrected at some point, and the surgery had gone well, so that all that was left was a tiny tough-guy scar, as if he'd taken one straight in the face at some point but kept on trucking.

Also he had an incredibly precious widow's peak. Some guys had all the luck.

"You've been short-pouring the Finns," she said.

"Yes," he said. "You have my pencils."

"Yes."

"It's not the pencils I mind," Wharton said, "so much as the case. And the knife. They're antique silver, Smith and Sharp. You can't find those anywhere anymore."

She took the case out of her pocket. She wasn't going to give an inch, not even after everything else. Especially not. To hell with the ghost, and to hell with Brakebills, and to deepest darkest hell with the Chatwins. The world had split open under her feet, and nothing would ever be the same, but she would still play her part to the hilt. To the end. They couldn't take that away.

"Why have you been short-pouring the Finns?"

"Because I need the extra wine."

God, was he really an alcoholic? Nothing should surprise her at this point, but still. He didn't seem like the type. Epifanio, maybe, but not Wharton. And Wharton wouldn't be an enabler like that.

"But what do you need it for?" Plum held the case just out of reach. "I'll give you back the pencils and all that. I just want to know."

"What do you think?" Wharton said. "I leave it out for the damn ghost. I thought the wine might keep it happy. That thing scares the shit out of me."

Wharton had a lot to learn about ghosts. She sighed and sat down on a crate. All her strength was gone.

"Me too." She handed him the case.

Wharton sat down next to her and pulled over a little table. He placed the two glasses on it.

"Wine?"

"Thanks," Plum said. "I'd love some."

If not now, when? He poured, properly this time, even a little heavy. The dark liquid looked black in the glass, and she had to restrain herself from gulping it.

Fresh tobacco. Black currants. God, it was so good. She kept it in her mouth for a count of ten before she swallowed. If there was any magic in this world that was not magic, it was wine. She smelled wet hay from a tumbledown field in Tuscany in the early morning, after the sky turned light, but before the sun burned off the dew.

It reminded her of somewhere else too, a place she'd never seen, let alone smelled—someplace green and unspoiled and far away, which she knew well even though she'd never been there, just as it knew her well. She felt its pull on her, as she always had. But for the moment she let its name escape her.

CHAPTER 9

They'd only been at the Newark Airport Marriott for a week and already Quentin didn't know how much longer he could stand it. This was not somewhere humans were supposed to stay more than one night in a row. It was not a long- or even medium-term residence. The walls were thin, the food was lousy, and the interior decoration was worse. This place was bad for your soul.

He didn't see much of the others, apart from Plum. Pushkar was busy overflying the East Coast at high altitude with Lionel and the bird, scouring it for any signs of the suitcase and/or the Couple. Stoppard was building something large and complicated out of tiny metal parts in his bedroom, from which he emerged only once or twice a day, at odd hours, wearing an oil-stained apron. The bird had sent Betsy off with a credit card to buy supplies. Meanwhile Quentin and Plum had been tasked with figuring out how to break the famous incorporate bond.

It was a bear of a problem, nasty and complicated, a real tarball. Quentin had heard about incorporate bonds, though he'd still never seen one in real life. The theory went as follows: picture a two-dimensional world, an infinite plane, full of infinitely flat two-dimensional objects. You, a three-dimensional being, could theoretically lean down from above it and fasten one of those objects in place, anchoring it permanently to its plane from above; if you did it carefully you might not even damage it too much. In the case of an incorporate bond the same operation was performed in three-dimensional space, using a four-dimensional anchor to fix the object immovably with respect to the fabric of three-dimensional space-time.

It was about as difficult as it sounded, and messy and expensive to boot. Four-dimensional paperweights didn't grow on trees, or at least not in this plane of existence they didn't. Incorporate bonds were the last word in magical security, and the Couple must have gone through a good deal of trouble to cast the spell, but in doing so they'd rendered the case unstealable. Except that the bird thought it wasn't.

In Quentin's experience magical creatures like the bird didn't tend to know a lot about magic from a technical point of view. They didn't work magic themselves, they just *were* magic, so the theory of it didn't really matter. Also a lot of them weren't terribly bright. But the bird had some ideas about it, or someone had supplied it with ideas, and on the face of it they weren't demonstrably nonsense. But carrying them out posed a raft of thorny practical issues, and the bird had generously left the working out of said problems to Quentin and Plum.

At first it was fun: it was a dense, rich, genuinely hard problem, and they attacked it with a will. The issue of the suitcase's Chatwin connection receded to the back of Quentin's mind as they scribbled flow charts on hotel stationery, then on reams of printer paper filched from the business center, then finally on a fat roll of butcher's paper from an art supply shop. The spell kept ramifying into more and more secondary and tertiary and quaternary spells, to the point where they had to color-code them, and the color-coding eventually ran to a full 120-count pack of Crayolas. Quentin and Plum argued more vehemently than was strictly necessary over which colors should go with which spells.

That should probably have been a warning sign. After a week they'd drilled down far enough that they were staring at some real bedrock problems, questions that looked like they ought to have answers but which kicked back everything they threw at them. He might have given up if it hadn't been for Alice.

For years, seven of them, he'd thought of Alice as someone who belonged to the past. She wasn't dead, but she was gone. He was resigned to living his life without her. But when he saw her that night in the mirror at Brakebills all that ended, and she came surging roughly back into his present.

He hadn't seen her since Ember's Tomb, and their reunion was so chaotic and unexpected that in the moment he didn't know what to think or feel or do—Fogg was right, he hadn't followed protocol, because the protocol was designed to banish or kill anything that made it inside the Brakebills cordon, and he wasn't going to do that. And he hadn't wanted to say why. Just like that Alice was there, right there, close enough to talk to, close enough to kill him. Or to kill Plum, whom until that night he knew only as a face in the crowd. But she hadn't.

There was a part of him that wished he hadn't seen Alice at all, that he hadn't been in the Senior Common Room that night, that it hadn't been his turn to eat with the First Years. It wasn't enough that he'd lost her once and spent seven years getting over it—now Alice had to hunt him down, cross worlds to find him and get him thrown out of the only home he had? When he kicked in that mirror part of him had meant it: he wanted to send her back, push her back down. He knew Brakebills was over for him even before Fogg fired him. He knew it as soon as he saw her.

Because he'd felt her presence. He was sure he had. She wasn't gone: her body had burned, but the essence of Alice was in there somewhere, the Alice he knew, trapped inside that toxic blue flame like a fly in amber. He'd recognized her, the old Alice, the one he used to love, twisted and distorted but real, and he couldn't leave her there. If there was some way to get her out, he would find it. That was his job now. Teaching would have to wait.

He was ready. The whole business of getting kicked out of Fillory had been good for him. It made him tougher, more grounded in reality, to the point where he could deal with getting kicked out of Brakebills. He was basically homeless, and getting increasingly less respectable, but he knew who he was and what he had to do.

He just needed a plan. He needed to get himself together—he needed resources, he needed somewhere to live. He needed to find out everything he could about niffins. For that he needed money, and to get money they would have to break this damn bond.

They weren't going to do that without help. Unfortunately the only magician Quentin could think of who was smart enough to help them was very far away, on another continent in fact. It was a place that he and Alice had known well.

When Quentin first suggested a field trip to Antarctica Plum wasn't enthusiastic. It was cold there, and a pain to get to, and also Professor Mayakovsky was kind of a dick. But Plum was a creature of enthusiasms, and it didn't take her long to come around to the idea. It would be an adventure! She could be a goose again! She'd loved being a goose.

"Except," she said, even more excited, "why be a goose? We've been geese. We could go as something else! Anything else!"

"I was thinking of going as a human being," Quentin said. "Like on an airplane."

Plum was already at her laptop and Googling.

"OK, check this out. What's the fastest migratory bird on Earth?"

"An airplane."

"Whatever, you are like the bullshittest magician ever. Look at this, it's called the great snipe."

"Are you sure that's a real bird? It sounds like something from Lewis Carroll."

"'Some have been recorded to fly nonstop for forty-eight hours over 6,760 kilometers.' I'm quoting here."

"From Wikipedia."

But still. He looked over her shoulder. The great snipe was a plump little wading bird, roughly egg-shaped, with a big long bill and zigzaggy brown stripes, like a not particularly exotic seashell. It didn't look like a speed demon.

"'Female great snipe are, on average, significantly larger than the male,'" Plum said.

"We'd need something to base the spell on, like some great snipe DNA. At least the first time we did it. I don't think we can do the transformation based on an image from a Wikipedia entry."

"Are you sure? They have it in hi-res."

"Even so. Plus I'm kind of concerned about the cold. That bird doesn't look like it was evolved for Antarctica."

"Except it'll still be summer," Plum said. "Backward seasons."

"Even so."

"Stop saying that." Plum frowned, then brightened up again. "OK, forget about birds. I don't know why I was even thinking birds. We could be fish! Or whales—blue whales!"

"We'd still have to go the last bit. After we got to Antarctica."

"We'd just swim under the ice!"

"That's the North Pole. Antarctica is a continent. Under the snow it's all rock."

She huffed her annoyance.

"Whatever, Nanook."

But of course she was right: it would be cool to be a blue whale. The idea grew on him. There was no particular reason to do it, other than it would be more interesting, but that seemed like enough. What else was magic for? It was safe: they were legally protected, and barring scattered orca attacks blue whales had no natural predators. The only downside was that even though they were fast swimmers by cetacean standards they turned out to be painfully slow compared with most birds, let alone the great snipe—20 mph was about a blue whale's top speed, at least over long distances. At that rate it would take them a couple of months to get to Antarctica.

"I doubt we could delay the job that long," Quentin said.

"Yeah," Plum said sadly. "It would have been nice though. Oh well, another dream dies."

But in the end they found a way to save it. They flew commercial most of the way, as far as Ushuaia, a small but unexpectedly charming port in Tierra del Fuego that claimed the distinction of being the southernmost city in the world. It was squeezed into a narrow strip of land between the Beagle Channel and the snow-covered peaks of the Martial Range behind it, as if it were backed up against them and trying not to fall into the freezing water. From there they could cross the Drake Passage to the coast of Antarctica in the form of blue whales.

From the airport they took a taxi to the waterfront. They'd brought no luggage. From the safety of a concrete wharf, the Beagle Channel did indeed look forbiddingly cold, a flat gray stripe of sea lapped at by glaciers on either side. But they couldn't do anything from dry land. For the actual transformation they'd have to be in deep water.

Chartering a boat would have been the sensible thing to do, if they were tourists, or sport fishermen, or smugglers. But Quentin and Plum were magicians, so they waited until midnight, then cast spells on their shoes and hiked out onto the channel on foot.

It was tricky at first, till they made it out through the mercifully light surf and got used to the rhythm of the swells. It was only their shoes that were buoyant, so if they fell over they'd get wet like anybody else. Once they were a couple hundred yards from shore, out beyond the glow of the lights along the beach, it got quiet and very dark and very cold.

"I feel vaguely blasphemous doing this," Plum said. "Like, only Jesus is allowed to do this."

"I really don't think he'd mind."

"How do you know what Jesus would mind?" She was silent for a minute, concentrating on the walking. It was not wholly unlike trying to walk on a black, cold, unusually violent bouncy castle. "Did you like Brakebills South?"

"I don't think anybody likes it. But it was good for me. I learned a lot."

"Yeah. I liked it when we were animals."

"That was good. Did they turn you into foxes?"

She shook her head.

"Bears and seals. For some reason they don't do foxes anymore."

When they'd gotten on the plane that morning Brakebills South had seemed very far away, but now they were here, just a short splash across the Drake Passage from Antarctica, and suddenly it was very close, and his memories of it felt very fresh. They'd been so innocent then, he and Alice, even after what happened when they were foxes. Their feelings had been so big and raw and urgent, and they'd had absolutely no idea what to do with them. He wished he had it to do over again. He would try to be a nicer, stronger person.

Except that wasn't quite it. What he really wished was that he had Alice back now, in the present.

"Did you do that thing at the end, where you race to the pole?" Plum said. "I bet you did."

"Yup. You win."

Plum just seemed excited about going back.

"I bet you got there first."

"That one you lose."

"Ha!" Her laughter got lost among the waves. "I can't believe the great Professor Coldwater got beat to the pole! Who beat you?"

"A better magician than me. Did you win your year?"

"I sure did," she said. "By a mile."

The moon came up, unnaturally bright, a wafer of white phosphorus, but the black water seemed to swallow light rather than reflect it. Even a ripple was enough to trip over, so they wound up taking big exaggerated steps. Farther out from the beach the water smoothed out but the swells got bigger. The few lighted windows in Ushuaia, which shut down after ten o'clock, looked inexpressibly cozy. Fortunately they were wearing warm clothes, parkas and long underwear, which if all went according to plan they would never see again.

They hiked out about a half mile, well out into the bay. According to the nautical charts Quentin had consulted that was far enough. They stopped and bobbed up and down on the water in place, comically, not quite in sync. They'd prepared as much of the spell as they could ahead of time.

Quentin took a deep breath and rolled his shoulders. It was rare for magicians to kill themselves with their own magic, but stories that ended that way usually began something like this.

"All right?"

Plum chewed her lip and nodded.

"All right."

Quentin peeled open a Tupperware container full of a revolting paste he'd ginned up back in New York based on whalebone dust scraped from some scrimshaw he'd bought at an antique store. They each dipped in two fingers and anointed their foreheads.

"Maybe we should stand farther apart," Plum said. "If this works we're going to get really big."

"Right."

They took a few steps back, like they were preparing to fight a duel, then faced the same direction. Quentin braced himself. Based on his memory of the goose transformation back at Brakebills he was pretty sure that this was going to be really unpleasant. He took a deep breath, held up his hands, and made a gentle downbeat, like he was cueing the start of a Mahler symphony.

It began. Surprisingly, it wasn't that bad.

Shrinking, having the mass squeezed out of him like toothpaste out of a tube, must have been the rough part of becoming a goose, because now the opposite was happening, Quentin was expanding, and it didn't feel that bad at all. He was inflating like a balloon, especially his head, which was getting absolutely huge. His parka strained and stretched and then burst apart in a cloud of down.

His neck and shoulders merged into his body as the Quentin-balloon grew and grew and his eyes zoomed off in opposite directions on either side of his gigantic head. His arms and hands grew more slowly, becoming proportionally smaller, then flattened and dearticulated into flippers—it was like wearing mittens—and slid smoothly down toward his waist. His legs fused together, and something *very* curious was going on with his feet, but he took note of this fact only in passing—it didn't especially alarm him. The most hilarious part was his mouth: the corners raced back toward his ears so that his head was practically split in half by a fifteen-foot recurved smile.

His lower teeth melted away completely. His upper teeth lengthened and multiplied crazily into a hairy overbite, more like a mustache than teeth.

The only real moment of panic came when he toppled forward into the water and went under. His human instincts told him he was about to freeze or drown or both, but he did neither. The water was neither warm nor cold—it was nothing. It was like air. He did utter some truly epic, booming whale-sneezes before his blowhole-based respiratory system got going. But even that was kind of enjoyable.

And then everything was still. He was hanging in the void, neutrally buoyant, twenty feet below the surface. The Quentin-blimp had been launched. He was a blue whale. He was roughly as long as a basketball court. He was in a really good mood.

For a few minutes he and Plum floated next to each other, eyeball to eyeball. Then at the same time—somehow they coordinated this—they surfaced, arched their backs, sucked in gallons of air through the tops of their heads, and dove.

Quentin didn't know when he'd ever felt so calm. Together with Plum he kicked with his flat, powerful tail and began undulating through the water. It took hardly any effort; it would have taken an effort to stay still. He sucked in a huge mouthful of water—his mouth and throat distended hilariously to take in more and more and more—and then squirted it out again through his weird front teeth (his baleen, that was the word) like he was spitting tobacco. It left behind a tasty residue of wriggling krill.

He'd imagined that he'd get some kind of deluxe ocean-vision as part of his package of new whale-senses, but in fact he didn't see much better than he had as a human. With his eyes on different sides of his head his binocular depth perception was shot, and having no neck, all he could do to change the view was roll his eyes around or steer his whole humongous body. Also, unnervingly, he didn't seem to have any eyelids anymore. He couldn't blink. The urge decreased over time, but it never completely went away.

Once they cleared Tierra del Fuego Quentin's sensorium expanded hugely. His world became enormous. His sight may have been crap, but his hearing was something else entirely.

To a blue whale the whole ocean was a vast resonating chamber, a great watery tympanum stretched across the earth, with fleeting, fugitive vibrations constantly zipping back and forth across and through it. Based on these Quentin could feel the shape and proportions of the world around him all the time, as if he were running invisible auditory fingertips across it. If he'd had hands he could have drawn you the coastlines of southern Chile and Antarctica and a relief map of the ocean floor in between.

And if the great blue chamber ever fell silent, he made some noise of his own. He could sing.

His throat was like a didgeridoo, or a foghorn, blasting out deep, resonant pulses and moans. The ocean was full of voices, like a switchboard, or an echo chamber, an Internet even, alive with encoded information passing through it in the form of calls and responses. The whales were always checking in with each other, and Quentin checked in too, in a language he knew without having to learn it.

They weren't just being social. Here was a great secret: whales were spellcasters. Jesus, the entire ocean was crisscrossed with a whole lattice of submarine magic. Most of the spells took multiple whales to cast, and were designed to bend and herd large clouds of krill, and occasionally to reinforce the integrity of large ice shelves. He wondered if he'd remember all this when he was human again. He wondered, but he didn't really care.

And there was something else—something down there in the black abyssal trenches of the ocean. Something that wanted to rise. The whales were keeping it down. What was it? An army of giant squid? Cthulhu? Some last surviving *Carcharodon megalodon*? Quentin never found out. He hoped he never would.

Much more than when he was a goose or a fox or a polar bear Quentin felt like himself as a whale. He had a big fat brain that was capable of running most of his personality software at the same speed he was used to. But he wasn't the same Quentin, not exactly. Whale-Quentin was a calm, wise, contented Quentin. He was colossal, planetary, moving through the blue gloom unthreatened by anything and requiring nothing more than air through his blowhole and krill through his mouth. Drake Passage was about five hundred miles across, and it would take them two or three days to swim it, but time was an idea that he was having an increasingly hard time being interested in. Time was defined by change, and very little changed for a blue whale.

He noticed everything but was concerned with nothing. Drake Passage had the worst weather in the world, literally, but all that meant was that when he surfaced for a breath, once every fifteen minutes or so, the waves broke a little harder against his wide, slick back. He and Plum were great blue gods, flying wingtip to wingtip, and everything around them paid homage to them. Fish, jellyfish, shrimp, sharks; once he spotted a great white, swaggering along by itself through the depths with its permanent shit-eating grin. It had so many teeth it looked like it had braces. Nature's perfect killing machine! Go on with your bad self. No, really. It's cute.

And then the ocean floor began sloping up to meet them. He'd almost forgotten what they were doing here, fumbled it away and allowed his mind to disappear forever into the endless blue whaleness of it all. But no: they were here for a reason.

This was always going to be the worst part. They were going to have to deliberately beach themselves, hopefully on nice soft sand, but more likely on some rocky shale, or worse. They just had to hope their skins were thick enough, and the terrain gentle enough, that their delicately flanged stomachs didn't get shredded in the process. They moaned a bit at each other, as one does, then they aimed themselves at the Antarctic coastline.

As they got closer emergency calls came in from some distant pod, warning them off, urging them to turn back for deeper water. Look out! Don't do it! It was surprisingly hard to ignore them—he felt like he was the pilot of a falling 747 and the air traffic controllers were begging him to for God's sake pull up, pull up! But they stayed the course, churning with their tails, pouring on speed, their massive bodies bulling through the water. If they'd had teeth they would have gritted them.

Then Quentin was lying facedown on black stones under a white sky, naked, with the weak surf of the Southern Ocean washing fiery-cold over his bare legs, which were already going numb. It felt like being born must feel, being spat out of the warm, enveloping, sustaining sea and up into the bright searing cold world. In short it sucked.

Quentin did the one thing he knew would feel good: he shut his eyes for the first time in three days and kept them shut for a good minute. He'd missed his eyelids.

Plum was lying next to him. A minute ago he wouldn't have had to turn his head to look at her, but now he swiveled his small, pale nub of a human head in her direction. She looked back at him, pale and shivering.

"Final leg," he said thickly.

Huh: lips and teeth. What a concept. He pushed at them clumsily with his tongue.

"Final leg," she said.

Quentin levered himself up off the shale and immediately fell over. Gravity, my old enemy. What a stupid way to locomote. Standing up felt like trying to balance a telephone pole on one end.

They were on a narrow curving beach, black pebbles and gray sand; it was just about the least tropical beach in the world. They were both naked, and there might have been a time when, as a human male, he was at least notionally interested in the sight of Plum without her clothes on, but he was still mentally more than half cetacean, and the relative nakedness or clothed-ness of a human of either sex really could not have been more beside the point to him. He could barely remember what they were doing here.

Fortunately they'd talked through what would happen next, drilled it into their brains, which they knew would not be functioning at full capacity. They both began searching through the rocks and tide marks, heads down. This had to be done quickly, before hypothermia set in. Quentin reeled like a drunk, cutting his strange, unbearably soft yellow-pink feet on the unsympathetic rocks, until—there. A feather. White flecked with gray. He plucked it out of a mass of sticky, smelly sea-trash. No time to be picky. Basically anything but a penguin would do.

It was coming back to him, the purpose of all this. He waited, bouncing on his toes, hands clumped under his armpits to keep his fingers warm, getting increasingly self-conscious about being naked, until Plum found hers. Then he clamped the feather between his chattering teeth, and they did the spells at the same time.

This time the change was bad, and he threw up when it was done, though granted throwing up isn't as big a deal to a bird as it is to a human. He made a neat, hygienic job of it—business as usual. After its brief reunion with humanity his brain went animal again, this time having to endure the insult of being squeezed into the tablespoon volume of a seabird's skull. He got oriented in time to watch Plum dwindle into the shape of a seabird twenty yards away, her pale body feathering over and collapsing in on itself into—he didn't even know what kind of bird she was. Or for that matter what he was.

He was whatever kind of bird that feather had belonged to. A moment of contact with Plum's turmeric-yellow, perfectly circular eye, then they both took flight.

Onward and upward.

CHAPTER 10

Quentin had never heard of anybody going to Brakebills South in the gap between fall and spring semesters, which this was, and he wasn't even a hundred percent positive they could get in. They might find the building shut down, Mayakovsky gone or in hiding, the whole place sealed off. If that happened they'd have to reassess pretty fast and make a break for one of the non-magical research stations on the coast, where their arrival would be hard to explain at best.

They spiraled in from above, balancing on their aching wings, steeling themselves for the moment when their webbed seabird feet would skip off the surface of some hard invisible dome—but the moment never came. Apparently Mayakovsky considered five hundred miles of Antarctic no-man's-land enough of a defense against home invasion. They alighted on the flat roof of one of the towers and became human again.

Quentin figured it was better to let Mayakovsky find them rather than the other way around—he didn't want to startle the old magician into some lethal display of defensive magic—so they made as much noise as possible coming down the stairs. First stop was the laundry, where they secured some Brakebills South robes: the nakedness issue was starting to feel urgent again.

The place felt off-limits, out of bounds. It was like they were hunting a minotaur in its maze. Quentin trailed one hand idly along a wall, and the smooth stone was cool and sticky with condensed moisture, something about the heating spells—it gave off a damp basement smell that brought back memories of the last time he'd been here, when they were all studying eighteen hours a day under Mayakovsky's rule of silence. There was something he didn't have to worry about at Brakebills South: nostalgia.

He was too hungry to feel anything anyway. They wound up in the kitchen, where they stuffed themselves on anything they could find that might possibly get the taste of bird beak out of their mouths. Quentin was keenly aware that Mayakovsky had no real reason to help them, even assuming he could. He'd always known he wouldn't have much to offer by way of compensation, aside from an intellectually interesting problem and some shameless flattery and, he supposed, the strictly— *strictly*—platonic presence of a smart and pretty young woman. But somehow it had all been more convincing when they were first setting out.

They never heard Mayakovsky coming, he just appeared in the doorway, silent as a ghost, looking grim and hungover and unbathed. His stubble was slightly frostier, his gut more prominent, his nails yellower, but otherwise he was perfectly preserved. It was like Antarctica had freeze-dried him.

He didn't kill them.

"Saw you coming," he growled. "Miles away."

He had on a dressing gown, unbelted, a white button-down shirt badly in need of bleach and a pair of very short, very un-professorial shorts.

"Professor Mayakovsky." Quentin stood up brightly. "I apologize for intruding on your privacy like this, but we're working on an interesting problem, and we could use your help with it."

Mayakovsky sawed the end off a stale loaf of bread with an unwashed knife, spread about an inch of soft, unrefrigerated butter on it and began to eat standing up. It was pretty clear he wasn't going to throw the ball back, so Quentin kept going: he explained about incorporate bonds, and what they were trying to do, and why he, Mayakovsky, alone among all practitioners of the arts invisible, could give them the assistance they so desperately needed. Mayakovsky chewed steadily and noisily, gazing into the distance with watery, rapidly blinking eyes.

When Quentin was done Mayakovsky swallowed, sighed, his round shoulders rising and then falling under his robe, and left the room. He came back with a piece of paper and a blunt pencil. He swept some crumbs onto the floor and put them down in front of Quentin.

"Write eet down," he said. He pointed at Plum. "You. Make coffee."

Plum made a monster face at him behind his back. Quentin turned up his palms: what are you gonna do? She made a monster face at him too.

"Fine," he said. "You draw. I'll make the coffee."

While Plum produced a crude approximation of their original flow chart, Quentin made coffee in a battered Soviet-era espresso maker. Mayakovsky came back for both the drawing and the coffee—he didn't bother to pour, he just took the whole machine—and left again. It was just as well, Quentin was getting tired. He hadn't slept for four days; there had been no breaks during the flight from the coast, and whales didn't really sleep at all. He found his way to the dormitory wing by memory and lay down on a cot in one of the empty cells and fell asleep in the milky white Antarctic light.

He had no idea how long he'd slept, but when he came back down to the dining hall matters had progressed. Mayakovsky was back, now wearing glasses with heavy black frames, sitting at a table talking heatedly at Plum and waving his arms. The flow chart was on the table in front of them; it looked like it had been repeatedly folded into two-inch squares and then unfolded again. Most of the white space was now full of annotations and calculations in Mayakovsky's tiny blocky handwriting, a jumble of numbers and letters, Roman and Cyrillic, and more obscure symbols.

Quentin pulled up a chair. Mayakovsky's body odor was sharp as cheese.

"It is crazy, what you are doing." Mayakovsky shook his head with Slavic melancholy, as if their sheer incompetence saddened him. "A valid exploit, yes. All right. Crude—this, here, totally unnecessary. Totally." He tapped the paper heavily. "And this, you transpose—it is working against your secondary effects, here and here. Spell is fighting itself. You understand? But the rest is not so terrible."

It was better than Quentin expected. Listening to him crisply parse their tangled, fudged work, he knew they'd been right to come to him, however much it had cost them and might still cost them.

"Thees, though, no." It was a round, resonant, definitive Russian *no*. He indicated one of the later stages of the spell with the back of his hand, like he didn't even want to touch it, it was that far beneath his contempt. "It is impossible. Waste of time. You need more power, much more. Is a simple matter of scale. You are—I don't know. You are trying to dig through a mountain using a toothpick."

Professor Mayakovsky shook his head again. His mood was darkening visibly, heading for black.

"You are needing more power, much more. See? Khxere. And khxere." He indicated two points on their flow chart; like a lot of Russians Mayakovsky had mastered many arcane points of higher mathematics but not the English letter *h*. "Between khxere and kxere."

"I said that!" Plum said. "Remember? That's basically exactly what I said!"

"I remember." Quentin stared at the chart. His confidence was flagging. It all seemed very inadequate now. "How much more power?"

"Much. Orders of magnitude." *Megnitude.* "You want to break the bond with these?" He grabbed Quentin's fingers in one pawlike hand and shook them in front of Quentin's face. "These little things? Waste of time. Would take one hundred years! Or one hundred Quentins!"

"Or a hundred Plums," Plum said.

"Feefty Plums," Mayakovsky said gallantly, with a quick yellow grin. "But you are nowhere near it. Nowhere near. Waste of time."

He crumpled up the diagram and threw it at the wall.

Quentin watched it roll to a stop under a table. He would have liked to take a few minutes to go back through the spell in a patient, civil, collegial fashion, looking for areas of flexibility, places where the multipliers could be tweaked, maybe, to make up the difference. But Mayakovsky rolled over him, frog-marching him briskly through the math of it, brutally multiplying three and four digits in his head as he went. It was all Quentin could do to keep up. There was nothing that Mayakovsky didn't know about incorporate bonds, apparently; it was like he'd studied up on them specifically in anticipation of their arrival. He understood their spell far better than they did.

Quentin wondered what Mayakovsky's own work looked like, if he did any. He was alone out here half the year every year. What the hell did he do with himself? With a mind like his there was no limit to what he might have accomplished, if he wanted to. But Quentin had no idea what Mayakovsky wanted.

Quentin closed his eyes and rubbed his temples. He could picture the whole spell in his head, and he could follow what Mayakovsky was saying, just, but he couldn't see an answer. There had to be a way through. He was damned if he was going to go back empty-handed.

"Maybe I could store it up," he said. "Build up the power over time. Construct a kind of containment device—I could cast the spell a hundred times, store it up, release it all at once."

"And you stabilize how? 'Store' how? What is storage matrix?"

"I don't know. A gem, a coin, something like that."

Mayakovsky made a rude noise.

"Bad magic. Dangerous magic."

"Or," Quentin said, "I could get a hundred magicians together. We'll cast it all at once."

"I think you will not be telling one hundred magicians about this little project."

Fair point. "Probably not."

"It would be very risky."

"True."

"I do not know why you want to break an incorporate bond, but whatever it is is not legal, I don't think. Even me you should not have told."

Mayakovsky was studying him across the table. Quentin studied him back. His stolid face was impossible to read. Plum watched the exchange alertly.

If he's bluffing, call it. If he's not, what the hell are you going to do about it?

"Maybe you should turn us in," Quentin said. "I mean, if it comes out that we were here, you could lose your job."

"Maybe I should."

Mayakovsky stood up and went to a cabinet and rummaged through it. He took out a bottle of something clear, without a label.

"I want you out of my house," he said. "I will make a portal."

But then, instead of throwing them out, Mayakovsky lapsed into a funk. He sat back down at a table in the corner and started drinking. After a few minutes he offered the bottle to Plum.

"Dreenk."

Plum sniffed, took a sip, coughed, wiped her mouth and handed Quentin the bottle.

"Dreenk," Plum said.

It smelled like radiator fluid.

"Christ," he said. "What is this?"

That got a rare laugh from Mayakovsky.

"Antarctic moonshine."

It wasn't a very reassuring answer. What could possibly grow here that you could even ferment? Lichens? He hoped it was lichens. The alternatives seemed even worse.

Mayakovsky lapsed back into silence. He seemed to feel no need to even acknowledge their presence anymore, though Quentin noticed he didn't leave them alone either. He and Plum exchanged flummoxed looks. Mayakovsky didn't seem to want to talk about incorporate bonds. They tried to engage him in small talk about life at Brakebills South, but he was impervious to banter.

"Are you related to the poet?" Plum asked him.

"*Nyet.*"

Mayakovsky added something snarly in Russian, probably about poets.

So Quentin and Plum compared notes about their experiences as blue whales, gossiping about the various pods they could remember, while Mayakovsky stared at the wall and drank steadily and mechanically. He brought out a loaf of dark bread and some pickles but he didn't eat, just picked the loaf up every few minutes and sniffed it and put it back down.

How long was he going to let this go on? Well, Quentin wasn't going to help him. He was going to drag this out as long as he had to, to the bitter end. He wasn't going to give up, not until Mayakovsky made him.

The Antarctic light outside was like an interrogator's lamp, steady and without mercy. It felt like they were the last three human beings on earth.

As much as he openly despised them, Mayakovsky couldn't seem to bring himself to banish them either. Maybe he was lonelier than he let on. Eventually he got out a chess set, with one pawn replaced by a knob from a cabinet. First he destroyed Quentin, then he beat Plum twice, the first time with some difficulty, the second time after three quarters of an hour and by the narrowest of margins. Quentin suspected Plum of pulling her punches.

Maybe Mayakovsky suspected too. Midway through their third game he stood up abruptly.

"Come." He set off out of the room with his rolling, purposeful gait. "Bring bottle."

Quentin looked at Plum.

"After you," she said.

"Ladies first."

"Age before beauty."

"P's before Q's."

It was starting to seem funny. They were a pair of comedy supernumeraries, Rosencrantz and Guildenstern to Mayakovsky's gloomy Hamlet. *Glean what afflicts him.* Quentin found some glasses—he was tired of sharing a bottle with Mayakovsky, though no doubt Antarctic moonshine had powerful sterilizing properties—and they followed him.

He led them through a door Quentin had never seen unlocked before and through his private apartment. Quentin averted his eyes from the many small, unclean garments scattered on the floor.

"Dreenk!" Mayakovsky roared as they walked.

"Thanks," Quentin said, "but I'm—"

"Dreenk! This is your professor speaking, skraelings!"

"You know," he said, "I'm a professor now too. Technically speaking. Or I was."

"I will show you something, Professor Skraeling. Something you will see nowhere else."

Apparently murderous drinking was the price of admission to Mayakovsky's inner sanctum, but Quentin was willing to follow any lead no matter how tenuous. He was still wobbly from the trip over, but the moonshine had ignited some smoldering heat source in his stomach, a sour, slow-burning peat fire. Mayakovsky himself didn't seem particularly drunk, except that his mood had flipped from depressive to manic.

He led them down two flights of stairs, down into the Antarctic rock itself. Maybe he was the anti-Santa, of the South Pole, and he was going to show them where the elves made lumps of coal for Anti-Christmas. Quentin prayed to every god he could think of, living and dead, that this was not a sex thing.

It wasn't. It was Mayakovsky's laboratory: a suite of dark, square, windowless workrooms, each one furnished with well-worn benches and tables and studded with silent heavy machinery: a drill press, a band saw, a small forge, a lathe. In contrast with everything else in Mayakovsky's domain it was all magnificently clean and orderly. The tools and instruments were polished and laid out in straight rows on cloths as if they were for sale. The machinery gleamed a dull matte blue-black. The room was still except for some quiet regular motion in the shadows: a softly swinging pendulum; a spinning top that for some reason didn't stop; a slowly turning armillary sphere.

The three of them stood looking around in the half-light, the lichen vodka or whatever it was momentarily forgotten. The silence was another level below the regular ambient silence of Antarctica: an absolute sonic vacuum.

"This is lovely," Plum said.

It was true.

"Beautiful."

"I know why you do this," Mayakovsky said.

He didn't so much answer them as continue a monologue that had been going on in his head.

"You"—he looked at Plum—"you, I don't know. Maybe you are bored. Maybe you are in love with him?" Plum waved that one off frantically, a full-arm gesture: *No, abort, abort.* "But you, Quentin, you I understand. You are like me. You have ambition. You want to be great wizard. Gandalf maybe. Merlin. Dumb-bell-door."

He spoke softly and, for him, gently. He drank, then cleared his throat and spat wetly into a handkerchief, which he stuffed into the pocket of his robe. He'd been living alone for a long time.

Did he? Quentin thought. Want to be a great magician? Was that the truth? Maybe it used to be. Now all he wanted was to be a magician period. He wanted to break an incorporate bond. He wanted Alice back. But truth was seeming pretty relative at this point. Truth was a substance soluble in lichen vodka.

"Sure," he said. "Why not."

"But you will not be great. You are clever, yes—you have good head."

He reached over and rapped on Quentin's head with his knuckles.

"Don't do that."

But Mayakovsky was unstoppable, a drunk best man hell-bent on giving an inappropriate toast.

"Fine head. Better than most. But sadly for you there are many heads like it. One hundred. One thousand maybe."

"I'm sure you're right." No point in denying it. He leaned against the cool, oiled metal of a drill press. It felt reassuringly stable, an ally at his back.

"Five hundred," Plum said generously. She boosted herself up on a table. "Be fair."

"You will never be great. You know nothing of greatness. You want to see? I will show you greatness."

He waved his arm expansively at the darkened workbenches, and all through the room metal and glass stirred and glowed and came alive. Engines moved, wheels turned, flames lit.

"This is my museum. Museum of Mayakovsky."

And he showed them what he'd built in the long Antarctic winters.

Mayakovsky's workshop wasn't just a marvel, it was a library of marvels. It was a catalog of answered prayers and impossible dreams and holy grails. Suddenly Mayakovsky was a showman, ushering them grandly from table to table: here was a perpetual motion machine, and a pair of seven-thousand-league boots. He showed them one drop of universal solvent, which no vessel could contain and thus had to be kept magically suspended in midair. He showed them magic beans, and a pen that would write only the truth, and a mouse that aged backward, and a goose that laid eggs in gold, silver, platinum, and iridium. He spun straw into gold and turned the gold into lead.

It was the end of every fairy tale, all the prizes for which knights and princes had fought and died and clever princesses had guessed riddles and kissed frogs. Mayakovsky was right, this was grand magic, this was what a lifetime of solitary practice and toil bought you. Later it was hard for Quentin to remember details—the moonshine bleached them out of his brain cells like an industrial detergent—but he recalled a player piano that would improvise according to your mood, never repeating itself, optimizing the music according to how you responded, becoming more and more beautiful until it was the sound of everything you'd ever wanted to hear.

After a few minutes it was painful—he had to tell Mayakovsky to stop it before he broke down sobbing. Later he couldn't have hummed the melody to save his life.

"This, Quentin. This is greatness. These are things you will never do. Never understand."

It was true. Even with the strength he'd gained after his father died, he would never be in Mayakovsky's league. It cost him nothing to admit it. He just wished that with all his genius Mayakovsky could help them.

But Plum was frowning.

"But I mean so why are you still here?" she said. "In Antarctica? If you're this great wizard? I don't get it. I mean, look at all this stuff! You could be famous!"

"I could be." Mayakovsky said it sourly; the showman was gone. "But why? Why should I care if people know my name? People do not deserve Mayakovsky!"

"So you like being here? Alone like this? I don't understand."

"Why shouldn't I like it?" He stuck out his lower lip. He didn't much care for being psychoanalyzed. "Here I have everything. Outside there is nothing for me. Here I can do my work."

"But she's right, it makes no sense." Quentin found his voice. "You've probably solved problems people have been banging their heads against for years. You have to go back and tell everybody."

"I have to do nothing!" And then more quietly: "Enough. I will never go back. I am done with that."

Even with his ordinary, averagely brilliant brain Quentin was beginning to understand. He knew a few things about Mayakovsky's personal history: how he'd had an affair with a student named Emily Greenstreet that ended so disastrously that he'd had to flee to Brakebills South. And Quentin knew something about hiding out from the world, too. He'd done his fair share of it. He'd been so depressed and traumatized after what happened to Alice that he withdrew from the world of magic and swore never to cast a spell again. If he never risked anything more—he reasoned—he could never lose anything more. He could never hurt anybody else.

But it hadn't lasted. It wouldn't do. Never risking anything meant never having or doing or being anything either. Life is risk, it turned out. Eliot and Janet and Julia had come for him, and he'd gone back to Fillory after all. He'd risked again, and won, and lost, and it hurt but he didn't regret it, not any of it.

"You're wrong," Quentin said. "Fine, you're a genius, but you're wrong about this. You could go back. It wouldn't be as bad as you think."

"Do not tell me what I can do. Do not tell me who I am. When you can do all this, little man, then you can judge me."

"I'm not judging you. I'm just saying—"

"You—you are not such a mystery." Mayakovsky jabbed Quentin in the chest with a finger like a dried sausage. "You think I do not know you? They threw you out of that place, that other world you go to. Yes? And you came back to Brakebills. But they would not have you there either! So out you go again!"

Jesus, he must know about Fillory, or at least the Neitherlands. Mayakovsky advanced on Quentin, who gave ground.

"Well, yeah," Quentin said. "But you'll notice I'm not hanging around my ice castle brooding about it."

"No! No! Now you want to be a criminal! But even that is too much! You have to come running to Daddy, begging for help!"

"My dad's dead."

Quentin stopped backing up.

"I may be a second-rate magician," he said, "but at least I'm not a weird recluse who yells at people. I'm out in the world trying to get something done. And I'll tell you something else, I think you know how to break an incorporate bond. In fact"—oh my God, maybe he actually was a genius—"in fact, I think you're under one yourself. That's what's keeping you here. Isn't it?"

Mayakovsky had been very well prepared for their visit. Too well, even for him. It was a long shot—but Mayakovsky hesitated, and Quentin knew he was close.

"Tell me how to break it." He pressed his advantage. "You must have figured it out, even if you're too scared to do it yourself. Tell me how. Help somebody for a change!"

He'd touched a nerve, because something went cold behind Mayakovsky's eyes, and he slapped Quentin across the face. Quentin had forgotten how he liked to do that. It stung like hell, though not as much as it would have if he hadn't already been drunk on lichen vodka. It made his ears ring, but his face was already two-thirds numb.

He was drunk enough that he did something he'd always wanted to do, which was to slap Mayakovsky back. With his grizzly hide it was like slapping a crocodile. Mayakovsky broke out in his sulfurous yellow grin.

"There it is!" he shouted. "Again!"

Quentin slapped him again.

With no warning Mayakovsky threw his thick arms around Quentin in a big Russian bear hug. It was hard to follow the emotional about-face, but Quentin went with it. Why not? Over Mayakovsky's shoulder he saw Plum watching them round-eyed—she looked like she was trying to teleport herself out of the room through sheer force of will. But fuck it, why shouldn't two men hug each other in a basement in the middle of Antarctica? He patted Mayakovsky's back with his free hand. This poor fucking guy.

And Quentin's father was dead. Who else was he going to hug? This must be what having a family is like, he thought. This must be how people hug their parents. Good old Mayakovsky. They weren't so different after all.

"I am a dead man, Quentin. This is my grave. I bury myself here."

"That's ridiculous," Quentin said. "It's stupid. You can break the bond. You can come back anytime. Come with us!"

Mayakovsky pulled away. He held Quentin at arm's length.

"You keep your shit world! You hear me? You keep it! I will stay here. I am done!"

He patted Quentin's cheek.

"It is over for me. You are a pathetic mediocrity, but you are braver than me. You will not end like Mayakovsky. It is not over for you."

He held out the bottle. Christ, Quentin thought they'd finally finished it, but there it was, practically full again. He must be refilling it by magic.

Quentin didn't remember much after that. Later he would have a hazy recollection of Mayakovsky singing and laughing and weeping but it all got mixed up with the lichen-flavored dreams he had after he passed out, and he could never separate the fact from the hallucinations. In his dreams, at least, they sat on the floor of the workroom, passing the bottle around, and Mayakovsky told them about how he'd been there in the Neitherlands too, when the big blue gods returned and tried to take their magic back. How he'd fought them, alongside the dragons, how he'd ridden bareback on the great white dragon of Lake Vostok. How he'd smashed the bell jar over the Neitherlands with lightning and thunder from his own hands.

The next morning Quentin woke up in his own bed. Not in Brakebills South, in his own bed back in the Newark Airport Marriott. He had no memory of how he got there. Mayakovsky must have sent them back through a portal after all, the same way he'd sent Quentin back to Brakebills after the race to the South Pole.

Though Jesus, it made him shudder to think of Mayakovsky opening portals in the state they'd been in. Alcohol and portal magic, not a great combination.

When Quentin sat up he immediately wished he had in fact died in a catastrophic teleportation accident. Every hangover feels like the worst hangover you've ever had, but this one was definitely a classic. One for the ages. He felt like all the water had been forcibly sucked out of his body, like an apricot in a dehydration chamber, and replaced with venom from an angry adder.

Slowly, carefully, he got to his hands and knees. He pushed his face into his pillow, abasing himself before whatever angry god had done this to him. Maybe there was some untainted blood left somewhere in his body, and it would run downhill into his aching brain. His fingers felt something under his pillow, something hard and round and cool to the touch. A gift from the tooth fairy. He took it out.

He was right, it was a gift. It was a coin, shiny and gold, the size of a silver dollar but slightly thicker. There were three of them. He turned one over in his hand. It gleamed like it was in sunlight, but the curtains were drawn. He knew what it was right away.

Quentin smiled, his dry lips cracking. Mayakovsky had done it, exactly what Quentin had said: he'd stored up power in these coins, the power he'd need to break the bond. Mayakovsky must have prepared them to break his own bond but then never used them. God bless the old bastard. Maybe Quentin's father hadn't had any power, but Mayakovsky did, and more than that he'd had the courage to pass it on to someone else. He was wrong about himself: he was a brave man after all.

Kneeling on the bed, his headache already fading, Quentin held one of the coins between two fingers and made it disappear—a one-handed sleight, stage magic—then brought it back. It felt like the present he'd been waiting for all his life. He wouldn't waste it. The plan was going to work, they were going to break the bond, and steal the case, and then he could start over. He could start his real work. For the first time since he'd left Brakebills his life was starting to make sense to him again.

The coin's edges were sharp and newly minted. On one side was the image of a wild goose in flight. On the other was a face, a young woman in profile: She was Emily Greenstreet.

CHAPTER 11

"Man," Josh said. "I can*not* believe the world is ending."

"Stop saying that," Janet said.

"Order," Eliot said, not for the first time, "in the court."

Poppy said nothing. She was thinking, her mouth twisted to one side. They were in the high square room in Castle Whitespire where the kings and queens met every day at five o'clock. The flaming ruins of a five-alarm sunset smoldered in the window behind her, which was currently pointing west.

"It can't really all be going to end," she said finally.

"And yet." That was Janet.

"I feel like I just got here. I did just get here! Do we have any other evidence that it's ending? I mean besides Ember's say-so?"

"Sweetie, He is the god of us," Josh said. "He probably knows."

"He's not infallible."

"How do you know?"

"Because if He were infallible," Janet put in, "He wouldn't be such a twat all the time."

Janet never shrank from taking both sides of an argument at once.

"You know," Josh said, "I bet it's because of sacrilege like that that the world is ending. Your earthy, irreverent sense of humor has doomed us all."

"Poppy does have a point," Eliot said. "Don't forget that the first time we met Ember He was a prisoner. Martin Chatwin had Him locked away in Ember's Tomb."

"So He's not omnipotent," Josh said, clinging to his point. "He might still be infallible."

"Either way, He never tells us everything He knows." Eliot adjusted his crown, which had gotten crooked. "Not till it's too late. I wouldn't be surprised if that's what's going on now. All Ember is saying so far is that if it continues on its present course, the world is going to end. That doesn't mean Fillory can't be saved. Necessarily."

He waited for somebody to jump in. Nobody did.

"What I'm suggesting is that maybe we, its kings and queens, could save it."

"Sure," Janet said. "We could put on a show! We could use the old barn!"

"I'm making a serious point."

"Yes, and I am mocking your serious point to show how ludicrous it is."

"Look, Ember is a god," Eliot said, "but He's a god only of Fillory. He's limited. He doesn't know everything there is to know about the wider universe. I think we should poke around some ourselves, see if He's missed something. See how far our royal power can stretch. See if we can get an advance look at this so-called apocalypse. Maybe we can head it off at the pass."

This was met with more silence, while everybody tried to think of a reason why what Eliot was proposing might be plausible or achievable.

"Yeah, no, of course," Josh said. "I mean, we're gonna go down fighting, right?"

"Right!" Loyal Poppy gave a swift nod of her sharp chin.

"So—what?" Janet said. "We just head back out into the wilderness? Looking for adventure? In whatever comes our way?"

"That's right," Eliot said. "That's what we do."

She weighed this suggestion.

"OK. But I'm coming this time. Last time I got stuck babysitting the country and you guys were gone for like a year and a half. When do we leave?"

"ASAP."

"And what if we can't?" Poppy said. "What if we can't head it off?"

Janet shrugged.

"I guess we go back home. I mean, to our other home. Our former home."

"That's what the Neitherlands is for," Josh said.

"Guys, listen."

Eliot leaned forward. He put on his High King face and his High King voice. At times like this he wanted to look as much as possible like Elrond, Lord of Rivendell, from *The Lord of the Rings,* and he didn't think he was a million miles off base. He made eye contact with each one of them in turn.

"I know I don't speak for all of you. Not in this. But if Ember is right, if Fillory really is ending, I'm going to stay and see it end. This land is where I became who I am, who I was meant to be. Who I am is who I am in Fillory, and if Fillory dies, then I'll die with it." He studied his kingly fingernails. "I think I made that choice a long time ago. I don't expect you to make it with me, but I want you to know, there isn't any going back. Not for me."

The crescent moon was already visible, early today, opposite the sunset, hooking a pale horn over the rim of the world. Eliot could picture it, the rim of the world, now that he'd been there, with its endless brick wall and its narrow gray strip of beach and its single door to the Far Side. The tower was high enough that sometimes you could kid yourself that you could really see it, on a clear day, which this was.

Josh cocked his head and screwed up his face and studied Eliot with one eye. He pointed at him, hesitantly.

"Fuck you."

Eliot cracked his crooked grin. Everybody relaxed.

"Look, it sucks," he said. "I hate it. But we'll take it as far as we can, then we'll walk away. We'll go back to Earth, have a decent drink for a change. We'll see what Quentin's up to."

"Oh, God," Janet said. "I think death might be preferable."

Everybody laughed except for Poppy, who was still thinking.

"I just wish—"

She broke off and gave a shaky sigh, to try to calm herself down. It mostly worked. Josh took her hand under the table.

"What is it, sweetie?"

"It's just that if it all ends then the baby will never see Fillory! I know it's silly, but I wanted the baby to be born here. I wanted him to see all this. Or her. I wanted us to have a little prince or princess!"

"They'll still be one, baby," Josh said. "Whatever happens. We'll be royalty in exile. It still counts."

"No," Janet said. "It doesn't."

In the end it was only Janet and Eliot who went, for the simple reason that Josh couldn't really ride a horse yet, not even a talking one who could coach him, and anyway Poppy was feeling sick, and Josh didn't want to leave her.

So it was just the two of them. It felt very different from when they'd set out to fight the Lorians, or even from when they'd gone hunting in the old days. It was quieter. More somber. They rode out shortly after dawn through a small stone arch in the rear of the castle that let out on a narrow trail, hardly more than a goat track, that ran along the tops of the cliffs overlooking the bay. No fanfare, no confetti, no loyal retainers. They went alone.

"Which way?" Janet said.

Eliot pointed north. No particular reason, it was just good to be decisive in these situations.

The grass was still wet. The new pink sun hovered low above White-spire Bay. Eliot felt very small and Fillory felt, for a change, very big and very wild around him. It was a while since it had felt like that. This was a serious quest, maybe the last one. What happened now truly mattered. Eliot had struggled before he found Fillory, he knew that: he drank too much, he found clever ways to be nasty to people, he never seemed to have an emotion that wasn't either ironic or chemically generated. He'd changed in Fillory, and the thought of going back to that, of becoming that person again, frightened him. He wouldn't die with Fillory, he'd meant that when he said it, but if Fillory died Eliot knew that something in him, something small but essential, wouldn't survive either.

He wouldn't miss this interminable summer though. It had a certain fiery majesty to it, and he appreciated that, but at this point he was dying for the heat to break. A hot early morning wind surged through the trees, thick and strong like a flowing river, combing through the leaves, which were green but yellowing in the drought. The trees must know what was coming, he thought. If Julia were here she could have asked them.

Whitespire—the town as opposed to the castle or the bay—was of modest size, and it didn't take them long to reach the outskirts. It was surrounded by a wall of irregular height and composition, a patchwork of building materials, brick and stone and mortar and timber and rammed earth, that had been demolished and rebuilt and then buttressed to keep the whole business from falling over as the town expanded and contracted over the centuries. Beyond the wall were fields full of people shoulder-deep in golden grain with huge baskets on their backs, like in a Brueghel painting. They fell silent as Eliot and Janet passed; most of them took a knee as well and bowed their heads. Eliot and Janet nodded—he'd long ago figured out that it was better to accept the fealty; modesty and self-deprecation were just confusing in a king. A half hour later they were through the fields and addressing themselves to the Queenswood north of the city.

They pulled up just short of it. There was no underbrush at the edge; the border with the fields around it was clean and clear. It wasn't a natural wood. Eliot had a formal feeling, as if they were presenting themselves at a ball. Good evening, my old friend. Shall we dance once more?

"After you," Janet said.

"Oh, fuck off."

If you rode with a queen, the queen must enter the Queenswood first. That was the rule. The trees—huge, crotchy, black-barked oaks covered with gnarls and knots that always seemed to be about to form a face but never quite did—slid smoothly apart like stage scenery.

Janet urged her horse forward.

"Any idea where we're going?"

"We discussed this. That's not how quests work. We're not going to think about it, we're just going to journey."

"I can't not think about it."

"Well, don't overthink it."

"I can't help it!" Janet said. "Whatever, you can do the not-thinking for both of us."

They left the bright morning behind for the permanent twilight of the deep forest. The clop-clopping of the horses' hooves became a deeper tom-tom thump-clumping as the way went from cobblestones to ancient packed loam.

"What if nothing happens?" Janet said.

"Nothing is going to happen. At least at first. We have to be patient. That's part of the quest."

"Well, just so you know, I'm doing this for a week," Janet said. "That's it. Seven days."

"I know what a week is."

"The way I think of this," she went on, "is it's like we're taking Fillory's pulse. This is a diagnostic quest. We're saying, Are you still functioning, you wondrous magic land you? Are you going to give us an adventure, and is this adventure going to be your way of telling us what's wrong with you and how to fix you? If so, great. But if by a week we haven't gotten into shit, I'm calling it. Time of death. Fillory's flatlining."

"A week is not a lot of time," Eliot pointed out, "in which to decide the fate of an entire world."

"Eliot, I love you like the brother I never had or wanted," Janet said, "but actually a week is a really long time. After a week you and I are going to be really really sick of each other."

Their path wound and wended and looped through the Queenswood, drawn apparently on the spur of the moment by the arboreal hivemind. One could try to steer one's way through it, but this time they set the autopilot and let it ride and took what came. It was eerily quiet: the trees of the Queenswood tended to pick off fauna they didn't care for—falling branches, strangling roots—which left only some deer and a few decorative birds. The forest floor was furred with vast herds of ferns and striped with light that slipped in through chance gaps in the canopy overhead. There were no fallen trunks. The Queenswood buried its dead.

The trees parted and parted before them—it was vaguely erotic, Eliot thought, like endless pairs of legs spreading, ushering them on and on into more and more intimate spaces. They burrowed deeper and deeper in. Occasionally the path forked and he picked one fork or the other, for no reason but always without hesitating.

Like a magician producing a dove from a hidden pocket, the wood abruptly brought them to the circular meadow with the giant clock-tree inside it, the one where they'd found the Seeing Hare, and where Jollyby had died. The tree had a deep sunken scar where its clock had been, a blinded cyclops, but at least it wasn't thrashing anymore. It was at peace. The sapling Eliot had extracted the watch from, to give to Quentin had died. He was sorry about that, but not so sorry that he wished he hadn't done it. It was worth it to know that wherever he was Quentin at least had that with him.

They decided to spend the night there. If history was any guide, it was a good place to await something fantastical and portentous. Janet swung down out of the saddle.

"I'll get us dinner."

"They packed us dinner at the castle," Eliot said.

"I ate it for lunch."

In businesslike fashion, Janet pulled a short staff from a pair she wore crossed on her back and trotted off into the trees. Eliot had never seen her wield a staff before, but she held it as if she knew what to do with it.

"Hm," he said.

It was a spooky place to be alone in, especially without his queen. The grass was dotted with wildflowers; he'd always meant to name some of the Fillorian flowers, but he'd never gotten around to it, and now he probably never would. It was too late. He heard a rustling, cracking sound from all sides which alarmed him until he realized that the trees along the edge of the meadow were helpfully dropping dead branches for firewood. They must have accepted his presence, he thought. It was strangely touching.

From one saddlebag Eliot extracted their tent, a neat canvas parcel, and tossed it on the soft grass. It unfolded and erected itself in the deepening twilight, with a sound like a sail being hoisted in a high wind.

In the morning a fine mist hung over the meadow, as if a heavy cannonade had just moments ago ceased firing, leaving behind puffs of silent white gunsmoke in the air.

They rode all day without incident—that's two down, five to go, Janet said—and by sunset they'd reached the end of the green splendor of
the Queenswood and entered the adjacent maze of gray firs called the
Wormwood. On the third day they forded the Burnt River, never a
pleasant experience, though rarely actually dangerous. Its black water
was always choked with ashes, nobody knew why, and the nymph who
lived in it was the glossy black of a beetle—a terrifying creature with
silvery eyes who went up and down the river at night screaming.

Eliot proposed trying to talk to her, but Janet shuddered.

"That's a last resort," she said. "That's like day six."

"Whatever. It's not the end of the world."

"FYI, you only get to make that joke one time, so I hope you enjoyed it."

Eliot would have preferred to head west from there, toward the lakes
called Umber's Tears, or maybe to Barion, a mellow walled hill-town
where they made an incredible clear liquor out of some native grain.
Eliot maintained a comfy royal townhouse there that he hardly ever got
to visit. But Janet wanted to ride north.

"That would be fine," Eliot said, "except that there's this horrible
thing called the Northern Marsh. It's north of here, hence the name."

"That's why I want to go north. I want to go there. I'm feeling the marsh."

"I'm not. I hate that place."

"Wow, I thought you were supposed to be all Johnny Quest over
here. Fine, I'll meet you in Barion."

"But I don't want to go to Barion alone!" Eliot said.

"Your whininess is beyond unattractive. Come with me to the marsh
and then we'll both go to Barion."

"What if I die in the Northern Marsh? People do, you know."

"Then I'll go to Barion alone. I like traveling alone. If you die can I
have your townhouse?"

Eliot said nothing. Privately, and very much in spite of himself, Eliot understood that Janet was having a hunch about the marsh, and you couldn't ignore those. Not in the context of a quest.

"Fine," he said. "I was just testing your resolve. Gloriously, you have passed. To the marsh we go."

The Northern Marsh wasn't actually as far north as all that. By late afternoon the ground had begun to get squishy, and they made camp on its outskirts that same night. The next day dawned gray and brisk, and they picked their way through cattails and coarse grass and chilly puddles until the horses refused to go any farther. Janet's was a Talking Horse, and he politely explained that he was speaking for both him and his dumb companion when he said that this was not a place you wanted to cross on hooves, not when your legs break as easily as horses' legs do. Eliot accepted their resignation graciously. The two of them went on on foot.

The air was full of the smell of warm mud and rotting things. They circled around big weedy expanses of standing water and occasionally waded through them when they had to. The Great Northern Marsh was a lonely, quiet place. You would have thought it would be full of frogs and insects and waterfowl, but nothing seemed to live there. Just a lot of plants and smelly microbes.

As they forced their way deeper in, the ground became mud flats and water punctuated by occasional stubborn hummocky tufts of grass. Their boots were getting hopelessly befouled, and Eliot felt the ratio of solid ground to water shifting slowly and inexorably in the water's favor. The way was bordering on impassable when they found a narrow board-walk which Janet had been looking for without telling him. It was just two thin weather-beaten gray planks laid flat over the sucking puddles, and in places elevated a few feet off the ground by stilts and pilings and opportunistic tree stumps.

Eliot took a minute to scrape his boots off, though he was pretty sure they weren't salvageable, then they set off again. There were no railings, and they had to balance their way along like a damn circus act. He tried to remember whether quicksand was a real thing or an urban myth.

"I wonder where all the birds are," he said, to take his mind off it. "I've seen, like, two birds. This place should be covered in them."

"Makes you wish Julia were still here," Janet said. "She was good with birds."

"Mm. Do you? Wish she were here?"

"Of course. I always liked Julia."

"You didn't show it very often," Eliot said.

"If you really got Julia," Janet said, "you would have understood that she didn't like people who were too demonstrative with their affections."

This caused Eliot to retroactively evaluate a lot of the interactions he remembered between Janet and Julia. Their footsteps sounded hollow on the boards in the marshy hush.

"Incredible that this thing is still standing," Janet went on. "I can't imagine who keeps it up."

"How do you even know this place?"

"I was out here once, when you-all were away at sea. I thought somebody should survey it. It looked weird and interesting. I ran into some scary shit and backed off, but not before I met some weird and interesting people."

Eliot wondered, not for the first time, what exactly Janet had gotten up to while the rest of them were off sailing the ocean blue. He'd gotten the official version of course, which was that she'd been running the country and doing an excellent job of it. But every once in a while Janet said things that made him wonder if that was the whole story.

"Do you ever wish you went with her? Julia, I mean? To that other-side deal, whatever it was called?"

"I think about it sometimes," Eliot said. "But no. There's no way I could have gone. Being king here is who I am. I wasn't joking about that part, before." He wobbled for a moment on a rocky board. "I wish I knew what it was like though."

"Probably it's not as marshy. You know the funny part?"

"Tell me."

"I know how Poppy feels," Janet said. "About the baby. I want that little guy to see Fillory too. I want it to rule when we're gone."

Eliot wasn't sure if a person born in Fillory *could* rule Fillory, but he was more focused at this exact moment on his own possible imminent death at the hands or other extremities of this horrible swamp and whatever lived in it. He supposed that if he sank to the bottom of it his corpse might be perfectly preserved, for later generations, like those bodies that got pulled out of Irish bogs. That would have a certain grandeur to it.

But probably he'd be eaten before that happened. And after that the world would end anyway. So.

"That's what happens to the birds, by the way."

Janet pointed. She was having no trouble keeping her balance; she didn't even look at her feet as she walked. In the distance something pale translucent pink floated, drifting, thirty feet above the cattails. It looked just like a jellyfish, with long floral tentacles dangling down.

It was an unspeakably sinister sight: an alien aerial parasite. A dying sparrow fluttered in one of the tendrils, stuck to it like a fly stuck to flypaper.

"Wow," he said.

"Don't touch one, the venom's really bad. Stops your heart."

"I wasn't going to. How do they fly? Helium or hydrogen or hot air or something?"

"Nah. Just magic."

They must have been getting close to the center of the swamp because the ponds were getting wider and deeper and darker and more still, and they were connecting up with each other, to the point where the swamp was on the point of just being a regular lake. A steamy mist was gathering around them. Here and there a lotus flower poked up above the surface, a rosy-white bulb the size of a softball on a thick green stem. Strange that something so pure and lovely could grow out of all that muck: one clean perfect thing distilled out of the filth.

Eliot had a hard time not thinking about the vast shape he'd seen last time he'd flown over the Northern Marsh. He hoped it stuck to deeper water.

Though that appeared to be where they were headed. The boardwalk rose high up above the marsh now on long spindly pilings, more like a narrow jetty, and it was taking them straight out over the lake. The banks vanished into the fog. Eliot felt disoriented, abandoned by the gods. If this adventure were working the way it should have been they would have learned something by now, he thought. Seen something, felt something. Instead they were nowhere, with nothing ahead of them and nothing behind them, suspended in midair, on dead wood, over a black mirror of dead water.

"How far are we—"

"This far."

The boardwalk ended abruptly. If Janet hadn't put her hand on his shoulder he might have walked straight off it. There was a rickety ladder leading down, in case he was overcome by the urge to do some recreational bathing.

"Got a question for an old friend," Janet said. "Hey!"

She shouted it out over the water.

"Hey!"

There was no echo. She looked around.

"Should have brought a rock to throw. Hey!"

They waited. Something jumped in the stillness, a frog or a fish, but Eliot turned his head too slowly to catch it. When he turned back the water wasn't still anymore.

The first sign of it was a broad, smooth bow-wave that rushed silently toward them, wetting the stilts halfway up. Eliot instinctively stood on tiptoe as it passed. Then a massive, ridged, warty olive shell broke the surface, fifty feet across, like a submarine breaching. It was a turtle, a snapping turtle by its beak, which was hooked like a falcon's. Christ. The thing was a leviathan.

No wonder nothing lived here. The jellyfish ate the birds out of the air, and this thing must scour the water of anything with more than two cells to rub together. Huge bubbles of methane were surfacing around it, released from the mud it must have been buried in. The smell was indescribable. Or actually no, it wasn't indescribable. It smelled like shit.

"Who calls the Prince of the Mud?"

The snapping turtle spoke slowly. Its voice was raspy, an old chain smoker's. Its head was blunt and blocky and a little bit comic, kind of like a talking thumb. Its piggy eyes were set deep in nests of horny skin, which made it look angry, which Eliot was going to assume it was until it proved otherwise.

"Oh," it said. "You."

"Yeah, me. Pooh, you smell."

"The smell of life."

"The smell of farts. Got a question for you."

"What else do you have for me? I cannot eat questions. The hunting has been poor."

Its huge face was all hide and beak. Its neck was as thick as its head.

"Oh, I don't know." Sometimes Eliot wondered if Janet were a little bit sociopathic. How else could she possibly sound bored and casual in this situation? Though Eliot knew she had feelings, she just kept them in different places from most people. "We've got a couple of horses. Answer my question and we'll talk."

Eliot kept his face blank. She had to be bluffing. No way was Janet giving this thing the horses.

"I'm High King Eliot," he said.

"He owns this shithole," Janet said.

"I am Prince—"

"Prince of the Mud," she cut him off. "Which Eliot owns. We know. You're a giant turtle."

"Your kingdom may be wide, but it is spread thin. Mine runs deep."

It turned its head slowly from side to side, studying them with first one matte-looking eye, then the other. A jellyfish drifted past, its tentacles limply brushing the turtle's forehead, but the leviathan didn't appear to notice.

"Ember says Fillory is dying," Eliot said. "What do you think? Is it true?"

"Death. Life. A fish dies. A billion mites eat it and live. In the swamp there is no difference."

"There is to the fish," Janet said. "You're a shitty philosopher, so don't try. Is Fillory dying?"

If turtles had shoulders it would have shrugged.

"Yes then. Fillory is dying. Give me horses."

"Wait, are you serious?" Janet was pissed now. She looked like she hadn't believed it until this moment. "It's really ending? Well, can we stop it?"

"You cannot."

"We can't," Eliot said. "But maybe there's somebody who could?"

"I cannot say. Ask the queen."

"I'm the queen," Janet said. "Or I'm a queen. I'm the main queen. I'm asking you."

"Queen of the dwarves. In the Barrens. Enough. Give me horses or let me be."

The turtle began to sink, slowly, withdrawing its head under the shelf of its shell, barely disturbing the black water till its chin rested on the surface.

"I don't know any dwarf queens," Janet said. "You know any dwarf queens, Eliot?"

"Heck no. Because there aren't any female dwarfs. They don't exist."

"She doesn't exist," Janet said to the turtle. "Try again."

"Listen closer."

The snapping turtle snapped. Its head shot out to maximum extension—Eliot wouldn't have believed anything that big could move that fast. It was like a Mack truck coming straight at them. As it bit it turned its head on one side, to take them both in one movement.

Eliot reacted fast. His reaction was to crouch down and cover his face with his arms. From the relative safety of this position he felt the day grow colder around them, and he heard a crackle, which at first he took for the pier splintering in the turtle's jaws. But the end didn't come.

"You *dare*?" Janet said.

Her voice was loud now—it made the boards vibrate sympathetically under his feet. He looked up at her. She'd gone airborne, floating two feet above the pier, and her clothes were rimed with frost. She radiated cold; mist sheeted off her skin as it would off dry ice. Her arms were spread wide, and she had an axe in each hand. They were those twin staves she wore on her back, each one now topped with an axe-head of clear ice.

The turtle was trapped in mid-lunge. She'd stopped it cold; the swamp was frozen solid around it. Janet had called down winter, and the water of the Northern Marsh was solid ice as far as he could see, cracked and buckled up in waves. The turtle was stuck fast in it. It struggled, its head banging back and forth impotently.

"Jesus," Eliot said. He stood up out of his defensive crouch. "Nice one."

"You dare?" Janet said again, all imperious power. "Marvel that you live, Prince of Shit."

The turtle didn't seem surprised, just mad.

"I'll have you," it hissed, and it surged and strained. The ice squeaked and groaned and started to split. Janet leaned into the casting, however she was doing it, and froze the swamp harder and tighter.

"I will freeze your eyes," she said, "and shatter them! I will split your shell and pick out the meat!"

Jesus, where did she get this stuff? The turtle strained once more and then was still, like a great ship frozen in arctic pack ice. It stared at them furiously, its eyes burning with murder. Janet let herself float down to the wooden boards.

"Fuck you," Janet said. "You know better. Next time I'll kill you."

She spat, and the gob froze in midair and slid across the ice. With that she turned and walked away. Eliot practically fell off the boardwalk getting out of her way. He didn't want to touch those axes.

He felt like he should say something too, before he went, so he did. "Dick."

"Worm," the turtle rasped back. Its breath smoked in the sudden cold. "You'll see. It's turtles all the way down."

"Yeah, sure," he said. "I've heard that before."

He trotted off after Janet. She left frost footprints behind her.

CHAPTER 12

It wasn't until a couple of hours later, when they were back on their horses and heading southwest, the direction of blessedly solid dry ground and, eventually, Barion and its clear alcoholic balm, that Janet cleared her throat and said:

"So I guess you're probably wondering how I all of a sudden turned into an amazing ice goddess with magic axes just now."

Eliot was, actually. But he was going to see how long he could go without mentioning it. It wasn't that he didn't want to know, they both knew he did. It was a game they played.

They both knew he would cave eventually.

"With what now?" he said airily. "Oh. Sure. I guess so."

"I call the right axe Sorrow," she said. "You know what I call the left one?"

"Happiness?"

"Sorrow. I can't tell them apart."

"Mmm. Mm-hm."

They rode together in silence for another five minutes. They were both seasoned players. Eliot kept looking over his shoulder—he was paranoid that one of those pink jellyfish things was going to come up on him from behind and drape its tentacles all over him. After it stopped his heart it would probably reel him up into its innards and you'd be able to see him being digested through its translucent flesh. It would all be very public.

Though again: what did it matter, if the world was ending? But it did matter. He knew that. Everything still mattered. Now more than ever. He decided to concede the loss.

"OK, so how did you all of a sudden become etcetera and so on?"

"I'm so happy you asked! Remember that time when you guys went off to sea and left me in charge of Fillory for like a year and a half?"

"And saved magic and by extension the entire world? I do."

"Well, it was fun running everything and making all the decisions and implementing long-overdue reforms, but then after a month things got a little slow, and I needed a project. So you know that desert that's south of Fillory, across the Copper Mountains?"

"I know of it."

"I annexed it."

"Wait." Eliot reined in his horse, and they both stopped. "You invaded the desert?"

"I *annexed* it. I was thinking how in the books other countries are always coming after Fillory and threatening it and so on. I figured why not turn it around? Let's go expansionist! Preempt some shit! I mean, we have all the magic and freaky monsters in the world. Just the giants alone are basically the equivalent of a nuclear arsenal. Oh and plus we have our own god, who's actually real. It's practically a moral imperative. Manifest destiny."

Eliot heeled his horse, and it ambled into motion again. He loved Janet, but she really was beyond belief. He waited what felt like a suitable interval.

"Don't think that because I'm not saying anything I'm not stricken with shock and regret," the High King said. "Because I am. That's *why* I'm not saying anything."

"Well, if you didn't want me to invade the desert, you shouldn't have gone off and saved the world," Janet said. "It was a very popular initiative internally. The people loved it. And our standing army was just standing there, and the lesser nobility were spinning their wheels looking for a way to climb the ladder. Earn some honors and titles and whatever. You have to use that stuff or it ends up going bad on you, like with the Fenwicks."

Eliot snorted.

"Well, this is why you don't understand politics," Janet said.

"Politics doesn't understand me!"

"And think of the mineral resources out there. Our raw materials are crap in this country."

"Please forbear to insult the High King's minerals."

"They're crap. So I took a regiment and a bunch of Talking Elephants and that ninja lady Aral—you know, the one Bingle beat in the tournament, which don't get me started on that travesty of justice—and we crossed the Copper Mountains. Which by the way, have you ever seen them? It's amazing. They really are practically all copper, and they've turned this great green oxidized color. There's even a special word for it: *aeruginous*. Aral taught me that. Turns out she's a demon at Scrabble."

"Copper is a mineral. And we call them brigades, not regiments."

"And I've never really been sure whether or not we owned the Copper Mountains, you know? It's not clear on the maps." It was like Janet couldn't hear him. "So now we do, because I annexed them on my way to the desert. It only took a couple of days. An elephant fell off a cliff, a copper cliff, which practically broke my heart. Elephants and gravity, not a great mix. But you know what? The other elephants immediately stopped and went down and found what was left of it and stood around it in a ring. I couldn't see what they did, but when they were done—it took a day— the one that fell was all back together and up and running again. They resurrected him. I've never seen anything like it. Elephants, they know some shit. I don't know why we rule them, they should rule us."

"That's treason," Eliot said lightly. "True, though. What was the desert like?"

"The desert? The desert was the most beautiful thing I've ever seen."

Having spent a lot of time around Janet, Eliot was used to the way she shifted smoothly and without warning from irony and aggression to honest expressions of actual authentic human emotion.

"You must go, Eliot. Go in winter. The Wandering Desert is like an ocean of sand, which I realize is a cliché, but it literally is like an ocean. The dunes move along like big swells in the open sea. Slowly, but you can see it. We spent a day just sitting on the slopes of the Copper

Mountains watching them roll in and smash themselves against the foothills, all in silence, like humongous breakers."

"And then," Eliot said, "realizing that you were about to invade a beautiful but otherwise useless and wholly innocent desert, you took stock of your tactical and ethical errors and turned around . . ."

"But I didn't. I didn't turn around. In fact that was when I knew why I'd come.

"I sent the elephants back. Elephants—God, I don't know what I was thinking, bringing a bunch of elephants over the mountains. Hannibal, I guess. They were nice about it, but it was no place for them. I told them they could go graze the Southern Orchards. That seemed to square it.

"I sent the regiment back too. Brigade, whatever. They were good sports, very valiant, and they didn't want to go, but I ordered them and they had to. I guess they were hoping for a fight, but there was nobody to fight. Once they were gone I walked out into the desert alone."

"Why," Eliot said, "the hell would you do that?"

As they rode the landscape around them was turning back from bogs into meadows again, going from squashy to firm, the dry land sorting itself out from the wet like it was waking up from a bad dream. But Janet was far away and seeing a different landscape entirely.

"You know, I don't think I'll ever be able to explain it. It was just so pure. Suddenly all this life, all this greenery, seemed so needlessly elaborate and wet and messy. The desert was honest and real: just dry sand making smooth curves against an empty sky. It was like I'd been floundering in the mud my whole life and here was the way out.

"I suppose I was taking my life in my hands, but it didn't feel like it at all. I felt safe there. Safer than I'd ever felt anywhere. I didn't have to seem anymore, I could just be." She sighed in frustration. "I'm not explaining it right. God knows I'm not a spiritual person or anything. I just felt like I could breathe out there."

"No, I get it. Keep going."

For a long time Eliot had had the theory that in Janet's mind everybody was as judgmental of her as she was of them, and if that was true then the world must be a pretty scary place for her. No wonder she liked it out there by herself.

"That night the most amazing thing happened: the stars came down from out of the sky. They weren't used to seeing human beings, so they weren't afraid. They were like tame birds—they were all around me, a few feet off the ground, each one about the size of a softball. Spiky, and a little warm, and they sort of squeaked. You could hold them." She sighed again. "I know that sounds weird even for Fillory. Sometimes I wonder if I dreamed it.

"I walked for three days, till my supplies ran out, but it never crossed my mind to go back. Not once. I kept waiting to lose my nerve, but I never did. I kept going south. The swells get big out there in the middle, in the deep desert, big as hills. At the top you could see a long way, but I never did see the edge. Maybe they go on forever.

"Well, you can guess what came next. I passed out from hunger and exhaustion and woke up in some guy's sand-boat, sailing across the desert."

"Really?" Eliot said. "I was going to guess that you realized you were going to die and went back the way you came. Either that or that one elephant who fell off the cliff before and came back to life showed up, galumphing majestically through the dunes, and rescued you. With Aral riding it maybe. I figured you were setting that up as a surprise twist."

"Well, I wasn't. I woke up on this guy's boat. It wasn't much of a boat—basically it was a board with a pole stuck in it and a sheet tied to the pole. It was more like a windsurfer. He sat cross-legged on it, with one hand on the tiller and one on the mainsheet—his forearms were like bowling pins—and the whole business went flying across the sand.

"He didn't say anything, but he was incredibly good-looking. Tall, lean, big nose, brown skin. He took me back to his home, which was in a huge rock outcropping sticking up out of the sand. At the top was a big crater full of black earth with things growing in it. A whole tribe lived in little cells carved out of the rock in a ring around it."

"Where did they get water?" Eliot asked.

"I wondered that too. I found out. But I'll get to that.

"They were a pretty hard crew. This guy who saved me, he was the leader, they called him the Foremost. I tried to explain to him that we were invading him, or that I was, and that this desert was all part of Fillory now. I thought about letting it go, since he saved my life and all, but come on: an invasion's an invasion. Or an annexation. Anyway I figured I'd better put it out there up front, that they were now free to enjoy the benefits of being a semiautonomous quasi-national territory within the larger embrace of the Fillorian empire.

"But the Foremost was having none of it! He was very firm. Said he'd never even heard of Fillory. I know right? It pissed me off, but it impressed me at the same time. So I hung around.

"I liked it there. For a bunch of people with no obvious enemies they had this dope fighting style: they all carried a personal weapon made out of this wicked black metal. Light and strong, and when it hit something it struck blue sparks—very mysterious, I couldn't figure out where it came from. The Foremost had a whole spear made out of it. He had a big speech about how great it was. Forged in the desert, slew a god, that kind of talk. He said it acted as a focus for magic—amped up your discipline—but I never saw him use it like that.

"I decided I was going to win them over. The charm offensive. I started helping out around the place, trying to get into the rhythms of the tribe. You wouldn't have believed it, a queen of Fillory on her hands and knees pulling parsnips out of the ground, eating these gross grubs they sieved out of the sand—I tried to think of them as lobsters, but they were grubs. And you know what? I didn't even mind it. It didn't make me angry. I can't remember when I've ever felt less angry than I did out there.

"And I slept with the Foremost. I didn't love him, but I liked him a lot, and I loved his world. I wanted to be part of that place. And God knows he was easy on the eyes. Sex with him was amazing. Like going to bed with the desert.

"After about three months—"

"Wait," Eliot said. "You've been in Rockville for three months at this point? What was going on in Fillory?"

"In Fillory matters were unfolding according to protocol. What did you think was going to happen? You set up a country right, it runs itself. I got those people thinking I could hear their thoughts, for Christ's sake.

They were scared to piss in the shower. No way were they going to try anything.

"Anyway after about three months the Foremost told me that if I was going to stay any longer I had to undergo their initiation rites. It was a major deal, every year a couple of people died. But I didn't care. I wasn't ready to leave. And if you passed, you got one of those black-metal weapons. Never say I do things by halves."

"I will never say that," Eliot solemnly promised. "Janet, this is kind of intense."

"I know. And you haven't even heard the intense part. So I'm breaking a sacred oath by telling you about it, but what the hell, here's what it was. The Foremost took me out of the city, back out into the desert, and then he kneeled down with me and picked up a handful of sand and told me that what I sought was in there. Well, what the hell right? But so I looked at the damn sand.

"And after a while I began to notice that there were little glittery bits in it. Not a lot of them, but every once in a while you'd come across a black grain with a shiny sheen to it. I started to get it. That was the black metal the weapons were made out of. It was all around us, in the sand. One grain in a thousand, the Foremost said.

"He gave me a canvas sack and told me that I had to sit alone in the desert until I'd filled the whole sack with just metal grains, one by one. I was like, filled-filled? Like overflowing? Or just, you know, a nice amount? He said I'd know because when I was finished, when the sack was full, something called the Smelter would come. It would turn the ore I'd collected into pure metal and fashion a weapon for me."

"Really?" Eliot said. "How incredibly nice of it."

"Well, I know. Pretty convenient. You'd think I would have been suspicious. But I had to have one of these things. Had to.

"So I stayed out there. I would take a handful of sand, make a little pile in my palm, pick out the black specks and sort of brush them off my palm into the sack. No magic, it was just me and my sack and my bare hands. After a few hours my eyes were red and streaming and just about crossed. By the time the sun rose the next day I was hallucinating.

The bag was filling up, you could weigh it in your hand, but it was going to be a race to see whether I finished or went insane first.

"It was pretty bad. All the usual stuff happened that happens in an ordeal. I peed myself. I practically went blind. I threw up at one point. It was really, really unpleasant. But at the same time I could feel the ordeal remaking me. You know? Like the desert itself was smelting me, melting away weaknesses and impurities and extracting what was hard and true. I thought a lot of that kind of crap while I was collecting my grains."

"Janet." Eliot didn't know what to say. He'd never heard her talk this openly about her feelings. Whatever happened out there, something about her really had changed. He hadn't seen it till now. "Janet, how could you do that to yourself?"

"I don't know, I just knew I had to. I picked and I picked and I picked. My hands were shaking like crazy. The sun was going down the third day when I started to feel like maybe I was pretty close to done. It wasn't a huge sack—more of a bag, really—but it was looking pretty full. If somebody asked you for a sack of ore you wouldn't be embarrassed to give it to them.

"Supposedly if you had even one grain of regular sand in there the Smelter wouldn't come, and I don't know if I believed that or not, but I kept shaking the bag and fishing around in it to see if somehow one had gotten in. I really loved my bag of black metal. It felt cool, and oily, and so dense. It had a special smell. I was proud of it. I just could not wait to see what kind of weapon came out of it. I knew that whatever it was would be like the sharp, unbreakable expression of my innermost will. It would be what I'd been waiting for my whole life.

"I guess my defenses were low, because a lot of stuff came back to me out there that I'd been pretty much avoiding thinking about for a long time. Like I thought about Alice coming to Brakebills for the first time, thrashing through the woods, not even knowing if they'd let her in. I thought about how shitty I was to her before she died or whatever. I thought about Julia waiting for Brakebills to come and get her, waiting and waiting alone in her room, and Brakebills never coming.

"I thought about you, and how I used to feel about you, and how bad that felt. I thought about how far you've come. You really got yourself together when you came here, Eliot, and I respect that. I guess I never told you that. Everybody does."

"Thank you." She hadn't. It felt good.

"I thought about this one time when I was at boarding school. I never think about my childhood, ever, but that night it all just came oozing out. You know my parents sent me away to boarding school when I was eight? Now I think it was too early, but at the time I just assumed it was normal. I don't even think the school takes students that young anymore. And as it turned out it was a rough year for my family— I had a baby brother die of SIDS—and I think they kind of forgot about me for a while there. What with all the grieving and such. They just figured I'd take care of myself.

"Which I guess I must have. But it was a pretty bad year."

"Why haven't you ever told me this?"

"Oh, I don't know. I guess I never really let myself feel how much it hurt. But I kind of relived the whole experience that fourth night, waiting for this Smelter thing to come. I literally regressed to being eight years old.

"Anyway then it was June, and the school year was all over. Time to go home. But on the last day there was some kind of mix-up, my dad thought he sent a car for me, I guess, but his assistant forgot, or the driver never showed, either way nobody came for me. I sat on my suitcase in the lobby all day, while the other kids got picked up one by one, and I kicked my legs and read one of those big floppy *Peanuts* books over and over again, and nobody came. That was before cell phones, and they couldn't track down my parents. The staff were whispering behind my back. They felt sorry for me, but I could tell they kind of wanted me the hell out of there too so they could go home.

"I can still remember the view from the lobby: the line of palm trees through the glass doors, the sunset highlights on the wobbly linoleum tiles, the smell of the varnish on the wooden benches. I'll never forget it. I'd look at the shadows and think, definitely he'll have come by the time the shadow of the window frame hits that corner of the bench, but then he wouldn't come, and I'd pick a new spot. I was realizing for the first time what a small part of my parents' world I was. They were everything to me, but I wasn't everything to them.

"The staff let me eat dinner with them, which ordinarily students never got to do. They ordered in from Popeye's. I felt so excited and special."

Eliot wished he could go back in time and get that mini-Janet, scoop her up and take her home. But he couldn't.

"Then after dinner my dad finally showed up. He came striding through the door, stiff-arming it open without breaking stride, tie loose, walking too fast. He was probably pissed off at himself, about the mix-up, but it came off like he was pissed off at me somehow. Like it was my fault. He was pretty much of an asshole about the whole thing.

"I guess you can see where this is going. I was seriously weak at that point. I had the spins. I was falling asleep every five minutes. I woke up at dawn on day five and I knew that the Smelter wasn't coming. And I gave up. It was over.

"Somebody stronger would have stayed out there till they died. Julia might have. Alice, maybe. I guess if somebody really wants to break me, it turns out I can be broken. There it is. I didn't know. Now I know.

"I walked back to the rock. I still had my sack of metal. I couldn't let go of it—maybe they could use it for something else, I don't know. I was not in good shape, I can tell you. I was so dehydrated I couldn't even cry. It was pretty much of a mad scene, like Ophelia in *Hamlet*. Except, you know, a lot drier.

"And then I was back in the city, and they were taking care of me, helping me to a table where there was all this food and drink. They were having a party. The whole tribe was there. Everybody was smiling. The Smelter hadn't come, but somehow it was all right. I'd failed, but that was just the way of things. The desert was eternal, and I had fought it and done my best and lost and that was all I could do. Everybody sat there smiling at me and after a while I was smiling too.

"The Foremost asked me to come up to where he was, at the head of the table, in front of everybody. He told me to kneel, and he took the sack of metal from me and held it up.

"*You are an outsider,* he said. *But you came to us, and you bowed before the desert, and you combed through its sands with your fingers.*

"Dramatic pause.

"*You thought the desert would grant you its treasures. The treasures of our people. You thought it would give up our secrets. Our metal. Our strength. You thought you would take our desert from us, and rule over us.*

"*Here is what the desert has given you: a bag of worthless sand.*

"And he poured my sack out onto the floor.

"*You will never find our metal. The desert guards its secrets. It shares them only with its sons and daughters. You may take this sand back to your High King of Fillory and tell him that I let you live. Tell him that he may send us more whores if he chooses, this one was adequate.*"

Janet rode in silence for a minute. Her back was to Eliot. He didn't know if she was composing herself at the memory or just lost in thought. He saw her touch her face once, that was all.

"Janet," he said.

"The Foremost got a good laugh out of that last one, believe me." Her voice was unchanged. "He knew his audience. All that black sand was in front of me on the floor in a little pile. It had seemed a lot bigger out in the desert. I still couldn't believe it wasn't metal. I almost died for it.

"But I didn't finish the story before, about when I was at boarding school. You know what I did that day, when my father came for me? I fucking spat on him. I told him I would never go home again. I tore his expensive shirt. He slapped me and dragged me out to the car kicking and screaming.

"But I'm not eight anymore. I'm not a little girl. And the Foremost wasn't half the man my father was.

"I whispered something to him. He had to lean down to hear me. I whispered: *I don't need your secrets, Foremost. But I'll take your weapons. And I'll take your desert too.*

"Then I threw a handful of that fine black sand right in his eyes. And I got up off my knees. And I stopped whispering.

"*And you can tell your god when you see him that I didn't let you live. But I guess that'll be kind of obvious.*

"See, he'd made a big mistake. He thought when he sent me out there that he was going to crush me, but he was wrong. He made me stronger. The desert made me look at my own secrets, the ones I kept from myself, and I did. When I came back I didn't have a weapon, I was a weapon.

"I can cast Woven Strength pretty quick when I have to. I was worn out from the ordeal, believe me, but nothing was going to stop me. Before he knew what was going on I punched the Foremost into the fucking wall. My hands were basically like stone. It felt good.

"For a minute everybody else just watched. I think they were thinking, OK, fair fight, let's see if the Foremost can get out of this by himself. Don't want to disrespect him by trying to help, sort of thing. By the time they changed their minds about that it was too late for him. And for them.

"Well, look, I was angry. I don't think I commit a lot of gratuitous violence, but this was war, and he was a jerk, and I made a mess of him. I threw him through a couple of doors, and he cried like a fucking baby. You know what they used to write on cannons? *The last argument of kings*. I guess you could say magic is the last argument of queens."

Eliot didn't say anything. For all the years of his life he'd spent with Janet, he'd never really known her, not deep down. Sometimes he looked at her and thought, Gosh, I wonder what's underneath all that anger, all that hard glossy armor? Maybe there's just an innocent, wounded little girl in there who wants to come out and play and be loved and get happy. But now he wondered if maybe that little girl was long gone, or if she'd ever been there at all. What was under all that armor, all that anger? More anger, and more armor. Anger and armor, all the way down.

Janet's face was white, but her voice was still calm.

"When the Foremost was done crying I made him show me everything. All their secrets. I didn't even care anymore, I just wanted him to know how beaten he was. That rock went deep under the desert—they'd cut shafts down through it—and underground it was all ice caves. That's where the water came from.

"No metal though. There wasn't any. Can you believe that? Those weapons were all they had—I think it must have come from a meteorite or something, a long time ago. Forged from star-metal, kinda thing. They just passed them down, father to son, mother to daughter. I locked the Foremost in an ice cave and left him there. I figured his buddies would find him eventually. Maybe he'd die, maybe he'd be OK, I don't know. What am I, a fucking doctor?"

Eliot urged his horse forward a bit, right up beside Janet's, and as well as his horsemanship would allow he leaned over, put his arm around Janet, and kissed her on the cheek. He felt her smile.

"Before I left I took his spear away from him. I still had the strength going, so I broke it in half with my bare hands, right in front of him, and I formed an axe-head on the end of each one, out of ice. Not bad, right? I was going to say, 'Consider yourself annexed, bitch!' or something like that, but sometimes an exit line just feels *de trop*, you know?"

"Yeah," Eliot said quietly. "I know. I really do."

"So anyway," Janet said, "that's how I got my new axes."

She spurred her horse down the trail toward Barion.

CHAPTER 13

One day, about a week after Quentin got back from Antarctica, Lionel knocked on his door. It was two thirty in the afternoon.

"Ten minutes." Lionel didn't wait for him to open it. "In the lobby. Bring your gear."

By the time Quentin got there Lionel was already down the hall at the other suite.

Mid-afternoon had become a dead time in the daily life cycle of their little criminal cell. They'd already gone over their parts in the plan one more time, as best they could in the confines of a hotel room, which was probably nothing like the field conditions, which they still knew way too little about. Stoppard didn't seem to mind tinkering with his apparatuses eighteen hours a day, but the rest of them were slowly going out of their minds. They'd spent the morning tweaking a couple of things that didn't really need tweaking. Quentin had taken this as far as he could, and he was impatient. Alice was out there somewhere.

It was too cold to go outside, and if they did go outside they were at Newark International Airport, so they played cards or read or watched TV or did finger exercises or ran on the treadmills in the athletic center. Betsy scribbled in a voluminous diary. Sometimes they swam in the shallow hotel pool, which was enclosed in a damp, dripping glass grotto on the top floor and was so chlorinated that they felt slightly poisoned for half an hour after they got out. Quentin was happy to have a break in the routine. Maybe they were going off-site, for a dry run of the whole business.

They met in the lobby, all except for Pushkar, who was nowhere in sight. Stoppard arrived carrying two hard plastic suitcases, one of which was obviously pretty heavy. Quentin brought a duffel bag with everything he figured they'd need to break the bond, if it could possibly be broken, which was still an open question. It wasn't like they had one to practice on. He had Mayakovsky's coins in his pocket.

Betsy came empty-handed.

"Field trip!" she said. "Thank God. Now I can say it. Are you ready? Plum snores. There, I said it."

"I'm glad it's finally out there," Plum said.

"Do you think this is it?" Stoppard said. "I mean, is this the job?"

"No." Betsy shook her head. "Dress rehearsal. Shakedown cruise."

"We'll meet the others on-site," Lionel said, and he led them outside. It was the white limo again. This time the driver got out, and Lionel got behind the wheel. The rest of them climbed in the back.

It was a good idea. Quentin was all for improvisation when there was absolutely no other choice, but it would be nice to be as overprepared as possible. Maybe the bird had even set up an incorporate bond for them to play with? The limo accelerated onto the highway, heading north.

The intercom clicked on.

"Cardboard box," Lionel said. There was one, on the floor in a corner. Quentin slit the tape with a key. It turned out to be full of clothes: shiny black parkas and black jeans and watch caps. "Find your sizes. Get changed."

It was all very black-ops. Stoppard rooted through the box excitedly till he found a parka that fit him. He pulled it into his lap and fingered it tenderly.

"I am in love," he said. "I am in love with this coat."

Betsy had already whipped off her pants, revealing practical white underwear and a pair of very pale legs, and begun pulling on her jeans.

"This tapered shit is so Jersey," she said.

"I think I'll wait," Plum said.

The limo crossed the Hudson into Manhattan, then forged on farther north, through Yonkers and then veering east into Connecticut. Quentin watched the world flow by: hulking overpasses, brick housing projects dense with too-small windows, strip malls with giant signs shouting at the traffic, more housing projects and then finally, like a sigh of relief, trees. In the permanent twilight of the tinted windows it all looked as far off and alien as the contents of an aquarium.

They stopped twice, once for gas and once at a long low brick building with a sign outside proudly identifying it as a rehab center, where Lionel took receipt of a long brown paper package from someone who barely opened the door. Stoppard fidgeted in his black coat, which he'd already put on even though it was too hot for it in the limo, and he'd added a pair of aviator glasses. His hands kept straying to the controls for the disco lights.

"Don't," Plum said in a warning tone.

There was a lot of pent-up energy in the car.

"So," Betsy said. "Stoppard. What the hell are you doing here? I mean, on this job?"

"Same as everybody else," he said. "I'm here for the money."

With startling quickness Betsy plucked the sunglasses off his face. Stoppard snatched at them but she made them vanish; she had a quick, fluid casting style that reminded Quentin powerfully of someone else's, he couldn't place it and then he could: Julia's. Without the glasses Stoppard looked a lot younger.

"Don't bullshit us, Maverick," she said. "You're like nine years old. You can have the glasses back when you tell us how you got here."

"I'm seventeen! For your information. And anyway how did *you* get here?"

"Well, let's see . . ." She put a finger on her chin and looked up and to one side, pretending to think. "I'm the best there is at what I do. I have some things I need to take care of, and it'll be a lot easier to do that with two million dollars. And I enjoy violence and riding around in stretch limos with nerds. The end!" She smiled. "Now you."

If Stoppard had not already had a raging crush on Betsy, he had one by the end of that speech. Either way some of the attitude went out of him.

"I just like building stuff, I guess?" He wanted to play the game the way she had, but he had nowhere near the necessary reserves of sarcasm and sangfroid, so he wound up just being honest. "I was into computers for a while, but it was hard to get what I needed, you know? Even when you build your own gear the chips are still pretty expensive. And I've been with a couple of foster families—you don't get any privacy. You can never hang on to your stuff. Especially when it's worth something.

"None of my families were magic. A couple of guys at the Best Buy, they got me into it, but pretty soon I kinda left them behind. When I get focused on something I just have to figure it out, you know? I don't stop. I wasn't going to school much at this point, and where I live you don't want to be outside too much . . . I had a lot of time on my hands. And my last family, I got my own room. Give a nerd enough time and a door he can close and he can figure out pretty much anything.

"But anyway magic plus computers, not a good combination, so I figured I had to choose one or the other. But then I found horology. Horomancy."

"Please tell me that word doesn't mean what it sounds like it means," Plum said.

"Clock magic. It was the best of both worlds really. I always liked the hardware side, and it's easier to scrounge parts for clocks than computers— you would not believe what people throw away. Plus you can, uh, steal stuff sometimes too, if you have to. After a while I got some pretty sophisticated apparatus going. Seeing what kind of magic I could get traction on—temporal effects, obviously, but that's just where you start. You work your way outward. Weather. Optics. Probability. Field effects.

"Mostly I was figuring this stuff out on my own. It has a different feel from all that gobble-gobble stuff you guys do." He waggled his fingers like he was casting a spell. "This is more slow and steady. Tick-tock, tick-tock."

Quentin was developing some respect for Stoppard. Genuine loners were rare in the magic world, but this guy was the real thing. A total outlier: self-motivated, self-taught, on the fringes even of the safe-house scene. He was his own one-boy, one-room Brakebills. He wasn't much to look at, but Quentin never would have gotten anywhere near magic all by himself in Brooklyn.

"Anyway I must not have kept it as quiet as I thought because one morning I woke up and there was a letter on my bed, about the meeting at the bookstore. After that it was a no-brainer. I mean, forget about the cash, the gear that bird got for me—he must have pretty much infinite money. Stuff I only ever read about. Pretty much my wet dream."

"Pretty much," Betsy conceded.

She could have made a joke, but somewhere in there she'd lost her bloodlust—Stoppard wasn't quite the juicy target she was hoping for. Too innocent. Too easy.

"If you're into watches," Quentin said, "take a look at this."

He fished his pocket watch out of his coat on the end of its silver chain and handed it across. Even with his newly discovered skill at mending he hadn't made any headway with it. Stoppard took it the way a vet would take charge of a wounded sparrow. He regarded it from different angles, held it to his ear. His manner became quick and professional.

"Doesn't run?"

"Not at the moment," Quentin said. "Think you could get it going?"

"I don't know. Probably."

Stoppard put it in his lap and cracked open one of the hard plastic suitcases, which was evidently purpose-built to hold a set of tiny, glittering steel tools. He took out a jeweler's loupe and selected one pair of tweezers and put another in his mouth, then he opened the back of the watch to look at the works—something Quentin had never been able to do.

A faint pale light filtered out. Stoppard's face went slack.

"Oh my God," he whispered. "Oh my God. Where did you get this?"

"It's come a long way."

"What is it?" Plum leaned over. "Ooh—so many little wheels."

"These mechanisms don't exist. Nobody does this. Look, it's got a second face."

He swung back the outer dial to reveal another one underneath it.

His expression communicated the fact that he had somewhat underestimated Quentin and that he was, to the extent to which he was capable of it, sorry about that. Then he went back to the watch, ignoring Plum's attempts to look over his shoulder.

He didn't say anything for the next hour, until the limo rolled to a stop. Lionel walked around to their door and opened it. Cold air washed in.

"This is it, guys," he said. "Keep it quiet. No magic till I tell you. We're still a couple of miles from the house, but we don't know much about the security."

"Wait, what?" Plum said. "But this isn't the real thing?"

"This is it," he said again, impatiently. He looked even paler and lumpier than usual, and he'd let his beard get even more unruly.

"For Christ's sake," Quentin said. "You realize we're nowhere near ready!"

"Then get ready. We're out of time. You guys are professionals, right?"

The answer to that was a rousing chorus of silence.

"Look, just do your jobs."

He disappeared, leaving behind a limo full of shocked silence. Plum turned to Quentin.

"What do you think?"

"I don't know," Quentin said. "We could walk away."

Giving up now would be hard. He'd be set back months, and that would hurt. But this was more risk than he'd signed on for.

"Oh come on," Betsy said. "It's just a job."

"That's my point. No way is this worth getting killed over."

"Just breaking the bond alone, I'm putting us at about a fifty-fifty shot," Plum said. "Let's think about that for a second."

"Let's think about this." Betsy leaned across from the seat opposite. She smiled as if she were confiding a wonderful, intimate secret. "If you leave now? I will hunt you down and kill you. I will never stop till I find you. I've given up too much, and I am too close. Do you understand?"

She stared at Quentin, not blinking.

"Not even remotely." Quentin didn't blink either. He didn't like being bullied. "Why do you care? What are you close to? It's only money."

"Do you know what's in the case?"

"No. Not even the bird knows what's in the case."

"I know what's in the case," Betsy said. "And I'll give you a fucking hint: this isn't about money."

"Maybe you could be a little more specific."

"You want to know what's in the case? Freedom." She held his eyes for another long second, then sat back against the banquette. Quentin looked over at Plum, then at Stoppard, who'd gone back to picking at the insides of the watch. The prospect of starting over again at the beginning, finding some new way in, was not appealing. If they could just get it right and get it over with he could move on with his life.

And there was the Chatwin connection, he couldn't let that go. And there was Alice. Who was he trying to fool? He wasn't going to walk away. He was in this much too deep already. He opened his eyes. Betsy was still watching him.

"You'd better believe," he said, "that if this starts getting ugly, I'm going to be the first one to bolt. Then maybe I'll hunt *you* down. Think about that." Quentin put a hand on Stoppard's shoulder, who looked up at him as if he were waking from a dream. "Better give me that back for now. You can look at it later."

Stoppard nodded and closed up the watch and mutely handed it over, though his eyes followed it until Quentin tucked it back into his jacket.

They climbed out of the limo. It was late March, around four in the afternoon, and the temperature hovered around freezing. They were on a back road, really just a gravel track, somewhere in rural Connecticut, with a row of trees running along one side and dead-looking blackberry bushes on the other. Hayfields were all around them. There were no houses in sight.

Plum stayed behind in the car to change, and when she got out they were all in matching black. Quentin wore his overcoat instead of a parka, because it looked more magicianly, and it was black anyway, and he had no idea when if ever he'd see the limo again. He had the page from the Neitherlands folded in an inside pocket, along with the watch.

"Well," Plum said. "This doesn't look suspicious."

The breeze was icy, and even though they weren't supposed to use magic Quentin quietly added a couple of charms to keep himself warm. Off in one of the meadows Pushkar was waving at them, and they struck out toward him through the dry, unmown grass. Lionel stood behind him, looking as big as a haystack, and the blackbird came winging over from the darkening trees to settle on his shoulder. It looked much more like a wild animal out here in the country. Quentin wondered what the other birds made of it.

Pushkar had an enormous rectangular oriental carpet unrolled on the grass, a gorgeous thing with a knotted floral pattern on it in cream and pale blue and lion-gold. Pushkar was studying it and nodding slowly, sometimes bending down and smoothing out folds and making small adjustments to the fringes and to the pattern itself—it looked woven into the material, but it altered at his touch.

A flying carpet. He'd never actually seen one. Pushkar wore a multicolored, utterly tasteless game-day sweater under his parka.

"Nice rug," Quentin said, since it was.

"Guess how much it cost?" He didn't wait for Quentin to guess. "Seventy thousand dollars. The bird paid cash, I saw it."

They stood around the edges. The gathering looked like a cold, formal, badly planned picnic. The bird addressed them from the top of Lionel's head.

"We found the Couple a week ago. They are in a house two miles northwest of here. A large estate, with nothing else near it. We have been watching it, learning their routines. This morning something agitated them. We are concerned that they are preparing for something—maybe they are going to leave, maybe they will upgrade security, we don't know. But there is no more time. We will make our attempt tonight. Questions?"

Quentin couldn't think of any. Plum sniffled in the cold. Stoppard picked up his cases.

"Is it OK if I—?"

"Sure." Pushkar nodded, and Stoppard stepped gingerly onto the carpet, as if he were worried it would scoot out from under him, or roll up with him in it.

He kneeled down and opened both suitcases; one was full of tools, the other one, the heavy one, contained a stumpy, silvery steel cylinder about a foot in diameter and two feet long. That's what he'd been working on in his room, apparently—Quentin had seen it in pieces, but never put together. It had a white enamel clock face on one end and a cluster of small wheels and dials on the other. Stoppard unfolded a spindly stand and placed the cylinder on it, then opened the steel case and started fiddling.

Lionel wandered off; he was wearing only a black sweatshirt, the same one he'd been wearing that night in the bookstore, but he didn't seem to feel the cold. At least they had a big bastard on their side. Betsy began a stretching routine.

"I feel like we should be doing something," Plum said.

"I wish I smoked. Do you want to go through the spells again?"

"Not really. You?"

"I would but I think my head would fall off."

So they sat down cross-legged on the carpet in the cold and waited. Quentin could feel Mayakovsky's coins in his pants pocket. They felt good. They felt like confidence. Stoppard took out a small metal crank, fitted one end into a socket on the back of the machine, and began furiously turning it.

"Mainspring," he said happily, over the ratcheting sound. His breath puffed out white. "White alloy. Constant even source of kinetic energy. Tough to mess with magically."

"What does this thing do?"

"Security mostly. It puts a bubble around us, makes us very hard to see or hear or detect magically. It should also keep us warm, which I personally can't wait for."

Quentin realized Stoppard didn't know even basic personal warmth spells, so he cast a few on him as he cranked the mainspring. The bird watched it all. If it was anxious or impatient, there was no way to tell.

Once the machine had been ticking for a few minutes Stoppard detached the handle and stowed it away. He made a couple of adjustments, and there was a soft whirring sound, a hummingbird's wings against a window, and the hands on the dials began to move. It chimed twice, clearly and musically, and light flashed deep in its gleaming innards like lightning inside a thundercloud.

The wind died around them. There were no other perceptible effects, but Stoppard looked satisfied. He shut the case. Lionel wandered over, frowned, and nodded.

"Good," Lionel said. "Everybody on. Pushkar, take us up."

At a word from Pushkar the carpet stiffened under them and smoothed itself out, as if the squashy grass it was resting on had been replaced by a smooth ballroom floor. They all instinctively clustered in the middle, as far as possible from the edges, and the carpet rose rapidly and silently up into the sky: fifty, a hundred, two hundred feet, high enough to clear the tallest trees. It was a restful, dreamlike feeling—less like flying than like being in a glass elevator with no building around it. Now Quentin could see that they were in a sparsely populated area, lightly wooded, the houses large and far apart, some of them dark, some glowing with friendly yellow light.

No one spoke. The carpet stopped rising, paused, and began to swim gently forward, smoothly, like a raft drifting on a calm river. The rug's tassels hung down limp in the still air. As they got less afraid of the edges they gradually spread out. From this height they could appreciate the meticulous work of whoever had been the last person to mow these fields: they'd left a neat, even, looping pattern of darker and lighter stripes.

After five minutes the bird said:

"There."

Lionel pointed for him.

It was a big gray-roofed mansion about a mile away. Not ostentatious, just a very big fieldstone house with white trim, in the Georgian style, though on a mega-Georgian scale.

"Tasteful," Betsy said.

"Lotta money out here," Lionel said. "Bankers. I hear Judge Judy's house is here somewhere."

It was hard to imagine a universe in which Lionel watched *Judge Judy*.

The shadows of the trees on the edges of the meadows stretched longer and longer, melting and running as the sun drifted downward. When they were half a mile from the house Pushkar stopped the carpet, and there was a rapid conversation between him and Stoppard and the bird as they dismantled some kind of invisible but ticklish outer security perimeter, which required a lot of careful massaging of Stoppard's machine. The speed and pitch of the whirring spiked and then slackened again once they were through.

Meanwhile Betsy removed a three-foot length of brass wire from Lionel's bag. She scored it every few inches with the blade of a Leatherman, then bent the ends with the pliers and hooked them together to form a rough hoop a couple of feet across. When she sang a couple of keywords—her voice was incongruously high and sweet—the area inside the hoop lit up with an artificially bright view of the landscape through it.

Holding it up, she turned in a slow circle, all the way around the horizon. She stopped facing east.

"Look," she said. "Lionel. Big portal over there. Five, six miles. Weird one."

Lionel squinted at it too. He frowned.

"Somebody else's party," he decided. "Let's worry about ours."

Betsy turned back to the house. The grounds were so neatly laid out they looked like they'd been sketched directly onto the gray-green grass by an architect working with compass and ruler. In the twilight it looked motionless, but seen through the hoop six or seven guards stood out against it, phosphorescent.

"This must be what a Predator drone feels like," Quentin said.

"Hold this steady." Betsy handed him the hoop. "Plum, you ready? Like we talked about."

"You can do it from here?"

"I can do it from here. Whenever you're ready."

Betsy didn't seem the slightest bit worried; if anything her tone had become gentler and more relaxed than Quentin had ever heard it before. This must be her element. The carpet's flight path angled lower.

"OK. Do that one first." Plum indicated the nearest guard, farthest out from the house, who was standing alone at a gate in the wall.

Betsy made a fist, placed it over the image of the guard in the hoop, and blew through it softly. The man slumped to the ground; it was as if she'd blown his pilot light out.

"Is he asleep?" Quentin asked.

"Sleep, coma. You say potato."

Plum was concentrating, whispering in some Arabic language.

"Faster," Lionel snapped. "Come on."

She picked up the pace. A few seconds later a guard, or the shadow of one, appeared to draw itself up out of the ground and take its place where the man had stood. It didn't glow in the hoop the way the man had, but otherwise it resembled him exactly. Plum let out a deep breath.

"OK?" she said.

Lionel studied it, then pursed his lips but nodded grudgingly.

"What did you make it out of?"

"Leaves. That's all there was. He'll look fine from a distance."

"OK. Do it faster next time."

The carpet drifted silently forward in its invisible bubble, now just fifty feet up, passing over the outer wall of the estate, then an outer lawn, a clay tennis court, a swimming pool, drained and covered for the winter. It was hard to believe no one could see them—Quentin didn't *feel* invisible—but there were no shouts and no alarms. They cast no shadow. When they spoke it was in whispers, even though Stoppard insisted that they could have had a rock concert inside this thing and nobody would hear it.

Betsy and Plum dropped and then re-created four, five, six guards. Plum's doppelgängers were convincing, at least from this distance. They were made from whatever she could grab from the immediate area—grass clippings, mulch, clay from the tennis court, just nearby shadows—but they wore the same clothes as their victims, and though they didn't walk, they could shift their weight and turn their heads alertly the way a real guard would have, like minor enemies in a video game.

"There," Lionel said. "It's that window. The wing on the right, top floor, middle window."

"That's where the case is?" Quentin said.

"That's where we get in."

For a second Quentin didn't know what was missing, then he did: Stoppard's machine had stopped ticking. Stoppard reacted faster than he did—he lunged across the carpet from where he'd been trying to talk to Betsy, fumbled the crank into its hole, and cranked the handle madly. The device started up again almost immediately.

"You fucking shitbag!" Lionel hissed. "How long were we visible for?"

"I don't know!" Stoppard didn't stop cranking. "Couple of seconds maybe! I'm sorry, I don't know what happened!"

They all waited for the alarm to go up. Everyone held still. It was not unlike being in a submarine and waiting for the depth charges to start dropping. The carpet kept sailing forward, unfazed. Quentin stepped rapidly through a very hard shield spell that would stop a bullet, probably, if he were facing in exactly the right direction.

But the depth charges didn't come, and they kept going. When Stoppard got tired Quentin dropped the spell and cranked instead, until the mainspring protested. This is ridiculous, Quentin thought, but coldly—he wasn't going to let himself panic. We're making it up as we go along.

Pushkar slowed them down and commenced fine adjustments, drifting a little left, then right, up and down, whispering patiently to his steed, a pilot steering a tanker into a narrow slip. They were close to the house now, passing over a tiled terrace strewn with weathered Adirondack chairs, and they could see into a few rooms where the lights were on. Quentin got a glimpse of a woman standing up at a counter, drinking coffee and reading a magazine. Two men stood outside on the patio smoking; they held their cigarettes Eastern European style, like darts. They could have been anybody, in any house, anywhere. The carpet was going to pass barely ten feet over their heads.

The invisibility field brushed a tree branch. Instead of just passing through it the branch snagged, as if the field were a bubble of tacky glue, then curved and bent. They watched helplessly until it finally gave and a handful of oak leaves tore off.

Quentin's toes curled. But at the same moment the oak branch snapped something fell inside the house—a coffee cup, it sounded like—and smashed on the floor. The two men turned. Someone swore, a woman. They were distracted. The moment passed.

That wasn't luck; luck doesn't come that good. Somebody must have—yes, Lionel was finishing up some arduous piece of probability-warping magic, breathing hard with the effort.

"Nice," Quentin said.

"Shouldn't have needed it."

"It's not his fault," Quentin said. "He never even got to test it. We're lucky we got this far."

Lionel looked at him more surprised than angry—like he didn't realize Quentin had the power of speech.

"Shut the fuck up," he said, and turned back to the house.

They came to a stop in front of the window and hovered there, the tasseled edge of the carpet pushed up against the white clapboard of the house. There was no light inside. Stoppard took out a little brass scarab from one of his cases and placed it on the window. It crawled around it in a large square, and wherever it crawled it left behind a cut in the glass. When it was done Stoppard placed the cut square on the carpet, carefully, and returned the scarab to its case.

"Quentin, you're up," Lionel said.

"What am I up for?"

"That." He pointed to the hole in the window. "Time to pull your weight."

It had actually occurred to him that he was the only one who hadn't done anything so far. Quentin peered into the hole. It was scary, but he was glad the wait was over, he needed something to do. Quentin thought back through his brief inglorious history with wet ops. Invading Ember's Tomb with Dint and Fen; attacking the castle on Benedict Island. He was less terrified than he had been the first time, and less manic than he had been the second. Maybe that was experience.

"Give me a minute. OK to do spells?"

Lionel looked at Stoppard for the OK, then nodded. Quentin closed his eyes, placed two fingers on each lid—opposite hands, so his wrists were crossed in front of his face—and pronounced the words of an Indian night-vision charm. When he opened them it was as if the brightness and contrast on the world had been turned up and all the colors dialed down. Pushkar shook his head pityingly.

"Later we will discuss your Hindi."

Stoppard was fussing with his clockwork.

"She's getting pretty warm," he said. "I'd say she's got about fifteen minutes."

He shushed it gently, as if it were a feverish child.

"Fifteen minutes?" Plum said. "It's going to take that long minimum just to break the bond. Minimum."

"So get moving," Lionel said.

Quentin stuck his head through the hole and saw perfectly clearly, though in slightly false pastel colors, a huge empty guest bedroom, lavishly furnished. It was a lot nicer than the Marriott. He crawled the rest of the way inside. The bird fluttered through and lit on his shoulder. He flinched, but not as hard as the first time.

"Walk out into the hall, turn right, then left at the corner, left again, then first door on your right. There is no one else on this floor. We will follow with the device. Just stay within its range."

As it turned out the device followed all by itself: the stand on which it rested clambered nimbly through the window on its six jointed legs, like a giant ant with one staring white clock eye. The thick white carpet swallowed their footsteps.

Quentin peered out into the hall, left then right, feeling like a kid sneaking out at a sleepover. The bird was right: no one there. The walls were bare of pictures; the house looked like the anonymous luxury vacation rental that it probably was. For just a minute Quentin allowed himself to think about what he would do if this actually worked. He'd buy a house. He'd study niffins. Could he summon Alice? Bind her? Was she a demon now? He would break back into Brakebills if he had to; maybe Hamish would let him in. He'd go back to Mayakovsky if he had to.

He turned left at the corner and immediately the corridor was revolving around him like a tunnel in a funhouse. He flopped over and hit the carpet hard. He gripped it, tried to wind his fingers into it, feeling gravity shift around him. Christ—what did he expect, invading a magician's house? He looked back over his shoulder, but he was alone, everyone else was gone, and the spinning corridor stretched out to infinity.

And then it didn't. The others were standing there watching him with expressions of mild concern as he lay flat on the floor, desperately groping for a handhold, and Plum waved away the last shreds of the illusion.

"Get up," Lionel said.

"Trap," Plum said. "You're fine."

He got to his feet cautiously. His heart rate was already easing off. She was right. He was fine.

Left again, and there was the door on the right. Quentin couldn't find a whisper of magic on it, but Betsy pushed past him and began taking a series of traps offline—weird, unpleasant psychic snares. He heard the muffled boom of faraway thunder: a storm, it must have blown in fast. He looked back at the others, strung out behind him down the hall. Pushkar and Lionel had rolled up the carpet and were lugging it with them on their shoulders.

When Betsy was done he pushed open the door. It wasn't even locked.

It was a pool room, long and well appointed, with a row of windows along one wall and couches along the other. The overall impression was of slightly artificial clubby gentility. Brown leather armchairs occupied the corners, and there was a cavernous fieldstone fireplace at one end that showed no sign of ever having been used. Boxes and crates of all possible sizes and shapes lay strewn around, which ruined the genteel atmosphere, along with some items too big or too unwieldy to be boxed or crated: a stuffed deer, a penny-farthing bicycle, an old-timey jukebox, a double bass made of dark wood.

An older man with thinning blond hair, not one of the Couple, was sitting on a couch playing with his phone. He looked up, surprised, but before he could speak Betsy calmly froze him in place with a spell she'd obviously had ready, then knocked him out cold with another one. He stayed sitting up, but his eyes were now closed.

The pool table itself was a beast, eight-legged and carved and inlaid to within an inch of its life, with a matching cabinet against the wall for cues and racks of scorekeeping beads and such. It must have weighed a ton; it looked like the kind of thing that shouldn't be on the second floor of a house. One end was half buried in boxes and teetering stacks of books. It also supported, in plain view, an old brown leather suitcase.

It was a little the worse for wear, but otherwise it was the twin of the one Lionel had shown them at the hotel. It had an oval sticker from the Cunard–White Star Line on one side.

"All right," Quentin said quietly. "Close the door. Nobody touch it."

It was his and Plum's show now. Stoppard crouched down and studied one of the smaller dials on his machine.

"Nine minutes," he said.

Working quickly, they cleared away everything around the case so that it sat by itself. He whisked the felt around it with a little broom, then dusted it with fine white ash. Plum stuffed a wet towel against the bottom of the door and got a little fire going in a brazier; she set it up in the fireplace. The room began to fill with aromatic smoke. In the background Quentin could hear Betsy laying down barriers and traps, prepping for the moment when Stoppard's bubble popped and the owners of the house abruptly and calamitously became aware of their presence. She was sealing the room off like a vault, from every side, floor and ceiling included.

Plum chalked off angles on the felt around the suitcase, using a ruler, doing sums in her head. Quentin bolted together a skeletal metal frame around it which they then strung with wires at high tension in an asymmetrical pattern. They used violin strings—E strings, the highest ones.

"Two minutes," Stoppard said.

"Not ready!" Quentin, Plum and Betsy said it together. Jesus Christ, it wasn't even going to be close. Thin white smoke drifted up from the works of Stoppard's device, and there was heat shimmer above it now. It was ticking more slowly. It looked about ready to melt down.

"You'd better believe the Couple's going to be ready," Lionel said.

"Dammit." Betsy pressed some soft red wax hastily into the door lock, then mashed a seal into the wax. Pushkar took down a pool cue from the rack and practiced a couple of businesslike bo staff strikes. He looked like he knew how to use it, though if it got to the point where they were fighting with pool cues they were all pretty much screwed anyway.

Pushkar broke off his routine.

"Something's coming." He tapped his temple. "Precognition."

"Get the carpet ready to go," Lionel said. "Quentin and Plum, how much longer?"

Still reciting smoothly, Plum held up four fingers. Quentin took a tuner out of his pocket and began plucking the strings on the cube—perfect fifths, and they had to be precise to within a couple of hertz. Betsy formally addressed herself to each wall, then the floor, then the ceiling, hands pressed together, her lips moving. Each wall flashed silver as she did so. Plaster dust drifted down from the corners.

Stoppard's device sighed quietly as something inside it snapped or melted fatally, and the ticking stopped. No one moved. For a long moment the only sound in the room was Plum whispering over the case. Quentin gripped one of Mayakovsky's coins in one hand.

Hoarse shouting came from somewhere on the first floor, then silence. A door slammed. Pushkar peered out a window, shook his head: nothing yet. Betsy was bobbing up and down on her toes, flexing her fingers, practically humming with excitement. Lionel stared grimly at the door, grinding his teeth. He squared off his blocky hands in front of him at chest height, fingers spread, thumbs touching.

The floor bounced once under them, hard, and then a second time—Quentin had to put a hand on the pool table to keep from falling over, and a couple of stacks of boxes toppled. They were trying to break through from below. He kept his place in the chant, just barely. Footsteps pounded by in the hall, then stopped outside the door. Something Betsy had left out there went off with a sharp *bang*, but it was hard to know if it did any good.

Almost time. Quentin and Plum kept their gazes locked to make sure they were in perfect sync. The door started to vibrate in its frame, hard, making an even tone that gradually rose in pitch. A thump, and a dent appeared in the wall at head height, then another, then a third.

But they had it. Time. The strings were chiming all at once, without even being plucked. If it was going to work, it was now. Quentin gripped the coin in his hand—he thought he could feel it getting warm, getting ready to give up its payload. He took a breath.

Soundlessly and all at once, the lights went out. Did he do that?

No—he hadn't said the keyword yet. Plum cocked her head in the semi-darkness, confused.

The windows blew in. Torrents of broken glass gushed onto the floor. The shockwave chucked Quentin carelessly against the base of the opposite wall. It wasn't enough to knock him out, not quite, but his brain got stuck for a few seconds, and he forgot where he was. When he'd recovered enough to get to his knees and take his hands away from his face, the room seemed to be full of struggling figures wearing robes.

"What the hell?" he whispered.

Something bad was happening. For a second he thought he'd lost Mayakovsky's precious coin, but no, there it was, a few feet away on the rug, still shining with unexpressed power, and he had just enough presence of mind to sweep it up and shove it in his pocket. The dimness churned with strange people—two of them had Betsy pinned against the wall, and she was screaming curses at them. There was something strange about them: their hands. They weren't flesh. They glowed a faint pale gold, and they were slightly translucent—you could see things through them.

He started to get up, but one of them was standing over him. She put a foot on his chest and pushed him over backward; it didn't take much. Quentin looked at the foot. It was an ordinary foot, a woman's foot, leather sandal, definitely human.

There were seven or eight of them—it was hard to get a good read in the dimness. Another woman stepped up to the case. Out of nowhere Pushkar popped up behind her and belted her in the back of the head with a pool cue, or he tried to: the cue snapped like balsa wood, like he'd hit a marble statue, and the one who had her foot on Quentin uncorked some spell one-handed that made him freeze and fall down flat, stiff as a board.

Ignoring the action around her, the woman studied the cage Quentin had set up; in the golden light of her hands her face looked mildly amused. She picked it up and tossed it aside, then she spoke a few words over the case in a businesslike tone—she could have been ordering a pizza. There was something weirdly familiar about the way she talked. She pulled the suitcase loose, just like that—there was a ripping sound, exactly as if it had been held down by nothing more than Velcro, then it came free. She tucked it under her arm.

These people were thieves, like them. They let Quentin and his pals be the fall guys and take out the security, then they walked in and robbed the robbery. In his concussed, addled state Quentin mostly felt admiration for their calm competence. They were doing a good job.

Moving in sync they backed away toward the windows, a coordinated withdrawal, each one keeping one of the opposition well covered. Quentin got his elbows under him and propped himself up to watch, trying not to pose a threat to anybody. They were organized as hell, whoever they were. Two of them were commandeering Pushkar's carpet, unrolling it flat onto the air outside.

"No!" Betsy said. "You can't!"

She was handling this way better than Quentin was. Already she was back on her feet and walking toward them, launching wild attacks with both hands, lightning and then fire flowing from her fingers, flooding the room with light. But three of the robed people had joined hands to create a defensive barrier, and her magic died against it. Quentin sat up all the way now. His head was clearing. She was right: this was their job. That case was theirs. Those people had no right to it. He got to one knee.

Now he knew why their magic sounded so familiar: they were speaking a distorted kind of archaic German, which he happened to know well, because it was the same language the page from the Neitherlands was written in.

The last one climbed out onto the stolen carpet.

"Stop!" Betsy shrieked.

She ran to the window as they slid away. The bird hopped out from under the pool table.

"They cannot open it," it said, maybe to itself. "They still cannot open the case."

Quentin staggered to the windows, but he could only send a futile, fugitive heat ray after them, which whanged straight back off their shield and burned a scribble on the wall of the house next to him. Plum was kneeling by Pushkar, who was shaking off the spell that dropped him. Lionel was still on his hands and knees staring spacily at the floor.

The banging on the door started again, more urgent now. The wood was splintering. Even the blond guy on the couch, the one Betsy had shut down, was stirring. But Quentin felt only calm. Fear and confusion were gone, he'd lost track of them in the fight. And they weren't done fighting yet. They were going to finish this thing if he had to do it himself.

"Pushkar." His voice sounded weird and distant in his bruised ears. He cleared the dust out of his throat. "Pushkar. Is there anything here that can fly?"

Still leaning heavily on the pool table, Pushkar looked around the room.

"Yes," he said.

CHAPTER 14

They swarmed out through the empty windows like angry bees out of a hive. Plum and Stoppard rode leather club chairs; Betsy had a small prayer rug that had been in front of the fireplace, which she handled standing up, surfboard-style; Quentin got the penny-farthing bicycle. Pushkar himself, along with Lionel and the bird, had taken command of the enormous pool table, which despite its size and weight had turned out to be surprisingly amenable to flight spells. It was slightly wider than the window frame, but it bashed its way out anyway in an explosion of brick and plaster dust, shedding a stream of multicolored billiard balls from its innards.

The sun was setting, and it was twilight at ground level, but as they surged up above the tree line the sunset picked them out in thin golden light. They raced up into the freezing blue air, up into the early evening sky, accelerating as they went, up and to the west, chasing the dwindling speck of the fleeing carpet.

Pushkar's spellwork was master-level, and the speed was exhilarating— Quentin had done a little flying on his own, but this was totally different. Already the house was shrinking behind them. The bike's leather seat was rock-hard, but beggars can't be choosers. At least it wasn't the double bass. He wondered if it would go faster if he pedaled.

Quentin stuck close to the pool table, drafting off it. Through it all Lionel had managed to keep that long brown paper package clamped under his arm. No one spoke, they just bent over their makeshift aircraft, eyes streaming, urging all the speed out of them that they could. Betsy already had a lead on them on her rug, her short hair blown straight back from her face, leaning forward on her toes staring fiercely ahead like a ski jumper in mid-jump.

Foot by foot they began to overhaul the carpet, reeling it in. The thieves—the other thieves—were using Pushkar's spells too, but he hadn't set the carpet up for speed. Whatever the hell was in that case, they were going to take it back. Mile after mile of Connecticut woods rolled by underneath them; maybe they were already out of state, he couldn't even tell. The carpet dove, skimmed the treetops, rolled and turned, then clawed back the altitude. Quentin shadowed it.

After ten minutes they'd closed the gap to a few hundred yards. The people on the carpet sent a couple of fireballs back at them, and something else that flashed and popped, but nothing they couldn't see coming in time. Stoppard was riding sitting down; Plum had turned her chair backward and was kneeling on the seat. There was no question they could overtake. But what were they going to do when they got there? Board it? Quentin was high on speed and risk now—he had to keep reminding himself that this wasn't a video game, he only got one life, and magic wasn't going to grow back any limbs he might lose along the way.

Maybe Pushkar could undo whatever he'd cast on the carpet, stop it in mid-flight. Quentin veered his bicycle over toward the pool table to try to talk strategy, but as he did a deep rumbling came from behind him, getting louder, and he risked a look over his shoulder.

Two blazing comets were ripping up at him through the still evening air, trailing smoke and sparks. They bulled right through the formation, overtaking him from behind like outbound meteors; one passed within five feet of him and the shockwave nearly knocked him off the bike. But it wasn't him they were after. The twin comets smashed hard into the carpet, one-two.

It was the Couple. They'd come to take their suitcase back.

The carpet dipped with the force of the double impact. Betsy dived after it, and Quentin followed. Shouts floated back to him on the wind, fragments of screams, obscenities, orders, spells, all instantly whipped away on the wind. A desperate close-quarters scrum was in progress.

One of the Couple, the woman, stood wreathed in light in the center of the carpet, surrounded by a circle of angry robed thieves. The man had caromed off whatever defensive shell was on the carpet but circled back immediately, like a moth pinging off a light bulb, and clung to the underside, where he began ripping his way up through it with both hands.

For the moment Quentin just watched and kept pace. He'd wait it out, then they could pounce on whoever survived, taking advantage of their hopefully weakened state. He looked around, picked out the others in the deepening twilight. They were doing the same—all except for Betsy, whom he'd now lost track of.

A lake flashed past far below, then more trees. They shot through thin wisps of low-flying cloud. The amount of magical energy being expended in the fight on the carpet was truly awesome; the Couple must have been carrying artifacts, because their energies were radically heightened. They might have been bad people, but they were terrifyingly strong spellcasters and apparently totally without fear. Thank God he hadn't had to face them toe to toe. Quentin saw the man—grinning his face off—punch a fist up through the carpet and get a grip on the ankle of one of the golden-handed monks, drag him scrabbling through and fling him spinning down and away toward the darkening landscape below. The woman was already closing in on the case itself, but she was fighting her way through a storm of defensive magic.

A monk stepped forward and squared off hand to hand. They closed, and then it was chaos, a blur of lights and speeded-up movement. In the middle of it something came careening down from above at a steep angle like a diving cormorant and hit the carpet with a solid *whump* that shook dust out of it.

It was Betsy.

"Dammit!" Quentin said.

She should have waited, but apparently whatever personal stake she had in the case, coupled with her native eagerness to get herself killed, had gotten the better of her. Dammit dammit dammit. Discarded, her rug flew by him in the wake of the fight. Quentin urged his ridiculous penny-farthing forward, slowly closing the gap between himself and the carpet. She was out of her mind, but a team was a team.

He recognized the feeling of cold inevitability that came right before a fight. This was going to be close-quarters action, and he hastily hardened his hands and face. He tried to focus on a sense of righteous anger: it was their case, they'd taken it, and he was going to get it back. For Alice. He ducked as a dark form came flipping back at him head over heels, nearly colliding with the pool table. It was the man of the Couple. He looked limp, barely conscious, but he wasn't falling, and Quentin let him go.

Now the trembling trailing tassels of the carpet were only a few feet ahead. He saw Betsy backhand the woman—a burst of light and a concussive thump accompanied the strike, which snapped her head around a quarter-turn—then clamp one hand on the handle of the case. The woman recovered and lunged for it too, while the remaining monks jockeyed around them, waiting to see who they had to take on. But before that could happen Betsy crouched down and placed her free hand on the carpet. He saw her mouth move but couldn't place the spell. It must have been some powerful antimagic because the carpet instantly lost all internal cohesion and dissolved into a cloud of threads.

A whole flock of bodies flashed past Quentin and fell behind and down. Quentin struggled to track Betsy: she was dropping like a rock, still holding the case with one hand. Incredibly the woman had a grip on it too. They spun around each other, their clothes rippling and burring frantically in the wind. Quentin pointed his handlebars at them and dived, as close to vertical as he could get.

He hit terminal velocity and kept accelerating, speed stripping away what was left of conscious thought. The land loomed up toward them, dark green and wrinkled with low mountains. He clenched his teeth and pushed the ancient bicycle down faster and harder, the wind singing in the spokes, the effort tearing at his chest from the inside. They were coming into focus now: neither woman could break her fall without letting go of the case first, and neither one was willing to let go, so they were going at each other with their teeth and free hands and whatever spells they could work one-handed under the circumstances.

Given time he might have stopped one of them from falling with magic, but there were two of them and there was no time. Details in the landscape were resolving themselves, magnifying and magnifying, a stream, a field, individual trees. He matched course with them, swayed over to them, bumped them—the woman grabbed at him but tore loose again. He wasn't going to be able to do this gracefully. He wasn't sure he could do it at all. Now the ground was close, very close. Quentin's knees were shaking, and the spindly front wheel collapsed and tore away. He bulled into them again, felt both of them clutch at him with their free hands. He heard the woman screaming wordlessly, and he felt her get a hand in his hair. She wasn't screaming, she was laughing.

He was going to slow gradually, then he checked the ground and panicked and braked hard. Underneath them a pine tree exploded from a toy into a grasping, pricking monster and together the three of them slammed into the penny-farthing and the penny-farthing slammed into branches. He had time to think: fuck them all if he died like this! For a case that he didn't even know what was in it! Pine needles slapped him and then they hit the ground and his vision went white.

Something was ringing like a bell. It was his head. His chest was empty, and he writhed on the ground like a grub. He tried to take in some air, any air at all, and weird creaking and crying sounds came out of his mouth. Either his ribcage had collapsed and crushed his lungs and he was dying, or he'd just got the wind knocked out of him and would be fine in a minute.

He pushed himself up. The world was turning around him like a carousel.

As it stabilized he saw Betsy already up and staggering in circles. Quentin started to say something, but he could only cough and spit.

"Where is it?" she said hoarsely. "Where is it? Do you see it?"

The woman was still down, ten feet away, but she was stirring. Quentin got a close look at her for the first time: tall and model-thin, older than her picture, with ringletted black hair and a bad cut on her forehead that would need stitches. Quentin spotted the case resting in a patch of ferns, as neat as if it had just come off a baggage carousel, a few yards from her.

The woman saw where he was looking. She made a noise in her throat and began to crawl toward it, but Betsy was way ahead of her. As she walked past her Betsy bent and put a hand on the woman's neck.

She spasmed, arching her spine like a cat. Betsy touched her with the other hand, then straddled her like a horse, pumping energy into her—her fingers sparked. The woman's body bucked under her like she was being defibrillated.

"Stop!" Quentin croaked.

But it was already too late. She let go and the woman fell face-first on the black earth, still twitching. Quentin smelled burned flesh.

"I stopped," Betsy said. She kept walking.

She picked up the case, examined it skeptically for damage, hefted it in her hands. It looked like it hardly weighed a thing. Quentin crawled over to the dying woman but stopped short of touching her. There was no telling what kind of fatal magical juice was still in her body. Smoke rose from her black hair. It was too late anyway.

Betsy watched him. She spat on the ground.

"I'll kill you too if you try to stop me."

The forest was quiet. It was early spring, the undergrowth was still recovering from the rude shock of winter, and only a few crickets chirped. The woman had been a murderer. Three minutes ago she would've let either one of them die. Betsy squatted down and laid the case down and fumbled with the latches.

"Shit." She strained at them, set herself and strained again. "Shit. I was afraid of that. Where the hell is Plum where you need her?"

"What do you want with Plum?"

More or less on cue Stoppard and Plum came crunching down through the branches, shielding their faces from the bristles. They were crowded together on the same club chair; something must have happened to the other one. Their landing was hard but controlled until the chair came down on a rock and one of its legs snapped off, spilling them onto the soft ground.

Plum got to her feet, rubbing her hands on her thighs.

"Jesus," she said. "What happened?"

"The girl bit it," Betsy said. "Open the case."

"What, now? Shouldn't we—?"

"Open it!"

"Better do it," Quentin said. "She killed the woman."

Betsy must be pretty worn out by now, he thought, but there was still no telling what she was capable of.

"Jesus," Stoppard said. "Why'd you do that?"

He seemed to really want to know, but Betsy ignored him. Her face was grim and set.

"Open it. Do it now."

"What makes you think I can open it?"

"You know what."

Plum sighed, resigned.

"I guess I do."

She sat down cross-legged in front of the case and snapped open the latches as if they'd never been locked. As soon as she did Betsy kicked her aside roughly.

"Hey!"

She rummaged through the contents. She picked up a book, tossed it aside, then she held up a long knife made of what looked like tarnished silver. It was a simple weapon, unornamented. It looked very functional and very old.

"Yes," she whispered to it. Her voice cracked. "Oh, yes. Hello you."

With a rush of air and a thunderous crackling *whump* the pool table bashed straight down through the canopy and landed solidly on its thick legs on the forest floor. Lionel rode it down standing up, the bird on his shoulder. There was no sign of Pushkar.

"Where's the case?" Lionel took in the corpse, Quentin and Plum and Stoppard, Betsy and the knife. "You opened it."

He'd unwrapped his parcel: it was a gun, a snouty-looking assault rifle that fit lightly under his arm. Stock and barrel were deeply engraved, swirls and tracery—it was obviously a hybrid weapon, high-tech but magically augmented.

"I sure did," Betsy said.

"Where's Pushkar?" Stoppard said.

Instead of answering Lionel smoothly raised the rifle to his shoulder, sighted down it and fired two controlled bursts briskly and efficiently at Stoppard's chest.

He should have died right then. But even before Lionel fired Betsy was between them, holding the blade—she'd moved faster than Quentin could follow. The bullets sparked and clanged off the silver knife, two quick metallic triplets, and ricocheted off into the bushes. Whatever that knife was, it came with a lot of fringe benefits, and one of them was that it wasn't going to let its wielder get hurt.

Quentin stared at Lionel.

"What the fuck? You fat piece of shit!"

Five minutes ago he'd felt so empty it was like he'd never cast a spell again, but there was power in fear, and in anger, and he got to his feet. He felt like he might be able to get a spell out of it, but before he could try Betsy took three running steps and launched herself at Lionel like a big cat—the knife must have given her a whole suite of powers, strength as well as speed and protection. Lionel turned quick and got off another burst, but the knife ate them up effortlessly, and then she was too close to shoot. They waltzed drunkenly around the pool table, Lionel grunting as she butchered him standing up.

Curiously, there was no blood. The knife met very little resistance— it sliced up through his torso, down through his collar bone, then she forced it deep into his chest. It went through him like a wire through wet clay. The next cut took his head off.

It fell and rolled through the leaves. It didn't speak, but its eyes blinked. The stump of the neck looked like gray stone.

"Huh," Betsy said, standing over the headless corpse. "Golem. It figures."

Huh. Though it seemed like a notable fact that she hadn't known he wasn't human before she started murdering him. Only now did Betsy start breathing hard, like it was all catching up with her at once: the job, the flight, the fall, the killing, the case, the whole comprehensive fiasco.

"Where's the money?" Stoppard asked.

"There isn't any," Quentin said.

It was catching up with him too. They'd been blindsided by the monks and then double-crossed twice: first by Betsy, then by the bird. It must have planned to kill them all along instead of paying them off. There never had been any money. He was farther back than when he started. Farther from home. Farther from Alice.

Though they did have the case, or whatever was left in it, unless the bird was coming back for it. For now it was gone; Quentin hadn't even seen it go.

Betsy jumped down from the pool table, and her knees almost buckled when she landed. All the strength had gone out of her.

"I thought they'd try that." She sounded weary and, for the first time since he'd met her, very young. She couldn't have been more than a couple of years into her twenties. "Figures. Never trust anything without hands. Or with hands for that matter."

"Thank you," Stoppard said. "You saved my life."

"Eyes are up here." Betsy pointed. "But you're welcome."

"What is that thing?" Quentin said.

"This?" Betsy held up the knife, studying its edge. "This is why I'm here. This is what I've always wanted. This is a weapon for killing gods."

"Why would you want to do that?"

"Have you ever met a fucking god?"

"I guess I can see your point."

Plum picked up the book that Betsy had tossed aside. It had a blank leather cover—it looked like a notebook or a diary.

"Are you sure gods can even die?" she said.

"I'm going to kill one and find out and then maybe I'll let you know." Betsy pushed the knife through her belt. "I'll see you guys around. Don't look for me."

"I wouldn't dream of it," Quentin said. "Take care of yourself, Betsy."

"Yeah," Stoppard chimed in. "Take care of yourself!"

"The name's Asmodeus, bitches," she said. "And if you see Julia, tell her I've gone fox hunting."

She turned around and walked away into the night.

CHAPTER 15

Following a restorative stop in Barion, Eliot and Janet forded the Great Salt River, half a mile wide and six inches deep, a vast gray-brown ribbon spilling through the green countryside like somebody left a hose on somewhere. They passed a low, grassy hill on which an enormous white figure was etched; the grass and soil had been cleared away in lines so that the white chalky substrate underneath showed through. It was a simple cartoon of a man holding a staff horizontally above his head. He was usually there, or thereabouts—sometimes he wandered, but he was there today. It was good to see him still at his post.

They trotted through open country, following paths in the grass like an old carpet that had worn thin. They crossed sun-blessed fields with stone walls crisscrossing them, real classics, almost pristine. Every way you looked the landscape of Fillory composed itself into even lines, ridgelines and tree lines, near, middle and far distance, each one a shade paler than the last, gently sloping to the left and the right and the left. A long, heavy tranche of cloud lay above the horizon, utterly still, its outline etched finely against the sky, like the silhouette of a breaking wave cut out of paper.

"Look at it all," Janet said. "Just look at it. It's almost like the world isn't ending."

"Almost."

Even now it still felt unreal. With so much beauty everywhere it was easy to forget that Fillory was a dying land. Maybe this was Fillory's hectic glow.

Then they plunged out of the sunlight into the gloom of the Darkling Woods, where they'd appeared the very first time they came to Fillory. This was a more chaotic scene than the Queenswood; not all the trees were sentient, and the ones that were tended to be loners, and not very civic-minded. They spent a morning looking for the exact spot on which they'd arrived—there was a clock-tree there, they remembered, and a sort of a gully—and there would have been a nice circularity to it, paying their respects to where it had all started. But they argued about where it was, and in the end it turned out that neither of them was right, by which time they were both in bad moods. They couldn't even find the Two Moons Inn, where they'd kind of hoped to stop for some lunch and a beer.

The next morning they broke out of the woods again and into the Clock Barrens, which turned out to be a vast flat plain sparsely covered with tiny twisted scrub trees, the tallest of them only waist high. It was a bonsai forest. The Barrens began more or less abruptly, as things tended to in Fillory: it was one of the peculiarities of Fillory that it bore an uncanny resemblance to a map of itself.

Eliot had never seen the Clock Barrens before. There had never been any particular reason to go here, and he guessed he'd just never gotten around to it. Good to check that box before it was too late.

"So that's it," he said.

Words failed him. They sometimes did. Eliot wondered if he was seeing it for the last time as well as the first, and what else he hadn't seen, and wouldn't ever see.

"I thought it would be . . ." Janet said. "I don't know. Clockier."

She poked at one of the stunted trees with a headless axe.

"Me too."

"Maybe it is and we're just looking at it wrong. Maybe from overhead it looks like a giant clock or something."

"It so does not look like a giant clock from overhead."

There were no paths, but they didn't especially need any. The little scrub trees were far enough apart that the horses could walk between them. Eliot had to fight a feeling of panic, an urgent need for decisive action. This was day six of Janet's timeline, and even though she'd made it up on the spur of the moment it had taken on an authoritative feel.

They had a lead, a slim one, but it was a stretch to call it an adventure. It wasn't much to hang a quest on. They were trotting along in search of they didn't even really know what, and there was no way to speed up the process, if there even was a process. It was quixotic, was what it was. Not even that, it was sub-quixotic. My kingdom for a windmill to tilt at.

"I had an idea last night," Janet said. "For saving the world. I woke up with it in the middle of the night but then forgot all about it till now. Are you ready?"

"Ready."

"We hunt the White Stag, like Quentin did. We catch it or shoot it or whatever you do with it. We get three wishes. We wish Fillory would last forever and not die. Done. Mischief managed."

Eliot was silent.

"You have to admit—"

"No, it's good," he said. "It's definitely good. You think the stag could do that?"

"No idea. But it's worth a try, right?"

"Definitely worth a try. Agreed. If this quest is a bust we'll do that."

"Plus we'd still have two wishes left over after we saved the world," Janet said. "One each. What else would you wish for?"

"I feel like I should wish for Quentin back."

Janet laughed.

"Then I could use my wish to wish him away again. *Psych!*"

They slept that night in the barrens; they had to burn flat a circle of ground to make room for their tent. The trees were surprisingly fireproof—the wood was fantastically hard and dense—but when they caught they burned like rocket fuel, hot on their faces, sending sparks and spears of light up into the night sky and leaving fountainous after-images on their vision. It made for a July Fourth atmosphere, a summer carnival in a wasteland, and they broke out the last of the wine. After a couple of bottles Janet suggested they start a huge forest fire, because it would look cool; Eliot thought it would be more prudent not to, but he agreed that if they couldn't save the world they might as well come back here and burn the Clock Barrens before the end.

By mid-morning the next day, day seven, they could see where they were going: a single clump of trees sticking up on the horizon, regular-size non-bonsai ones. As they got closer they saw that the trees stood in a circle, a thin ring one tree deep, and that there was a house in the middle.

"Barren, or barrens?" Janet said. "Can you have just one barren? Or multiple barrens? Barrenses?"

"Hush. This is it."

They drew up a hundred yards from the ring. They were all clock-trees, every one. It was a strange and beautiful tableau. Eliot had never seen more than one full-grown clock-tree at a time; Quentin used to joke that there was probably only one clock-tree in Fillory, it just moved very fast when they weren't looking. But here were twelve of them, and all different kinds: there was a gnarled oak; a slender birch with a rectangular dial; a needle-straight pine; a melted-looking, morbidly obese baobab.

The house in the middle was perfectly square, with a steeply pitched shingled roof. It was made of a pale stone that looked like it had been brought from a long way off.

"Very Hansel and Gretel," Janet said.

"It's not like it's a candy house."

"You know what I mean."

He did actually, there was a fairy-tale feel to it all. Nobody answered when they knocked so they walked around to the back, where they found an old woman on her knees working in a vegetable garden. The resident witch, obviously. Her hair was gray but pulled back in a girlish ponytail. A small woman, she wore a long brown dress, coarse and practical. When she stood up to greet them her face was pleasant and peaceful, though there was something mischievous in it too.

"Greetings," she said, "to the High King of Fillory. And to Queen Janet, of course."

"Hi," Eliot said. "Sorry to drop in like this."

"Not at all. I knew you were coming." She crouched down again and went back to what she was doing, which was fixing a little wicker cloche that stood over some sweet peas. "I figured you weren't trying to be stealthy when you lit those trees on fire. Are you wondering how I know your names?"

"Because we're famous?" Janet said. "Because we're the king and queen of you?"

"I know your names," the woman said, "because I'm a witch. I'm a bit famous too. Jane Chatwin. Or as I used to be known, the Watcher-woman."

"Jane Chatwin," Eliot said. He felt something very close to awe. "Well. We meet at last."

She was right, she was famous: she was one of the first children to come to Fillory, decades ago, and she had haunted it for decades as the mysterious Watcherwoman. It was she who, with the help of a magic watch that controlled time, helped orchestrate their journey to Fillory in the first place, and their disastrous confrontation with the Beast, who had once been her brother, Martin Chatwin.

"Or are you still the Watcherwoman? What shall we call you?"

"Oh, Jane is fine. I haven't been the Watcherwoman for years now."

"Somehow I thought you'd be hotter," Janet said.

"You've been talking to Quentin. Why don't you come inside, we'll have some tea."

The cottage was well kept, neat as a pin and swept to within an inch of its life. The décor was a crude Fillorian approximation of the interwar English drawing rooms that Jane must have remembered from her childhood. Funny that for all the effort she'd put into escaping the real world, she'd wound up re-creating it here. She summoned a blue bloom of fire out of her stove and placed a teakettle on it. Hard to say where she got a natural gas hookup out here.

"One could boil the water with magic," she said, "but it never tastes quite the same."

While they waited they sat around a sunny-yellow wooden table with a water glass full of wildflowers on it. Now that they were here Eliot thought he'd wait a bit before he popped the big question.

"How long have you been living here?" he asked. "We didn't even know you were still in Fillory."

"Oh, I never left. I've been here for years, ever since that business with you and Quentin and Martin. Since I broke my watch."

"I've always wondered about that," Janet said. "Is it really gone?"

"It's gone. There's nothing left. I broke it and jumped on the pieces."

"Darn."

Eliot hadn't even thought of that. It might've been handy, if they could've put it back together. Though he wasn't sure what they would go back and do differently. Maybe they could just relive the same couple of years forever. Was that how it worked? It was confusing. And irrelevant now.

"Not that I don't miss it," Jane said. "As it turned out, it was all that was keeping me young. When I broke it I went from twenty-five to seventy-five overnight, or thereabouts—with all that back-and-forthing I'd lost track of how old I really was. Now I know." She looked down at the backs of her hands, which were ropy and mottled. "I wish the dwarfs had warned me. They must have known."

"I'm sorry," Eliot said. He tasted his tea; it was bitter, and it tingled on his lips. "Fillory owes you a debt."

"We all owe each other debts. I always thought you must hate me, for the way I used you."

Janet shrugged.

"You did what you had to. It's not like you got off easy—your brother's dead. And without you we never would have found our way to Fillory at all. Call it a wash. Though I did wonder what happened to you. What the hell are you doing all the way out here?"

"I study with the dwarfs now. They're teaching me clockwork."

"I didn't know there were any dwarfs out here," Eliot said. "I thought they only lived in the mountains."

"There are dwarfs everywhere. They're like ants—for every one you see, there's fifty more you don't. These ones are underground." She tapped her foot on the floor. "There's tunnels all the way under the barrens. You're sitting over one of the entrances."

Huh. Janet had the wrong fairy tale, she should have said Snow White. He suppressed an urge to look under his chair. It made him a bit uncomfortable to think that Fillory might be riddled with dwarf-tunnels. They'd never done anybody any harm, yet, but Jesus. They were like termites.

Though it did explain who'd run a gas line into her cottage.

"There's an entire city down there. I would show you but the dwarfs are touchy about their secrets. They're terribly polite, but they'd find some reason not to let you in."

"How come they let you in?" Janet said.

"I've paid my dues. Plus I did them a few favors."

"Like what?"

"Like saving Fillory."

There was a funny kind of competitiveness in the room, a rivalry: the first generation of Fillorian royalty versus the second. Jane Chatwin didn't seem especially fazed by Janet's bluntness. On the evidence it was hard to imagine Jane Chatwin being fazed by anything.

"We saved Fillory," Janet said.

"Twice," Eliot said.

"But who's counting."

"It's a start," Jane said.

When they'd finished their tea she showed them into the next room, which had a pleasant smell of very pure mineral oil and raw-cut metal. The walls were studded with hooks, and on each hook hung a pocket watch. There were brass watches, steel watches, silver and gold and platinum watches. They had white faces with black numbers and black faces with white numbers and clear crystal faces that showed the movements behind them. Some just told the time, some were crowded with tiny subdials that displayed the temperature and the season and the positions of celestial bodies. Some of them were as fat as softballs; some of them were the size of cuff links.

"Did you really make all these?" Janet said. "They're awesome."

You could tell she really thought they were. Eliot also got the impression Janet wanted one but wasn't quite up to asking.

"Most of them," Jane Chatwin said. "It keeps me out of trouble."

"Oh my God," Janet said. "You're trying to rebuild the watch, aren't you? The time-travel one! Aren't you? You're going to reverse-engineer it or whatever!"

Jane shook her head solemnly.

"Oh. Well, I wish you would."

"If they don't control time, what do they do?" Eliot asked.

"They tell time," Jane said. "That's enough."

When the tour was over they went back outside and admired the garden again. Behind it, rusted and half drowned in grass, were the broken remains of what Eliot took to be the Watcherwoman's famous ormolu clock-carriage, run down at last. He wanted to ask about it, but he sensed that from Jane's point of view the visit was coming to an end, and he wasn't leaving without what they came for.

"What are the dwarfs doing all the way out here anyway?" Janet asked. "Why build a bunch of tunnels in the middle of nowhere? Or under the middle of nowhere?"

"I'll show you." Jane took a spade that was leaning against the house and stuck it into the ground with a coarse *chuff.* When she turned over the shovelful there were glints of something in it. "Didn't you ever wonder why it was called the Clock Barrens?"

"I guess I did."

Jane bent down with a groan and picked a couple of the shiny things out of the soil, three or four of them, and held them out. In the palm of her hand lay two tiny, perfect gears, a brass wheel as thin as paper, and a delicate coiled mainspring.

"Clockwork," she said. "It's naturally occurring here. You should see the big stuff they mine, deep down. You could make Big Ben out of it. I'm not entirely sure that they didn't."

She flung them away into the grass. Eliot had to suppress an urge to go after them. This kind of thing, totally inexplicable random strangeness like this, made him want to save Fillory more than ever.

"Plus they like the dwarfiness of the trees," she added.

"Jane," Eliot said, "we came here for a reason. Ember says that Fillory is dying. The end of the world is coming."

She nodded but didn't answer at first. The setting sun caught the bezel of a clock-tree and flashed off it, orange light on silver.

"I suspected something like that," she said. "Did you notice the clocks? They don't agree anymore. They used to keep perfect time, but now look at them. Their hands are going everywhere. It's like they're panicking. Little idiots."

She frowned at the fairy ring of clock-trees like they were disobedient children. He supposed they were all the children she had, or would have.

"What do you think it means?"

"Hard to say." Lost in thought, for a moment she looked young and beautiful and intensely curious, the way she must have looked to Quentin when she first recruited him back in Brooklyn, dressed as a paramedic, all those years ago. "You know, these were the last clock-trees I ever made. I always thought I'd think of a better name for them.

"Their roots go very deep into Fillory. Not all the way through to the Far Side, I don't think they've made it that far, but more than halfway. They're like a nervous system, very quick to register systemic change. They're useful that way.

"But they shouldn't be able to disagree with each other. It shouldn't be possible. They're all one big tree below the surface—they reach out for each other and grow together at the roots. The dwarfs hack through them sometimes, but they grow right back. Except that this time they haven't. Deep underground, something must be tearing them apart. Tearing Fillory apart."

Jane walked over to one of the trees, the smallest one, knobby and broken-backed like an olive tree—it was bent over so far she'd had to prop it up with a board. She knocked twice on the crystal face of its clock; it was on a section of trunk that ran parallel to the ground, and its face looked up at the sky. It swung open, first the glass, then the dial, to reveal the works inside, gears and catchments turning and meshing silently.

She bit her lip.

"What should we do?" Eliot said.

"Damned if I know." She slammed the clock face shut like it was the door of a washing machine. "Listen. Eliot."

"Your Highness," Janet prompted. She felt free to disrespect Eliot—very free in fact—but she didn't like other people doing it. Jane ignored her.

"Look at me: this is what an ended story looks like. I was giving my life for this country, this world, before you were born. Everyone I've ever loved is dead. I had my own brother killed. I have no partner, no children. I've done my great deed, and it took everything I had. I won't be dragged back into another adventure. I've made a separate peace."

"Well, and we would rather not drag you," Janet said. "But, see, apocalypse."

"Has it occurred to you that you might just accept it?" She was a small woman, but she drew herself up, and there was some Edwardian dignity in her manner. "Has it crossed your minds that you don't have to go off on a holy crusade every time things don't go your way? You children and your adventures. Stories have ends! Why don't you let Fillory die gracefully, in its own time and its own way? Maybe it wants to let go! I was never a real paramedic, but a phrase comes back to me: do not resuscitate. Let it go. Let Fillory die in peace."

"No."

"We're not asking you to come with us," Eliot said. "Just tell us what you know. There has to be something. Please."

The High King of Fillory went down on one knee before the Watcherwoman.

"Please. Our stories haven't ended yet. Yours may have, but ours haven't. If it's time, then it's time, but I am not the last High King of Fillory. I don't believe it. This land isn't ready to die."

Jane stared at him for a long time. Then she made a disgusted noise in her throat and turned away and boosted herself up onto the bent trunk of the clock-tree.

"All right," she said. "All right. I'll tell you what I know, but it isn't much. I feel like I know less and less every day. Maybe it's the time travel—some days I wonder if I'm starting to live backward, like Merlin. God, I think I would kill myself. Or would I already have killed myself? My brother could have helped you, but he's dead. Long ago."

"What, Martin? Not likely."

"Not him, the other one. Rupert. He spent a lot of time in Fillory. He was close to Martin."

"That's not actually a huge plus in our book," Janet said.

"It should be. Martin was an asshole, but he was smart. He found out things about Fillory that you and I will never know, and he was only thirteen when he did it. Have you ever wondered where he got all that power from? How he became what he was?"

"I guess I have wondered that," Eliot said.

"I have too. I never knew. But I think Rupert did. He was with Martin the day he disappeared. He always said he didn't see anything, but I think he did. He was an open book, our Rupes, no good at keeping secrets, though he thought he was.

"If I were looking for missing puzzle pieces, I would start there. Go back to Earth. Find his things, see what he left behind. Maybe he wrote something down. And I think he nicked something—you weren't supposed to bring things through, from Fillory back to Earth, or not big things anyway, but I think Rupert did. I think he stole something. At any rate when he left here there was a big stink about it. No one ever pinned it on him, and by then Martin was raising hell so it rather got lost in the shuffle, but I think he had something he wasn't supposed to.

"That's what I would do: go back, all the way back to where this whole disaster started. You weren't there, and even I wasn't there. But Rupert was."

That was all they got out of her. Eliot asked her some polite questions about the garden, while Janet walked from clock-tree to clock-tree, knocking on the faces, trying to get them to open for her the way they did for Jane; Jane claimed not to know why they didn't. After ten more minutes Eliot said they should be on their way, and Jane didn't disagree.

She walked them to their horses. They hadn't wanted to come inside the ring of clock-trees.

"Good luck," the Watcherwoman said. "And I do mean that."

"Thanks," Eliot said. "Good luck with your clockwork lessons."

"Thank you."

"I bet you wish you hadn't broken that watch," Janet said.

She wouldn't leave it alone.

"Wishes are for children," Jane Chatwin said. "I grew up."

CHAPTER 16

It was like a really terrible party where on top of everything else at the end it turns out your ride bailed and you have to walk home. It was cold, and Plum kept worrying that the bird would come back at any moment with reinforcements to claim its stolen goods. Or the surviving half of the Couple, if he had survived. She worried to the point where she kept losing her shit every time anything cawed or hooted or one of them stepped on a stick. It had to be after them. No way would it let this go, not after the lengths it had already gone to. The only question was when.

After Betsy left, or Amadeus, or whatever her name was, Stoppard had departed the scene too at top speed on the busted club chair, with promises to reconnect back in New York once the coast was clear. Plum and Quentin were going to take the pool table, but when they tried to shift it they discovered that they lacked the necessary motive power. All their magical strength was spent. So they set off on foot instead.

Maybe they should have taken Lionel's gun, for added protection, but they didn't. They just didn't want it.

It was a long night, and a long walk, but then again everybody had a lot of explaining to do, and a lot of thinking to do too. Quentin told her what he knew about why Asmodeus (that was it) would have wanted the knife, and after hearing the tale of Reynard the murdering rapist fox-god she thought it was pretty understandable. She must have been planning to steal it all along, that was the whole reason she was there. All else being equal Plum wished her well.

But how had she known it was in the case in the first place? Plum didn't even have a guess. Quentin didn't either, or if he did he didn't make it.

More disquieting was the fact that Asmodeus obviously knew about Plum's family. She'd realized a while ago that the bird must know; now it was clear that her secret identity wasn't anywhere near as secret as she thought it was, and that being a Chatwin meant that she was already part of a lot of other people's stories in ways that she was only now becoming aware of. She figured she might as well tell Quentin at this point; she felt safe with him. She'd almost told him once, at the hotel bar, and anyway he asked why she could open the suitcase when nobody else could, because *of course* he wasn't going to let that go, and that had to be the answer. Her great-grandfather had locked it and made sure only a family member could unlock it. She could have made up something, but she was so tired she couldn't think of a lie, and anyway what was the point.

For the record Plum thought it was pretty rich that Quentin turned out to be connected to a hard case like Betsy, if only indirectly. But he was turning out to be a pretty hard case himself, in his way, or at any rate harder than she'd thought based on first impressions. And everywhere she looked things were getting connected up, or rather it was becoming clear that they were already connected in ways that she was only just now picking up on. It was a worrying trend. Everybody else was deep into their own stories, and all the stories were woven together just beneath the surface into a web that included Plum. But what was Plum's story?

Toward dawn they'd recovered enough strength from the spellcasting orgy of the day before that they could risk some low flight, just above the trees. They had no idea where they even were. Once the sun was up they found a road and walked along it looking sufficiently pathetic and unthreatening that some guy out for an early-morning drive in his Honda Element gave them a ride into the nearest town.

The town was called Amenia, as it happened, like Armenia but without the *r*. It was in Dutchess County, New York, and it turned out to be the very last stop on the commuter train line to Manhattan, two and a half hours away. So they steal-o-mancied some dollars out of an ATM and bought tickets, plus some bad coffee and rubber croissants at the snack bar in the lobby of the train station. Then they sat on the old red bench in said lobby. It was nine in the morning, and the next train wasn't till noon.

It had been a long night, and a long day before that, and Plum needed to go to sleep and perchance to dream—maybe dreaming she could begin to process and understand the sight of a roomful of robed figures with golden hands, and Betsy standing over an electrocuted corpse, and Lionel opening fire on Stoppard, and Asmodeus née Betsy carving a suddenly nonhuman Lionel to pieces with a knife . . . thinking about it again she started to shake. Things had gone much too far, and her brain felt raw and scarred from it all.

It wasn't how she'd imagined spending what should have been her last semester at Brakebills. It wasn't even how she'd imagined spending her post-Brakebills life of crime. As soon as she read the letter she found on her bed the night of the ghost, she knew she was going to take the job. Keep moving, keep busy, that was rule number one of being Plum. And yeah, part of her got an illicit thrill out of it. She'd never had a rebellious phase, and she wasn't sure she wanted one, but she'd sure as hell gotten one. It was crazy and weird and kind of sleazy but she embraced it.

At least she'd learned some new magic from Quentin and Pushkar. Maybe she could spin it to her parents as an internship. What she really wanted was something she could fall in love with the way she loved Brakebills, but at this point she wasn't sure she would ever find it.

Even after her dramatic reveal she and Quentin had eventually run out of conversation, and now they just sat there on the bench in the empty waiting room of the Amenia train station, looking out at the cement platform, and the empty tracks, under the empty white sky, feeling the weight of the sleepless night pressing down on their shoulders like a mile of ocean, and them sunk to the bottom of it. Plum let her mind spin off its axis. Her brain wasn't up to thinking about the future right now, or about the past. It wasn't functioning on that level. So she hung out in the present, second by second.

It was a surprisingly substantial train station for a town this tiny, this far from New York City. A flat-screen TV wedged into one corner of the lobby showed local news, including shaky iPhone footage of strange objects seen streaking across the sky last night. Plum wondered if people actually commuted to Manhattan from here. She wondered what it would be like just to be a regular civilian person who lived in Amenia, New York. She thought it might be pretty nice.

Quentin kept taking out his pocket watch and looking at it. Plum wanted to find it annoying—it was kind of a hipster affectation, that watch, like a novelty beard, especially since it didn't appear to work in spite of Stoppard's attentions—but it was such a strange and beautiful object. It drew her gaze, magnetically. It must have been a gift, she supposed, from someone who loved him. That Julia person maybe. More stories.

"Do you want to read the book?" he asked.

Oh, that. The leather-bound book that had been in the case. They'd taken it with them, of course, humped it through the woods, but now the thought of opening it filled her with dread.

"Maybe we should burn it," she said. "Sooner or later the bird's going to come after it. So maybe when it does we're going to want to not have it."

"The bird will have to hire some new muscle first. Round up more stooges like us. That'll take time. In the meantime maybe it would help if we knew why the bird thought it was so important."

"I guess. We could always burn it later."

"Now you're talking."

"Lemme see it."

It was an old leather notebook, or maybe ledger was a better word for it. The kind of thing an accountant with a green eyeshade might have written in, in an old-timey bank. The cover had the same monogram as the suitcase: *RCJ*. The spine was oddly mottled, blue and green.

"This was my great-grandfather's."

"I figured."

"What do you think's in it?"

"Diary?" Quentin said.

"What if it has dirty parts in it. Like intimate confessions, that sort of thing."

"One way to find out."

She nodded, resigned, but still she let the book lie in her lap. It felt heavy, too heavy to lift. She was at a crossroads, but the kind that had no signs at it. She wondered what could possibly be inside the book that people should have died for it; she was assuming that Lionel had done away with Pushkar too. She wondered if later on she would wish she hadn't looked. That was one thing about books: once you read them they couldn't be unread.

But she could feel Quentin practically panting with excitement at her elbow—whatta dork. Always the eager beaver. Suddenly a wave of physical and emotional exhaustion just steamrolled over her, and Plum did want to be reading something, anything at all, rather than sitting in this empty train station lobby staring at the cinder block walls. She was too tired to feel anything more, she wanted a book to do to her what books did: take away the world, slide it aside for a little bit, and let her please, please just be somewhere and somebody else.

She was ready to sink, really sink, to the black, airless bottom of where this all began.

"OK," she said. "Bottoms up."

"*Skoal.*"

That made her wish she had a real drink instead of this shitty coffee. She opened the book.

From the first page it was evident that Great-Grampa Rupert had had literary aspirations, and that he'd undertaken this project with some actual seriousness of purpose, because he'd arranged the page like a formal title page. He wrote with a fountain pen, the blue ink faded now from midnight blue to midday, but still elegant, a diligent schoolboy's handwriting. The pages weren't ruled for prose, they were set up for columns of numbers, but Rupert had filled them with letters instead.

Plum's heart went out to the guy. Probably he was having a midlife crisis, and this was the novel or memoir or whatever that he just had to get out of him. This was how he was going to make his mark, have his say, show the world he wasn't like the others. (But if that was true why lock it in a case?)

With great ceremony, in the deliberate hand of a man who genuinely believed he was making a new beginning for himself, a clean breast of things, Rupert had written and then crossed out two possible titles:

~~THE FRIENDS OF FILLORY~~

and then

~~OF CLOCKS AND KINGS~~

before he settled for good and all on:

THE DOOR IN THE PAGE

My Life in Two Worlds

By Rupert Chatwin

"Good call," Quentin said.
"I think he nailed it."
"Third time's the charm."
She turned the page. The next one began:

> *We all thought Martin would get into trouble one day and in the*
> *end he did. It just wasn't the sort of trouble we were expecting.*

Evidently Rupert was happy with that first line, but then not with what
came next, because the rest of the page was ripped out, leaving the sentences alone on their own orphaned strip of paper, a single accusing
finger. The next page was gone too—in fact there was a thick chunk of
stubs where somebody, presumably Rupert, had ripped out four or five
pages at once.

Plum realized she wasn't as eager to go on as she thought she would
be. She'd kind of forgotten that her great-grandfather was a real person,
and his brothers and sisters too. They'd lived real lives. They'd had real
hopes and dreams and secrets, and none of it had worked out the way
they wanted it to. They'd felt like the heroes of their own stories, just
like she felt like the hero of hers, but that was no guarantee that everything would work out. Or anything.

After that false start Rupert wrote quickly, fluidly, with minimal punctuation and only occasional corrections. Plum got the impression he'd never even reread it after he started writing.

It was at one of Aunt Maude's parties that it happened for the first time. She often entertained in those days, in a lavish style that some people thought was not entirely in line with the sacrifices that we all, as loyal subjects of the King, were expected to make on behalf of the war effort.

I suppose hers was a glamorous life, but it never seemed so to us. We all know what it is to be a child, to be innocent, to understand nothing. We understood nothing, the five of us. Not anything. But we watched everything.

We watched the hired musicians fuss with their instruments, rosin their bows and empty their spit valves into wineglasses. We watched the ladies wince at their uncomfortable shoes and the men tug at their uncomfortable collars. We saw the faces of the servants assume a practiced blankness the moment before they entered a crowded room. We stole canapés off the trays, and loose change from the coats of the guests.

But talk of the war bored us, and flirtatious chatter bored us just as much, and none of the guests cared about anything else. The scene may or may not have been glittering, as such parties are always described, but either way it was wasted on us. The only ones who paid any attention to us were the interchangeable young men who passed through the house in an endless parade, and they did so only to try to gain favor with Aunt Maude.

Their efforts were misguided—an interest in children was not a quality Aunt Maude prized. In her eyes it only made them weak and sentimental.

An hour or so after the first guests arrived the dancing would begin, and Aunt would drape her long limbs and eventually her entire upper body across the back of the piano, to either the consternation or the delight of the pianist, depending on who was playing. Our various bedtimes would come and go, but nobody put us to bed. *Eventually we Chatwin children would retreat, yawning and fractious, to the back halls and upper stories of Dockery House, as it was known, though Aunt Maude didn't like the name—she thought it sounded fussy and Victorian. Which it did, which is precisely why we children liked it.*

It was on one such occasion that Martin began playing with an old grandfather clock that he found standing by itself in a back hallway. He was mechanically minded and could never resist a chance to tinker with something complicated and valuable.

As the other boy in the family I suppose I might have been expected to share his enthusiasm, but I did not. I wasn't one of those keen children with well-defined, clearly articulated interests—I had very few enthusiasms at all apart from books. I was no good at games, or music, or drawing, or figures. I don't wonder that Martin, as I later found out, thought I was weak, like those young men who were always wooing Aunt Maude. But it was in the nature of the calamity that followed that it took the strong and spared the weak.

I remember Fiona telling Martin to stop, he would break it, and Helen defending him—Helen never tired of scolding the rest of her siblings, but she worshipped Martin, and he could do no wrong in her eyes. I didn't think it mattered either way, as Maude rarely visited this part of the house. If the clock stopped running it would be years before she discovered it, at which point she would decide that it had been that way all along. She was a careless woman.

Jane said nothing. She rarely spoke unless someone questioned her directly, and sometimes not even then.

Once he had the cabinet open Martin began repeating "bloody hell" under his breath. Even Helen shushed him when he swore, which he had been doing a great deal ever since our father went to France—the year was 1915, if I haven't mentioned it, and father was a lieutenant in the Artists Rifles, a regiment that, its whimsical designation notwithstanding, was about to embark on a tour of the most brutal battlefields the Great War had to offer. I had wandered a little way down the hall to examine an interesting spiderweb in an angle of the ceiling, but upon hearing Martin I came back. I believe I was hoping that he and Helen might have a row.

The clock was a monster, its flat brass dial so richly studded with circles and hands and curious symbols that it looked like a cross scowly face. Martin dragged over a stool, the better to study it eye to eye, as it were. Cool, damp air breathed from inside its cabinet as it would from the mouth of a cave. As we watched the clock whirred to life and chimed the hour: nine o'clock at night.

Little Jane yawned. Martin stared at the clock furiously, meeting its crooked gaze, mussing his own hair without noticing it, as he did when something vexed him.

He hopped down.

"Bloody hell," he said. "Rupes, take a look inside. What do you see?"

I obediently bent my head to look into the cabinet, and Martin pinned my arms and attempted to shove me inside. It was his idea of a joke. He was always shouldering me into closets and down stairs. There was nothing sinister in it, we were just bored to sobs.

"Leave off, Martin," Fiona said, but without much conviction.

We tussled; the clock wobbled dangerously; he was stronger, but leverage was on my side, and eventually I got my shoulders jammed in the opening in such a way as to make further progress impossible. I sometimes wonder if things would have been different had he succeeded. But as it was he saw there was no more fun to be had, and he let me up. I was red-faced and breathing hard, my collar popped up on one side. He swaggered away in a circle to show that he hadn't really meant it.

"Really, have a look," he said. "There's no works inside. No pendulum. What makes it go?"

No one was much intrigued by this mystery. Jane picked at a bit of peeling wallpaper. Fiona leaned against a wall and rolled her eyes at boys.

"All right," he said. "I'll get in myself."

Martin was determined to get some comic material out of this empty clock, one way or the other. As the eldest I think he felt responsible for entertaining us. He began stuffing himself into the clock's wooden body. I don't think he expected to succeed—his shoulders were filling out even then—and I remember his curious frown when he reached an arm in and couldn't find the back. He ducked whole upper body inside. It looked like stage magic, one of Houdini's trapdoor boxes.

I saw him hesitate, but only for a moment. He put one foot in, then the other, then he was gone. We all looked at each other. Fiona, irritated at the idea that a trick was being played on her, put her head in next. Only seven and small for her age, she barely had to duck. She disappeared inside too.

Helen and I stared.

"Jane," I called, for she was still busy fooling with the wallpaper. It seems impossible to me now, but she can only have been five years old. "Jane."

She came trotting over, incurious.

"Where's Fi?" she said. It was a lengthy soliloquy by her standards.

At that moment first Martin and then Fiona came spilling back out of the clock, Martin spitting mad, Fiona in something like a blissful daze. The first thing I noticed, even before their clothes, was that they both looked suntanned and fit, and their hair had grown by an inch. They smelled like fresh grass.

Time runs differently in Fillory. To them, a month had passed. Just like that Martin and Fiona had had their first adventure there, which Christopher Plover would later write about in The World in the Walls. *That was the beginning of everything for us Chatwin children, and it was the end of everything for us too.*

CHAPTER 17

Much of what follows has already been described by Christopher Plover in Fillory and Further, *his beloved series of novels for children, and ably enough too as far as it goes. I don't take issue with his work. I've made my peace with it. But as you will see his story was not the whole story.*

One difference I must insist upon, before and above all else, is that what Plover naively presented as fiction was, apart from some details, entirely true. Fillory was not a figment of our imaginations, or his, or anyone else's. It was another world, and we traveled to and from it, and we spent a good part of our childhoods there. It was very real.

Rupert had stopped and traced and retraced these last letters—*very real*—over and over again, until the paper had begun to shed little shreds of itself, as if it couldn't support the full weight of the meaning he wanted it to carry, the burden he wished to unload onto it. And onto Plum.

At first Plum couldn't have put her finger on what exactly it was that was freaking her out about this story. But that was it: she'd expected Rupert's memoir to be a typical upperish-crust jolly-hockey-sticks account of an English boyhood, enlivened by a behind-the-scenes look at the making of the Fillory series. But it was dawning on her that Rupert was going to persist with the joke. He was going to stick to his story, and the story was that Fillory was real.

Maybe this was the Chatwin legacy: full-on insanity. There was madness in the family. Plum put a finger on the wounded paper and felt its roughness. She wanted to heal it.

But she couldn't. She could only keep reading.

It is difficult to write those words, knowing that they will not be believed. If I were in your place I wouldn't believe them. I would stop reading. But they are the truth, and I can't write anything else. I am not a madman, and I am not a liar. I swear it on everything I hold sacred. I suppose I ought to say that it is God's truth, and it is. But perhaps not the god you are thinking of.

After Martin and Fiona went into Fillory through the grand-father clock, I went through with Helen, and that is how all the events described in The Girl Who Told Time *came to pass, more or less—a lifetime's worth of adventures, all of which happened in the space of five minutes in a dusty back hallway of an old house during the first war. By then Jane was awake and alert again, so all five of us went through together.*

Already I can see you shaking your head: no, you've got it wrong, they always went by twos. Well damn you and damn Plover too. We often went together, all of us. Why wouldn't we have?

The truth is, there were many adventures we never told Christopher Plover about, and many more that for his own reasons he didn't see fit to include in the books. I suppose they must not have fit neatly into the plot. I can't help but feel that I myself was some-what slighted in Fillory and Further. *It's petty of me to say it, but I do say it. I stood vigil at the gates of Whitespire during the Long Evening. I claimed the Sword of Six, and then broke it on the peak of Mount Merriweather. But you wouldn't know any of that from reading Plover.*

I was perhaps not a pretty young man. I wasn't as appealing as Martin. I didn't make good material, as they say in the literary business. But I suppose if he didn't write about me at my best, he didn't write about me at my worst either. He never knew the worst. None of them did, except Martin.

Regardless, all of our lives split that night. They became double. A more alert guardian than Aunt Maude would have noticed the change—the whispered colloquies, the tanned faces and uncut hair, the extra half-inch or so of height we would gain during an especially long trip to Fillory. But she didn't notice. People are very determined to see only what they can explain.

Anyone who has led a secret life—spies, criminals, fugitives, adulterers—knows that a façade is not an easy thing to maintain, and some people are better at it than others. I, as it turned out, had something of a gift for lying to adults; I sometimes wonder if I was left out of certain expeditions simply because I could be relied on to cover for the others. I don't know how many times I found myself forced to invent stories—outlandish but far more mundane than the reality—to explain why one sibling or another hadn't turned up for Mass or lessons or tea.

We were always scrambling to change in and out of our Fillorian things before they could be discovered. Our feats of arms often left us covered with scratches and bruises that had to be accounted for too. Martin's shin was split wide open once by an arrow, hunting bandits near Corian's Land, and he spent a month in Fillory convalescing.

Perhaps the greatest indignity was having to pretend that we didn't know things that we'd learned in Fillory. I still remember falling over laughing watching Fiona, the great huntress of the Queenswood, laying it on thick at the archery range, getting tangled up and finally sitting down on her bum trying to string a bendy little schoolgirl's bow.

We gave that up, in the end. Jane just didn't care enough to dissemble, and one day she simply galloped away from her riding class, hallooing wildly in centaur as she cleared the stone wall at the end of the meadow and disappeared into the forest. After that we all stopped caring. Let people be amazed, if they absolutely must.

Very often, when the way to Fillory was closed to us, and we had exhausted the limited possibilities of Aunt Maude, her house, her *library, her staff and the grounds, we crossed the road and picked our way through the trees and through a gap in the hedge to Mr. Plover's house. I know now that he cannot have been over forty, but we thought of him as a very old man because his hair was already grey. I think he was quite terrified of us at first—he had no children himself and was not much used to their company. And as children went we were very childish indeed. At that time in our lives Martin was the closest thing we had to a parent, and although he did his best he was still only twelve. We were loud and obstreperous and very nearly feral.*

Even on the first day we invaded Plover's house we sensed the conundrum that Americans are faced with in England: they're too frightened of English people to behave rudely to them, and too ignorant to know how to behave politely. We exploited it. Unwilling to throw us out, incapable of entertaining us properly, unable to think of anything else to do, he offered us tea, though it wasn't yet three in the afternoon.

It was an inauspicious start. We threw our crusts and dueled with our spoons and tittered and whispered and asked rude questions as we ate—but we did eat, for it was a very good tea, with nice biscuits and homemade marmalade. Plover can't have enjoyed himself much, but he was wealthy and unmarried and had already retired from business, and he must have been nearly as bored in the country as we were. So we all soldiered on.

In most respects the occasion was very unsuccessful, and we couldn't have guessed at the time that it would be the first of many. I realize now that we, all five of us, must have been very angry children: angry at the absence of our parents, angry at the presence of louche, neglectful Aunt Maude and her many suitors, angry at the war, angry at God, angry at our own strangeness and seeming irrelevance. But people are slow to recognize anger in little children, and children never recognize it in themselves, so it comes out in other ways.

Whatever the reason, we competed to see who could push the boundaries of propriety the furthest. It was Fiona who won that contest—and I recall her doing it triumphantly, with an almost sensual pleasure—by mentioning Fillory.

This was a transgression not only of earthly rules but of Fillorian ones. The disrespect was not toward Mr. Plover, who was merely baffled, but toward Ember and Umber, who had sworn us to secrecy. Up until that moment none of the five of us had ever said the word "Fillory" within earshot of an adult. We weren't even positively certain that we could. Would the rams' magic reach across the void between worlds and seal our lips?

It would not. There was silence at the table. Fiona froze, alive and trembling with delight at her victory, and with terror at her sin. Had she gone too far? Nobody knew. We waited for the thunderclap of retribution.

"Fillory?" asked Mr. Plover innocently, in his flat Chicago tones. He seemed happy to have found a question to ask us. "What on Earth is that?"

"Oh," Martin said airily, as if the admission cost him nothing, "it's not on Earth at all. It's a place we go to sometimes. We found it inside a clock."

And after that the boundary was breached, and the walls crumbled, and we all rushed ahead, the stories tumbling out one after the other, none of us wanting to be left behind.

It really was too funny, Plover listening away and, after a while, making notes on some loose paper. He was wide-eyed at the treasure trove of childish whimsy he'd stumbled on—he must have fancied himself a latter-day Charles Kingsley, the Charles Dodgson de nos jours. He would never ask about it right away, instead he would work his way around to it circuitously—he would chat and nod and observe the niceties, but always the moment arrived when he would reach for a notebook, which he never seemed to be without, hoist one leg over the other, lean forward and say, in his queer accent, neither American nor English, "And what's the latest from Fillory, huh?"

But it made a difference to us, being able to tell someone, anyone, even a no-one like Plover. It made Fillory more real to us, and less of a game. Now we at least had an audience.

Sometimes we really would make it up, laughing hysterically to think what Sir Hotspots or the Stump King would have thought of our tales of birds made out of leaves and giants who ate clouds. What rot! Helen was particularly bad at that game: she could only ever think of stories about hedgehogs. Sea-hedgehogs, were-hedgehogs, a Hedgehog of Fire. Hedgehogs were the sole extravagance of which her imagination was capable.

But Plover took it all in, indiscriminately. The only stories he balked at were the ones about the mammoth, velveteen Cozy Horse, and those were actually true. Eventually we prevailed on him to write them down too, if only because we couldn't bear the thought of the poor thing's feelings being hurt.

Looking back on it now I can see more clearly the strain we were under, continually negotiating between two realities, one where we were treated as kings and queens, one where we were invisible, inconvenient children. The shock of those sudden elevations and demotions would have given anybody fits.

Plover has the stories divided up very neatly into five different volumes, but the reality wasn't anything like that tidy or simple. Plover conveniently has us going to Fillory only during the summer hols—except the once, in The Girl Who Told Time—*but really we went there all year round. It was never our decision, not after that first night, we went whenever it suited Fillory to summon us. We never knew when the door would open, summer or winter, day or night. Sometimes months would pass without a portal opening, and we would start to wonder if it was all over, this grand hallucination, and it was as if one of our senses had gone dead. We would grow increasingly snappish, turning on each other, everybody blaming someone else for having ruined it, for having offended Ember or Umber or broken one or other of Their laws, thereby queering the deal for the rest of us.*

Sometimes, during these long lulls, I would start to suspect the others of sneaking off to Fillory behind my back without telling me. I imagined them freezing me out of the game.

And then with no warning it would all start again as if it had never stopped. On some otherwise nondescript afternoon, devoid of hope or interest of any kind, Fiona or Helen would come rushing into the nursery wearing a formal gown we'd never seen before, color in her cheeks, hair in outlandish court braids, shouting "guess where I've been!" And we would know it wasn't over after all.

It was feast or famine. One year, I think it must have been 1918, it seemed as if we spent half the summer in Fillory. It even became unnerving. You'd go to the closet for a clean shirt and you'd find yourself staring through it at one of those beautiful lumpy Fillorian meadows, or one of its curving shell beaches, or into the still heart of a forest at night. To my knowledge none of us ever refused; I don't know if we even could have. Once or twice it was a genuine nuisance—you'd be about to go into town with nanny, you'd have been given a shilling for sweets, and the groom had promised you a turn with the good grey mare after, and you'd bend down to look under the bed for your other boot, and before you knew it you were picking yourself up off the floor of Castle Whitespire. And by the time you got back—three weeks later for you, five minutes later for everyone else—you'd have lost the money and forgotten what you'd been doing in the first place, and everyone would be cross with you for keeping them waiting.

That summer it was as if Fillory was hungry for us, reaching out and grabbing us greedily whenever it could. It was an insatiable lover. I remember riding into town on our bicycles and seeing a little whirlwind of leaves wandering in our direction. All Martin had time to say was "bloody—!" before it was on him. It whirled him away, and Helen too, off to the other side.

That was the adventure of the Hog Knight, which I don't know whether Plover records or not. I've forgotten now, it all runs together, and here in Africa I haven't got the books with me. I do remember that the bicycles never came back. Even Aunt Maude was cross about that.

In some ways Fillory drew us together, but in many ways too it pushed us apart. We got into terrible disagreements over silly things. Fiona told us once that Umber had taken her on a special trip, just for her, to the Far Side of the World. He showed her a wonderful *garden, where all the thoughts and feelings that had ever been thought and felt existed in the form of plants, blooming and green as they passed through people's minds and lived in their hearts, and then drying up and turning brown and crisp as they passed out of mind, sometimes to bloom again in another season, sometimes gone forever.*

It was a lovely story, and it must have been true, Fiona couldn't have made it up. She didn't have that sort of imagination. But it left a sour taste in my mouth. Why her and not us? And not me?

Privately we argued about Ember and Umber. If we believed in Them, and we certainly did, then was it not blasphemous to go to church in the real world, and mouth prayers to God, who had after all never showed us a secret magic garden, or a castle all our own, or even so much as a single pegasus? Or did each world have its own God or gods, and one should simply worship the God of whatever world one happened to be in? Or were all the gods one God, really? Different aspects of each other?

Nonsense, Jane said, she'd never heard such rot. We had furious, hissing quarrels about this, and in the end we splintered into the Ramsians, as we called those who worshipped only the rams Ember and Umber, namely Martin and Helen and Jane, and the more pragmatic Anyone-ists, namely myself and Fiona, who prayed to the twin rams in Fillory and God in the real world.

After that Helen was always finding reasons not to go to church. Jane, who had the zeal of the martyr, would go on purpose and cause the most awful scenes with her laughing and have to be removed.

Martin was simply staunch and grim, wherever we were. Of us all I think he may have loved Fillory the most, but it was a fierce, angry, watchful love, forever alert to the possibility of betrayal. I don't mean to defend Martin, but I do think I understand him. When our parents left it was Martin, more than anyone else, who filled the void in our lives. He was the one who picked us up when we fell, and sang us lullabies at night. But who filled the void for

Martin? It can only have been Fillory. And she was a fickle, capricious parent.

One thing we did not argue about was why, among all the children in the world, we had been given the gift of Fillory. Why us and no others? Why did Ember and Umber and all the rest of the Fillorians show us such special favor, when in our own world we were just ordinary people? I believe that I alone among us five was troubled by this. To the extent that I, at the age of ten, had a soul, the question gnawed at it. A mistake had been made, I was sure, a real blunder, because I knew that I was not strong or clever or even particularly good. I knew I didn't deserve Fillory.

And when the truth finally came out, and the hoax collapsed, the punishment would be terrible indeed, and our suffering would be hot and sharp, in proportion to the blessings that had been showered on us.

I didn't even notice about Martin until he told me. We were at school, St. Austol's in Fowey, and he took me with him on a long freezing tramp around the Upper Meadow, a frosted, rotted rugby pitch where one went to exchange confidences and discuss matters of consequence.

I was grateful to be asked. Martin was my senior by two years, and older boys didn't generally acknowledge younger siblings at St. Austol's. We were halfway around the track before he spoke.

"D'you know, Rupes," he said, "it's been three months since I last went over?"

We called it that: going over. He didn't have to say where. He spoke with an elaborate casualness that I'd learned to recognize as a warning sign from him.

"As long as that?"

"Yes, as long as that! It was you and Fiona in August, then Helen and Fiona, then Jane and Fiona, then Helen and bloody you again two weeks ago. Where does that leave me?"

"On Earth, I suppose." I hadn't meant to be smart.

"That's right, on bloody Earth! I'm bloody well stuck here! Do you know, I've taken to cramming myself into cubbies and closets and I don't know what else just on the off chance I'll find a way through? Whenever I see a squirrel I take off running after it, in case it might be a magic one on its way to Fillory. The other boys think I'm mad, but I don't care. I'd do anything to get out of here."

"Come on, Mart," I said. "You know how these things are. It'll come around to you again."

"Did the rams say anything about me? I'm out of favor, aren't I?"

"Honestly, they haven't! Half the time I can't understand what They mean anyway, but I'm sure They haven't said anything about you. I would've told you."

"But you'll ask Them, won't you? When you see Them?"

"Course I will, Mart. Course I will."

"I have to do something."

He kicked at a heavy black lump like a shrunken head that might once have been a cricket ball.

"But look," I said. "I know how you feel, I hate it when I'm not asked. But it's not as bad here as all that, is it? I mean, Fillory isn't everything."

"But it is." He stopped walking and looked me in the eye. "It is everything. What else is there? This? Earth?" He picked up the dead cricket ball and threw it as hard as he could. "Listen: will you come and get me?"

He grabbed my arm—he was pleading with me.

"You know sometimes it comes on slowly. Like that time it was you and Jane, and it was just patterns in the wallpaper at first, you said. Took you ten minutes to go all the way through. You could come get me when it starts. We'll go together, like back in the old days."

"I'll try, Mart. I really will." But we both knew that wasn't how it worked. Ember and Umber decided who came, and that was that. "You were the first one in. You started it all. You found the way. We both know you'll go again, it's only a question of when. You're the High King!"

"I'm the High King," he repeated unhappily.

At the time I believed it, mostly. I was ten, and he was twelve, but the gap between us had always seemed wider. I looked up to Martin. I literally couldn't imagine myself having something he did not, doing something he could not.

But by the next summer it was clear that something had changed between Martin and Fillory. The romance was over. In all that school year he'd only gone over once, and then the rams let him stay only two mingy, grudging, uneventful days. He spent those days sulking, ruining them out of spite, even though he knew they would likely be his last. He barely left the palace library. The rams shunned his company. He was on the way out, and we all knew it.

It wouldn't have been so bad except that out of all of us it was Martin who needed Fillory the most. Honestly by that time I think Fiona could have taken or left it. She was already growing out of Fillory. For Jane, who was five when it began, it was just normal. She couldn't imagine life without it—it was barely even special. If the rams had turned Helen out, she would have accepted it, no questions asked, thy will be done. She would have taken a perverse pleasure in her martyrdom.

As for me, I never believed it would last anyway. Every day, every second, I expected it to end. On some level I would have been relieved.

Maybe it was just that Martin was older, that he had lived longer without Fillory. He remembered what life was like without it, and he understood better than the rest of us did how strange and precious it was. The rest of us made friends outside the family, in the real world, but increasingly Martin did not. He shirked his lessons, and filled his exercise books with winged bears—they'd been seen circling over the Hen's Teeth—and Fillorian coats of arms. A natural athlete who barely had to try at games, he stopped trying at all. He scorned everything in this world, heaped contempt on it. He even ate less and less, as if a bite of shepherd's pie would trap him down here in the darkness, like Persephone. He lived for Fillory.

But Fillory didn't live for him. In my later life I have known alcoholics, more than a few, and I recognized in their faces some of what I saw in Martin's. Loyal prophets of an indifferent god.

Martin might have fallen out of favor with Fillory, but never with Plover—whatever happened at Whitespire, at Darras House he was always the favorite. If anything Plover's affection for him seemed to grow in inverse proportion to that of the rams, or maybe it was the other way round. Whatever the reason, Martin was the only one of us whom Mr. Plover ever invited to visit him alone. What they discussed in their private lunches and teas Martin never told me, but as far as I can tell those occasions didn't give him any special pleasure. He often returned from them in a brown study, and sometimes he made excuses to avoid them altogether.

Now of course, as a grown man with some knowledge of the world, I cannot help but wonder whether Plover's interest in my brother was entirely appropriate. Such speculation is inevitable, but as both parties are dead, or as good as, I suppose we should be charitable, and assume that Plover merely took a fatherly interest in this bright, sensitive, fatherless boy. A mentor's interest.

And yet. Martin and I only ever spoke about it once, and the memory is not a pleasant one. I asked him what they talked about, the two of them, on his visits, and he snapped at me. "If Plover ever asks you to come by yourself, don't go. Never go to that house alone." He made me promise, and I did. Though Plover never did ask.

At the time I thought it was his pride—I thought he was jealously protecting his status as the favorite. But now I think it is possible that he was trying to warn me, even protect me. I wish I knew. I haven't seen my brother in twenty-five years. But I sometimes think, when I am brooding on the past, that that must have been part of Martin's need for Fillory, his addiction to it. He went there to escape from our saintly benefactor Christopher Plover, and to find better, wiser, or at least safer mentors in the form of the rams.

And if that is the case I cannot help but wonder too if, in a terrible irony, that was precisely why the rams stopped bringing

Martin to Fillory. Martin was fleeing from Plover, but Fillory didn't want him anymore. Because Plover had sullied him.

At the time these worries and doubts didn't trouble me, or not much. Not enough. In the years since then the shadows have grown deep and long, but at the time the sun of Fillory was at its zenith, and I was a child, and any shadows were barely visible.

That summer the topic of Martin's mysterious exile was much whispered about in the relative privacy of our large, crumbling bedrooms at Dockery, especially when he wasn't there. What was the cause? And what could be done about it?

We'd all tried to raise the matter with the rams, but with no success. "This is not his time," They would say. "When he comes, he will come." And so forth. There was a great deal of that kind of talk, and what a lot of trash it all was.

Pious Helen thought it was a shame, but it was the rams' will, and we had no business questioning Their wisdom. Jane sided with Helen, something I believe she came to regret when she was older. Fiona didn't like to take sides against Ember and Umber, but she thought that if we formally petitioned Them, as a group, They might agree to bring Martin back, or at least tell us what his offense had been and give him a chance to atone for it. We had all done a great deal of service for the rams, fought on Their behalf, risked our lives for Them. They owed us that much.

To Martin we made a great show of sympathetic concern, and we were sympathetic, and we were concerned, but some of the concern was for ourselves, too. Martin was getting older. He was on the cusp of puberty, which was something we knew very little about, but we knew that adulthood followed hard on its heels, and we had never heard of any adults making the journey from our world to Fillory. We understood instinctively that Fillory was a world that ran on innocence, demanded it as an engine demands fuel, and Martin was running out.

Sooner or later we would all run out. Adulthood would come for Helen next, and then me. Like all children we were selfish little creatures. I hope that this will in some way explain, if not excuse, what we did next.

Martin did what he did, but we helped him. We wanted him to do it, because we were afraid. We made a pact: the next time any of us were summoned, we would do what we could to hold the doorway open, and we would try to get Martin through. We would jam the door, take control of the bridge that connected Earth and Fillory, and force Martin across it. Probably it wouldn't work, but who could say till we tried? It was counter to the spirit of the enchantment, but you could never tell with enchantments. Sometimes the spirit was what mattered. But sometimes they were just letters on a page, words in the air, and it was only a question, as Humpty Dumpty said, of which is to be master.

CHAPTER 18

This is a story we never told to Christopher Plover.

Some days you could feel a portal coming on. To everyone else the day might be sunny and clear, but to us five the air would feel clammy and charged the way it does before a storm. You could sense the world building up to something, screwing itself to the sticking point. Then we would look at each other conspiratorially and pull our ears—that was the agreed-upon sign—and from that point on we'd be no good for anything else. The madness was on us, and we would fidget feverishly, unable to sit still or read or follow our lessons. Nothing else mattered until someone vanished and the tension finally broke.

On other days Fillory would wrong-foot everyone. You wouldn't see it coming at all. You might not even be in the mood for it, but suddenly there it would be, and all you could do was give in to its spell as it tore you free of this world.

It was one of those days, the second kind, when it happened: a lazy Saturday when the summer sun seemed to be leaching all the energy from the world, leaving us listless and immobile. We couldn't play, we couldn't study, we couldn't stop yawning. Even the effort of going outside to visit the giant, bug-eyed goldfish in the stone-rimmed pond in back of the house would have been unimaginable.

Fiona and I were in the library, which was a pleasant room, two stories high, with two movable ladders which when rolled into each other at a high rate of speed produced a very satisfying bang. But as a library it was largely useless. The books were locked away in cabinets—you could see their spines through metal grills, like a forbidden city hidden in the jungle, but you couldn't get at them. As far as I knew no one could: the keys were lost.

There was exactly one book in the library that you could read— somehow it had escaped being incarcerated with the rest of them. It was a catalog of seashells, a huge volume I could barely lift, and its spine cracked like a pistol shot when you opened it. The photographs were black-and-white, but about one in fifty pages had been hand-tinted in full color, and those shells had a special vivid feel to them. A Fillorian feel.

That morning Fiona and I were leafing through it. The pages were thick and sticky in the heat; they were made of a special glossy paper that was almost rubbery, like the leaves of some huge tropical plant. As usual we debated the aesthetic merits of the various shells, and the possible poisonous properties of their various residents, un-til suddenly Fiona stopped. She'd slipped her hand under the next page, hoping it would be a colored one, but her fingers found only empty air. It was as though the book had suddenly become hollow.

She looked at me and pulled her ear. The page turned all by itself, flipped over by a gust of wind from beneath it. From Fillory.

The portal was set directly into the book's enormous page. Ap-propriately enough it opened onto the seaside—I recognized it right away as the coast north of Whitespire, where there was a long, graceful bridge of living rock that led to a nearby island. We were looking straight down onto the powdery white sand from above, and the urge to clamber through immediately was almost overpow-ering. As I watched Fiona actually did—forgetting Martin, forget-ting our pact, she stepped up onto her chair and onto the table and dropped through the page as neatly as if she were jumping off a high bank into a pond.

I didn't. With a titanic effort I pulled myself away, feeling like I was leaving skin behind, and ran to find my brother.

He was by himself in an empty spare room. He was supposed to be working on a sketch of a vase for a drawing class, but when I came in he was just watching listlessly as the wind pushed a blind in and then sucked it out again. He stood up as soon as I entered. No words were necessary. He knew why I'd come.

I was sure the portal would be closed, but when we came pelting into the library together it was still there, waiting for us, or at any rate waiting for me. From a distance the view of the beach through the open book was a perspectival impossibility, a trompe l'oeil. It did strange things to my depth perception.

When Martin approached it the book shifted on the table and tried to shut itself—it seemed affronted, as if we'd surprised it in a state of undress. But Martin was ready for that. He pointed at it with three fingers and shouted a phrase I didn't understand—it might have been dwarfish, it had those scraping fricatives dwarfs use. Until then I hadn't understood that he'd been studying magic. Perhaps he hadn't just been sulking there in the library at White-spire after all.

The book trembled, straining now to shut itself. Martin and the book, Martin and Fillory itself, were fighting, and it was an awful sight, because I loved them both.

Martin gripped it in both hands and pulled, grunting, trying to rip it in half—I suppose he thought that then it couldn't close at all. But it was too thick, and the binding was too strong, so instead he forced its jaws back open like a man wrestling an alligator and pinned it down. He climbed up on the table and slowly, awkwardly, he got his feet and then his legs and hips through the door in the page.

As he did it the book began to groan horribly, as if the wrongness of it, the violation, hurt it physically. When he was all the way through I thought it would snap closed but instead it fell back open again, limp and unhappy at having been force-fed a meal it didn't want.

Ashamed, I climbed through quickly and dropped onto the beach. Looking back I saw Jane appear in the doorway of the library, and our eyes met across the gap between worlds, but it was too late for her. The book had had enough Chatwins for one day, and it closed over my head. The portal vanished.

The tide was out and the wind was slack. The sea was flat as a made bed. It looked about eleven in the morning.

Martin was halfway up the dunes already. He had had plenty of time to think through what he would do in Fillory, if he ever got the chance. He was here on borrowed time, and he wasn't going to waste it.

"Hey!" I called after him. "Wait for us!"

Fiona was watching him too, but she wasn't following. The joke had gone far enough for her.

"He's not going to Whitespire," she said quietly.

"He's not? Martin!" I shouted. "What are you doing?"

"I think you should go with him," Fiona said. "Someone should."

Martin had paused at the crest and was considering us.

"Well, come on then," he said, "if you're coming."

I did. Fiona stayed where she was.

Nothing happened the way Plover said it did later. All that business with Sir Hotspots in The Flying Forest *is his invention—pure fiction. In reality it was just me and Martin. I was the only witness.*

Martin's gait was a stolid, purposeful tramp, and I had to skip every few strides to keep up with him.

"Where are we going?"

"I'm not going back," he said.

"What?"

"I'm not going back to England, Rupes. I hate it, I hate England, and everybody there hates me. You know that. And if I go home I'll never get back here again, we both know it. You saw the

book, it almost had my legs off. If the rams want me out They'll have to throw me out, and when They try by God They'll have a fight on Their hands."

There was no point in arguing with him. There was a bit of our father in Martin, and just then he sounded like Father cursing the Germans, something he used to do often and at great length.

"What are you going to do?"

"Anything," he said. "Everything. Whatever I have to."

"But what?"

"There's something I want to try. I had an idea about a trade."

"A trade. With who? What have you got to trade?"

"I've got me!" he snarled. "For what that's worth." And then, less angrily, in the voice of Martin the little boy, who would exist for only an hour or so longer: "Will you come with me?"

"All right. Where are we going?"

"We're going to see someone. Who knows, might be you could do a trade with him too."

He looked over his shoulder, to make sure Fiona hadn't followed us, then he quickly sketched a square in the air with his fingers. The shape became a window, looking out over a marshy landscape, and he stepped over the sill and through it. The casual speed with which he did this shocked me deeply. We'd seen magic practiced by Fillorian sorcerers, but none of us had studied it, or not as far as I knew. Martin must have been practicing secretly for months, leading an entire life that he concealed from us. A secret life within a secret life.

I followed him through.

"Where are we?"

"Northern Marsh," he said. "Come on."

The ground here was boggy, but Martin picked his way through it with confidence, ever the intrepid explorer. I tried to step where he stepped, but I lost my balance and put a hand down, and it came up covered with black muck. Soon our shoes were full of water, and the marsh was sucking at them as if it liked the taste. I wasn't dressed for this; I was lucky I'd had shoes on at all.

After a quarter-hour of this I climbed up on a round rock, an oasis of solidity, and stopped. Ahead was just black puddles and reeds and more black puddles and then open water.

"Mart! Stop!"

He turned and waved at me. Then he took a last look around at the horizon, pressed his hands together in front of him, prayerfully, and dived headfirst down into a puddle.

The water barely looked deep enough to reach his ankles, but it swallowed him as completely and easily as if it were an ocean. I watched the surface settle and reseal itself behind him and turn glassy again.

Only then did I become truly afraid.

"Mart! Martin!"

I left my shoes on the rock—for all I know they're still there—and thrashed ahead to where he'd disappeared and shoved my arm into the puddle up to the shoulder. It had no bottom. I took a deep breath and put my head under.

My inner ear spun. I tried to steady myself and instead fell forward. There was a moment of nausea and weightless confusion, then I was lying on my back on wet ground gasping like a fish. Gradually everything began to right itself.

I was lying on the underside of the swamp—the reverse side of the muddy plain I'd just been tramping through. Gravity had turned upside-down. If I looked down I was looking up through the puddles at the blue sky of Fillory. If I looked up there was only darkness overhead. It was nighttime in the world under the Northern Marsh, and before me, across a flat plain of black mud and sun-filled puddles, was a fairy castle made of black stone. Its towers pointed down instead of up, but so did everything, including me.

This was new. Martin had taken us somewhere truly strange. Fillory was a land of wonders, but this place had an uncanny quality that I can only describe as not correct. *It was a place that shouldn't have been, somewhere off the edge of the board, where you weren't meant to put a playing piece down. This wasn't an ordinary adventure, another legend in the making. I knew already that Plover would never hear about it. This was happening off the books.*

I could have turned back, but I knew that if I did I would never have a brother again. I also knew that what was happening to him would happen to me too. I would have two more years, three at the most. I didn't want the game to be over yet. I'll follow behind Martin at a safe distance, I thought, and watch what he does. Maybe he's found a way out of the maze.

I stood up, fighting vertigo. Martin was waiting for me in front of the great door to the castle. He was sopping wet and smiling, though a little sadly I thought. I picked my way toward him, avoiding the puddles.

"This is it," he said. "Just like they said in the books, but it's different when you really see it."

"Like who said? Martin, what is this?"

"What does it look like?" he said grandly. "Welcome to Castle Blackspire."

"Blackspire."

Of course it was. It was just the same as Whitespire, stone for stone, but the stones were black, and the windows were empty and dark. It was Whitespire upside-down and backward and in the middle of the night, the way it must look when we were all asleep and dreaming. Martin pulled his sopping sweater off over his head and dropped it with a smack on the smooth stone.

"But who lives here?"

"I'm not sure. At first I thought it might be backward versions of us. You know—Nitram, Trepur, that sort of thing. What's Fiona backward? I can't do it in my head. And we'd have to fight our opposite numbers to the death. But I'm starting to think it's not like that at all."

"Well and thank God for that. What is it like?"

"I don't know," he said. "Let's find out!"

He heaved on one of the big doors and it opened silently on oiled hinges. The great hall inside was lit by torchlight. Pale silent footmen in black livery stood against the walls.

"Right." Martin seemed not at all disconcerted. I think he was
past fear by then. He raised his voice—he was full of a kind of
hopeless bravado. "Is your master at home?"

The footmen inclined their heads, silent as chess pieces.

"Good. Tell him the High King has arrived, and his brother.
We'll wait for him in his throne room. And light some damn fires,
it's cold in here."

Two of them withdrew, backward, showing proper deference.
Or maybe everybody walked backward at Castle Blackspire.

We were far off the track here, off the script and improvising.
Everything we'd done till now in Fillory was like a game, dress-up,
good fun and then laughing all the way back to the nursery. But
Martin was entering into a darker kind of play. This was a double
game: he was trying to save his childhood, to preserve it and trap it
in amber, but to do that he was calling on things that partook of
the world beyond childhood, whose touch would leave him even less
innocent than he already was. What would that make him? Neither a child nor an adult, neither innocent nor wise. Perhaps that
is what a monster is.

I didn't want to follow him. I wanted to stay behind and be a
child for a little while longer. But I couldn't stand to lose him
either.

He led me deeper into the castle—we both knew the way. I
dragged my feet, but he strode along like he was on his way to his
own birthday party. He was going to make an end of it, one way or
another, and he couldn't wait. He was so relieved he was practically
glowing.

"I don't like this, Mart. I want to go back."

"Go then," he said. "But there's no going back for me. This is my
last stand. I'm breaking the rules, Rupe. Either I'll break them or
they'll break me. I don't care anymore, not since Ember and Umber
decided to punish me for nothing at all."

"What rules?" I was on the point of tears. "I don't understand!"

He steered us into a dressing room off to one side of the throne
room, a chamber where up in Castle Whitespire, up in the world

of light and air, foreign dignitaries visiting Fillory would await our pleasure. There was a fire here, and I was grateful for the warmth. There were dry clothes too, in Blackspire colors, and Martin began stripping off. I kept my wet clothes on.

"I'll tell you how I came to it," he said. "I was thinking, isn't it funny that we get to be kings and queens here? We're children. We're not even from here. There's nothing special about us, not that I can see. But we must have something special, mustn't we? Something you can't get in Fillory?"

"I suppose."

Fully naked, unembarrassed, he warmed his bare pale skin in front of the fire. He was happier than I'd seen him in months.

"What is it? I'm damned if I know. My humanity, I suppose. But whatever it is, it means nothing to me, so I'm going to see how much it's worth to them. I've put it up for sale, on the open market, and now I've found a taker. We're here to see how much I can get for it."

"I don't understand. You're going to buy your way back into Fillory?"

"Oh, I'm not doing it like that. I'm not asking for favors. What I want is power, enough power that even Ember and Umber won't be able to send me home."

"But Ember and Umber are gods."

"Then maybe I'll be a bit of a god too."

"But what if—?" I swallowed, simple child that I was. "If you sell part of yourself, what if you aren't Martin anymore?"

"What if I'm not?" he said. "What good is Martin? Everybody hates him, me included. I'd rather be somebody else. Anybody else. Even if it's nobody."

He picked up a dry shirt from a neat stack of clothes on a chair.

"I suppose I'm like one of those guests at Maude's parties, the ones who won't go home when it's over, not even after she turns the lights on. But I've got no other home to go to, not anymore. When I look at England now I see a dead place, Rupert. A wasteland. I won't live in a wasteland. I'd rather die in paradise."

The clothes looked rich, and they fit him perfectly, as I knew they would: cool, shadowy colors, black velvets and small silvery pearls like the little sugar balls they use to decorate cakes. He looked very much like a king.

"Mart, come on," I said, even though I knew from experience that begging only made him angrier. "Leave it alone. Let it be how it was."

"Don't!"

He jabbed a finger at me. I felt more than two years younger than him then—somewhere he'd learned the secret of a richer, more powerful adult rage.

"It isn't how it was! It never will be again! They changed the rules on us, so as far as I'm concerned all bets are off." He cinched his belt tight. "If They apologized, if They showed any regret, then maybe. Maybe. If They would even say why.

"But They wouldn't. Not Them. So I'm off to war, like Daddy. They can't give us Fillory and then just take it away again. The rams have sunk low, but I'll sink lower. They're bad, I'll be worse."

He flung open both doors to the throne room.

"Mart, who lives here?" I asked. "Whose house is this?"

He went in; I hung back in the doorway. The walls of the throne room were lined with more footmen, still and heavy-lidded as frogs. The torches burned strangely, not warm and yellow but sparking and spitting like holiday fireworks.

"Here I am!" Martin shouted.

I couldn't see his face, but I could hear the joy in his voice—he was relishing the rage and shame. I think he'd been keeping them down for a long time, trying to feel nothing at all, and after so much numbness anything felt sweet, even pain.

"Well, come on!" He spread his arms wide. "I've got what you want. Come on and take it!"

I think I knew then why They did it—why Ember and Umber wouldn't let us stay in Fillory. It wasn't that we were too old, or too sinful. It wasn't so that we could spread Their wisdom in another world, our world. It wasn't that being in Fillory made you happy, and in its way too much happiness was as dangerous as too much sadness. That is a lie that even Ember and Umber never told.

No, it was that Fillory was cruel, as cruel in its way as the real world was. There was no difference, though we all pretended there was. There was nothing fair about Fillory, just as there was nothing fair about people's fathers going to war, and their mothers going mad, and the way we among all animals were cursed with a longing for somewhere better, somewhere that never existed and never would. Fillory was no better than our world. It was just prettier.

I didn't think those things, not then, but I felt them all when I looked past Martin into the golden barbell eyes of the great ram Umber, the Shadow Ram. Castle Blackspire was His house. Umber was Martin's buyer.

Give him credit, Martin took this in stride.

"Oh, it's You, is it?" he said. "Well, come on, you old faker. It's all here, and only slightly soiled. Are you ready?"

"Yes," came the resonant reply. Not like Ember's voice: higher, and calm and civilized, even urbane. "I am ready."

"So go ahead. Take it. Take it all, you bloody coward, and give me what I want!"

I gave up then. I could have tried one last time to change Martin's mind. I could have tried to drag him out of that room. I could have tried to take his place, or to fight a god, but I didn't. I was afraid, and I fled. I ran through the empty halls of the night palace and didn't stop till I was lying on my face in the cold mud on the edge of the Northern Marsh. I never saw my brother again.

Martin's disappearance made headlines all over England, pushing even news of the war below the fold. The English love a good tragedy, especially when it involves a child, and this one was a nine-days' wonder. Detectives were dispatched to Fowey from Penzance and London and farther away. Dockery House was turned upside down, from attic to basement, and Plover's house was too. Notices were circulated. Dogs were loosed. Gardens were dug up. Ponds

*and fountains were dragged. Men with slight builds were lowered
into abandoned wells.*

*An amazing number of lost things were recovered: bicycles, pets,
keys, odd items of silver, one or two petty criminals, in one case a
rogue bassoon which had been stolen and then apparently abandoned in a ha-ha when it proved impossible to sell. The bassoonist
having by that time pined for it and then passed away, the instru-
ment was lodged temporarily and then eventually permanently by
the police at Dockery House, as if by way of an apology—a sort of
replacement for the child they never managed to find. Jane, in her
inscrutable way, learned to play it passably well.*

*A cloud of suspicion settled on Christopher Plover, but over time
it dispersed, as clouds will, pausing on its way to shadow a few of the
less savory locals in turn, but always inconclusively. Truth to tell
Plover was a little heartbroken when Martin disappeared. There
was no evidence, and no arrests were ever made. We children knew
where Martin had gone, of course, more or less, though I never told
the others everything I knew. I never told them it was Umber who'd
taken Martin's offer. I didn't have the heart to do it.*

*I think the adults knew we were keeping something to ourselves,
but they could never put their big, clumsy, groping fingers on what
it was. It was our shared secret.*

*But we didn't all feel the same way about what he'd done.
Helen in particular—always the arch-Ramsian—was scathing
about it, excoriating Martin for defying Ember and Umber's will,
as she saw it. But I believe that we all understood it and even, on
some level, admired it. I know that I did. It must have taken great
will and resourcefulness to seek out Umber, to strike the deal and
then to go through with it. He was many things, and God only
knows what he is now, but Martin was not stupid, and he wasn't
a coward.*

*Though it was difficult to reconcile Martin's escape into Fillory
with the damage it caused in the real world. One of the secrets
Martin must have learned down below the Northern Marsh was
how not to care about some things, and there was power in that,*

the power to live as though his actions had no consequences. It fell to us to witness the consequences, and they were ugly. Our mother's nerves were always fragile, and Martin's disappearance finally and permanently annihilated her. We saw her more and more rarely, and when we did, in one or other dispiriting institutional setting, she never failed to accuse us of keeping Martin from her. Her own children seemed sinister and alien to her. She knew, somehow, that we knew. And she was right.

But I never saw Martin again. I always looked for him, though as time passed I became more and more worried about what would happen if I found him. He could or would not show himself to me. I've never understood why not.

He certainly had the chance. There were more adventures left for us in Fillory, most of which ended up in A Secret Sea *and* The Wandering Dune. *I didn't turn them down. Even after what I'd seen that day, even with my heart half broken, I still could never say no to Fillory.*

And then Fillory said no to us. By the end of A Secret Sea *I was twelve, and after that I was never asked back. One by one we became too old. Helen had one final adventure, in the company of Jane, and the two girls returned bearing a box of magical buttons which Jane claimed could have given them free entry to Fillory forever. But Helen considered the buttons to be a perversion of magic, she thought using them would be a blasphemy against the rams, and she disposed of them immediately and could not be persuaded to divulge their hiding place. Her arguments were very Ramsian indeed, and everyone sided against her, even Jane. It was a schism, and after it we Chatwin children were never as close again, and our integrity as a tribe was diminished even further.*

Maybe the strangest consequence of Martin's disappearance was that Plover started writing. Whatever went on between him and Martin, when that ended, the writing began, and one day Plover surprised us with a book. He'd had it privately printed. He called it The World in the Walls. *The cover was his own charmingly amateurish drawing of Martin and the grandfather clock.*

It will sound strange, but after the initial surprise the book never interested us much. We took one cursory glance at it, made fun of the illustrations—Plover had the most ignorant, sentimental ideas of what a dwarf looked like—but we already knew everything in it. People like to call the Fillory books magical, but they never seemed that way to us. If you've seen magic, then the Fillory books are very pale imitations indeed. Plover's words were like dried flowers, stiff and crumbling, crushed flat between pages, when we'd had the living, blooming blossoms all around us.

Now all I can see is how simple he made everything sound. Reading the Fillory books you would think that all one has to do is behave honorably and bravely and all will be well. What a lesson to teach young children. What a way to prepare them for the rest of their lives.

We each of us on our own found ways to get on without Fillory. The real world was not as fantastical and brightly colored as Fillory, but it was very distracting nonetheless, and if it didn't contain any pegasi or giants it was absolutely teeming with girls who seemed almost as magical and dangerous. Fillory was sweet, but this world was very savory. It was easy to let Fillory go when every football match and scholarship examination and furtive kiss told you to stop fighting, forget it, let it be, leave it behind. We talked about Fillory less and less among ourselves, and we went to Plover's less and less, and the whole business began to seem less and less real.

By this time the books had begun to sell, too, and a miraculous rain of money began to fall upon us. We wouldn't have said it out loud, or even to ourselves, but it was as if we had sold Fillory itself—or rather we'd sold its realness, reduced it to the status of a children's fantasy, in exchange for regular and startlingly large payments into accounts which would come under our control when we were twenty-one. By the time I was seventeen and sitting an entrance examination for Merton College, Oxford, I'm not entirely sure I believed in Fillory at all anymore.

Jane did. She never stopped looking for the buttons that Helen hid, and when she disappeared at thirteen I believe that she found

*them. But she knew better than to try to take me with her, and
none of us tried to follow her. When she did not return, I could only
assume that she went down the same path that Martin did.*

*It has been years now since Helen or Fiona or I have mentioned
Fillory to each other, except as it pertains to our finances. We don't
talk about Martin or Jane—in their way they've come to seem as
fantastical to us as the Cozy Horse. Without those things we've got
very little to talk about at all, and I would pay any price not to have
to suffer any more of Helen's glittery-eyed, American-accented chatter about Jesus. It's as though we three are the survivors of a great
disaster—like the bombing of a city, the way London is being
bombed to pieces now—and to even mention what happened would
be to risk calling back the planes to blast us to pieces all over again.*

*I wouldn't even have written this much had it not been for the
events that have overtaken Britain and the world in the past three
years. They have driven me to extremes of desperation I would
never have thought possible. There is no telling now who will triumph in the present conflict, and there is every chance that the
Germans will overrun England itself before it is all over.*

*Perhaps help will come. Perhaps Martin is able to perceive events
in this world, from wherever he is, and he will come back; if he doesn't
care to I would think that at least Jane would. If they are unable to
intervene in the affairs of this world, perhaps Ember or Umber could.
That would be a welcome sight: my long-lost brother and sister and the
two Great Rams of Fillory, aflame with power, marching abreast on
Berlin to chivvy Hitler out of his bunker like a stoat.*

*But they haven't come. And I am beginning to think that they
are not going to come.*

*And that is why I am writing these words. This book is a mem-
oir, a secret history, but it is also an act of calculated provocation.
I am at present with the 7th Armoured Division in Tobruk, in
Libya, preparing for a battle tomorrow with Rommel and his Pan-
zers. I, Rupert Chatwin, a king of Fillory, who rode a griffin
against the armies of the Whispering King, who beat the Wight of*

the West in single combat and broke his back, will fight the Germans in an obsolete Crusader tank full of lice and the stink of me and my comrades-in-arms, that has already leaked oil across half of northern Africa.

If I survive I will send this home with instructions that it be published six months from now unless word arrives from me. The news that Fillory is real will be splashed across every paper in Britain— unless you agree to take me and my family back. Yes, I address you directly: Ember and Umber, Martin and Jane. If not me then save my wife and my child, your only nephew, that is all I ask. Surely it is within your power. Surely you can find it in your hearts.

But if that is still not enough, then I offer you goods in trade. I was not completely honest before: when I left Castle Blackspire that day I did not leave empty-handed. Blackspire is Whitespire's twin, and I knew where the treasure room was, and I knew how to open it. Even in my fear and grief, I was still selfish enough and spiteful enough to plunder it for whatever I could carry. I wasn't an adept like Martin, but even I could recognize power when I saw it. I took a blade, and a spell, and I believe they are very powerful indeed. They are of the old workings. The very strongest stuff.

You can come and try to take them from me, but I think you will not. Here: I offer them to you freely if you will do this thing.

For the love of God, Ember and Umber, Martin and Jane, or for the love of whatever it is that you hold sacred, if you are reading these words, take us back to Fillory. For all the ways I have betrayed you I beg your forgiveness. I will atone for my sins any way you like, if you will open the door again, one last time, for me and my family. I was once a king of Fillory, but I will return as your lowliest servant if you will only open the door. I am begging you now. When I turn this page I want you to open the door.

The book ended there.

Plum let it lie open on her lap. It felt like it weighed approximately one thousand pounds. She couldn't look at Quentin. She didn't want to share this moment with him. Maybe she would in a moment, but not yet.

They hadn't come. They hadn't saved him, and Rupert's stolen goods had stayed stolen, and he'd died there in the desert. Though his wife and child—Plum's grandfather—had survived anyway. The blade: that was what Betsy took. At first Plum wondered about the spell, but it was there too, cut up and bound into the notebook at the end, on lumpy parchment slightly smaller than the pages around it: a dozen leaves of close writing in a foreign script.

Then it all went blurry, because Plum's eyes were full of tears. She had denied it all her life, that any of it was real, but not anymore. Not after this, and not after what the girl in the mirror had shown her. It had really happened. It wasn't just a story, it was a true story. It had found her, drawn her into its pages, and now it was time for her to play her part in it. Fillory had chewed up her ancestors and spat them out. Now it was hungry again and coming for her, and she would have to find a way to face it.

She put her head in her hands and leaked some more tears, there in the lobby of the Amenia train station. After five minutes she got up and went to the snack bar for some napkins to blow her nose on.

"Quentin," she said when she got back. "I think Fillory was real." It was hard to force the words out. They didn't want to be said. "I know it sounds crazy, but I think he was telling the truth. I think it was all real."

Quentin only nodded. He didn't look surprised. If anything she suspected him of having dabbed away a tear or two when she wasn't looking.

"It is real, Plum," he said. "I've been there."

CHAPTER 19

The townhouse stood on a back street in the West Village, one of the oddly angled ones where the orderly grid of Manhattan starts to break down into chaos below Fourteenth Street. It didn't get much traffic, which was part of the point: it was a discreet address. Plum said she'd bought it with money from her grandparents, her share of the Fillory royalties that they'd put in trust, intending to use it as a crash pad during her glorious postgraduation future in New York. Now she and Quentin were crashing there a little early.

From the outside it looked dark and deserted, and they were careful to maintain that appearance. A lot of people wanted that suitcase, and Quentin didn't know who they would come after first, him and Plum or Asmodeus, but they would be coming sooner or later, and probably they would hit the softer target first, and that was not Asmodeus. For now they would lose themselves in the big city.

Nobody had touched the house since the previous owner moved out. There wasn't even any furniture, so they sat on the dusty wooden floor in the front room. They were running on empty, worn out from the disaster of the robbery, and then worn out all over again in a different way by reading Rupert's journal, but Quentin forced himself to set up a thin perimeter of magical defense before they slept. Nothing fancy, standard magical tradecraft, and the bare minimum of it, but it was enough to take the house off the grid and make it opaque to anybody who was poking around, though not so opaque as to be suspicious.

He didn't bother with the upper floors. They'd just stay out of them for now.

Then they collapsed on the floor of the living room, still in their coats and hats. They'd have to get some couches in here, or at least some sleeping bags. And some food. And some heat. But not yet. Quentin hadn't slept the night before, and he'd thrown his back out in the fall, and he was starting to be in some serious pain. It had happened to him a couple of times before. Up through around twenty-five he'd never even thought about his back: it was a balanced, frictionless, self-regulating system. Now it felt like a busted gearbox into which somebody had chucked a handful of sand.

Lying on the hard floor made it hurt less. Quentin thought about how wrong things had gone. Things so often went wrong. Was it him? Was he making the same mistake over and over again? Or different mistakes? He'd like to think he was at least making different mistakes.

Plum did fall asleep, right there on the floor, with her face smushed into her black parka from the limo for a pillow. But Quentin didn't, not yet.

The journal had affected them in different ways. For Plum it had been a reckoning, a massive correction, that finally forced her to see that Fillory was real and that in some inescapable way she was part of it. On the train he'd told her the whole story of his life there, from beginning to end, as bridges and stations and other trains flashed by in the window, and lots full of idle municipal snowplows, and backyards full of overturned play structures. He told her about everything, Alice and Julia and all the rest.

But for him it was different, and while Plum slept he sat up, leaning against the wall, and read the journal again. There was news in it: if Rupert was to be believed then Umber was the one who'd turned Martin into the Beast, in exchange for some obscure, grotesque sacrifice. That threw Quentin as much as anything else. There was something seriously wrong with one of Fillory's gods, or at least there had been. And if Umber did help Martin, why would Martin have killed him, as Jane Chatwin said he did? It made no sense.

None of it got him any closer to Alice either, or not that he could see.

They needed a new plan, a way forward, maybe even another job. They'd be ready next time—the bird had betrayed them, it hadn't played by the rules, but now Quentin got that there never had been any rules. But first they had to rest and build themselves back up. Quentin had to get his back working again. He also had some hard thinking to do.

Plum woke up at dawn, bursting with energy again—she was indefatigable that way. She always had to be doing something. Going outside seemed like a bad idea, with the whereabouts and intentions of the bird still unknown, so they stayed in. They ordered in a lot of take-out food and some cheap insta-furniture, and Plum set about fixing up her house.

Somebody had disco-ized it in the 1970s, and then later it had been de-disco-ized, mostly, but there were still trace amounts of avocado carpeting, and the outlines of mirrored tiles that had been glued to the walls. A space-age chandelier that looked like Sputnik had escaped the purge too. But the house had good bones, and it still had its broad-planked wooden floors, and its elegant many-paned, energy-inefficient wooden-framed windows with nice old shutters. There were a lot of nice twiddly plaster ornaments around the ceiling. It had some integrity, this house.

Plum knew more about this kind of magic than Quentin did, and Quentin was hobbled by his bad back, so he acted as semiskilled magical laborer-consultant to her hypercompetent general contractor. Under her direction they arrested the slow collapse of the back wall, which was being undermined by rainwater because the drainpipe was busted and the drain in the back patio was clogged. No one had updated the electrics and plumbing since approximately the 1930s, and the walls were stuffed full of ancient cloth-wrapped wiring and lead pipes that were right on the point of dissolving. They shored everything up as best they could. It felt good to be doing something simple and concrete and achievable.

They cast all the cleaning spells they could think of, until they'd removed enough dust and dirt and scum and nicotine residue from the walls and floors and sinks and tubs to make a whole other house out of. They got the furnace going, and the gas and water. But while Quentin was working with his hands his mind was working on other things. All his enterprises were in ruins. He should have been thrashed by this,

flattened, but instead . . . with all of that gone, and his father dead, and
Mayakovsky's coins in his pocket, he felt strangely free. It was time to
take stock.

At some point somebody had gone through the top floor of the house
and demolished all its interior walls, leaving behind only four lonely
load-bearing columns of brick with bits of plaster still clinging to them,
thus making a single long chamber, front to back. Plum continued to
roam the house wearing overalls and work gloves, attacking and repairing targets of opportunity; she didn't want his help, and moreover his
back was still killing him. So he went up there to clear his mind.

Using a chunk of kids' street chalk recovered from a locker under the
stairs Quentin traced out a classical labyrinth pattern on the floor. He
did it from memory, based on the ancient Greek Lemnian pattern, and
it took him quite a few tries to make the geometry of it work out, but
that itself was a solid meditative exercise. The path wound and coiled
around the four pillars. Labyrinths were old sorcery, and subtle: good
for recharging one's magical resources when they were running low.

When it was done he hung sheets over the windows, which looked
cheap and tatty but produced a dim, diffuse, immaterial light. He
started at the beginning and slowly limped through it, again and again.
The walking freed his thoughts; it also made his back feel a bit better.

His mind wandered back to Rupert's journal, and on the spell bound
into the back of it. Rupert had never cast it, as far as Quentin could tell,
nor had he been able to figure out what it did. Now Quentin wondered.
It was a treasure pillaged from the black underbelly of Fillory. It had to
be something valuable.

And there was something fateful in the way it had come to them.
What had Rupert called it? One of the old workings? Maybe it was war
magic, something that could help them if the bird came after them.
Maybe it was something deep and strange and strong enough that it
could help Alice.

He went and got the spell and read through it as he walked. Before
long he could walk the maze without even looking up from it. His work
on the page from the Neitherlands wasn't going to go to waste, that was
for sure, at least in terms of having sharpened his ability to construe

gnarly magical rhetoric in languages that he had a very dim grasp of. It had been a long time since he tried to read archaic Fillorian, let alone its associated notations for magical gestures.

The further into it he got the less it looked like what he'd expected. He was anticipating something military: either a very powerful shield or a very deadly weapon or both. Maybe concealment, maybe some kind of cataclysmic weather effect. But it didn't feel like any of those. It wasn't shaped right somehow.

For one thing the spell was long as hell—you could transcribe most spells in a couple of pages, max, because there just wasn't that much to them, but this one went on and on for a good twenty. There was a lot of formal business toward the front end of the casting that looked purely ceremonial, but you never knew for sure what you could leave out, so you had to do it all.

What's more it required a lot of materials, including some pretty exotic items. All in all it was a bear, and it would have cost somebody a lot of time and effort and money to cast it. It was worse than the bond-breaking spell (which they'd never even got to cast at all, dammit).

Still, there was something elegant about it too. It was a mess, a rat's nest, but under all the fiddly bits and the ornamentation there was a structure, a complex one. Later stages of the enchantment looped in elements of earlier ones, piling effect on effect, each one multiplying the next—in its way it was a thing of real beauty. For a while he wondered if it might be a summoning, along the lines of the one Fogg used to harvest his cacodemons, or the spell that Julia and her friends had attempted at Murs with such disastrous results.

But he didn't think so. This wasn't like any magic he'd ever seen before. Something about the spell made his fingers twitch—it was as if it wanted to be cast. He left the labyrinth and took it to Plum.

"I've been reading through that spell," he said. "The one your great-grandfather left you."

"Uh-huh."

Plum was down in the basement, standing on a ladder and doing something involved to the joists, Quentin couldn't tell exactly what.

"It's interesting," he said.

"I would imagine."

"I've really never seen anything like it."

"Uh-huh."

She put her palm on one massive beam and pressed, and it cracked and groaned, and the whole house seemed to shift slightly. Plum studied the results.

"Structural stuff," she explained.

"So you don't mind if I check it out a little further?"

"I give you my blessing."

"Don't you want to look at it yourself?"

She shook her head without looking at him. She was completely absorbed.

"From what I saw I couldn't read the script. Can you?"

"More or less."

"Well, keep me apprised."

"I will."

Starting small, he began to make preparations. The spell would require the magical equivalent of a clean room at a semiconductor factory, so Quentin cleansed and warded the top floor in any and all ways he could think of. He shocked the walls and timbers and joists and whatever else so hard the dust jumped out of the cracks, and then he shocked the dust.

Reluctantly, he took a wet cloth to his chalk labyrinth, but it had served its purpose. He floated a couple of big worktables up the stairs, bumping them against the walls of the stairwells and taking a few divots out of the plaster on the way, which Plum frowned at. He had to take them apart on the landing because he'd misestimated the size and they wouldn't go through the door.

When you got down to brass tacks the spell wasn't really one spell, it was more like fifteen or twenty different spells meshed together, to be executed in an overlapping sequence and in some cases simultaneously. Some of them could be cast in advance, some the day before, but most, the really big stuff, had to be done on the fly, in the moment. He had trouble holding it all in his head at one time. But what was it Stoppard said? Give a nerd a door he can close.

It was a detour from his search for Alice, but they were effectively under house arrest anyway, and something hunchy and instinctive kept egging him on. He made cautious forays out into the city for supplies, creeping along under domes of magical camouflage. The walls of the top-floor workshop began filling up with old books—reference books, botanicals, atlases, huge black split-spined grimoires, the leather all *craquelured* like desert hardpan, in tall wobbly stacks that swayed worryingly if you brushed against them. The tables began to be populated by a weird menagerie of steel tools and brass instruments and odd, asymmetrical glass containers.

Even as he ground away at the technicalities, some of the larger functionality of the enchantment was becoming clearer to him, its outlines picked out in a thousand trivial practical details. A lot of it seemed to have to do with space. There were spells in here designed to make it: literally to fabricate room, to weave together new space-time out of whole cloth. Here was a spell that expanded the space, blew it up like a balloon. This one shaped it. That other one stabilized the borders and made sure it didn't collapse again into the nothingness whence it came.

But after that it got really arcane and hard to follow. There were spells to summon matter into being. This part sucked entropy out of the system, forcing the matter to organize; these pushed it through a series of very obscure transforms, some of which appeared to do nothing at all, or cancel out earlier ones. There was a lot of fiddly magical-matter stuff that would have mystified him if it didn't overlap in places with the page from the Neitherlands. There was a whole laundry list of botanical spells, weather and water and wind magic, spells for shaping living rock. There was some really head-cracking bits that looked like attempts to reset the basic physical parameters of the universe: elementary charge, speed of light, gravitational constant. For all its elegant complexity the spell had a primitive, primordial feel to it. It was an old working, and a weird one, a relic of another age of another world. It felt like it hadn't been cast in a thousand years.

One thing was clear: this was grand magic. It was sorcery on a scale he'd never attempted before, and it was going to test him severely. Until now he'd been a journeyman magician, and a competent one, but if he could execute it this spell would make him into a master. It would force him to become one. It would accept nothing less.

Early one morning a dawn thunderstorm woke him up, and as he was lying there wondering if he was going to be able to get back to sleep an image of the whole thing appeared in his mind all at once. It assembled itself spontaneously, unbidden, as if it had been waiting for him to just get out of its way and let it form. There it was, dim and shimmering but complete, with all its parts working together.

It wasn't war magic. The spell didn't shield you, and it didn't hide you. It didn't kill, and it didn't summon something to kill for you. It wasn't going to restore Alice either. But it did do something wonderful. This was a spell that created something. It was a spell for making a land.

He actually laughed out loud when he thought of it. It was too funny—too insane. But now that he saw it he couldn't un-see it. He could follow it like a story that wound crookedly through the various sections and paragraphs and subclauses of the spell like a thread of DNA. This thing was intended to make a little world.

It was ruthlessly ingenious. It wasn't a cosmic act of creation, a thunderbolt from Olympus, it was much more subtle than that. It was more like a seed, the dry, tear-shaped germ of a little world—tiny, the kind of thing that could fall through a crack in a sidewalk, but full of sand and rain and stars and physics and life, all flattened and dried and compressed into words on a page. If you cast it right it would expand and unfold into a place, somewhere hidden away from the real world. A secret garden.

Quentin could already see it in his mind's eye, fresh and new and still undiscovered. Green fields of matted grass, deep silent lakes, the shadows of clouds, all spread out beneath him like an Escher etching, the way the Earth looked when he was a goose. Birds flitted between bushes, deer stalked stiff-legged through the woods. You wouldn't own it, or rule it, but you could take care of it. You could have stewardship of it.

Lying there in bed in the half-light, rain spattering on the window, he forgot all about the bird and the Couple and the money. All that seemed beside the point now. He forgot about Brakebills. He even let himself forget Alice for a minute. This was new magic: half enchantment, half work of art. He'd spent too long searching for new kingdoms. He wanted to make one of his own, a magical place, a place like Fillory.

But not in Fillory. He would build it here on Earth.

"I don't want to make you sound like a crazy person," Plum said, "but just then it sounded like you said you were going make a land."

"I am. Or we are. We could. That's what it does, Rupert's spell."

Plum frowned.

"I don't get it," she said. "You can't just *make* a *land*."

"It helps if you don't say it like that."

"You mean with rocks and trees and stuff?"

"That's exactly what I mean."

"Wow." She stretched, then plunked her chin in her hands. They were having breakfast at their brand new Ikea dining table. "Wow. Well, that would be a hell of a spell. Great granddad wasn't much of a writer, but you gotta admit he was a pretty good thief. Do you think it's actually possible?"

"I think we should find out."

"But I don't get it. Why? I mean it's cool and all, but it sounds like a gigantic pain in the ass."

It was hard to put into words. The land would be a good place to hide from the bird, if they needed to hide, but that wasn't the point. This meant something to him. It would be like Prospero's island, but in a good way: not a country of exile, a model world, safe and peaceful and private. A magician's land.

Plum, a highly perceptive person, could see that he wasn't going to change his mind. She sighed.

"So if we do make a land, what does that make us? Are we like the gods of it?"

"I don't think so," Quentin said. "I don't think this land would have any gods. Or maybe it would. But we'd have to make those too."

With Plum on board, or at least not actively resisting, things progressed more quickly. Quentin made contact with a very dodgy and unappealing wizard in the South Bronx who sold him a steaming, lightly buzzing metal box which he swore up and down contained a sample of ununoctium, a synthetic element with an atomic number of 118, the very last entry on the periodic table. Its existence was still mostly theoretical—laboratories had only ever put together a few atoms of it at a time, and ordinarily it decayed in about a millisecond. But the atoms in this sample were chronologically frozen, or at least vastly slowed down. Or at least they were supposed to be. It had cost him a good chunk of the money left over from his first-day payment from the bird.

"Do you think it's really in there?" Plum studied the box skeptically.

"I don't know," Quentin said. "We'll find out."

"How?"

"The hard way, I guess."

Quentin had a very expensive, very cool-looking staff purpose-built for the project. It was made of pernambuco—the dense, black, almost grainless tropical wood cello bows are made of—and shod and chased with silver. Quentin didn't normally work magic with wands and staves, but in this case he thought he might need it as a last resort, a panic button, if things were coming completely apart.

He had to hide it all, to avoid attracting the bird's attention, but it went beyond that: Quentin was pretty sure the spell would be highly illegal from the point of view of magical society. There weren't very many laws among magicians, but synthesizing an entire land and concealing it inside a Manhattan townhouse would violate a goodly portion of them, so as far as magical energy was concerned the house had to be watertight. The power levels required would be massive too, and he could only be grateful they hadn't used up Mayakovsky's coins on the incorporate bond. He'd have to use one now. It wasn't what he'd made them for, but Quentin thought Mayakovsky would like the idea anyway.

Quentin dug seven long lines of Fillorian script into the hardwood floor of the workshop with a gouge and a mallet. He went at the ceiling too, embedding long curls of platinum wire in the plaster. In places he stripped the walls and nailed more wire along the bare studs. The only piece of the puzzle that was completely missing in action was that damned plant, the one from the Neitherlands page. Incredibly it had turned up in Rupert's spell as well. Quentin wasn't sure it was absolutely crucial, but either way he still couldn't identify it, so they'd just have to scrape by without it.

One night, after they'd both worked themselves into a state of exhaustion, he and Plum were lying limply on couches in the ex-disco room like they'd been flung there in the aftermath of an explosion. They were too tired to go to bed.

"So how big is this land of yours even supposed to be?" Plum said.

"I don't know yet. Not giant, I don't think. Ten acres maybe. Like the Hundred Acre Wood in *Winnie-the-Pooh*."

"Except with ten."

"Yeah. I'm trying to specify it in a couple of places," Quentin said, "but it's hard to know exactly what goes where."

"But it won't take up any space in the real world."

"I hope not."

"Quentin, why are you doing this?"

He recognized the importance of the question. He was going to fall asleep right there on the couch, he felt like he was melting into it. But he tried to answer it before that happened.

"What do you think magic is for?"

"I dunno. Don't answer a question with a question."

"I used to think about this a lot," Quentin said. "I mean, it's not obvious like it is in books. It's trickier. In books there's always somebody standing by ready to say *hey, the world's in danger, evil's on the rise, but if you're really quick and take this ring and put it in that volcano over there everything will be fine.*

"But in real life that guy never turns up. He's never there. He's busy handing out advice in the next universe over. In our world no one ever knows what to do, and everyone's just as clueless and full of crap as everyone else, and you have to figure it all out by yourself. And even after you've figured it out and done it, you'll never know whether you were right or wrong. You'll never know if you put the ring in the right volcano, or if things might have gone better if you hadn't. There's no answers in the back of the book."

Plum was silent so long that Quentin wondered if she'd dozed off while he was talking. But then she said:

"So—what? So you figured it out, and magic is for making lands?"

"No." Quentin closed his eyes. "I still have no idea what magic is for. Maybe you just have to decide for yourself. But you definitely have to decide. It's not for sitting on my ass, which I know because I've tried that. Am I making any sense?"

"You have not been making sense for some time."

"I was afraid of that. Well, it'll mean something when you're my age. You're what, twenty-two?"

"Twenty-one."

"OK, well, I'm thirty."

"That's not that old," Plum said.

"Don't patronize me."

"Fair enough. So what do you think the land is going to look like?"

"I don't know that either," Quentin said. "I try to picture it sometimes, but it's always different. Sometimes it's meadows. Sometimes it's an orchard, just rows and rows of apple trees. Maybe it looks like whatever you want it to."

"I hope it looks like the Hundred Acre Wood," Plum said. "I think you should concentrate on that."

CHAPTER 20

Plum needed a night off. It was early April in Manhattan, and winter break was almost over at Brakebills, but some of her former classmates were still in the city. Knowing they were so close she was overcome by a fit of longing for her old life. She decided to indulge it.

She wasn't even completely sure if she was still received in polite company, after her dramatic departure from Brakebills, so Plum was relieved when they turned up. The venue was a basement bar on Houston Street with a low ceiling and a lot of busted couches and a decent jukebox; it had survived untouched by the rage for elaborately perfect artisanal cocktails. Most of the old League was there, plus a few extras, including Wharton—their impending entry into the wider world seemed to have brought him and the Leaguers together, to the point where they were all more or less on the same side. Plum got the impression that the League had pretty much gone dormant in her absence anyway.

Well, time to put aside childish things, as the verse sayeth. At least they'd gone out on top.

They drank pints of IPA and attempted observational humor about the civilians or muggles or mundanes or whatever you wanted to call them all around them. They made bets about what people were feeling, and then Holly, who had a knack for it, did a mind-reading to see who was right. She couldn't get anything too specific, not words, or images, just the emotional tone, but that was usually enough. Bars were a good place for it. Alcohol had a way of making people's minds more transparent, like oil on paper.

Plum knew they were going to talk about Brakebills, and she knew that it was going to hurt. It was partly what she came for, the pain. She was going to test her new sense of herself as someone who was past all that now, who'd had a taste of life in the real world, even though it was turning out to be something of an acquired taste.

Fortunately the pain, when it came, came in bearable quantities of ache. Hearing news from the candlelit bubble-world of Brakebills helped her mourn for the comparatively simple, hopeful Plum who used to inhabit that world. Tonight would be a wake for that other Plum, the Plum who'd never tried that stupid prank. Rest in peace.

She interrogated them methodically for gossip. They were absolutely teeming with it: with graduation coming the Fifth Years were reverting to a state of nature. Everybody who'd been holding their breath for the past five years was letting it out. Even socially anxious, authority-respecting students had begun conducting risky experiments with sass. The candlelit bubble-world was on a collision course with the hard and rocky rogue planet of reality, and when they hit the bubble would pop.

And it was all happening without Plum. She felt like she'd been born too soon—she was a sickly, withered preemie next to a bunch of healthy pink full-term babies.

Most of them already had postgraduation plans. Darcy was going to work for somebody who was working for a judge in the Wizard's Court (that word, *wizard*, being an anachronism that cropped up mostly in legal contexts). Lucy was going to assist some possibly fraudulent but indisputably famous artist who constructed enormous invisible magical sculptures in the sky above the city. Wharton would be doing environmental stuff. Holly was part of a hard-core quasi-vigilante group bent on anticipating and averting violent crime among civilians.

The others were busy planning to give themselves over to pleasure, or if not pleasure then at least sloth. Life was already sorting them into categories, whether they liked it or not. All they could do was stare at each other dumbly across the widening gaps.

Plum found herself sorted into an extra ad hoc subcategory of one.

Nobody felt comfortable asking her about life after her career-ending and, from their point of view, essentially life-ending disaster. So she volunteered that she was currently working with ex-Professor Quentin Coldwater on an Absolutely Fascinating Research Project the exact nature of which she couldn't reveal.

Heads turned. This was gossip of the very first water—pure pharmaceutical-grade gossip.

"Oh my God," Darcy said, hand over her mouth. "Oh my God. Tell me you're not sleeping with him. Lie to me if you have to, I just want to hear the words."

"I'm not sleeping with him! Jesus, what an idea." Fortunately Plum didn't have to pretend to be appalled at the idea. Quentin was like her know-it-all older brother. "Who do you think I am?"

"So you're just . . . living and working with this mysterious brooding older man twenty-four-seven," Chelsea said.

"I have the phrase 'Girl Friday' in my mind for some reason," Wharton said.

"Guys. It's not anything like as intimate as you're imagining. We live in the same house. I'm assisting him on a project."

"Because, see, any amount of intimate there would be, you know—" Chelsea wrung her hands frantically. "Squick."

"I don't know," Lucy said loyally, raising the flag for the backlash to the backlash. "I mean, come on, guys. He's only what—forty?"

"He's thirty," Plum said.

"Sorry. It's hard to tell with the, you know, the hair. I just meant that we're not in Humbert Humbert territory here. Not quite."

"We are not in any territory at all! God! There is no territory!"

"All right, all right." Darcy held up her hands: we surrender. For now. "I just wish you'd give us a hint about what you *are* doing."

Plum did. She'd had enough. Something in her wanted to rise to the challenge of defending herself, and Quentin too. At some point, she couldn't have said when, this had gone from Quentin's weird impulse project to something she cared about too. She wanted it to work.

"Look," she said, "I know it sounds weird. And I have total respect for everything you guys are doing. I do. Even if you're just going to get high all the time and make light shows on the ceiling."

Chelsea gave the double V-for-victory sign.

"Those are your paths, and they're awesome. I'm just on a different one, and it's definitely a path, but it's different because I don't know where it's going. What Quentin is doing—look, I don't want to get into details, but it's pretty brilliant, and he's after something real. He's taking a big risk. I like that. I think one day I might want to do something like that too."

She finished her beer in silence. Everybody was a little embarrassed that Plum had made a speech that wasn't self-deprecating or funny. Well, so be it, she thought.

"So . . ." Darcy broke the silence.

"So you want to know what we're doing? We're doing magic. And if it comes off it's going to be a fucking masterpiece."

That was magic for you, right? The thing about magic, the real kind: it didn't make excuses, and it was never funny.

It wasn't completely true. They hadn't done any magic yet. But they would soon. The elaborate preparations in the fourth-floor room were starting to have an effect. One morning Plum walked in and noticed something funny about one of the windows, a little square one set in the back wall. It looked dark, like something was covering it from the outside, whereas the others were full of Manhattan sunlight. The window wasn't blocked, but the view had changed. It looked out at somewhere else now, or maybe somewhen else: a silent steel-gray marshland in early evening. Miles of swaying drowned grass, in fading light, stretching out to the horizon.

Plum touched the glass. Where the other windows were cool, it was unseasonably warm.

"Weird. Where the hell is that?"

"I have absolutely no idea," Quentin said.

Plum was enjoying her stint as a sorcerer's apprentice more than she would have thought. Morale was high. Once she'd learned that Fillory really was real, she'd braced herself for an assault from her depressive streak. The revelation seemed like the kind of thing that would give her depression a scary power and substance. But instead she'd found the news left her unexpectedly light, and free, as if maybe it wasn't her Chatwin-ness at all but rather the bracing-against-it that had caused her so much trouble over the years.

They spent a long cold day up on the house's flat, sticky tarpaper roof finishing out the magical security up there. If any passing satellite happened to snap a picture, some truly weird shit was going to turn up on Google Earth.

"So tell me about Alice," Plum said. She was painting sigils, black paint on black roof. "I mean, more about her."

This kicked off a long pause from Quentin, and Plum wondered if she'd crossed a line. She knew the basic facts, but he hadn't been forthcoming with a lot of details, probably because he didn't want to talk about them. But Plum did. She figured since Alice almost killed her, probably, she had the right to subject Quentin to a little exploratory interrogation. He obviously hadn't given up on his whole Alice project. It was lying fallow for the moment, but Plum wasn't fooled.

"What do you want to know?"

"What was she like, what kind of stuff was she into, that kind of thing. I mean, I met her ghost or niffin or whatever, but I didn't get a good sense of her day-to-day interests."

Quentin stopped working and stood up and massaged the small of his back.

"Alice was great. She was kind, she was funny, she was weird. She was smart—smarter than me, and a better magician too. She did things I still don't understand. It was sort of part of who she was—there was a force to her, a power, that I've never seen in anybody else."

"Were you in love with her? I mean, I know you were boyfriend-girlfriend, but."

"Totally." He smiled. "Totally in love. But I wasn't ready for her. She was more grown-up than me, and I had a lot of stuff left to work out. I made some mistakes. I thought some things were important that really weren't."

Plum stood up too. She was windburned and tired, and the fabric of the seat of her pants disengaged from the roof in such a way as to suggest that the tarpaper had probably wrecked them.

"I feel like you're talking around something here."

"Yeah. Probably it's that I slept with somebody else." Ah. Kind of sorry she asked there, but Quentin kept going. "Then she slept with somebody else. It was bad, I almost ruined everything. Then just when I was starting to really figure things out, that was when she died."

"That sucks. I'm really sorry."

"It took me a long time to get over it."

Plum's own romantic history so far had been pretty limited, with minimal drama. It was one area where she felt comfortable lagging behind her peers. But she prided herself on her powerful philosophical insights into other people's relationships.

"So if you do end up somehow, you know, bringing her back, do you think you'll be together? I mean are you still in love with her?"

"I don't really know her anymore, Plum. It was a long time ago. I'm a different person now, or at least I hope I am. We'd have to see."

"So you'd start over."

"If she wanted to. Though I feel like we were only just about to get started. We wouldn't start over, we'd just start."

Deep orange rays of sunlight meandered past, slowed by the viscous urban air they were passing through, full of floating particulates and toxic emissions. Bubbles popped in Plum's knees.

"Here's what I don't get. If you were so unready, if you had all that stuff left to work out, why do you think she loved you?"

Quentin went back to mixing the smelly reagent he'd been working on before.

"I don't know," he said. "I never did know."

"That would be a good one to figure out. Maybe before you bring her back?"

The next morning was the dress rehearsal. They broke the enchantment down into its component spells, running through each of them individually, then in small groups, being careful all the while not to let them combine into anything that was actually live and volatile. In cases where the spell involved some exceptionally expensive component, or it was physically dangerous, they just mimed their way through it.

Though once Plum forgot and spoke something she was supposed to skip, and just like that there was bright light and heat in the room. For an instant it was unbearable, like when there's bad feedback in an auditorium.

"Shit!" Quentin bolted, and she heard water running in the bathroom. When he came back his fingernails were still steaming slightly.

"Sorry!" Plum said. "I'm sorry."

"Don't worry about it." Though you could tell he was annoyed. "Start over. From the beginning."

It was funny about magic, how messy and imperfect it was. When people said something worked like magic they meant that it cost nothing and did exactly what you wanted it to. But there were lots of things magic couldn't do. It couldn't raise the dead. It couldn't make you happy. It couldn't make you good-looking. And even with the things it could do, it didn't always do them right. And it always, always cost something.

And it was inefficient. The system was never airtight, it always leaked. Magic was always throwing off extra energy, wasting it in the form of sound, and heat, and light, and wind. It was always buzzing and singing and glowing and sparking to no particular purpose. Magic was decidedly imperfect. But the really funny thing, she thought, was that if it were perfect, it wouldn't be so beautiful.

On the big day they agreed they would start at noon, but like anything else involving more than one person and a lot of moving parts—band rehearsals, softball games, model-rocket launches—it took about five times longer to get ready than they planned. They cleared away the books and stacked them tidily in the corners, and they laid out all the tools and materials on trays, neatly labeled and lined up in the order they'd be needed in. Quentin stuck a list of the spells on the wall, like the set list for a gig. There were a lot of things that they had, by mutual consent, skipped in the dress rehearsal but which it turned out were really time-consuming, like reading out the full text of one of these old cultic chants ten times.

They started in on the low-hanging fruit, making sure that conditions in the room were optimal and were going to stay that way. Constant temperature; a little extra oxygen; low light from the chandelier; no weird magical incursions. They cast spells on each other to ward off any weird charges or energies and to speed up their reaction times just a touch; some of this stuff you just couldn't cast right at baseline human speed. Caffeine helped with that too, so they kept plenty of that around.

The air in the workroom became still and cool, and it began to smell very slightly sweet—jasmine, she thought, though she wasn't quite sure. She couldn't remember when they'd arranged that.

By around five o'clock in the afternoon they realized they were putting off casting anything that would take them past the tipping point— that would commit them to doing this thing right here and now, tonight, and not tomorrow or some other day. The train was still in the station, it could still be delayed. But they'd run out of bullshit prep work. It was in or out.

Only now did Plum realize how nervous she was.

"I'm calling it," Quentin said. "If we're doing this let's do it."

"All right."

"Go ahead and cast Clarifying Radiance."

"OK."

"I'll start prepping the Scythian Dream."

"Check."

"OK, go."

"Going."

She went. Plum turned to the first set of materials on the shelf: four black powders in little dishes and a silver bell. Clarifying Radiance. Meanwhile Quentin said a word of power, and the light in the room became a shade more sepia, like the sunlight moments before a thunderstorm. Everything began to sound echoey, as if they were in a much larger room. Just like that they crossed the Rubicon. The train left the station.

From that point on it was controlled chaos. Sometimes they worked together—one or two of the spells were four-handed. Other times the flow diverged, and they'd be doing totally different spells in parallel, stealing glances at the other one's work to make sure they finished up at the same time.

There was a steady flow of cross-talk.

"Slow it down, slow it down. Finish in three, two—"

"Look out, the streams are forking. They're forking!"

A single curve of Irish Fire delaminated into two, then four, curling away to either side. The curls started pointing worryingly back toward Plum, who was casting them.

"I've got it," she said. "Dammit!"

The fire went out.

"Do it again. Do it again. There's still time."

It went on like that for three or four hours—it was hard to keep track. By then they were deep into it, and the atmosphere in the room had gotten thoroughly dreamlike. Huge shadows stalked along the walls. The room seemed to list and bank like it had taken flight with them inside it. She banged a tray down onto the work table in front of Quentin, and he began picking what he needed off it without even glancing down at it, and she was shocked to realize that it was the second-to-last spell on the list. This was almost it.

Plum had run out of things to do so she just watched him, drinking a glass of water she'd placed under the table when they started and had somehow managed not to kick over. The rest of it was all him. She was dizzy, and her arms felt weak. She folded them over her chest to keep them from shaking.

Plum didn't think her friends would have made fun of Quentin at that moment. For a while she'd fallen into the habit of thinking of him as a peer, basically, but over the past week she'd been reminded that he was a decade older and doing magic on a different level from her. Right now he looked like a young Prospero in his prime. He'd taken off his jacket and rolled up the sleeves of his white dress shirt, which was wringing with sweat. He must have been tired but his voice was still firm and resonant, and his fingers were working with a practiced crispness through positions she'd never seen before, the tendons standing out on the backs of his hands. This was the kind of magic, Plum thought, she would do when she grew up.

Big surges of power were flowing through the room. It crossed her mind that spells like this were exactly what turned people into niffins, when they got out of hand. Huge tranches and structures of magic that so far she'd only ever seen in isolation were colliding and interacting like weather systems. The intensity doubled and redoubled itself. Without warning the room juddered and dropped, leaving them in free fall for an instant—if it had been an airplane the oxygen masks would have come down. Quentin's voice sounded artificially deep, and he'd started to tremble with the effort of keeping everything together. He hastily dragged an arm across his forehead.

"Staff," he said. "Staff!"

The second time he barked it, loudly, and Plum snapped awake and turned and grabbed the black wood staff from where it stood leaned up in one corner.

He was hitting the panic button. Quentin grabbed the staff from her quickly, blindly, and as soon as it was in his hands it began jerking and vibrating, like it was attached to a line with an enormous fish on the other end, or a giant kite caught in a high wind.

She moved to help him, but he shook his head.

"Better not touch me," he said through clenched teeth. "Could be bad."

The air was thick with the smell of burning metal and the sweat of tired magicians. She could sense it in the room with them now, the land itself: an angry, hungry, thirsty infant thing demanding life, ready to take it from them if it had to. It cried out with an almost human voice. A spray of golden light erupted from between one of Quentin's fingers: that must have been one of Mayakovsky's coins going. Scenery raced past the windows, all of them now, too blurred to make out.

Space distorted grotesquely, and for an instant the room looked stretched out of all proportion, fish-eyed, as if a bulbous blister had formed on the surface of reality itself. Plum was scared of what would happen if it burst.

Quentin shouted, in pain or triumph or despair, Plum couldn't tell which:

"*Nothung!*"

He spun the staff and banged the silver-shod end against the floor with a sound like a gunshot. She felt the shock through the soles of her feet. The wires in the ceiling and walls went red hot, and the letters on the floor burned white like magnesium.

Then they faded again, and bit by bit it all stopped. The floor stabilized. The air was still again; a couple of candles hadn't blown out, and their flames wobbled and then straightened up. Quentin collapsed forward onto the table. The room was silent except for a faint high silvery tone, though it could have been her ears ringing.

The world outside the window had become lower Manhattan again, even that odd little window in the corner. Quentin raised his head and straightened up. He peered around, up at the ceiling, into the dark corners of the room, curiously. He looked over at Plum.

She pointed behind him.

A red door had appeared in the wall. It was painted wood banded with black iron that had been worked into elaborate curves and fairy spirals. Quentin dropped the staff, and it clattered to the floor.

CHAPTER 21

Plum watched him take a few slow, cautious, disbelieving steps toward the door and then stop again, as the dust settled and the ringing died away. Plum felt wrung out, shivery, like she'd gone for a run on an empty stomach, but she couldn't take her eyes off the red door.

"We did it," Quentin said solemnly. "It really worked. We made a new land."

It had one brass knob, placed in the center. Quentin touched it and then put his hand on it, hesitantly, as if he expected an electric shock, or as if he thought his hand might go right through it. But it was solid. He turned the knob and pushed—wrong—then pulled the door toward him. It opened easily.

A cold wind breathed into the room. It cooled Plum's overheated forehead, but it chilled something deeper inside her.

"Quentin," she said.

He didn't move, and she stepped forward to stand beside him on the threshold.

"Are you going in?"

Like he was waking from a dream Quentin looked over at her.

"In a minute." He held up his hand. "I was sure I was going to have a scar there from Mayakovsky's coin. Like in *Raiders*. It felt like it was burning. But there's nothing."

Plum had no idea what he was talking about, but she didn't say anything. It didn't seem like the moment.

The land didn't look like the Hundred Acre Wood. It wasn't even an orchard. It wasn't even outside. Looking through the door was like looking in that mirror back at Brakebills, after Darcy's reflection had vanished: it was exactly like the room they were standing in, except for the fact that they weren't standing in it. And it was all reversed.

"Through the looking glass," Quentin said.

This wasn't what she'd expected. Quentin picked up a long-handled spoon from the worktable and tossed it underhand through the doorway. It clanged and slid along the floor in the other room. It seemed safe enough.

"What is this?" she said.

"I think it's our land."

"But why does it look like that? Is that what it's supposed to look like?"

"I don't know."

"Was this what you were expecting? I thought you were going to do an orchard. Is this what you were trying to do?"

"No."

"Why would you make a land that looks exactly the same as the one you're already in?"

"That's a good question."

Quentin walked through the door and into the other room. She watched him look around. She had to hand it to him, he didn't look all that freaked out. Just checking out the scene.

"Classic," he said. "It's completely reversed. It's opposite-land. You gotta like the respect for tradition."

He spread out his arms.

"Come on in if you want to, I think it's safe."

Plum went on in. It really was the weirdest thing. It was like the house had acquired a Siamese twin, attached to it at the door. She was struggling with a sense of anticlimax.

"It sort of worked," Plum said. "I mean, we did make a land, right?"

Quentin nodded.

"Or a house anyway. Let's be careful, Plum, this feels a little off."

It was a very, very quiet house. The original house was magically soundproofed, so it was quiet too, but this was different. This place was sonically dead—it was as if the walls were covered in that egg-carton foam they used to line the walls in music studios.

And there was something else. The place had a claustrophobic feel. She couldn't put her finger on it till it was literally staring her in the face.

"Look at the windows," she said. "All the windows. They're not windows, they're mirrors."

It was like the eyes of the house had gone blind.

"Huh. I wonder what the mirrors are."

Yeah. Good question. There was one in the little half bath out on the landing. She steeled herself for some horror-movie shocker and then poked her head in.

Curiouser and curiouser. The mirror was still there, and it was still a mirror, but inside the room in the mirror it was snowing—blowing snow, bordering on a real blizzard. It was starting to drift on the floor, the towel racks, the rim of the sink. It settled on her hair and her eyelashes. But only in the mirror: reflexively she touched her hair, but it was dry. The snow wasn't real. Quentin appeared behind her.

"Eek," he said.

Clearly this was affecting them in different ways.

They strolled through the house, lord and lady of their uncanny new domain. Everything was there, more or less, except when it wasn't. The furniture, the drapes, the silverware, the glassware. The doors were ordinary doors. But there were no computers and no phones. The books were there, but the pages were blank. No toiletries in the bathroom, no clothes in the closets. Nobody lived here. Water came out of the taps, but cold only. They disagreed over whether one of the oriental rugs was left-right inverted—Quentin was sure it was—but Plum remembered it differently, and neither of them felt like going back and checking the original.

Fatigue and disappointment were giving them both a slightly hysterical edge.

"It's like a giant closet," Plum said. "We could store stuff in here. We'd have more closet space than anybody in New York City."

"We're not going to store stuff in here."

"Put a couple of flat-screens in here, Xbox, easy chair: man-cave!"

They'd made their way up to the top floor again when they heard a heavy *clunk* from the floor below. Her bedroom.

"I guess that's the other shoe," Quentin said. "Wands out, Harry."

Plum snorted—charitably, because she was a good person—but she took his point. She went defensive: a nice hard blocking spell. Charge it up and you could hold it back till you needed it; it would just take a gesture to release it. Whatever Quentin was prepping, it gave off a high rising whine.

But when they got there the bedroom was empty, except that Plum's desk chair was now lying on its back, its little feet in the air, like it was playing dead: *ah—they got me!* Slowly Quentin lifted it up and set it on its feet.

"The chair fell over," he said brightly.

"All right, all right."

It was like they were daring each other to be the first to lose their nerve. They tromped downstairs to the second floor. Another thing: color photographs had faded to black and white.

"I wonder—" But Quentin was cut off by that same *clunk* as before, from over their heads now. The chair again.

"Huh." Neither of them wanted to look. "I wonder what's outside?"

"I don't," Plum said. "And I dare you to not look."

For a second they both thought there was something in Quentin's bed, but he jerked the covers back and it was just a pillow. This was seriously creeping her out. Something shattered downstairs in the kitchen—it sounded like somebody dropping a wineglass.

Obediently, they both trotted downstairs, Quentin first. Lo, a lone wineglass lay in pieces right in the middle of the floor. Lookee there.

"Must have been the wind," Plum said.

Now she was doing it. Her shrink would say she was using humor to avoid deeper feelings. She would be right.

They rummaged around aimlessly; they were both hoping to stumble on something that would make the land exciting, and magical, and Romantic, the way they were hoping it would be, but they didn't. She didn't like this land. It was like they'd dialed a wrong number. This wasn't what they'd ordered.

"I wonder, if there's food here, if you can eat it?" Quentin said.

She nerved herself to open the fridge. There had been a bowl of green grapes in it, but the grapes had become green glass marbles.

Quentin was picking up books one after the other and opening them.

"Dude. They're all going to be blank."

"Maybe. This isn't what I expected, but I don't know why it's not what I expected. It felt right when we were casting it, but something must have gone wrong."

He put the book down and walked boldly over to the front door, but before he could open it there was a muffled thud from the second floor. It might have been a lamp falling over onto a rug. He stopped, his hand on the doorknob.

"Quentin—"

"I know," he said. "This is definitely a land, but I'm not completely sure it's our land."

"Whose then?"

He shook his head. He didn't know. It was literally everything she could do not to start humming "This Land Is Your Land."

"Well, we made it," Plum said.

"I know, I know. Want to go see who knocked over the lamp?"

"Let's go."

She followed Quentin up the stairs but he stopped halfway, listening.

"Why do I feel like we're getting decoyed here?" He turned around and edged past her, back down the stairs. "I'll be right back."

"Famous last words."

She watched him reach the bottom of the stairs and freeze, staring at something out of view.

"Shit."

"What is it?"

Except that she knew even as she was asking him. There were blue highlights on the polished banister next to him. She knew that blue.

"Run!"

He pelted up the stairs at her, white-faced.

"Jesus, run!"

He would have run straight over her if she hadn't snapped out of it and taken off like a shot ahead of him. It shouldn't be here. It was like something from a dream had followed her into the real world, or maybe it was the other way—she'd followed it into the dream. Quentin covered a lot of ground with those long legs—he overtook her on the second floor, sprinting right past her, but he grabbed her hand as he passed her and pulled her along, practically yanking her arm out of its socket. He barked his shin hard on an ottoman as he ran, which must have hurt like hell.

"Run run run! Come on!"

On the third-floor landing Quentin paused and sent a spell down the stairs over her shoulder, something that flashed hot on her face, then they were running shoulder to shoulder up the stairs and into the workroom and through the door and out into the real world.

She slammed the door behind them, then blasted out the blocking spell she'd had ready for good measure. She'd totally forgotten about it till then. The air in front of the door shivered.

They looked at each other, both breathing hard.

"I don't," Quentin panted. "Think. She can. Come through."

He looked like he was going to cry or be sick or both. She really hoped he did neither of those. They shouldn't have cast the spell. Jesus, how stupid did you have to be—ancient enchantment rouses primal horror, it was the oldest story there was. Hubris. They were such idiots.

"How the fuck did she get here?" Plum gasped.

Quentin didn't answer. His face looked weird: happy and sad and terrified all at once.

CHAPTER 22

Quentin didn't sleep that night. He did try, because it seemed important, because sleeping was something you did at night, but it was never going to happen. After a couple of hours of staring at the ceiling shivering, his mind spinning and lurching like a dryer with a shoe in it, he gave up and got dressed and climbed the stairs to the fourth floor. It was three in the morning. He stood in front of the red door for a good half hour, nervously jiggling his knee, clenching his jaw till it ached.

Then he began plastering himself with wards and boosting his reflexes and doing whatever else he could think of that might come in handy. He was going back through.

The safeguards were probably beside the point. Alice had been stronger than him when she was human, and now she was on another power scale entirely. Now she was plugged into the main line. But he had to get closer to her. He didn't understand why she was here. Maybe he'd summoned her somehow, without even knowing it, trapped her and bound her in this weird mirror-house. Maybe she'd come on her own—Alice had found him at Brakebills, and now she'd found him again here, wriggled her way into his land like a worm into an apple. She was the snake in his Eden.

It didn't really matter. He hadn't managed to make a land, or not much of one, but this was better. Making a land was a distraction anyway. So was the robbery. This was what he wanted.

But what did Alice want? To haunt him? Laugh at him? Hunt and kill him? The scholarly literature on niffins was pretty thin. Their behavior was unpredictable at best. But whatever she wanted, he knew what she needed, and that was to be human again. He couldn't have asked for a better chance.

And he needed her too: he needed to see her again, she was the only person he'd ever felt completely at home with. He knew he should wait and eat and sleep and talk it over with Plum, but—he told himself—it was hard to know how long he had. The whims of a niffin were pretty much the definition of perverse. If she left now he might never find her again. He was going to finish this.

And plus Plum would try to talk him out of it.

The house was quiet. He wasn't even remotely tired. Staring at the red door he tried to summon up in his mind the Alice he knew. Did he really remember what she was like? Maybe he was pursuing a ghost, the ghost of a ghost, a figment of his own memory. It had been seven years: that was longer than he'd known her as a human. Maybe he was chasing some long-gone, never-was fantasy-Alice. If he could bring her back, who would she be?

Quentin was going to find out. He opened the red door but didn't cross the threshold. The other room was still there, the mirror room, with its mirror windows. He sat down on the floor, cross-legged, and waited.

He'd been sitting there for ten minutes when Alice swam by, slowly, in profile, her legs trailing lightly behind her, as silent and malevolent as a shark in an aquarium. She was slightly smaller than she had been in life, like an expensive doll of herself. She didn't see him; if she knew he was there she didn't bother to turn her head.

Once she was out of view he stood up, waited five more minutes, then stepped through the door. Everything was just as it had been. There was the same deep muffled quiet. No wind from outside rattled the mirrored windows. Nothing moved. Or almost nothing: there was an unnerving flicker at the corner of his eye, like a television left on without the sound. It was the mirror in the bathroom, where flakes of snow were still drifting down.

He stood at the top of the stairs, swung his arms and bounced on his toes. He had not even a glimmer of a plan. How did you turn a monster back into a person? It took a long time for Alice to appear again, and he was starting to wonder if he should call her name when he heard a muffled, fumbling clatter in the room below, like somebody kicking something small and heavy across a rug. A minute later that thin blue radiance came filtering up the stairwell. Whatever he'd been about to do or say or cast exited his head, and he got up and walked stiff-legged back to the door. He couldn't stop himself. It was like his legs were bionic and somebody else was controlling them.

That was what it was to fear for your life. He stopped himself in front of the door, breathing hard, not quite going through, not yet. What was he going to do? He wanted to shout at her: *Wake up! Remember who you are! I need to talk to Alice!* But the thing about monsters was, you couldn't talk to them about it, because they wouldn't admit they were monsters in the first place.

She came rising up right through the floor. Quentin bounded away from the door, out of the room and down the stairs like an athlete. He heard laughter, creepily familiar. It was hers, but cold, musical, mechanical, somebody tapping on a wineglass. She came floating down the stairs after him, and he backed away into the mirror-version of Plum's bedroom. He caught a glimpse of her—she wasn't quite Alice, not exactly. She blurred out for a second, a low-res hologram of herself. Her hair floated weightless around her head.

And she never stopped smiling. Never. Blue lips, blue teeth. Maybe it was fun being a niffin. Maybe everybody had the wrong idea about it.

She followed him down to the first floor, through the dining room and back up the stairs, back down, back up, then back up to the third floor. She didn't hurry, though when he hurried up so did she, as if that were one of the rules of the game. It might have been comical if he weren't being chased by a blue demon who could burn him to nothing just by touching him, and probably without touching him. Sometimes she paid attention to the walls and the floors and the ceilings, sometimes she passed through them with no resistance.

Maybe the weirdest thing about this surreal duel was that he was starting to enjoy it. However distorted or transmuted she was, she was still Alice. He was spending time with her. She was pure magic now, pure rage and power, but he had always loved her rage and her power. Those were two of the greatest things about her. She wasn't Alice, but she wasn't quite not-Alice either.

At this rate he could stay ahead of her forever as long as he avoided dead ends. It was like he was a ghost, he thought giddily, and she was Pac-Man, or the other way around. (Though no—Pac-Man could eat the ghosts when they were blue. Never mind. Focus.) He wondered how long till she lost patience and went for him. It was like swimming with sharks, except that he knew what sharks wanted. He couldn't guess within a million miles what Alice wanted.

There were moments when he wanted to throw himself at her, right into her arms, and let her burn him up in an instant. What an incredibly stupid fucking idea.

After half an hour of this he doubled back through the red door, back home. This wasn't getting them anywhere. He sat on the edge of the work table, gasping a little from all the stair climbing. He was still alive, but he wasn't making progress. Someway or other he was doing this wrong.

He was still there when Plum came up around seven with coffee.

"Jesus," she said. "Are you playing chicken with that thing?"

"With Alice." He corrected her automatically. "I guess I am."

"How's it going?"

"Pretty well," Quentin said. "I'm not dead."

"And Alice—?"

"She's still dead."

Plum nodded.

"I don't mean to sound at all critical," she said, "but maybe you should just leave this alone? Stop tempting fate? I feel weird just being in the same house with it. Her."

"I want to learn about her."

"What've you got so far?"

"Not much. She likes to play. She could've killed me by now, but she hasn't."

"Christ! Quentin!"

They both watched the open doorway like it was a TV, or a hole through which they were ice fishing.

"It's weird to think that she killed my great-great-uncle Martin," Plum said. "But then it sounds like she had her reasons. Is she really alive in there?"

"I don't know. It feels like she is."

"OK. I'll leave you to it." Plum paused in the doorway. "Just—I know you're going to get obsessed with this, so try not to forget the big picture. If there's no hope, you have to promise me you'll let her go."

She was right, of course. Where did she get off, being wiser than him at twenty-one?

"I'll let it go. I promise. Just not yet."

"I'll leave you alone."

"I'm not alone," Quentin said. "Alice is here."

Later that day he tried fighting her. He'd watched Alice face down Martin Chatwin himself, with a whole arsenal of magic that he'd never seen before, but that was a long time ago. Now he knew his way around a ward-and-shield or two. He could chuck a magic missile with the best of them. He was a damn one-man magic-missile crisis.

And Alice was playing with him. This was a game to her. Quentin had this advantage at least: he wasn't playing. It made him feel sick, fighting somebody he wanted to love, but right now Alice was in no condition to love, or be loved.

He looked up the thickest, baddest-ass shielding spell he knew about and crudely attached a couple of hardening enhancements to it. Taking a deep breath, he stepped through the closet door and as quickly as he could cast the shield six times in a row, one after the other, six magic shields hanging invisibly in the air in front of him, or all but invisibly. Looking through six of them at once turned the air a little rosy-pink.

Any more than six and they would have started to interfere with each other. Diminishing returns. Plus he didn't think he could do another one right now anyway.

Then the missiles. He'd made them in advance, with all the trimmings: treble-weight, electrically charged, armor-piercing, viciously poisoned. He wouldn't have dared to even prep the spell on Earth, let alone cast it, if the house hadn't itself been so heavily shielded. If he missed they'd go through the wall like paper, plus they were a long way from street legal. Technically he was going to cast them in another dimension, so maybe he'd get off on jurisdictional grounds.

Alice rose to meet him: feeding time. She never quite touched the ground, he noticed, though when she saw him noticing she gave a little kick with her legs, balletic almost, a joke—as if to say, remember when I used to walk with these things? Sure you do. Remember when I used to spread them for you, my darling?

Quentin tried to kill her. He knew he couldn't, but he thought she might feel it, and as long as she was a niffin this was virtually the only interaction they could have together. He cast the magic missiles, full strength and then some; they practically took his fingertips off. They were green, seething things that darted at Alice like hungry fish.

But about ten feet from her they slowed to a crawl. She looked at them, pleased, as if Quentin had made her cookies. You shouldn't have! Under her gaze the missiles lost the courage of their convictions. They formed a line, single file, and obediently encircled her waist in a sparking, fizzing green ring.

Then the ring burst out in all directions. Two of the missiles whanged resonantly off Quentin's sextuple shield. He flinched. He wouldn't have survived even one of them.

Then Alice was across the room and hanging in the air right in front of him. He couldn't tell if she'd teleported or just darted straight at him, she was that fast. For the first time she looked pissed off. She bared her sapphire teeth. Was it being a niffin that made her this angry? Or had she been this angry all along? Maybe the rage had been inside her already, and becoming a niffin had just revealed it—burned away the protective shielding.

Either way she was Alice to the life, he'd know her anywhere; she was more than alive, she was humming and crackling with energy. Her eyes were the brightest, angriest, most magnificently amused eyes he'd ever seen. She reached out and put a hand on the first of his six shields, pressed on it with two blue fingertips, then put them through it. The shield flared and died.

The second shield buzzed angrily when she touched it. That should have killed her too; he'd laced it with a magical charge he'd only read about, and in a book he shouldn't have been reading. She wiggled her fingers with sensual pleasure. Delightful! With both hands she grasped the third shield and *picked it up*—set it aside as if it were a physical object, an old picture frame maybe, and leaned it against a wall. It was a joke, magic didn't even work that way, but if you were a niffin it worked however you wanted it to. She did the same thing with the next one, and the next, stacking them neatly like folding chairs.

Quentin didn't wait around for the ending. He could see where this was heading. Ceding the field of battle, he stepped back through the doorway. Let her follow him if she could, but she couldn't. It was hard and smooth as glass to her. She mushed her face and her breasts against the barrier, like a kid squishing her face against a window, and looked at him with one antic eye, blue on blue.

She was daring him, baiting him. Come on! Quit moping around! Don't you want to have some fun? When she opened her mouth it was bright inside, like in a photographic negative.

"Alice," Quentin said. *"Alice."*

He closed the red door. He'd seen enough.

She was the madwoman in the attic. It was weirdly intimate, this one-sided duel, just her and him, one on one. Not like sex, but intimate. He was like a free diver trying for greater and greater depths, forcing himself down, lungs bursting, then kicking frantically for the surface with his puny human flippers, the big blue nipping at his heels.

Quentin kept records of his trips in a spiral notebook: where he went, where she went, what he'd done, what she'd done. There wasn't much point to it, because the performance went more or less the same way every time, but it helped him fight off sadness. And he did notice one thing: Alice liked to herd him toward the front door of the house, like she was daring him to open it. That seemed like a dare he'd be better off not taking.

But if there was nothing else on offer? Their little dance was like the endgame of a disastrously bloody chess match, just a queen chasing a beleaguered king around an empty board, sadistically refusing to checkmate him. It was difficult to know what if anything was going on in the queen's mind, but one thing was clear: Alice was better at this game than he was. Apart from everything else she knew him better than he knew himself. She always had.

So that night, close to midnight, when Plum was safely in bed, he reversed tactics again. Alice wanted him to open the front door? He was going to head straight for it. Give her what she wants, see what she does with it. He still didn't know what he was looking for, but maybe he'd find out what she was looking for.

He prepped a couple of spells in advance, and cast the first one as soon as he'd stepped through the door. It created a reasonably lifelike image of him in every room in the house.

It didn't confuse her, but it might have pissed her off, because Quentin barely made it to the stairs before she banished the illusion so harshly that he felt like somebody had scrubbed his brain with steel wool. Go on or go back? In an undignified panic he feinted for the stairs, dodged past Alice at close quarters, arching his body like a bullfighter, and locked himself in the half bathroom off the landing.

Now he'd trapped himself, but good. He fumbled in his pocket and whipped out a Sharpie he'd been keeping on him in case of emergency. Scribbling at top speed he wrote an inscription in Swahili across the door, then sketched a big rectangle around the whole frame, with fiddly ornaments at the corners, all executed in one unbroken line. It was just a ward to insulate against magic, because, he reasoned hopefully, Alice was made of magic now. It was all he could think of.

The door shook with an impact, bulged visibly inward, air puffing in around the edges as if a grenade had gone off behind it. It held, but immediately it began warping in its frame, and the paint started to blister. It wasn't going to hold for long. It wasn't meant to be a magic barrier, it just wanted to be a bathroom door.

He turned around and his eye fell on the medicine-cabinet mirror, in which it continued to snow. Experimentally he put a hand through it—no resistance. Another portal. He put one foot on the toilet, planted his knee on the sink and fed himself through the narrow opening.

It was cold in the other bathroom—the other-other bathroom. He crawled desperately down off the sink and half fell onto the bathroom floor, which was slick with slush. Where was he now? Two worlds removed from reality now, a land within a land. Another level down.

What would he do when the door failed? He might be able to slip past her again, get back through, but then what had he gained? He didn't want to leave empty-handed, not again. This free diver was going to touch bottom, even if it meant he wasn't coming back up. There must be something interesting down here. At this depth maybe some of the rules would start breaking down.

Slipping and sliding to his feet, he half walked, half skated out into the hall and into the mirror-image of the mirror-image of the workroom. The lights were out in this one, and he hastily summoned some illumination—the palms of his hands glowed like flashlights. Something was different here. He could almost feel the increased pressure of the multiple layers of reality above him. This land was heavier somehow: like it had been put through a photo filter that saturated the colors and made the black lines thicker and darker. It tried to push into his eyes and ears. He couldn't stay here long.

But where to? He went over to the windows and heaved one up and open.

The street was recognizably their street, or almost: there was a road, and streetlights, but there were no other houses. It was like a desert housing development that had suffered some financial calamity just as construction began. All around in the distance cold sand slid silkily, hissing, over more cold sand. It was night, and instead of light the streetlights poured down rain as if they were weeping. The sky was black, no stars, and the moon was flat and silver: a mirror, reflecting a ghost earth. This wasn't something he was supposed to see. It was an unfinished sketch of a world, a set that hadn't been properly dressed.

He shut the window. This workroom had a red door too. He opened it and stepped through.

Now he was getting close to the heart of something, he could feel it. Three levels down, the innermost chamber, the littlest Russian doll—a tiny wooden peg with smeary features, barely a doll at all. This room looked nothing like anything in the townhouse, but he recognized it anyway. The hushed carpet, that warm, fruity smell—a stranger's house, that he'd only been in once, and that for about fifteen minutes, but it was like he'd never left it. He was back in Brooklyn, thirteen years ago, back at the house where he'd come for his Princeton interview.

It was like he was burrowing deeper into his own mind, back in time, back into his memory. This was where it all began. Maybe if he stuck around he could finally have his interview after all. He could go back and get his master's degree. Was this really it, or just a simulacrum? Was there another, younger Quentin waiting just outside the door, getting even more depressed than usual as he stood there fretting in the cold rain? And his friend James, young and strong and brave-o? The loops were getting stranger, the time lines were in a Gordian knot, the thick was plottened beyond all recognition.

Or was this a second chance? Was this how to fix her? Change it all so it never happened—rip up the envelope and walk away? He heard the sound of cracking wood, a long way off, in another reality. Two realities up. Last time he was here he went for the liquor cabinet. Lesson learned. He looked around: yes, a grandfather clock, just like in Christopher Plover. It was so obvious now. He opened the case.

It was full of shining golden coins. They poured out onto the floor like a Vegas jackpot. They were like Mayakovsky's coins, but there must have been hundreds of them. God, the amount of power here was unthinkable. What couldn't you do with it? He had his master's now, he was a master magician. He could fix Alice. He could fix anything. He stuffed his pockets with them.

Speaking of whom: Alice came drifting through the doorway behind him, slow-rolling languorously onto her back like an otter. Time to go. He juked past her and back through the door the other way.

In the workroom the snow was turning to rain, and the parquet had an inch of gray slush on it, and he half fell sprinting across it, his pockets heavy with treasure. He slammed shut the bathroom door but then fumbled the Sharpie and dropped it. No time. He spat out a spell that doubled his speed and scrambled up and over the sink and felt the hot prickle of way too much magic way too close on his trailing ankle. Alice was a blue blur behind him, and he wasn't faster than she was but he was fast enough, just, to make it back across the landing and through the workroom and the red door and out into the real world.

She hadn't gotten him. Not today. Not today. He stood there for a minute, puffing and blowing and pulling himself together, hands on his knees. Then he dug his hands in his pockets and spilled the gold out on the table. Show 'em what they've won.

He should have known. It was fairy gold, like in the stories—the kind that turns to dead leaves and dried flowers when the sun comes up. That's what he'd found. The coins had turned to ordinary nickels.

It was never going to be that easy. This wasn't working. There had to be another way. He needed sleep. His ankle was starting to burn where his close call with Alice had scorched it.

"Quentin."

Eliot was standing in the doorway, looking in his Fillorian court finery like he'd just detached himself from a Hans Holbein painting. He held a tumbler from the kitchen in one hand, full of whiskey, which he raised in greeting.

"You look like you've just seen a ghost," he said.

CHAPTER 23

Quentin hugged him so hard that Eliot spilled his whiskey down his front, which he complained about loudly, but Quentin didn't care. He had to make sure Eliot was real and solid. It made no sense that he was here, but thank God he was. Quentin had had enough of sadness and horror and futility for one day. He needed a friend, somebody who knew him from the old days.

And seeing Eliot here, out of the blue, for no reason whatsoever, felt like proof that impossible things were still possible. He needed that too.

"It's good to see you," he said.

"You too."

"You met Plum?"

"Yes, charming girl. I assume you're—?"

"No," Quentin said.

"Not even—?"

"No!"

Eliot shook his head sadly.

"I can see I came not a minute too soon."

They stayed up late filling each other in on everything that had happened, then they slept late and drank too much coffee and went over it all again. Eliot's news brought Quentin up short and sharp: whether or not he was in it, whether or not he could see it or touch it, he'd thought there would always be a Fillory out there somewhere. He loved knowing it was there. It anchored his sense of happiness, the way a distant stockpile of gold might underwrite the value of a paper bill. It was incon-ceivably sad to think of it ending. And where would they all go—all the people and animals and everything else? What would happen to them?

"But you think there might be something here that could save it?" he said. "Something Rupert had?"

Eliot paced around the living room in circles. Plum and Quentin sat on separate couches watching him. While they slept he'd been up even later, going through Rupert's notebook. He'd been excited at first when he realized that his search had converged with theirs—he'd come to Earth on a quest, and his best friend had already done it for him! But he'd gone back to being frustrated.

"Maybe it was the knife. But what would I do with it? Who would I stab with it? I never know who to stab. But I don't know what to do with the spell either."

"It's not for reviving a dead land," Quentin said. "It's for making somewhere new."

"There must be something else in that manuscript then, a clue or something. And why would the bird want it?"

As urgent as this was, Quentin's mind was still with Alice upstairs. Part of him wanted to snap into hero mode, to leap to Fillory's defense, but saving Fillory was Eliot's business now. It was hard to admit it, but it was true. He would do what he could, but right now his job was Alice.

"But so Martin made his deal with Umber?" Eliot said finally. "I thought Umber was good. And then didn't Martin kill Umber?"

"He still could have," Quentin said. "The classic double cross."

"Or, maybe Umber's still alive somewhere. Maybe we're just sup-posed to think He's dead."

"Ooh, I like that one," Plum said. "How do you even know Martin killed Umber? God, I still can't believe I'm talking about Them like They're real people. Or animals or gods or whatever."

"Ember told Jane Chatwin," Quentin said. "Jane told me. But you're right, maybe this is all Umber's fault. Maybe He's the hidden hand or hoof or whatever behind the apocalypse."

"But why?" Eliot rubbed his face with both hands. "Why would He do that? How can He be alive? Where's He been all this time? How can

He be evil? What, is He Ember's evil twin? It's a bit of a cliché, even for Fillory."

Buckets of sunlight were pouring overenthusiastically in through the bay windows. It was claustrophobic in the house—Quentin hadn't been outside for days. As tired as he'd been he hadn't slept well the night before. It was hard knowing that Alice was right there, burning, always burning, with just a thin slip of world between them. He wondered if Alice ever slept. He didn't think she did.

"And Castle Blackspire?" Eliot was getting more and more animated. "What's that? It screws up the entire structure! Where does it end? Umber's got to be the key, one way or the other. Got to. That must be the clue Jane wanted us to find." Coming to the end of his caffeine fit, he dropped bonelessly into a vinyl armchair. "I'm going to send a message to Janet. She should know about this."

"You can do that? Send a message to Fillory?"

"It's not easy. Kind of like a very expensive telegram. But yeah, RHIP. Let's talk about something else. What've you learned about your dead girlfriend?"

"She's not dead," Quentin said.

"*Bzzt!*" Eliot pressed an imaginary game-show button on the arm of the chair. "The answer I was looking for was, 'She's not my girlfriend, she's a crazy magic rage-demon.' Maybe you should just take the land apart. Scrub it out. Cut your losses."

"What, with Alice inside?"

"Well, she'll survive, probably. You can't kill those things. She'll just go back where she came from."

"But she's still alive, Eliot, and she's right there. Right there! If there was ever, ever going to be a chance to change her back, this is it."

"Quentin—"

"Don't Quentin me." Now he was the one getting animated. "This is what I'm doing. What I have to do. You're saving Fillory, I'm doing this."

"Quentin, look at me." Eliot sat up. "You're right. If there was ever a chance this would be it. But there isn't a chance. That's not Alice. Alice is already dead. She died seven years ago, and you can't bring her back."

"I went to the Underworld. She wasn't there."

"You didn't see her, but that doesn't mean she wasn't there. We've been over and over this. Quentin, I could really use your help. Fillory needs your help. And I hate to be crass, you know I do, but Alice is one person. We're talking about Fillory, all of it, the entire land, thousands of people. Plus a lot of cute animals."

"I know." They were wasting time, he had to get back upstairs. "I know. But I have to try."

"What's your plan there?" Plum said.

"I don't know. Run around some more, cast some more spells. Maybe I'll stumble on something. Trial and error."

Plum tapped her lips with one finger.

"Not my place, but it sounds to me like you're a little stuck."

"I am stuck."

"It sounds to me," she said, "like you're dicking around. Sneaking, dodging, avoiding confrontation."

"I'm not disagreeing with you, I just don't know what else to do."

"Against my better judgment," Plum said, "I'm going to give you the benefit of a woman's perspective on this one."

"I am so excited to see where this is going," Eliot said, "I can't even tell you. Keep talking."

"What I mean is, meet her head-on. Stand and fight. Quit sneaking around. See what happens."

"I tried that. I lost."

"It sounds to me like you tried hiding behind like ninety shields," Plum said. "That shit probably just pissed her off even more, and from what I've seen she was already plenty pissed. You know what makes people angry? When they're trying to tell you something, and you're not hearing them. Then they feel like they have to get louder and louder and louder, and then you're still not listening. You're just getting all scared."

"Because it's fucking scary!"

"She wants you to stand and face her, Quentin. What I'm talking about is walking in there and dealing with her. You want her to be a person again? Try treating her like one."

Quentin shook his head.

"That's suicide."

"Is it? It sounds to me like a relationship."

"You're being glib," he said.

"Am I? Why hasn't she killed you yet?"

A heavy silence fell in the room. The trouble was that she was right. However Alice got here, it wasn't an accident. He'd tried to make a land, and it hadn't worked. He'd wanted to create something, make something new, be somebody new, but it was becoming apparent that he couldn't, not until he'd dealt with something old. Not until he'd cleared his debts and laid his ghosts to rest.

The way he really knew Plum was right was that it was what Alice would have done.

"I still think you should scrub it out," Eliot said, obviously disappointed. "Fresh beginning. Start over."

"I have a feeling," Plum said, "that it's a little bit late in the day to start over."

Back in the fourth-floor workroom, Quentin opened the red door again. He was starting to hate the sight of his land. It was a stillborn thing: he'd meant to make something fresh and real, and instead he'd produced this cold, sterile photocopy. Something had gone wrong, and more and more he was starting to think that the problem was him.

He sat down at the worktable and stared at his notes, thinking about what Plum had said and waiting for some kind of signal to emerge out of the noise. Should he just walk in, stand there, look her in the eye? Maybe he should.

There she was, right there in the doorframe, watching him as if she knew what he was thinking.

"I'm here," he said. "Alice. It's time we talked. It's time we figured this out."

She floated there, free-falling in place, staring right through him. Something was missing: if they were going to talk, and if it was going to count, it should be here in the real world, not the copy. He wanted to bring her through, to force her out into the open, onto his ground. It would be a terrible risk. A niffin in lower Manhattan—if he lost control he could be looking at a magical September 11th. But you could talk yourself out of anything.

"Come here." Could she? "Come out here. Let's finish this."

Faint smile, but nothing more. Alice couldn't or wouldn't come through on her own. That meant he had to help her.

He began with a series of erasures and banishments and antimagic attacks, each one more powerful and violent than the next, but the land was tougher than it looked. They didn't scratch it. It wasn't going that easily, not without a fight.

He changed tacks: he picked up his staff, his lovely black wood and silver staff. It took five tries, whacking it against the brick pillars in the workroom, but he broke it in the middle and then twisted apart the two halves.

And even then the land persisted. Alice looked like she was enjoying the show. Maybe this wasn't a question of brute force.

He walked up to the threshold and stood six inches away. Closing his eyes, he willed the land to go away. He imagined it giving up, surrendering its existence, letting its cold substance dissolve as if it had never been. It never should have been. It didn't want to be. Let go.

Yes. He opened his eyes.

"Out, brief candle," he said, and blew softly, one puff.

The mirror-house collapsed from the outside in. There was a moment of silence—Quentin imagined the cold sandy outskirts dispersing outside, the raining streetlights ceasing to be. Then came a distant bang as the lower floors began contracting like an accordion. Quentin backed up as far as the doorway. Alice looked over her shoulder—if a niffin could disbelieve, there was disbelief on her face. Then the banging came closer, and finally the room behind her shut like a trash compactor and she was shoved rudely through the doorway into reality.

When she turned to face him again there was a new seriousness of purpose on her face. She wasn't playing anymore either. Quentin called down the stairwell.

"Guys! Plum!"

Alice smiled at him as if to say: sure, go on and call your little girl-friend.

"It's not like that."

As she passed the table her fingers brushed it and it began to burn. He backed down the stairs gingerly, never taking his eyes off her, as if she were a wild animal.

"Plum?" he called. "Eliot? Alice is out. I collapsed the land and she came through."

He heard Plum stir in her room.

"What?" She opened her door in a sweatshirt, hair loose, and saw Alice at the top of the stairs. She must have been taking a nap. "Oh. Was that a good idea?"

"Probably? Eliot!" Where was the High fucking King?

What was weird was, Quentin wasn't afraid. Usually in moments of crisis he was lost in a swarm of choices, paralyzed by the possibility that he might do the wrong thing—there were so many wrong things to do, and so few right ones! But not this time. This time the throughline was clear to him. There was only one right option, and it could be fatal, but death would be preferable to a life spent doing either the wrong thing or nothing at all.

"Plum, get behind me."

She did, for a wonder, and together they retreated downstairs to the living room, where he tried to stall Alice by blocking off the doorway. Kinetic magic: crude, but he had to try it. He threw together a barrier out of books, dishes from the kitchen, the pillows from the sofa, whatever he could get a magical grip on. But she passed right through them, and where she touched them they burned.

"Quentin!" Plum said. "This is my house! That I own! Don't break it!"

She put the fires out, but the air smelled like burning insulation.

"Plum, you have to get out of here," he said quietly. "Find Eliot and go."

Whatever he was going to do, he couldn't do it if he was worrying about Plum too. He couldn't hold back, and his control wasn't going to be good. In fact if he was lucky his control would be really, really bad. It was going to end here one way or the other: he was going to fix Alice or he was going to die trying. She'd died for him once already, he couldn't do any less for her.

An experiment: he brought his hands together, laced his fingers, and all the electrical cords in the room made for Alice like striking snakes. It was a trick he couldn't have pulled off before his father had died, but he carried that extra strength with him now. Current flowed, the lights browned out, and Alice's blue aura flickered. Quentin smelled melting plastic. Alice slitted her eyes with pleasure.

What next. He'd already tried magic missiles. A magnetic cage maybe. No? Just force then: wards, shields, thick invisible layers of power, one after the other, like he'd done when he was working on the page, wrapping around her and then contracting and then having the next one wrapped around it. Light refracted and bent around Alice, producing incidental distortions and rainbows. The spells shed little orbital sparks and streamers. He felt her pushing, probably with a tiny fraction of her strength, but she hadn't burst through yet. The mere fact that she felt resistance was progress.

Maybe it was love, or courage, or the plastic fumes, but Quentin felt strength building up in him, a rising, cresting flood of it. He'd felt this way once before in Fillory, on Benedict Island. And even farther back, that first night at Brakebills, when it had all come tearing out of him for the first time. But he was even stronger now.

It felt good.

Not much time left. Thank God the building was already warded up tight, because he could feel the energy in the room pressing at the walls, bulging them outward, threatening to blow out the windows. Alice shoved harder at the envelope of force, frowning. His eyes flicked around the room for anything metal, found the bare steel frame of the couch, jerked it to him with a magnetic spell. Amping up his strength, toughening his hands, he bent it into the shape of an arch with two feet: an omega.

He was almost too late. Like tearing tissue paper Alice was through her prison and on him. Her blue hands gripped the sigil just above his, but she couldn't get past it. Their faces were close together now. She was smiling as usual, showing her perfect sapphire teeth, as if she could barely keep from laughing her head off. Quentin smiled back.

This, at last, was right. He was meeting her head-on, like Plum said.

Strength to strength. He braced one leg behind him. No more skulking around in shadow worlds, this was real. He could feel the power of her, the buzz and snap of it. Could she feel him too? God, it was a relief to let go, to completely lose his shit and give it everything he had and find out once and for all if it was enough.

"Is that all, Alice?" he said. "Is that it? I want more. Give me everything."

The metal glowed red and white around their hands now. Instead of shielding his own hands he made them metal too: he borrowed the steel of the couch frame and drew it into them. They started to glow as he dumped more and more of his precious energy into keeping the ward going and keeping himself from catching on fire. He was going to beat this thing, this magical abomination that had Alice trapped inside it, he was going to pry it open and pull her out like the jaws of fucking life.

His magician's sixth sense warned him just as the balance shifted: this thing was going critical. His omega was steel, but at the end of the day it was only a couch frame, and he was asking more of it than it had to give. He managed one last shield, this one just around himself, then he let go. The metal glyph exploded into vapor in Alice's hands.

The blast pushed them apart—he skidded backward a few feet across the living room floor. He let it all drop. His shield evaporated. His hands and arms were flesh again. It was just him and her, nothing between them, just empty air and silence and seven years of lost time.

All through the fight he'd kept expecting himself to panic, but the panic never came, and now he knew it wouldn't. The old Quentin might have done it, but he wasn't a creature of fear anymore, jumping at his own shadow, never knowing who he was or why. When he was younger it seemed like the only time he wasn't afraid was when he was angry. He'd been so full of fear and self-doubt that the only way he could think of to be strong was to attack the world around him.

But that wasn't real strength. He understood that now. They'd both come so far to be here. He was getting a second chance, and he wasn't going to miss it.

"You," she said.

"I'm not the boy you used to know, Alice," he said. "Not anymore. That boy is gone. I know who I am now. But you don't know me."

A great, warm calm was in him, welling up out of the hidden reservoir where it had been waiting all this time, if only he'd known where to find it. Alice's eyes narrowed. She hung back, suspicious, studying him. Quentin began pulling his shirt off, started unbuttoning it and then just tore it off. It was time to go all in.

He nearly missed his chance. Having decided, evidently, that Quentin was bluffing, Alice went for him, and this time she was coming to kill him. He turned away and shouted a word he hadn't heard since he was twenty-two. He didn't know if Alice was technically a demon or not, but either way he had an empty demon trap tattooed on his back, and he was going to use it. It was all he had left.

He didn't see it happen, but there was a great inrush of air, like a giant gasping in surprise, and Alice cried out angrily—

"No. *No!*"

—and he heard the cry go up an octave and then cut off sharply.

Then the room was silent, and he was alone except for drifting motes of couch-fluff in the air. At the same moment his tattoo lit up with cold fire; it was like somebody had dumped liquid nitrogen on his back. When Fogg put a cacodemon in his back the night before graduation he'd felt nothing at all, but this wasn't nothing. This hurt. And there was pressure inside him, massive pressure. He couldn't breathe. He groaned like a woman in labor, trying to let some of it out, but it only got worse.

He could feel Alice in there. He felt her rage and her power and something like ecstasy. Quentin pressed his back against the coolness of the wall to try to ease the burning, but it did nothing. He felt like his rib cage was cracking. The veins were glowing in the backs of his hands.

The front door slammed open.

"What did you do? Where's Alice?"

Plum and Eliot were staring at him. They'd burst in ready for the fight of their lives.

"And you took your shirt off," Plum added.

"She's in my back," he whispered. He couldn't speak any louder. "I know."

He detached himself from the wall and began walking stiffly up the stairs. Sweat was starting out across his forehead, trickling down his chest.

"You should go," he whispered.

"What are you doing?" Plum asked, but he couldn't even answer her. He could feel Alice stirring inside him like a genie in her lamp. She wanted out by whatever exit she could find or make. In his mind he was putting things together, doing back-of-the-envelope calculations and then ignoring the answers when they weren't reassuring.

"What are you doing?" Plum shouted after him.

"Come on," Eliot said. "We have to help him."

They followed him up. He couldn't stop them, and Eliot was right, he needed their help. He climbed the stairs to the fourth-floor work-room, the skin on his back sore and stretched tight like a third-degree sunburn.

"Coins," he whispered. "Mayakovsky's."

There was enough room here. The spell came to him easily, auto-matically, like it had worn a deep channel right down the middle of him, even though he was casting it for the first time. He could see the page from the Neitherlands in front of him in his mind: the columns of num-bers, the turning orbits that spun around each other like a magician juggling rings, the plant with its long leaves rustling demurely in a wind from somewhere out of frame. He knew the whole thing by heart. Until now he just hadn't understood why.

This was what it was for. This was why he'd snatched it out of the air and saved it. Matter and magic. He'd thought it was about making mat-ter magical, but now he had something that was pure magic, and he was going to give it matter. Reverse the flow. He was going to bring Alice back into the world of the physical.

He snapped out orders—there was no time to be polite—and Plum and Eliot handed him things as he called for them: powders, liquids, books open to such and such a page, one of the gold coins. He took them without looking, like a surgeon up to his elbows in a patient.

It was like he'd been assembling the pieces without knowing it. He couldn't have done it without his newfound strength, and not without minor mendings either: he knew how to knit broken things together. He scraped at his insides for every last scintilla of magical strength. He was feverish, and his knees felt like they could buckle at any moment, but his mind was clear. He knew what he had to do, if he could just stay upright long enough.

When everything was complete, when the enchantment was hovering latent in the air like a thundercloud about to burst, he turned his back to the room and opened the trap.

It was like letting out an enormous breath that he'd been holding for way too long. The room flooded with blue light, the light in a swimming pool on a summer afternoon. Quentin almost blacked out with relief. Later he would look at his tattoo and find a raised, blackened scar in the center of the star.

Alice's blue form was floating limp in the center of the room, on its back, listless but stirring. She wasn't smiling now, not at all. Her expression, when she focused on him, was black. She was angry, a wasp who'd been trapped in a jar and then shaken, and she was ready to sting. She was the most beautiful, terrible thing he'd ever seen, like an acetylene flame, an incandescent filament, a fallen star right in front of him.

He met her gaze and held it and spoke a word in a language so old that the linguists of the world believed it to be lost and forgotten forever. But magicians had not forgotten.

Mayakovsky's coin, the second coin, flared in his hand, and he forced himself to grip it tight even though it felt like a fistful of molten gold or dry ice—like his fingers must be melting or blackening and curling up. Alice startled as if she'd heard a sound. Not his voice, but something else, something far off. A distant church bell tolling at dawn.

Then the air around her darkened, and the world began falling into her. It had begun: the spell was pulling atoms from the room around her. Her skin darkened and became dull and opaque. She writhed as particles swarmed around her like insects, embedding themselves in her form. Matter rushed at her, crowded into her, substituting crude substance for her luminous, translucent blue flesh.

Quentin stumbled back, and Plum and Eliot caught him, and together they staggered out through the doorway; it wouldn't do to be too close, to have any of their atoms pulled into Alice. The spell would do it if it had to, the spell didn't care. Alice was convulsing now, growing heavier, condensing out of the air, being forcibly embodied. She moaned, a deep agony moan, already half human. Her niffin-light was fading. She sounded like she was dying, and for a horrific second Quentin wondered if he'd been wrong, if he was killing her instead of saving her. But it was too late to take it back.

When it was finished, when the blue was all gone, Alice fell to the wooden floor with a dull smack, hard enough to bounce once and lie still. The room reeked of rarefied gases, sharp spikes in his nostrils.

Alice lay sprawled on the floor on her back, her eyes closed, breathing shallowly. She was flesh again. The old Alice, human Alice, pale and real and naked.

He knelt down next to her. Her eyes opened, just barely, narrowed against the light.

"Quentin," she said hoarsely. "You changed your hair."

CHAPTER 24

L isten up, everybody. I got a letter from Eliot."
    Janet felt comfortable in Eliot's chair in the meeting room in Castle Whitespire. She could have conducted business from her own official chair, but she liked Eliot's. It didn't look different from the other thrones, but there was something about it that felt more . . . pleasant. Accommodating.

Power, she supposed it was. It suits me.

"Point of order," Josh said. "Are you, like, High Queen now? Like with Eliot gone?"

Was she?

"Sure. Why not."

"It's just—"

"Your constitutional arguments are kind of *de trop* at this exact moment, Josh. Also I wrote most of the constitution, so you will definitely lose them. All of them." Josh opened his mouth. "Bup bup *bup!* Do you want to hear the letter or not?"

"Yes," Josh and Poppy said together. Then they gave each other a loathsome little miniature married smile.

"Sure," Poppy added.

Their deaths would be awesome—I mean the balcony was *right there*—but hard to justify politically. Janet moved on. For now.

"It goes like this." She held up the little paper tape, like a ticker tape, or a fortune-cookie fortune. "THICK PLOTTENS STOP UMBER

WAS SLASH IS EVIL AND MAYBE ALIVE STOP WHO KNEW
RIGHT STOP FIND HIM ASAP STOP MIGHT SAVE WORLD
STOP TRY UNDER NORTHERN MARSH MAYBE STOP BACK
SOONEST KISS STOP."

There was silence in the room.

"That's it?" Poppy said.

"You were expecting . . . ?"

"I don't know. Something a bit more formal maybe."

"He doesn't even say hi to us?" Josh said.

"No. Other questions?"

"Does he really have to do it like that? Like a telegram?"

"No, not really. I think he just enjoys it. Any questions of a more
substantive nature?"

Josh and Poppy shared another marital glance.

"I don't know how to phrase this exactly but what the fuck?" Josh
said. "Umber's not evil. Or wasn't evil. He was Ember's brother. Plus
He's been dead for like a million years or something. Martin Chatwin
killed Him."

"Or," Janet said, "maybe he didn't. Or He came back to life or something."

"Why hasn't Eliot come back?" Poppy said.

"That I don't know. I'm a little peeved about it myself. A little worried too. I've become quite attached to our High King. Maybe there's
something more interesting going on on Earth, but I can't imagine
what. Josh?"

"How does Eliot send you letters?"

"Oh. We rigged it up before he left. They sort of float to the surface
in that little gazing pool in the courtyard outside my bedroom, on these
strips of paper. It's very picturesque. Then you dry them out, and the
words develop like a Polaroid. Poppy?"

"Should we do it? Should we try to find Ember? I mean, Umber?
Sorry, I get Them mixed up. Baby brain, it's started already. Seriously, we
have to get moving with this because I'm almost in the second trimester
here. We've got six months."

One thing about Poppy, she had a can-do attitude. It was one of the things Janet liked about her. Maybe the only thing. Or she guessed Poppy's hair was all right too.

"But hang on," Josh said. "What if we do find Umber? What do we do with Him? I mean, you gotta figure He's pretty far up the power scale. It's not like we're going to intimidate Him."

"Well, I've been thinking about that," Janet said. "Maybe we stick Him in Ember's Tomb. Martin managed to trap Ember in there once, and He couldn't get out. Seems to me that thing is like a ready-made purpose-built ram-god-containment facility."

"But it's risky," Poppy said. "Could we even get Him in there? Maybe this is all a little precipitous?"

Just then Janet was overcome by the strangest sensation. She felt herself pulled ever so slightly to one side, her whole body, like she was starting to lose her balance. Then the room gave a little bump and jostle, and the feeling was gone again. It affected the others, too, she could see it.

Josh figured it out first.

"The room's stopped moving," he said.

Castle Whitespire was built on clockwork foundations that rotated its towers very slowly in a stately, never-ending dance, like the teacups in a really slow, boring carnival ride. They were driven by windmills. Ordinarily you hardly noticed it, but they noticed now, because it had just stopped. As far as she knew Whitespire's towers had never stood still before, even in the dark times, the worst times.

"Does that answer your question?" Janet said. "This world is falling apart. We have to do something, and this is the only lead we've got. I think we'd better use it."

"I'm just saying, we're talking about hunting a god here," Poppy said. "It's not going to be easy."

"If it were easy everybody would do it."

As soon as the tower stopped moving Josh had gone out on the balcony and leaned on the stone railing, looking down. Now Janet and Poppy followed him. Far below tiny people were spilling out of doorways, into the streets and courtyards, staring around them uncertainly, blinking in the late-afternoon sunlight. One by one they stopped and

looked up, looked to the three of them, shading their eyes, as if their
kings and queens could possibly have any answers.

"Idiots," Janet said, softly, but just for form's sake. Maybe the great
ever-spinning towers of Whitespire had ground to a halt, mayhap even
the heavenly spheres themselves no longer danced to the music of time.
Who the fuck knew. Maybe the only place she'd ever been happy was
about to fall apart. But not even the end of the world was going to stop
Janet from being a bitch. It was the principle of the thing.

They all went, all three of them. Four counting the baby. Josh and
Poppy had bickered—it didn't quite rise to the level of a fight—about
whether Poppy should come, but Poppy came out on top.

"You're worrying too much," she said. "I'll take good care of the
baby. You just take good care of me."

The trip to the Northern Marsh went more quickly this time. No
need for gallant-but-aimless diagnostic wandering in the wilderness.
This time they could take the direct route, the express train: hippogriffs,
the fastest fliers in the fleet.

You couldn't use them all the time. They were independent bastards,
valued their freedom, practically libertarians, and they were very fussy
about their feathers too, which you always ended up pulling out a few,
it was impossible not to. But desperate times, etc. They were better than
the pureblood griffins anyway—those things were just anarchists. Chaotic neutral all the way.

Janet's particular hippogriff had a funny red crest between its ears, a
feature she'd never seen before. It made a show of ignoring her as she
mounted, with the help of a boost from a loyal retainer. Just once before
the end of the world she wouldn't have minded a little gesture of respect
from one of these things. Ah well.

It was good to get a hippogriff's-eye view of Fillory, anyway, because
it at least confirmed that the halting of Whitespire wasn't an isolated
phenomenon. There were signs all over that things were seriously out of
joint. It was nothing like when she and Eliot had been traveling, just a
few days ago, and thinking about that she already felt nostalgia for it.

Now the grass in open fields waved and bent in strange, regular patterns, expanding circles and moving lines—from high overhead they looked like old-fashioned analog TVs on the blink, their vertical hold shot.

Then the eclipse that was a daily event in Fillory simply failed to happen. At first Janet couldn't put her finger on what was missing, but then she looked up and saw it: the moon and the sun were out of true. Where they should have lined up at midday, they missed each other, the horn of the moon just grazing the sun's corona and moving on, like a doomed aerialist who'd missed the catch.

"Shit!" Josh called out. "The Chalk Man's down!"

It was true: he had dropped to his hands and knees on his hillside, his featureless head drooping as if overcome by gravity, or just despair. His staff had fallen from his blobby hands. It floated beside him, in mid-hill. It was an incredibly pathetic sight.

And there was this endless goddamned summer. She had had enough of heat. Josh and Poppy were if anything even more shocked by all this than she was. They'd been snug in Castle Whitespire this whole time, breeding. They'd seen even less of it than Janet had.

The hippogriffs wouldn't set them down right in the swamp, because sure the world was ending, but that was no reason why they should get their precious talons and hooves muddy. But they found a reasonably clear, solid helipad-type spot on the perimeter and came in for an admittedly supernaturally graceful landing.

"Wait here," she told them. "Give us twenty-four hours. If we're not back by then you can go."

The hippogriffs stared at her with their angry yellow eyes and gave absolutely no sign as to whether they would or would not give her twenty-four hours. Janet struck out into the mud with Poppy and Josh trailing behind her.

"Not being critical at all," Josh said, "but if I were High King or High Queen or whatever, I would have brought maybe a detachment of soldiers with us? Like in a support capacity? Maybe that elite Whitespire regiment thing that's so hard to get into. You ever seen those guys drilling? It's nuts the stuff they can do."

Janet took a deep breath. Patience.

"We're hunting a god, Josh. You know how that movie goes. You send the shock troops in first, the really bad-ass ones, the definitely undefeatable guys, and what happens? They get slaughtered like instantly. And it's like *ooo, scary, nuh-uh, those guys were supposed to be undefeatable!* Then the heroes go in and do the real work. It's all just to build dramatic tension. I thought maybe we'd skip that part and cut to the chase."

"But I love that movie," Josh said, a little forlornly.

"That raises a good point though, Janet," Poppy said. "Since we're cutting to the chase. How are we supposed to go about fighting a god?"

"Not fighting," Janet said. "Hunting."

Even she wasn't that clear on the distinction she was making, but she thought it might shut them up for a few minutes so she could think. Somebody had to.

"And not we," Josh said. "You're not fighting. You're taking care of the baby."

"I'll take care of the baby," Poppy said, "by fighting."

It was warm and muggy, but the mud-water that kept oozing up through the sodden grass they were walking on was bitter cold. There were depths to this place that the sun couldn't touch. Fortunately Janet had on awesome boots.

"Anyway," she said, "Martin Chatwin beat Ember. So it can be done. What's Martin Chatwin got that the three of us don't have?"

"Like about six more fingers," Josh said. "For starters."

It was good to be out in the field again, whatever the odds. And it was good to be in charge. Before the desert she'd never really given things her all, at least not when the others were around to watch. It was too vulnerable-making; in a way she hadn't really had her all to give. No wonder the others hadn't taken her as seriously as they should have. Plus she'd done a few fucked-up things. She wondered whether Quentin felt angry about what happened that night. Like it was her that broke up him and Alice! She'd only done it out of habit. If you've got a junkie in the house, you don't leave your meds just lying on the table.

And like they would have lasted two more weeks anyway, given what a loser Quentin was back in those days anyway. The funny thing was, the more Quentin got his shit together the less she wanted to sleep with him. Weird how that worked.

When they found the boardwalk Janet started trotting along it, double-time. Poppy jogged along behind her but Josh called out "Hey, wait up!" and when they didn't he started sort of slowly motivating his doughy body along. Guy lives in a fantasy world without junk food or cars or trans fats or TV and he's still fat. You had to admire his dedication to the cause.

On the way Janet noticed a pair of child's shoes, ancient and weathered, abandoned on a rock. It was the oddest thing. They looked pitifully small. She wondered what could have brought a boy that young—they were a boy's shoes—all the way out here, this deep into the Northern Marsh, and what could have happened to him. Nothing good.

When the pier was in sight she drew the crossed axes from her back.

"Awesome axes," Josh said. "Where did you—"

"Your mom gave them to me," Janet said. "After I fucked her."

"Why—"

"Because she enjoyed it so much."

Not her best work maybe, but they couldn't all be winners. And she really didn't feel like telling that story again.

Janet stopped at the very end of the pier and looked around, hands on hips. Everything looked normal. Not a lot of apocalypse going on here. But then swamps already looked like the end of the world anyway. Maximum entropy, land and water commingled chaotically. There wasn't much farther downhill they could go.

Stray windlets roughened the surface of the bog. A couple of dead, thunderstruck trees poked up in the middle. I was just here, she thought. Like a week ago. Suddenly she felt powerfully aware of the circularity and futility of life.

Eliot had said Umber was under the swamp, which was both very specific and very vague. She thought about just jumping in blind, a leap of faith in Eliot and his intelligence-gathering skills. But then, giant turtle. While she was weighing the options, Poppy passed her and began climbing down the ladder. It was a slight breach of discipline, but this once she was going to let it pass. Poppy dipped an elegant toe in the water, then put her whole foot in.

"Huh," she said.

"Careful."

Poppy wasn't careful. With the traditional Australian's indifference to personal dryness and venomous underwater predators, she dived right in. The bog swallowed her up in one gulp, her entire lean length.

"Poppy!" Josh peered down after his vanished wife-and-child. "Poppy! Jesus!"

Nothing. Then Poppy's hand broke the still surface of the water, like the Lady of the Lake, except in this case instead of offering up a magic sword the hand just delivered a big enthusiastic thumbs-up.

"Oh, thank God."

Josh executed a well-practiced cannonball off the dock. Bombs away. So much for stealth. Janet descended the worn wooden ladder in a dignified fashion, like a normal person, until she was immersed up to her knees. She saw what Poppy meant—it did feel weird under there. Not wet, somehow, and like there was something trying to push her back up and out. She leaned down and put her head under.

And collapsed in an upside-down heap on wet ground. Janet felt thoroughly nauseated; her inner ear was objecting strenuously to what it was hearing from the rest of her senses. Something violently disorienting had just happened.

"Jesus!" She spat to keep herself from throwing up. Josh was already on his feet and jumping up and down.

"Again! Again!"

At least somebody was enjoying themselves.

They were under the water, the three of them, but inverted; that's what had happened. They were standing on the underside of the surface of the swamp, which now was hard and slick. It was dark down here, but it was pretty clear what the main event was, namely a big castle that looked exactly like Whitespire but creepier, its battlements all lit up with flaring white torches. The sky above it—or the lake bed, or whatever it was—was black.

"An underwater, upside-down Castle Whitespire," Josh said. "I'll admit, that would not have been my first guess."

"It's a mirror image."

"Mirrors invert left-right, not up-down," Poppy said, with tedious correctness. "Plus the black-white thing isn't—"

"OK, OK, I get it."

They met no resistance, but the drawbridge was up, so the three of them flew over the wall and into the courtyard. They saw no one. Josh knocked on the thick door to the outer hall. No answer, but it opened easily. The place looked empty but not abandoned—it was neat and clean, and more torches smoked and sputtered along the walls.

"Spooky," Poppy said.

They'd been standing there looking around aimlessly for a good minute before they even noticed the two guards standing frozen at the far end of the hall. Their eyes were dead—they looked about as alive as a couple of decorative urns.

"Oh," Josh said. He called to them. "Hey, guys! What is this place?"

The guards didn't answer. They wore somber, funerary versions of the Whitespire uniform, and that's what it was with their eyes: their pupils were really dilated, like they were on drugs. Which you couldn't really blame them, working down here. When Josh approached them they didn't salute him or even come to attention, but they did move: they crossed their halberds in front of the door to bar his way.

"Oh, come on," he said.

They lowered their weapons in his direction. Josh backpedaled.

"Got left!"

An ice axe from Janet took the one on the left straight in the forehead, sticking in his skull like it would have in a stump, splitting his helmet and his head right between his eyes. It was a beautiful throw. He dropped his weapon with a clatter and sank to a kneeling position but by some quirk of anatomy he didn't quite fall over. He did bleed though, the dark flood pouring over his face and spreading out across the stone floor.

"Or," Poppy said, "we could try diplomacy."

Josh and Poppy both cast kinetic spells on the one on the right, lofting him bobbing into a corner of the ceiling like a lost balloon at a birthday party. He dropped his halberd, and it clanged and bounced once on the floor. Janet felt a little embarrassed for him.

"I can't believe you killed yours, Janet," Josh said.

"Please. I don't even think these guys are human. They don't make any noise, did you notice?"

"Bleed though."

"Your mother bled when I—"

"Shh!" Poppy peered into the darkness the guards had been protecting. She held up a hand.

"—when I popped her cherry," Janet finished in a whisper.

"That doesn't even make sense!" Josh hissed.

"Shh!"

They shushed. In the silence, the dry, irregular sound of trotting hooves on stone. With some effort, her foot on the guard's cloven head, Janet rocked her axe back and forth till it came free.

A half hour's worth of not very dignified hide-and-seek followed. It was hard sometimes to figure out where exactly the sound was coming from. They padded along as silently as they could, trying to get a fix on it, cocking their heads and whacking each other on the shoulders and pointing and accusing each other of making too much noise in heated whispers.

Every once in a while they could hear a voice along with the hooves, muttering to itself, just on the edge of hearing:

"Yes, yes, just along here. Up we go. Right this way. Carefully now."

Who was He talking to? It was annoying.

The voice didn't sound at all like Ember's Olympian baritone. One time they realized they could take a shortcut, and they nearly headed Him off—they got a glimpse of His flickering haunches disappearing up a spiral staircase.

"A close shave!" they heard Him say. "Nearly caught!"

This was followed by a weird high quavering moan.

The three of them stopped in a vaulted gallery they knew from Castle Whitespire. Aboveground it would have been brimming with sunlight. Here they looked out the windows into depthless blackness. They could see the bright ring of water far below them, the surface of the upside-down swamp, a drowned sun swimming in it like a yolk in a silvery egg. Once in a while a few upside-down fish skittered past the windows.

The hooves started again, closer.

"I don't get this," Josh said. "Dude is a god. If He really wanted to get away from us He would just apparate or whatever. Either He wants to be caught or He's leading us into a trap."

"Let's find out," Janet said.

Now that was some leadership right there.

"I think He's heading up to the solarium," Poppy said.

"Great, then He's stuck. No way out."

"So we've got Him trapped."

"We could even just stay down here," Josh said, "and not go up there."

"What, and starve Him out?"

Even Poppy rolled her eyes.

"Let's get this over with and get out of here. This place is creeping me out."

"Yup." Janet was coming around to Poppy. 'Nother couple of decades and they might even start getting along. Janet unslung her axes, her Sorrows, and took the stairs at a sprint. You don't live in a castle full of spiral stairs without getting calves of adamantium. She heard Poppy whoop and head up behind her.

That quavering moan again.

"Goodness!" the voice said, up ahead, a genteel English tenor, not in its first youth, with a wee bit of a chuckle in it. It was an Edwardian comedy voice. "Alarums and excursions!"

It pissed her off. The fucking Chalk Man was down on his hands and knees. You think this is a joke? Alarums and excursions? I'll show you a fucking alarum. Pounding up the steps, right behind Him now, she got a whiff of His divine oily wool, weirdly sweet. Even she was feeling the burn in her legs. She should have stretched.

"Stop! Jesus! We just want to talk!"

We just want to talk about how fucking dead You'll be after we kill You.

Topside the solarium was a lovely domed chamber, but down here it was miserably gloomy in spite of the four torches that guttered in its four corners. Umber paused just long enough for Janet to get her first good look at him: He looked like His brother, obviously, enormous, with big ribbed horns swept back from his brow like they'd been brilliantined, except that where Ember was golden, Umber was a deep stormcloud gray.

"Off we go!" He called.

One of the windows lit up with sunlight; after an hour under the swamp it was like looking straight into an arc lamp. Umber had opened up a portal to the world above.

He surged forward, made one preparatory gallop and then leaped through the window, did a half barrel roll in midair, and landed upside-down on—the sky? The ceiling? No, it was just grass. Up there the gravity was flopped the other way. He stuck the landing.

"Haven't been up here for a while," Umber remarked, trotting away. "Closer than you think!"

Janet's shoulders sank. Dammit! We could chase this guy forever and never catch him. But Poppy, just reaching the top, was totally undaunted. Without breaking stride—in fact she picked up speed—she ran straight at the portal, planted her hands on the windowsill, did a handstand, let the gravity flip as she broke the plane, and landed on her feet on the grass, upside-down with respect to Janet and facing her.

It made Janet want to puke just watching her. And she wasn't even pregnant.

"Come on!" Poppy said brightly.

She spun around to face the receding ram-god. Even Umber seemed dismayed by her sprightliness. He startled like a mountain goat hearing a distant gunshot.

"Good-bye!" He called, and He was off like a greyhound, and the portal winked out.

Janet took a half step toward it, too late.

"Just like a fucking god," she said.

She was still standing there, arms crossed, glaring at it, when Josh came heaving up the top step like he was trying to get himself out of a swimming pool.

"I am gonna sack that guy's nutcastle," he croaked.

She brought him up to speed on the departed god, his absent wife, etc. He seemed oddly unperturbed.

"By the way, your wife is pretty impressive. I think I underestimated her. So kudos on that."

"Thanks, Janet." Josh was pleased. As he should be. "I never thought I'd hear you say the word *kudos*."

"Doesn't count cause we're underwater."

"So he did a portal, huh," Josh said. "Did you get a good look?"

"Hills," Janet said. "Grass. Sky."

Josh nodded, saying nothing, but his eyes were busy. He sketched rapidly in the air with his thick fingers, invisible diagrams and sigils.

"East coast. Northeast."

"What are you doing? Oh." She forgot Josh knew like three times as much as anybody else about portals.

He was already lost to concentration and his imaginary magic finger painting, which he accompanied now with satisfied grunts and hums. Janet had to give him credit: when he understood something, he really understood the hell out of it.

"Pfft," he said. "You gotta be kidding me."

He got up and began pacing around the room, looking around like he was tracking a mosquito nobody else could see.

"I figured He must be working on some, like, special secret divine transport grid that us mere mortals are locked out of, by virtue of our fallen mortal nature. Right? But not even! So where exactly was He standing when He threw this thing open?"

Janet gestured vaguely.

"Show me," Josh said. "I need to see it or it doesn't work."

Janet sighed.

"If you look at my ass I'm telling Poppy."

She got down on all fours, Umber-style, and reenacted the sequence exactly. Josh nodded gravely, staring at her ass.

Then he walked over to the window where the portal had been and pressed his palms against it. He rubbed the glass in slow circles, and it was like he was doing a grave rubbing: wherever his hands went, a ghostly, silvery afterimage of the portal appeared, or rather the view through the portal: a range of low hills, but oddly regular. Each hill was perfectly smooth, and more or less the same height as the others, and they were arranged in perfect straight rows. On top of each hill was a single tree, an oak tree by the look of them.

"Where the hell is that?" Josh said.

"Chankly Bore," Janet said. It had to be. Nowhere else like it. "Up north next to Broken Bay."

"Weird." Josh leaned in to study it, put his nose against the glass. "Chankly Bore. Is 'chankly' an adjective? Modifying 'bore'?"

"Some mysteries it doesn't pay to pry into. Josh, can you get us there?"

"Can I?" He snapped his fingers, once, twice. "Almost had it." Snap. On the third try the ghostly image burst into full color, hi-def, streaming live. "There you are, my queen."

Janet wound up inching herself across the low windowsill feet first, on her bum, her face chalk white, allowing the gravity to get a grip on her feet and drag them downward to where Josh could reach up to receive them from the other side. The gravitational sheer was just not something she could get her mind around, let alone her body—she froze halfway, looking a bit like Winnie-the-Pooh stuck halfway in and halfway out of Rabbit's burrow. In the end he had to yank her bodily through.

Then she was standing on Fillorian soil again, less than four hours after she had boldly set forth in search of the rogue god Umber, of Whom there was no sign. She ruminated, again, on the eternal return, the widening gyre, that seemed to govern human history. There is a tide in the affairs of men. A slack tide, that heaves up wrack and slime and rotting seaweed and deposits them on the sand, like a cat leaving the corpse of a rat on your doorstep. Then it slinks back in search of more.

They'd been so close. They could have solved everything. And now they wouldn't. He'd gotten away.

At any rate the Chankly Bore was a majestic sight in person. The hills ran on into the distance in their rows, not perfectly regular, she saw now, but almost, like the rubber dimples of a nonslip mat writ very, very large. Each one had its own tree at the summit, like a candle on top of a cupcake, and each tree was different. In places the flanks of the hills had been bleached a tawny golden yellow by the endless unyielding iron summer.

There was Poppy, waiting for them, a quarter-mile off. She pointed—wait a minute, maybe all wasn't lost after all. Umber wasn't hiding, He was standing right there, looking at them, at the summit of one of the hills—one row in, three over. He wasn't even moving! They could see Him totally plainly!

She started toward Him.

"Don't run!" she shouted, pleaded even, as if the sound of her voice could keep Him there. "Don't run away! Please! Just stay there!"

Umber didn't run. He waited for them.

He didn't even look especially concerned as the three humans, two queens and a king, plus a royal heir in utero, came straggling up the slope. As backdrops for earthshaking events went, the Chankly Bore was a corker. The view was sublime. Janet wondered if someone had planted the trees on the tops of the hills or if they'd just grown like that.

Actually the entity most likely to know the answer to that question was ten yards away and closing. As she came up to Him she slowed, hardly believing that He wasn't going to bolt the moment she came too close. His stupid woolly face was impassive.

"So," Janet said, breathing hard from the climb, hands on knees, "did somebody plant these trees or did they just grow like that?"

"Do you like them?" Umber said. "They're Mine of course. My brother did the hills, though I don't think He meant to leave them like this. I'm sure He planned to scatter them about artfully later on, here and there. He liked to create the appearance of deep geological history. But I said, 'No, no, they're wonderful just as they are.' And I put a single tree on top of each one, and they've stood like this ever since. From the First Day.

"One of them is a clock-tree now." That short quavering moan again—that was how He laughed, it turned out. How incredibly annoying and affected. "Don't know how she did that. A marvelous facility, that witch has."

His manner was different from Ember's. He was genteel, a little distracted, a little amused, a touch effeminate. Like if He'd been wearing any clothes He would have worn a bow tie and a purple waistcoat. She couldn't tell if He was sort of lofty and above it all or just a bit dotty.

But it didn't matter because either way the moment was here. This was it, exposition time, He was going to tell them everything, all the missing pieces, and then they would know what to do to make Fillory live again—oh God, she realized, how she wanted it to live! She didn't want to go back. She wanted to stay a queen!

Another case solved. After all that urgent chasing Janet suddenly felt like she had all the time in the world. A deep red sunset was getting going on the horizon, like a livid bruise just starting to show.

"You seem different from Your twin brother," she said.

"From who?"

"Your brother? Ember? Your twin?"

"Oh! Oh." He had a bit of a selective deafness thing going on. "We're just fraternal."

"We thought You were dead."

"Oh, I know!" Whinnying laugh. Umber actually trotted once in a circle, like a cat chasing its tail, such was His pleasure. "But I was just pretending. Martin wanted it that way. Such a strange boy. Never came out of the Oedipal phase, I don't think. He was always talking about his mummy in his sleep, wondering if his father was alive, that sort of thing.

"But of course You can get so much done when everyone thinks You're dead. No interruptions. No one prays to a dead god, why would they? Though I did spend a while in the Underworld. Not that I had to, but I was getting into the spirit of the role. They wanted Me to be the lord of it, the dead did, but I wouldn't. Imagine that—Me, god of the Underworld! I much preferred something less grand. More like, I don't know, a visiting research fellow.

"But I did enjoy My time there. It's so quiet. And the games are so charming! I could have stayed forever, I truly could have.

"And then I spent a few years as Ember's shadow, following Him everywhere, trotting around under His feet. He never knew! I would have thought it would be obvious, with My name. But you know, Ember doesn't think that way. He never did. He's very literal about things."

"But why would You do it in the first place?" Poppy was frowning and shaking her head. "I mean not the shadow thing, but why would You turn Martin into the Beast?"

A deep sigh from Umber. He dropped His golden eyes to the turf.

"That turned out very badly. Very badly. He wanted it so much, and I thought it would be good for him. But in the end I was so disappointed in Martin—his behavior. Disgraceful. Do you know what it was about Martin? He had no self-control. None!"

"I would say that yes, that turned out extremely badly," Josh said. "Not a lot of winners there."

"Not even Martin, in the end," Umber said sadly. "Poor boy. He wanted so terribly to stay here. He never stopped talking about it. And he was very brilliant. I couldn't say no, could I? I wanted to give him what he wanted, I only want to give everybody what they want! But then the things he did. He gave up his humanity, you know, in order to stay here in Fillory. He sacrificed it to Me, and there's a great deal of power in that. Even I was surprised at how much he got out of it.

"But then would you believe it, it was the best part of him! The rest of him turned out to be an absolute turd. I just went into hiding—he really might have killed Me if he could have found Me. Then later he said he did, and I let it stand. It's disappointing." Umber sighed and settled down onto the grass, making Himself comfortable. "So disappointing. We had to change the rules because of it. That's why We let you lot stay, you know. We don't send the kings and queens home anymore."

"But why did you take it?" Josh said. "I mean his humanity?"

"Well—" And the ram looked down again, this time coyly embarrassed. He trailed one of His fore-hooves in the grass. "I suppose I had a notion that if I possessed Martin's humanity, I could be king of Fillory. As well as god. A god-king, you might say. It was just an idea. But then I've been enjoying being dead so much, I haven't even tried!"

This conversation wasn't going quite the way Janet had thought it would. She didn't expect to like Umber, but she hadn't expected to hate Him so much. She was hoping for more of a charming-supervillain type. That she could relate to. But Umber wasn't charming. He had a way of not taking responsibility for things. She may have been a bitch, but at least she copped to it.

"This is all really fascinating," she said. "Truly. But it's not actually why we wanted to talk to You."

"Isn't it?"

"Which by the way," Josh said, "since we're talking, why did You sort of run away just then, and then stop running away?"

"Oh!" Umber looked surprised. "I thought you'd like that. Bit of a chase. Wasn't that what you wanted?"

"Not really, no," Janet said.

"Though I did like the part when I saved everything," Josh said. "That was good. You know, with the portal."

"There!" Umber said. "You see? And you needed the exercise too."

This had the effect of canceling out Josh's triumph. Poppy patted his arm.

"Well, whatever," he said. "Look, what about this apocalypse thing? End of the world. How are we going to stop that? That's Your thing, right?"

Umber actually looked wounded.

"The apocalypse? Oh, no. That's not one of Mine."

"It's not?" Janet said. "Wait."

"Goodness no. Why would I do that?"

The two queens and the king looked at each other. Something began dying a little inside Janet. Oh yes—hope. That's what people called it.

"But if You're not—?" Poppy said. "Then how are we going to—?"

The astonishment was plain even on Umber's inhuman face.

"Stop it? You can't think I would know! I don't think you *can* stop it. How would you stop an apocalypse? It's just nature. It happens by itself."

"So you can't . . ." Josh said, but he trailed off.

"But then—" Janet said. She couldn't finish her sentence either. She'd been sure this was it. The answer, the end of the quest, at last. She'd been so sure.

The impulse came over Janet out of nowhere; nowhere was where she got a lot of her best impulses these days. It suddenly all linked up in her head: Umber had taken Martin's humanity, and He made it all sound like a lark, like what else could He do? But Martin had become the

Beast, the Beast had bitten off Penny's hands and crushed Quentin's collarbone and made Alice turn herself into a niffin. And he'd eaten that girl back in school, what was her name. That all went back to Umber.

She ripped one of her axes from its strap on her back and in the same motion clouted Umber in the head with it. She didn't even have time to put an ice blade on it, it was just a cold steel spanner straight to the ram-jowls.

"Yah!"

Umber's eyes went wide. She did it again, a lot harder this time, and His front knees buckled.

These crazy axes. She'd give the Foremost that, he hadn't oversold them. They were everything he'd said they were and more. You could hit a god with them, and He would feel it.

Umber started to rise, shaking His long muzzle, befuddled more than anything else, and Janet hammered Him again, and again, and again, and His legs folded under Him and He sank down and lost consciousness. Then she hit Him once more, cracked Him right on His ear, knocked a tiny chip out of one of those big horns. Blue sparks flew.

"That's for everything You did! And everything You didn't do! You fucking jerk!"

"Janet!" Poppy said, losing her cool a bit for once. "Jesus!"

"Who cares? It's not Him. He can't help us. He doesn't know anything." Plus who knows when was the next time she'd get to beat down a god? Especially one who so obviously deserved it? Umber sprawled on His side, unconscious, the tip of His thick tongue poking out of His slack mouth.

"Loser." She spat on Him. "You could never have been a king anyway. You're too much of a pussy."

The others just stared at her, and at the slumbering god, laid out on the putting-green grass under a tree on top of a hill in the Chankly Bore.

"That was for Alice," she said. "And, you know, Penny's hands. All that stuff."

"No, we got it," Josh said. "Message received."

"We should go," Poppy said.

But they didn't, or not yet. In the distance, through a gap in the

Nameless Mountains, they could see that the sun had almost reached the rim of the world. They watched it setting.

But then it didn't quite set. It didn't quite make it. Instead of dipping below the horizon, the sun seemed to come to rest on it. Bit by bit, increment by increment, its lower edge flattened, and distant flares and gouts of flame began to rise up around it, complicating the sunset. There was a flash of light, then another, a distant bombardment. The sound reached them a few seconds later, a crackling boom, and the tremor a few seconds after that, a heavy industrial vibration passing through the earth, like someone was applying a belt sander to the rim of the world. A few leaves shook down from the tree behind them.

"What," Josh said, "the fuck is that."

Janet wished she didn't get it, but she did.

"It's the end." She sat down on the crown of a hill in the Chankly Bore and hugged her knees. "It's starting. We're too late. The apocalypse has begun."

CHAPTER 25

Alice slept. She slept for twenty hours give or take, in Quentin's bed, flat on her back, mouth propped open, perfectly still under a thin sheet, not once stirring or rolling over. Quentin stayed awake as long as he could watching her, listening to her faint wheezing. Her hair was long and lank and matted. Her skin was pale. Her fingernails needed cutting, and she was bruised on one arm from when she'd fallen to the floor. But she was healthy and whole. She was her.

Quentin looked at her and looked at her: she was finally back. He felt like the rest of his life could begin now. He didn't know if he was still in love with Alice, but he knew that being in the same room with her made him feel real and whole and alive in a way that he'd forgotten he could. When he couldn't stay awake any longer the others took over.

He was downstairs eating breakfast at noon, getting ready for another shift, when she woke up.

"She said she was hungry," Plum said.

Quentin looked up from his Cheerios to see her in the doorway, wrapped in Plum's pale blue bathrobe, looking like the palest, most wan, most precious, most vulnerable creature he'd ever seen. There were purple shadows under her eyes.

He stood up, but he didn't go to her. He didn't want to crowd her. He wanted to take things at her pace. He'd had a lot of time to think about this moment, and his one resolution was that he wasn't going to get too excited. Calm was what she needed. He was going to pretend he was greeting her at the arrivals gate after she'd been away on a long, disastrous journey.

It was easier than he thought. He was just happy to see her. There were no road maps for this, but they would figure it out. They had all the time in the world now.

"Alice," he said. "You're probably hungry. I'll get you something to eat."

Alice didn't answer, just shuffled over to the table, then stared down at it as if she were uncertain as to how precisely this apparatus worked. He put out a hand, to guide her maybe, but she shied away. She didn't want to be touched.

She lowered herself cautiously into a chair. He got her some Cheerios. Did she like those? He couldn't remember. It was all they had. He placed the bowl in front of her, and Alice regarded it like it was a bowl of fresh vomit.

Probably niffins didn't eat. Probably this was her first meal in seven years, because this was her first time having a body in seven years. After another minute she clumsily dipped a spoon in it. There was a sense of everybody trying not to stare at her. She chewed for a few seconds, robotically, like somebody who'd seen some crude diagrams of what chewing food looked like but had never actually tried it before. Then she spat it out.

"Told you we should've got Honey Nut," Plum said.

"Give her time," he said. "I'll run out for some fresh fruit. Fresh bread. Maybe that would go down easier."

"She might be thirsty."

Right. Quentin got her a pint glass of water. She drank it in one long swallow, then she drank another, gave a colossal belch and stood up.

"Are you all right?" Plum said. "Quentin, why isn't she talking?"

"Because fuck yourself," Alice said in a hoarse whisper. She went back upstairs and back to bed.

Quentin and Eliot and Plum sat around the kitchen table. The fridge had developed an annoying fault whereby it hummed loudly until somebody got up and gave it a shove, the way one would get a sleeper to stop snoring, whereupon it fell silent for half an hour and then started humming again.

"She should be eating," Quentin said. He got up. He couldn't stay sitting down; as soon as he sat he bounced back up. He'd sit down when Alice was better. "She should at least be hungry. Maybe she's sick, maybe we put her body back together wrong. Maybe she has a perforated liver."

"She's probably just full," Eliot said. "Probably she ate a bunch of people right before we turned her back and she just has to sleep it off."

Quentin couldn't even tell if it was funny or not. He didn't know where the line was anymore. And whatever Eliot said, he'd spent almost as much time at Alice's bedside as Quentin had.

"She'll be fine," Plum said. "Stop fussing. I mean, I was sort of expecting her to be grateful for us having saved her from being a monster, but that's OK. I don't need to be thanked."

"She looks good, anyway. Hasn't aged a day."

"I keep wondering what it was like, being a niffin," Quentin said.

"Probably she doesn't even remember."

"I remember everything."

Alice stood at the foot of the stairs. Her face was puffy from all the sleep. She came in and sat down at the table again, moving more confidently now but still like an alien unaccustomed to Earth's gravity. She seemed to be waiting for something.

"We got some fruit," Quentin said. "Apples. Grapes. Some prosciutto." He'd grabbed whatever looked yummy and reasonably fresh at the fancy market around the corner.

"I would like a double scotch with one large ice cube in it," Alice said.

Oh.

"Sure. Coming right up."

She still wasn't making eye contact with anyone, but it seemed like progress. Maybe it would relax her—help her get past the shock. So long as her liver wasn't actually perforated.

Quentin took down the bottle, feeling very conscious that he was making things up as he went along. He clunked an ice cube into the glass and poured whiskey over it. The thing was not to be afraid of her.

He wanted her to feel loved. Or maybe that was too much, but he wanted her to feel safe.

"Anybody else?" he called from the kitchen.

The silence in the room was stony.

"Right then."

He poured one for himself too, neat. He was damned if he was going to let his newly resurrected ex-girlfriend have her first drink in seven years alone. Plum and Eliot were both for once at a loss for anything to say. He poured them scotches too, just in case they changed their minds.

Alice slurped her whiskey down thirstily, then she took Plum's and drank that too. When she was done she stared into the empty tumbler, looking disappointed. Eliot discreetly moved his glass out of her reach. Quentin thought of getting her the bottle, then thought maybe he shouldn't. She should have more water.

"Do you want—?" he began.

"It hurt," Alice said. She let out a shuddering breath. "If you want to know. Have you ever wondered, Quentin? Did you ever really try to imagine what it felt like—really try? I remember thinking, maybe it won't hurt, maybe I'll get off easy. You never know, maybe magic fire is different. I'll tell you something: it's not different. It hurt like a bastard. It hurt approximately as much, I would guess, as being on fire with regular fire would. It's funny, the worst pain I ever felt till then was getting my finger caught in a folding chair. I guess I'd been lucky."

At the memory she stopped and looked into her glass again, to make absolutely sure she hadn't missed anything.

"You'd think your nerves wouldn't go up that high, but they do. You'd think they'd have an upper limit. Why would it be possible for people to feel so much pain? It's maladaptive."

No one had an answer.

"And then it didn't hurt at all. I can remember when the last bits of me went—it was my toes and the top of my head at the same time—and then the pain was completely gone, and I wanted to cry with relief because it was over. I was just so relieved that my body was gone. It couldn't hurt me anymore.

"But I didn't cry, did I? I laughed. And I kept on laughing for seven years. That's what you'll never get. You'll never, never, never get it." She stared down at the tabletop. "It was all a joke and the joke never got old."

"But it wasn't a joke," Quentin said quietly. "It was the most terrible thing any of us had ever seen. Penny had just gotten his hands bit off, and I lost half my collarbone, and Fen got killed. And then we lost you. It wasn't a joke."

"*Shutthefuckup!*" Alice barked. "You whining little shit! You'll never understand anything!"

Quentin studied her. The thing was not to be afraid. Or failing that not to look afraid.

"I'm sorry, Alice. We're all so very, very sorry. But it's over now, and we want to understand. Try. See if you can explain it to me."

She closed her eyes and breathed deeply.

"You don't understand, and you will never understand. You never even understood me when I was human, Quentin, because somebody as selfish as you are could never understand anybody. You don't even understand yourself. So don't think you can understand me now."

Eliot opened his mouth to say something but Alice cut him off.

"Don't defend him! You never had the guts to have a real feeling in your life, you're so drunk all the time. So shut up and listen to somebody tell you the truth for a change."

They listened. She looked like Alice—she was Alice—but something wasn't right.

"Once my body was gone, once I was completely a niffin . . . do you know, I kept thinking of this old toothpaste commercial. I don't know why I thought of it, but the slogan was 'that fresh-from-the-dentist feeling.' And that's what it felt like, exactly that. All the scum had been scrubbed away. I felt fresh and light and icy-clean. I was pure. I was perfect.

"And all of you were standing around looking so horrified! Do you see what's funny yet? I remember what I thought then. I didn't think about Martin or Penny or you or anything. The only thought in my head was *at last. At last.* I'd been waiting for this moment my whole life without knowing it.

"When I did it, when I cast the spell, I thought maybe I could control the power long enough that I could use it to kill Martin. But once I had the power, once I was a niffin, I didn't want to control it anymore. I didn't care, not in the slightest. You're just lucky I did kill him, very lucky. I never would have lifted a finger to save people like you.

"But I wanted to know if I could do it. When I pulled his head off it was more like a toast, like popping a cork. A toast to my new life! You want to know what it's like to be a demon? Imagine knowing, always and forever, that you are right, and that everyone and everything else is wrong."

She smiled at the memory.

"I could just as easily have killed you all. So easily."

"Why didn't you?" Quentin honestly wanted to know.

"Why would I?" she spat. "Why would I bother? There was so much else to do!"

This had gone badly wrong, and he should have seen it coming. Her body was back, but her mind—you don't spend seven years as a demon without consequences. She was traumatized. Of course she was.

"So you left."

Keep her talking. Maybe she would talk herself out.

"I left. I went right through the wall. I barely felt it, it was like mist to me. Everything was mist. I went right through the stone into the black earth. I remember I didn't even close my eyes. It was like swimming in a tropical ocean at night, warm and rich and salty and dark."

Alice paused there, and she didn't speak for a full minute. Quentin fetched water for her. She seemed to have lost track of the desire to keep on talking, but then it found her again.

"I liked it in the earth. It was dark and dense. Remember what a good girl I was? Remember how meek and pleasing I was to everybody? For the first time in my life I could just be. That was always part of the problem, Quentin. I felt like I had to be *interested* in you all the time. You wanted love so desperately, and I thought it was my job to give it to you. Poor little lost boy! That's not love, that's hell. And I was getting a taste of heaven. I was a blue angel now.

"I swam through the ground for months. It's full of skeletons. Magical dinosaurs, miles long. There must have been a great age of them.

I followed the spine of one for a whole day. Caves, too, and ancient earthworks, and many, many dwarf tunnels. I found a whole underground city once, where the roof had fallen in, a long time ago. It was full of bodies. A hundred thousand dwarfs buried alive.

"Even farther down there are black seas, with no outlets, buried oceans full of eyeless sharks that breed and die in the darkness. There are stars down there too, the understars, burning underground, embedded in the earth, with no one to see them. I might have stayed down there forever. But in the end I broke through to the other side."

"We know about the Far Side," Quentin said.

"But you haven't been there. I know that. I watched you sometimes. I was there at the End of the World, watching from inside the wall, when they turned you away. I followed you there in your little ship, nine fathoms deep, like the spirit in the *Ancient Mariner*. I watched your friend die on the island. I watched you fuck your girlfriend. I watched you go to Hell."

"You could have helped us, you know."

"No, I couldn't. No, I couldn't!" Her face was full of a crazy joy. "That's the thing! And do you know why? *Because I didn't care.*"

She stopped and sniffed.

"Funny. I couldn't smell when I was a niffin."

But she didn't laugh.

"Then I went the other way. I let myself rise and float up and out like a balloon, into the outer darkness. I jostled the stars on my way up. I entered the sun, spent a week in its heart, riding it around and around and around. I was indestructible, nothing could touch me, not even that.

"I went farther. Did you ever wonder, Quentin, whether the universe of Fillory is like ours? Whether it goes on and on, and there are other stars and other worlds? There aren't. Fillory is the only one. I went out there, out past the sun and the moon, out through the last layer of stars—the stars were the only things in all my time as a niffin that I couldn't pass through—and then nothing. I flew and flew for days, never getting tired, never getting bored, and then I turned around and looked back, and there was Fillory. It looks hilarious from far away, you can't imagine: a flat whorled disk, in a crowd of stars, balanced on a tottering tower of turtles like in Dr. Seuss. It's ridiculous. A little toy land, looking for all the world like a piece of spin art, inside a buzzing swarm of white stars. I watched it for a long time. I didn't know if I would ever go back. It's the closest thing I ever felt to sadness."

She fell silent. The fridge buzzed. Eliot got up and shoved it.

"But you did go back," Quentin said.

"I went back. I did whatever I wanted. Once I boiled a lake with everything in it. I chased birds and animals and burned them. Everyone was afraid of me, I was a bluebird of unhappiness. Sometimes they screamed or cried and begged me. Once—"

Alice gasped suddenly, as if something cold had touched her.

"Oh God. I killed a hunter." A quick, convulsive sob gripped her, almost a cough. "I'd forgotten that till just now. He was going to kill a deer. I didn't want him to. I burned him to nothing. It took no time at all. He never saw me."

She was breathing hard, hoarsely, one hand on her chest, like she was trying not to pass out or throw up. Her gaze darted around the room.

"It's all right now, Alice," he said softly. "It's not your fault."

That seemed to revive her. Alice slapped her palms down on the table. Her expression was angry again.

"It is my fault!" She shrieked it at him, as if he were trying to take away her most precious possession. "I killed him, me! I did that! No one else!"

She put her head down on her arms. Her shoulders were tense.

"I hated him. But I hated everyone. And more than anyone I hated you, Quentin. Hate isn't like love, it doesn't end. It goes on forever. You can never get to the bottom of it. And it's so pure, so unconditional! Do you know what I see when I look at you? I see dull, stupid, ugly creatures full of emotional garbage. Your feelings are corrupt and contaminated, and half the time you don't even know what you're feeling. You're too stupid and too numb. You love and you hate and you grieve and you don't even feel it."

Quentin stayed very still. It wasn't even that she was wrong. It was true, that's what people were like. But she'd forgotten that he knew that too, and that once upon a time that was part of what brought them together.

But he didn't say that. Not yet. She stopped and sat up again.

"I'm having weird cravings. Mangos. Marzipan." She frowned. "And—what's it called? Fennel? Then it goes away. It's been so long since I tasted anything."

Her voice when she said that last was the closest thing to the old Alice that he'd heard since she woke up.

"I had so much power. So much power. After a while I realized I could let myself slip backward in time. It was easy. If you think about it you're moving through time all the time, one second forward every second, but you don't have to. You can just let yourself stop. I could almost do it even now—it's as if you're on a rope tow, up a ski slope, and you just let your mittens go slack, let the rope slide through your fingers, and you slow down and stop. There goes the present, rolling on without you, it's gone, and just like that you're in the past. It's a wonderful feeling.

"But you can't change anything, you can only watch. I watched the Chatwins come to Fillory. I watched people be born and die. I saw Jane Chatwin have sex with a faun!" She snorted with laughter. "I think she was a very lonely person. Sometimes I just watched people read or sleep. It didn't matter, it was all funny. It never stopped being funny.

"Once I let myself go all the way back, all the way to the beginning of Fillory. The beginning of everything, or this everything anyway. It was as far as you could go. You bumped up against it, like you'd reached the end of your string.

"You couldn't call it a pretty sight, the dawn of creation. It was more like the corpse of whatever had come before. Just a big desert and a shallow, dead-looking sea. No weather, no wind, just cold. The sun didn't move. The sunlight was . . . unpleasant. Like an old fluorescent light that a bunch of flies had died in. Looking back now I think the sun and moon must have collided and melted together into one single deformed heavenly body.

"I watched the sea for a long time. You wouldn't think a body of water that big could be so still. Finally a big old tigress came loping down to the water. Her ears were notched, and she'd lost an eye and it had healed shut. You could see her padding along from a mile away. I thought she must be a goddess.

"She came down to the edge of the water. She looked at her reflection for a bit, then she went trotting into the water, up to her shoulders. She stopped then, and shuddered, and sneezed once.

"Obviously it was distasteful to her, but she did it anyway. She seemed very brave to me. She kept on going until she was totally submerged. And then nothing. She had drowned herself. I saw her body float up to the surface, on its side, slowly turning in place in the slack tide, and then it sank again for good.

"For a long time after that nothing happened. Then the water kind of gathered itself into a wave, and the wave threw up two big curly shells on the shore. They lay next to each other for a while, and then another wave came and left behind it a sheet of foam. The sand underneath them kind of stirred and shook itself and it sat up, and that was Ember. The foam was His wool. The shells were His horns.

"Ember went trotting down the beach until He found a couple more curly shells, and He nudged them around for a bit till they were next to each other and then stood next to them so that His shadow fell over them, and then the shadow stood up, and that was Umber. They nodded to each other and then went trotting together up into the sky.

"They took turns licking at the big moon-sun in the sky until it split into two things again, and then Ember butted the sun in one direction and got it moving, and Umber butted the moon, and the whole business started again. And that was the beginning of Fillory.

"But mostly I didn't give a shit about shit like that. Do you know what my favorite parts of the past were? I liked to watch myself sleep with Penny, because it hurt you. And most of all I liked to watch myself burn. I liked to go back to when I died and hide in the walls and watch it happen. Over and over again."

"Could you see the future?" Eliot asked.

"No," she said, in the same lightsome, detached tone. It was all the same to her. "Something to do with timelines and information flow, I think."

"Maybe it's just as well," Quentin said.

"If I could have I sure as shit wouldn't have come back here."

"That's what I meant."

"At first I couldn't even get to Earth, but something changed. The barrier softened and I could. I found out by accident: I liked mirrors— I liked looking at myself without flesh—and then one day I touched one and went through into a weird space inside it. It was in between, like the Neitherlands. Mirrors within mirrors took you farther down, deeper and deeper, and at some point they became mixed up with the mirror-spaces of other worlds. I spent months in there. It was cold, and empty, or almost—I met a lost bird once, fluttering around, trying to get out. When I came back up it was into this world, not Fillory.

"I didn't mind. Brakebills was interesting. Lot of magic there, and a lot of mirrors—it had a very complex mirror-space. I thought I might find my brother there, but I didn't. But I found you, Quentin. You were a scab I wanted to keep picking. You hurt me, even then, and pain was something I enjoyed.

"And the people were interesting. I could tell Plum was connected to Fillory, though I'm still not quite sure how. I was so sure you were going to fuck her."

"Why does literally everybody think that?" Plum muttered.

"And then you tried to make a land!" She was speechless with silent laughter for a few seconds. "Oh my God, it's so pathetic! You—Quentin, you could never make anything! Don't you see? How could somebody like you create something that was alive? You're a hollow man! There's nothing inside you. All you could make was that cold, dead mirror-house.

"And do you know why? Because all you ever do is what you think people expect you to do, and then you feel sorry for yourself when they hate you."

"I've changed a lot, Alice," Quentin said. "Maybe that was true once, I don't know. But I've changed a lot in seven years."

"No. You haven't."

"Think about this: could the Quentin you knew have made you human again?"

Alice was silent for a few seconds, long enough that Plum jumped in.

"Why are you telling us all this anyway?" Plum appeared to have had enough of Alice. "I mean it's fascinating and all, but it's sort of not what we expected."

"I am telling you this," Alice hissed, "so that he knows *what he did*." She was answering Plum, but she stared at Quentin.

"Tell me what I did." Quentin stared back at her. Her eyes had changed—they weren't quite the same eyes she'd had before. "I want to know."

"Then listen: you robbed me." She spat it. But she was already losing steam, she didn't even have the energy to be angry anymore. "I was perfect. I was immortal. I was happy. You took all that away from me. Did you expect me to be grateful? Did you? I didn't want to be human again, but you dragged me back into this body."

She held up her hands like they were low-grade meat, a butcher's discards.

"I lost everything, twice. The first time I gave it up. But the second time you stole it."

CHAPTER 26

Another tremor. It shook Umber awake. He opened His eyes.
"My heart," He whispered.

But when Janet looked away from the sunset, the sunfall, the god was already gone.

Lots to do. World ending. Can't hang around. He bounced back pretty fast from His beating, she would give Him that. It crossed her mind that maybe He'd been faking—maybe He'd gone down easy, taken a dive. It would have been like Him.

Either way she was kind of relieved Umber was gone. She didn't especially want to spend the end of the world with Him.

Meanwhile the action on the edge of the world was deeply, sublimely awful. The sun was squashing there like a rotten pumpkin—it hadn't just grazed the rim of Fillory, it was definitively, agonizingly bottoming out there, grinding itself flat, spending its remaining thermal and kinetic energy on destroying itself and throwing stupendous curling gouts and ferns of fire in the air and erecting a vast pillar of steam reaching up to the sky.

She'd never even seen the edge of the world. The others had, but now she never would. Or even if she did it wouldn't be the same: now it would have a big cigarette burn on it. Janet looked over her shoulder at the other horizon and saw that the moon was rising, as per usual. Good old moon. It must orbit twice as fast as the sun, she thought, to get in its eclipse at noon and then get back around again to rise in the evening.

Or no, it would have to go even faster than that. Variable speed? Multiple moons? She started trying to figure it out and then stopped. What did it even matter now.

"We shouldn't be here," Poppy said. "We should be back at the castle."

"What does it even matter," she said, out loud this time.

She wished Eliot were here. Or Quentin. Josh and Poppy were all right, but come on, they were short-timers, rookies. She would have liked the company of another old-schooler like herself. Even Julia.

"This means we're the last," she said. "The last kings and queens of Fillory, ever. I suppose that's a claim to fame."

"It's not over yet. We should go back to Whitespire. The people need us."

That's the spirit.

"Go," Janet said. "You're right, take care of them. I'll catch up. I'm going to stay here for a bit."

She couldn't have said why, but being here felt right. The weird, evenly spaced hills, lit up by the flickering, flaring light from the dying sun, casting long shadows back and away—she felt calm here. They would be fine back at Whitespire. What on earth would her presence add? She would sit her final vigil here, in the hills of the Chankly Bore.

Josh started to say something, but Poppy touched his arm and he shut up. She got it: they were out of their depth. In a quiet, businesslike way Josh began the portal ritual.

"I'll leave it open after," he said.

"Yeah."

"When it gets too bad," he said, "we'll come back for you. With the button."

"Yeah. I'll be here."

Then they were gone. Overhead the sky was a deepening blue, and with the green of the hills and the gray of the mountains and the flaming red-orange of the horizon it was a pretty striking scene. Too bad she didn't have a camera, or an easel, or a powerfully developed aesthetic sensibility. Janet wasn't much for rapt contemplation. She sat down on the chilly grass with her back to the hard, lumpy oak at the summit of

the hill. Maybe she should be wearing sunglasses, like those people who
went out to the desert to watch the early atomic tests.

Janet shivered. It seemed wrong that of them all she was the one to
bear witness to this. Her—the cynical one. No shits or fucks given.
Well, maybe it's better this way, better than somebody with a lot of big
weepy feelings. Quentin would be a Trevi fucking Fountain of tears by
this point. Somebody or something west of her winded a great deep
horn, a massive sustained brass pedal note. There were a few seconds of
silence, then it was answered from off to the south by a piercing silver
trumpet tone, the same note a fistful of octaves higher. Then six or seven
notes followed in unison, from all points of the compass, even out to sea,
shifting between major harmonies and clashing tritones.

Who the fuck is playing that shit? Janet thought. How do they even
know what notes to play? Probably it was Written somewhere, probably
there's always been a big alpenhorn somewhere under glass, with a sign
that says *In case of Ragnarok break glass and play an E flat.*

Where's my horn? It would have been nice to at least have a horn, she
thought, allowing herself some bitterness, some self-pity, because if not
now then when. It would have given her something to do. As one, all
around her, the clock-trees began to toll. She didn't know they could.

She got to her feet. This would never do. She was moping, and it
wouldn't do. She needed to get involved, find out what was happening.
She stood up, and on cue the grass in front of her practically exploded
as a hippogriff slammed down onto it, landing at speed and skidding
halfway down the slope on its talons and hooves and ripping up half the
hillside with it.

It gathered itself and trotted back up the slope to her. It had come to
find her.

"Your highness, Queen Janet, ruler of Fillory. This hippogriff awaits
your pleasure."

Respect. From a hippogriff. It really was the end of the world. She
strode to him, set a foot on its thigh and swung her leg over its broad,
tawny, close-furred back. It helped that the slope of the hill was on
her side.

She realized she knew this one—it had a red crest. She'd ridden it to the Northern Marsh before.

"Let us fly then, you and I, brave beast," she said. "Though it be for the last time, on the last day."

Whatever, she told herself. Don't judge. If there was ever a time for this kind of talk, this was it. She wasn't sure if it was tears or the wind or both, but her eyes were streaming as they took to the sky, and she had to blot them with her sleeve.

Janet gave the hippogriff its head, and it spiraled up over the Chankly Bore (was it a tidal bore? No, that was something else, she was almost sure) and turned south. The light was indescribably weird: dying, flickering sunlight from the west, on her right, and on her left the light of the rising moon, the two meeting and mingling into a silver-gold radiance unlike anything she'd ever seen.

"Higher, higher!" she called, and the hippogriff obeyed. As it did Janet laid a few spells on herself, specifically on her eyes: distance, focus, resolution, night vision. If she was going to witness this she wanted to see everything, to spare herself nothing. Ears too; she jacked up her hearing. She would be the recording angel, this night.

The effect was disconcerting—data came flooding in, more than her brain was really meant to process, and she literally jerked her head back as her vision exploded with detail. But she had to see it all. It was on her now, no one else.

Fillory seethed with motion—it was a restless night for the magic land, and everybody was out on the town. Even the trees were moving: the huge inky mass of the Darkling Woods to the west was no longer keeping to its customary outline. The trees, or the animate ones anyway, had pulled up their roots and were marching east in the direction of Castle Whitespire, cracking their gnarly knuckles as if to say, oh yeah, at last, we're going to get this done. It must have some ancient beef with the Queenswood, she thought, and now they were going to throw down. The trees left behind them a five-o'clock shadow of regular inanimate trees, a skeleton crew where the original forest was.

Yup: the Queenswood was in turn adopting a defensive crouch, elongating itself into a protective crescent around the borders of Whitespire.

Moving from the south to intercept the Darklings (presumably, it was what she would have done) were the smaller but no less game trees of Corian's Land, bolstered by the plucky little apple and pear trees of the Southern Orchard.

Fateful. Like Birnam Wood to Dunsinane. It's so *Macbeth*. Or *Hamlet*, I forget which.

Whitespire itself was lit up, every window; it looked like a Manhattan skyscraper full of high-powered lawyers pulling an all-nighter. The courtyard was full of men armoring up. Who were they going to fight? They must have no idea what was going on. Or maybe it was her, Janet, who was out of the loop. They'd probably read a bunch of prophecies. It's not like she had a fucking horn, was it?

Her eyes were two invisible searchlights, pitilessly clear, and she swept their twin beams over the eerily lit grassy hills of Fillory. It wasn't just the trees that were moving, animals were running below her too, and galloping and scampering and lumbering and fluttering. Deer, horses, bears, birds, bats, smaller things that might have been foxes or weasels or something. Wolves and big cats coursed along side by side—my but this was a biodiverse nation she presided over, at least for, oh, the next couple of hours anyway. All of them, all of them were flowing in vast numbers on various vectors in the direction of Castle Whitespire.

Or whoops—her eyes cut over—not all. Some of them were already there. More animals were already formed up around Whitespire to meet them. The penny dropped. God, all the buried tensions of this gorgeous, fucked-up place were just spilling over tonight. Those must be the talking animals at Whitespire, and the regular animals were marching to war against them. She knew they'd always avoided each other, but she never realized that they actually loathed each other. They must have been planning for this night for centuries.

The nonspeaking animals came on in a massed rabble; the talking ones stood stock-still in neat squares in the fields outside Whitespire, trampling the crops the way crops had been trampled by every army since the beginning of time. It was a black mass, a night with no rules. In the vanguard for the nonspeakings were a few of the very fastest beasts, bounding singly and in pairs over the low stone walls, clearing them by ridiculous margins that bordered on the show-offy: cheetahs and antelopes, ignoring each other for once, or maybe they were gazelles, plus a couple of lions and wild horses and some gnuey-looking motherfuckers that might have been wildebeests. Who knew those bastards could run like that? It was pretty awesome actually. Behind them, just ahead of the second wave, came a pack of very large, ambitious, energetic dogs.

They crashed straight into the impeccably ruled lines of the talking animals, a few of them meeting head to head with a brain-jellying smack that made you want to cringe and maybe vomit, even from this distance. It made it all ten times realer, that horrible sound, more even than the sun. It was the sound of death, the ultimate irreversible. This was really happening, and nothing would ever be the same.

Though more often the animals went in tearing and scrapping, and when they did they went for their opposite numbers, head to head, speaking versus nonspeaking. The cats went down immediately, snarling and pawing at each other in a haze of dust. You didn't see any dog-on-cat action, or not yet.

The talking animals were calling out in the fray, just the way human soldiers would:

"To me! To me!"

"On my right! The right flank, right flank!"

"Hold, damn you! Hold the line! Hold! Hold!"

It was a pretty even matchup. The talking animals were smarter and more organized, and they were, on average, a bit bigger than the dumb kind, but the dumb animals had the numbers. Janet found herself rooting for the talkers, instinctively, but then asking herself why. Were they morally better than the dumb ones? Did they deserve to win? Maybe she was just prejudiced. The talking ones at least got to talk. Maybe she should give the dumb ones this much, a victory in the last battle, the one that didn't count for anything.

Janet thought of the sloths. Probably there was a contingent of sloths like fifty miles from here, a whole fighting regiment of them, and they wouldn't get here for a month, and by then it would all be over. Or maybe the sloths didn't care enough to fight at all? Good God, was that

Humbledrum the bear, laying about him in the press? Slow to anger, that one, but my God. What a monster. He had a steel collar protecting his neck, and he was in full-on berserker mode, no doubt fueled by a barrel or two of schnapps.

She hoped he survived. But then again none of them were going to survive, were they, so maybe it was better if he died like this, in the thick of it, rather than watching the ruins of his world break apart under his feet. The hippogriff soared on, and Janet lost sight of Humbledrum in the chaos and the gloom. She would never know.

She was dimly aware that there was fighting in the air around her now too, birds having at it, complex dogfights, sprays of blood and feathers. Once in a while a pair would lock together and go twirling down out of the sky, neither one willing to release the other to save itself. Janet wondered if they'd break apart before they hit the ground, but she could never follow a pair long enough to see.

Men were fighting now too, around the castle. She squinted at them, focusing her magically augmented, telescopic vision. Who were they going to fight? Lorians? Monkeys? No, just those beast-people, half animal, half human, the ones Ember's Tomb had been full of, and a unit of dark elves in shiny black chitinous-looking armor. Where had they been all this time? Josh and Poppy were playing defense, Josh on the battlements, Poppy flying over the press like a leggy Valkyrie, taking some incoming fire in the form of spears and arrows that she was having trouble managing.

There, she was backing off, floating higher, out of range. She'd be all right. She'd better, she and Josh were her ticket out of this shitshow. The last chopper out of magic Saigon.

Janet swept her gaze across the landscape, searching out more bad news. It was all very voyeuristic, like porn. More! More apocalypse! And there was more. Loads more.

The centaurs were coming thundering down from the Retreat where they hung out. Strict formation for these guys, they'd probably been drilling for this shit for generations. They mixed into the fray—they mostly fought two-handed, heavy short swords in both hands, or with bow and arrow—and holy shit! They were going after the talking animals? There—that guy lopped the head clean off what had clearly till moments ago been a talking deer. A spray of blood mounted up over the heads of the struggling fighters, then it weakened and subsided.

Those fucking dicks. Nobody liked them, and now she knew why. They were probably total Nazis—figured if they could take out the other sentient beings they could run everything according to their weird fascist philosophy. Even Janet couldn't sit back for this. She sent a couple of bolts of lightning into their column, and got back a volley of arrows that the hippogriff evasively maneuvered around, after which it cocked its head back at her, just for an instant, to say with its furious yellow eye: WTF, I did not sign on for this.

"Sorry," Janet said, and patted its neck. "I just can't stand those guys."

For a minute it looked like the centaurs were going to make the difference, but then boom: a spearhead of unicorns rammed into the side of their formation. Jesus. Janet had to turn away. You only had to see a unicorn lay open the side of a centaur once, the ribcage flashing white when the ripped skin flopped down, to swear a mighty oath never to fuck with or even look at another unicorn again. I'm putting down the hearts and fluffy clouds and backing away slowly. Don't want any trouble here. You can have all the rainbows.

It was—viewed from a certain detached, clinical angle—like Fillory was playing chess with itself. A band of minotaurs straggled up, panting, having been outdistanced by the centaurs but plainly on their side. But just as they did flocks of griffins and pegasi began crisscrossing the battle space from above, kicking and raking and tearing. Actually the pegasi appeared to be worth fuck-all from an offensive perspective—their little hooves were too light and delicate to do much damage to anybody, and they were too fussy to beat anybody with their wings the way a swan might. But still, total respect to them for showing up. And what did it matter, because the griffins were cleaning house. Jesus, those guys were like flying tanks. Beak and claws. Built for war.

"Hey!" Janet said to the hippogriff. "You want to get in on this? You want to fight?"

But the beast shook its head. Ferrying Queen Janet around was enough for it. Its ambitions went no further. Which she totally got. This would be its war effort.

"What's your name?"

"Winterwing!" it squawked back at her. She patted its neck again.

"Well flown, Winterwing. Well flown. Fillory is grateful to you this night. Take us higher now."

No part of Fillory was untouched by the conflict. Here and there along the rivers and streams the nymphs had surfaced, the water around them reflecting the weird mingled light, though they only watched for now. Janet didn't imagine they'd be drawn into a fight unless their interests were directly threatened. Some of the dryads took the same tack, standing by their trees, leaning against them or twirling their staves the way a cop would twirl a nightstick.

God! She'd totally forgotten about the forests. They were almost into it now. A grove of the forwardmost elms and birch from Corian's Land (Corian: who he? Another thing she'd never know) had already jumped a big outriding oak from the Darkling Woods. The oak was a monster, and it had uprooted a couple of the lighter trees and was waving them over its head like a kraken, but it was being overrun. A few of its branches were cracked off already, and the leaves were flying. Trees were fucking mental in a fight, it turned out.

Janet looked up to see the moon tumbling overhead. It was still up there but way off course, spinning slowly end over end, aimless, lost in space. For some reason that was what did it. Janet threw her arms around the hippogriff's neck. She sobbed into its soft feathers, and got snot on them too. Whatever, it probably had bird mites. This was it, she thought. This was my best thing. My best thing. I thought I would always have it, but I was wrong.

The hippogriff's neck was stiff and proud against her face. It didn't turn to look at her. Maybe it wasn't very comfortable with displays of emotion. Well, tough. Since her nights in the desert Janet was all about being in touch with her emotions.

Janet heard and felt a deep boom, and she looked up mid-weep. Half the mountains in the Northern Barrier Range had just erupted, blown

their tops off like ripe pimples. She hadn't even known they were vol-
canic, but now they were lobbing big seminal gobbets of lava all over
their lower slopes, like a drunk prom queen puking on her dress. Shit
was getting geological, yo. Fillory was bleeding its hot arterial blood.

She made a visual survey of the coast. Broken Bay was overflowing
its banks, drowning the lower reaches of the Chankly Bore in seawater;
some of the hills were gone, you could just see the trees poking up out
of the water. Farther out to sea she thought she saw a couple of sentient
boats trying to ride out the tempest. To the south monstrous dunes from
the deep desert were slamming into the headwall of the Copper Mountains and threatening to bury the lush southern plains in sand. No!
Keep out! She wanted to stretch out her hands and push the desert back,
stick her finger in the dike. Probably the Foremost's gang were shivering
down in their ice caves.

Fillory was under siege, and the boundaries were failing everywhere.
The center cannot hold, and the edges are in pretty fucking dire shape too.
A crack opened, zigging across two open fields, glowing hot and red, the
grass crisping up at the lip. She wanted to throw her arms around Fillory,
hug it and squash it back together. But she couldn't. Nobody could.

Now something was harrying the Darkling Woods in the rear, and
Janet focused in on . . . *Jane Chatwin, come on down!* The former Watcherwoman looked pissed off, gray hair loose and flying, and whenever she
pointed her finger at an ambulatory tree it stopped, its shoulders sort of
sank, and it rooted itself back down to the ground again. Looks like she
was planning to ride this bomb down like Slim Pickens.

All the heavy hitters were checking in now. Up in the Barrier Range
the giants—for lack of anybody their own size to pick on, and because
they knew they were all going to die anyway—were fighting each other,
brawling and weeping huge tears as they did so. Over by Whitespire the
battle lines parted to make way for a large flightless bird, proceeding in
a stately fashion between the two sides of the Battle of the Animals, and
that could only be the Great Bird of Peace, one of the Unique Beasts. It
had the gait of a cassowary, or what Janet imagined the gait of a cassowary to be, lifting its feet carefully with its inverted knees and swaying
its head backward with every step.

When it reached the center of the field it paused, gazing around it calmly as if to say, now then, my lovelies, isn't it time to put an end to this foolishness? Do you not feel the love in my heart, and in your own? Then two big cats, a panther and a leopard, swarmed it, and it went down without even a squawk. It might have had love in its heart, Janet thought, but it also had a hell of a lot of blood.

Along with her regular serving of horror Janet felt an extra cold chill. Whatever magic gave the Unique Beasts their mandate, that was the foundation of Fillory, the rebar in the cement. Even the Deeper Magic wasn't cutting it tonight. If that was failing then all bets were really off.

The Northern Swamp was disgorging its beasts, some real sick fucks, chief among them that snapping turtle, the Prince of the Mud, and some huge wet lizard thing banded in yellow and black, flat and wide and squashed-looking. A grotendous big salamander. Even as she watched it it paused, trying to focus its wide-set eyes on something tiny, or relatively tiny, directly in front of it.

It was a white stag. It was the Questing Beast, standing before it, alone and unafraid. Oh, thank God, she thought. She couldn't hear, but as she watched it said something. It said it again, and then a third time, like someone trying to strike fire from a wet matchbook. The salamander closed its huge eyes and settled down on its belly. It was dead. The Questing Beast had wished it dead.

It had taken three tries, though, and apparently even the Questing Beast only got three. It had saved its wishes all those years, all those centuries, and now they were gone. It seemed to shrug, if a stag can shrug, and then the snapping turtle snapped, and the beautiful beast's white legs were sticking out of its mouth for a second, and then it was gone.

That seems unfair, Janet thought. A bad trade. The Questing Beast for some big salamander I never even heard of before. A rook for a knight.

She checked back in on the sun. Still boiling and thrashing on the horizon, spreading out laterally, like dropped ice cream melting on a hot sidewalk; probably it would take like a million years or some other cosmic span of time to expend all its energy and die. She checked back in on Josh and Poppy. Poppy was taking a break on top of one of Whitespire's walls, which were holding pretty well so far. Janet supposed that if things got bad they'd have to open the gates and retreat into the bailey, but it hadn't come to that yet. She missed Josh for a minute, till she found him down on the battlefield itself. He was in magic armor, sealed up tight—she was amazed he could even breathe in there—clumping around the field with a mace (always the fat man's weapon of choice, for some reason), whacking at whatever got in range. An angry elephant put its foot on him, and Janet's breath caught in her throat, but Josh's armor held. In fact it was so smooth and frictionless that he squirted out from under the elephant's foot like a pumpkin seed and flew twenty yards.

Josh picked himself up. He'd dropped his mace, but he was completely invulnerable anyway. Janet wondered what he thought he was doing, if hitting some wildebeests or whatever with a stick was making him feel better.

Let them join the fray, she thought. Let them have their fun. She just hoped the baby was safe. And at that moment, out of nowhere, Janet knew that she herself would never have children. Probably she'd known it for a while, but it was the first time she'd admitted it to herself. Let others breed. Let them, and God be with them. She would be the witness—she was tough enough to see everything break and not break herself. They also serve who fly around on hippogriffs and watch.

There was a lot to watch. It was all on now, Fillory had gone all in, the whole fucking pub quiz. Probably even the bugs were fighting each other. Where were the dwarfs, she wondered? Sitting it out underground? A tall and rather august man in a tuxedo had joined the fray, fighting bare-handed, and Janet thought she recognized him from Quentin's stories about the edge of the world. The battle was dissolving into frantic scrums featuring all kinds of weird shit she'd never even seen before: a burning suit of armor, a man who seemed to be woven out of rope, another who was just built out of pebbles. To the south a towering dune had finally crested the Copper Mountains, and surfing on it like a mad thing was a tremendous clipper ship crewed by—rabbits? For real? Was that something from the books? It had been so long. They came ripping down the steep slopes, heeled over.

It should have been exciting—bunnies! A magic clipper ship! That goes on land!—but all it provoked in Janet was exhaustion. What next? Sir Hotspots? Fuck all this, she said, and she squeezed her eyes shut for a minute. There was no end to Fillory, no end to the beauty and strangeness, except that there was, and this was it. She had to force herself to let go of it, and it felt like tearing off a piece of her own flesh. It was ending too soon, the way everything did, everything except Ebola viruses and really bad people like psychopaths. Those things never ended. How was that fair? Fuck it, it was stupid. Theories about life were always bullshit.

The chaos itself was momentarily, unfairly beautiful. The thrashing sun, the spinning, looping moon, Fillory half light and half shadow, dotted with flashes of fire, lava and flame and magical strikes from magical beings. Ignorant armies clashing by night. And way off in the distance, but still visible to her far-sighted eyes, came the glow of the Clock Barrens going up in flames and fireworks, all at once. So at least she'd seen that after all.

Then Janet saw maybe the most flat-out marvelous thing she had ever seen or ever would see in her life. Overhead a constellation in the shape of a lanky, loose-jointed person detached itself from the night sky, hung by one stellar hand for a second and then dropped, falling for a long minute and sending up a shower of sparks when it hit on its back, its component orbs embedding themselves in the turf of a meadow. It was immediately engaged there by the only other two-dimensional combatant on the field, the Chalk Man, who had recovered his spirits and repaired his staff. Puffs of limestone flew, and motes of light.

It's like Revelation, she thought. It's Revelation, and I'm the Scarlet Woman.

"Winterwing," Janet said. "Back to Whitespire. It's time."

The hippogriff set them down on top of the broad wall of Whitespire, which looked like it was going to finally see the battle it was presumably built to withstand, because the humans and the talking animals were giving ground now, falling back toward the great gates, which even Janet had never seen opened.

She dismounted and walked over to where Poppy stood. Neither of them said anything. The last queens of Fillory.

An almost infrasonic bass rumble had been building for a while, down beneath the general din, and now it rose into the realm of the audible, and they could feel it too. The fighters on the battlefield lost some of their interest in fighting and looked around for the source. Then it became really obvious, because the ground in front of the castle began to hump up and anybody who was caught out in the open on the hump began to run full out, and just in time too.

The ground at the top of the hump broke open, and a spray of something weird and alien erupted out of it. Roots, Janet realized—it was a spreading crown of enormous pale roots, cracking and writhing, and at the center of it stood Julia, eight feet tall and beautiful and glowing with her own magnificent radiance.

"Look," Janet said. "It's the Lorax."

A foolhardy panther sprang at her, and Julia smote it—there was no other word for it—out of the air with her staff one-handed and sent it spinning off and up into the darkness.

"Enough," she said.

Her voice must have been audible across the entire dying land. She was the brightest thing in Fillory at that moment.

"It is time."

That word *time* echoed from coast to coast. Everyone on the battlefield, beasts and humans and whatever else, stood still. Julia commanded bipartisan support.

She walked toward Janet and Poppy; as she walked one of the roots extended and flattened itself and made a bridge to the parapet where they stood. Another root scooped up Josh from where he'd been sitting, exhausted, on the ground in front of the gates, and set him down next to them.

"Insert joke here," Julia said, in something like her normal, nonamplified, predivine voice, "about how I leave you alone for five minutes and all of Fillory goes to shit."

Janet didn't know what to say. She had nothing left. She embraced Julia. It was a bit awkward, what with her being so huge and all, Janet more or less had to throw her arms around Julia's waist, but it felt wonderful. Her robes were the softest thing ever. Janet thought it might be beneath Julia's dignity, to be hugged by a mortal, but she allowed it.

"Queens of Fillory," Julia said. "And king of Fillory. This is it. It is time to go."

"Where are we going?" It was Josh who asked, in the voice of a lost child. "Can you take us to the Far Side of the World?"

Julia shook her head, no.

"The Far Side is ending too. We are cooling the sun and stilling the waters. We are rolling up the meadows and pulling down the stars."

"Then where are we going?" he asked again.

"I don't know," Julia said. "But you can't stay here."

She held out her hands to them. Janet got it; they had to be touching each other for the enchantment to work. Poppy took Janet's hand on one side, and Julia—her fingers felt big and tingly—took the other.

Janet bent her head and let herself cry. Her face streamed with tears. It wasn't going to kill her, she thought. She would live. Of course she would, she didn't have a scratch on her, for Christ's sake. Everything was going to be fine. It was just that she would never have a home again.

CHAPTER 27

I'm sorry," Quentin said, when Alice had finished.

"No, you're not. So don't keep saying it."

"I'm not sorry I brought you back. I'm sorry it all happened. I wish it hadn't been you. But no one else had the courage and the selflessness and the cleverness to do what you did."

"Fuck your courage and whatever else. I'm glad I did it. I'm just sorry you ruined it."

Alice continued to regard him with a contempt as inhuman as a human being could make it.

"It's hard to come back. I get that. I didn't understand how hard it would be." Quentin soldiered on under withering fire. "It's hard to be human, but there's more to it than that. You knew that before. You don't remember it yet, but it'll come back to you."

Quentin didn't know if it would or not, but he wasn't about to give ground now. He sensed that if he even flinched, she would take that as proof that she was right about everything. And she wasn't right—was she?

Eliot cleared his throat tactfully.

"There's no very good time to say this," he said, "but I have to leave." He clapped his hands on his knees. "The end of the world is coming, and I should really be there for that."

"Sure," Quentin said. "OK."

"Probably I should try to stop it. Probably I shouldn't have stayed this long."

"I know. You should go."

He was being uncharacteristically hesitant. Quentin made him promise to come back as soon as he could, and to give his love to Josh and Poppy, and oh my God they're married? You didn't tell me that? Amazing. And pregnant? Good for them. OK, now really get out of here.

"I'll just get my things."

"I understand."

"Actually I haven't got any things."

Having gone through the formalities, Eliot still couldn't bring himself to leave. He of all people was struggling to find the words to say something. He cleared his throat again.

"Will you come with me?" He blurted it out. "If anybody can figure this out, it's you. Or Julia, but Julia isn't taking my calls. We need you, Quentin. Come back."

"To Fillory." It hadn't even crossed his mind. "But you know I can't go back. I can't leave Alice now, and Ember would never let me in anyway."

"I've been thinking about that second part. I told you how the Lorians invaded us, even though they aren't supposed to be able to? And then Alice found a way to get here through the mirrors . . . I'm starting to think that Fillory is getting a bit porous in her old age. Border security isn't what it used to be. If there was ever a moment to get you through, it's now."

There was a time when Quentin would have seized on that possibility like a drowning man. Now it gave him a pang, the dull ache of an old wound, but that was all. That time had passed. He shook his head.

"I can't, Eliot. Not now. I'm needed here."

Alice snorted at the notion that anybody anywhere might need Quentin.

"I was afraid of that," Eliot said. "Well look, just come with me as far as the Neitherlands. That's all I ask. For all I know there's a smoking crater where the Fillory fountain was. I don't want to face that alone."

"Ooooh," Plum said. Her eyes went round. "I want to go to the Eitherlands!"

"Neitherlands," Eliot said, suddenly peevish. "And it's not a field trip for interns."

They were interrupted by something scratching at the front door. The room fell silent. They weren't expecting visitors. Nobody knew they were here, or nobody should have. Quentin put a finger to his lips.

More scratching. It stopped and then started again. He got up and walked as quietly as he could over to the door and peered through the spy hole. Empty street. There was nobody there. He looked at the others. Eliot shrugged.

He cracked the door a few inches, keeping the chain on, and something small and frantic burst in past him, and he reeled back a step. It was the blackbird.

It flapped crazily around the room for thirty long seconds, with that special horror that birds have of being indoors, before it settled on the Sputnik chandelier. Even then its gaze darted everywhere, constantly, like it was expecting danger from any and all directions. It looked different: thinner and more bedraggled. It was missing some feathers, and the ones it still had had lost their gloss.

"Do not kill me!" it said.

Plum and Eliot were on their feet. Only Alice hadn't moved.

"What are you doing here?" Quentin said. "Are you alone?"

"I am alone!"

"Why should we believe you?" Plum said. "You fucking asshole. You betrayed us. And you probably murdered Pushkar. He had a family, you know. Quentin, should we kill it?"

"Maybe. Not yet." If this was a trap, or a feint, or a diversion, it was a weird one, if only because he figured the bird for a physical coward. It wasn't like it to lead from the front. "Plum, watch it. I'm going to look around for anybody else."

But there was no one else, not in front or in back or on the roof or in any immediately adjacent planes of existence, not that he could detect. Maybe it really was alone.

"I take it this is that bird," Eliot said. "The one who hired you."

"It's that bird. What are you doing here?"

"I have no more money," it said. "I tried to hire more magicians, but without Lionel it went poorly."

"No money, no magicians," Quentin said. "Those are the breaks. I think you should leave now."

"I did not want Lionel to kill Pushkar! I did not tell him to. I don't know why he did. I was afraid of him!"

It already seemed incredible that they'd been so scared of the blackbird. It wasn't very frightening now. It must have run through all its resources staging their job, and without Lionel and its hired hands it was just a talking bird, nothing more.

It didn't appear to want to leave.

"You have to help me."

"No," Plum said, looking up at it. "We really don't."

"The birds here despise me. I am very hungry. I have eaten garbage."

"I don't care what you've eaten," Quentin said. "We've got more important things to worry about. Leave or we'll throw you out."

Though he wasn't exactly sure yet how they were going to catch and expel the thing. He wasn't looking forward to that chase scene.

"Please," it said again. "He will kill me!"

"Who?"

The blackbird didn't answer, just stared around the room anxiously, from one to the other of them. It didn't want to say. Quentin didn't feel the slightest bit sorry for it.

"It's talking about Ember."

Even the bird jumped, as if it hadn't realized Alice could talk. Her expression didn't change. She wanted everybody to know that her emotional investment in this drama was nil.

"What did you say?"

"That's Ember's bird. I met it in the mirrors. It begged me not to kill it. I can't think why I didn't. I'm going to bed."

On her way out she nearly walked into a wall out of habit—as a niffin she would have gone right through it. She left an uncomfortable silence behind her. From behind the drawn curtains they heard a truck come rattling slowly down the narrow street. Quentin waited for it to pass by.

"Is that true? Ember sent you?"

"Please." It had lost all of its avian loftiness now. It trembled. "He will kill me."

"He won't," Plum said, "because we'll kill you first."

"He sent me to get the suitcase. I do not know why. He would have sent a bigger animal," it added almost apologetically, "but He needed one capable of flight. To go through the mirrors. He gave me some money, and the spell to make Lionel once I got here."

"Why did He want the case? Was it the knife, or the book? Or both?"

"I don't know!" the blackbird wailed. "I don't know! I didn't know what was in it! Truly!"

And it began to cry. Quentin thought he had never heard a more pathetic sound. The bird fluttered down from its perch on the chandelier like a pheasant creased by a bullet. It landed on the coffee table and squatted there, sobbing.

Something coherent was forming in Quentin's exhausted brain, like a crystal forming in a murky liquid. He'd been looking at chaos for so long, he barely remembered what a pattern looked like, but now he thought he saw at least a fragment of one.

"Hang on," he said slowly. "Let's think this through. Rupert stole the stuff in the case, Ember wants it back. He sends a bird to Earth to recover it for Him. The bird hires us to find it."

Plum picked up the thread. "The stuff in the case was Umber's, not Ember's, according to Rupert, but I guess they're brothers so it's all in the family. But so why would Ember want it?"

"Why wouldn't he? Cool knife? Spell for making a magic land? Who wouldn't want that?"

"A god?" Eliot said. "Who already has a whole magic world?"

"Except He doesn't." All the lights came on in Quentin's head at once. "He doesn't though. Fillory is dying, and Ember has nowhere to go. He wants the spell so he can use it to make a new world! He's going to give up on Fillory—abandon it and start over!"

It came out in a rush, which was followed by a pause. Plum made a skeptical face.

"But it fits!" Quentin said. "He's not even trying to save Fillory! He's a rat who won't go down with his ship!"

"That," Eliot said, "is a mixed metaphor. And listen to me: I know you've got no reason to love Ember, but that seems a little cowardly."

"Yes, because He's a coward!"

"Plus you know the spell doesn't make a whole world, right?" Plum said. "Just like a land?"

"Maybe that's just us. Maybe a god could do more with it."

She looked up at the ceiling, considering. The blackbird watched all three of them desperately.

"Even if that's true," Eliot said, "what would we do about it? It's kind of depressing me actually. Just more proof that there's no way out of this."

Quentin sat down. Maybe he was getting ahead of himself.

"We still have the spell," he said.

"Destroy it," Eliot said.

"No." He couldn't do that.

"We have the bird," Eliot said. "We could turn the tables. Take it hostage."

"Oh, come on. Ember doesn't give a crap about the bird, the bird's expendable." The bird didn't object to this; it would've been hard to argue with. "We should go to Fillory, confront Him, make Him stay there and try and save it. He is the god of it. And we've got the spell. God, what a bastard!"

"Or," Eliot said, cautiously, "maybe we want to get in on this shit. Maybe he's got the right idea. Maybe we should give Him the spell and tell Him to make a new world and take us with Him."

"Eliot," Quentin said.

"I know, I know. It would be a lot easier though." Eliot heaved himself wearily to his feet. "Fine. Come on, let's go yell at a god. If nothing else I want to hear Him admit it. I want Him to say it to my face."

"I'm coming." Plum got up too.

"Somebody should stay here with Alice," Quentin said.

"Somebody young and inexperienced in the field," Eliot said.

"No." Plum glared at him, uncowed. "No way. I'm not babysitting the Blue Meanie."

"Maybe Alice will come with us. Maybe she can help. Alice!" Quentin shouted up the stairs. No answer. "I'll go talk to her."

"Good luck with that."

"Give me an hour."

"I can help!" the bird said.

Quentin's reflexes were good, but it still only worked because he had the element of surprise. He darted his hand out and caught the bird around the neck. Ignoring its hysterical thrashing, he walked over to a window, opened it, and threw the blackbird out.

Alice lay on her back on the bed with her eyes open. She heard the sounds of the house below her—walking, talking, shouting, slamming—but they were very far away. She stared at the ceiling. She felt like a marble figure carved on a tomb, her own tomb. This body was her coffin. She breathed shallowly; even that was an imposition she could barely tolerate.

She would not indulge this body. She didn't owe it anything. She wanted to feel it as little as possible.

Clumping footsteps coming up the stairs. The door opened.

"Alice."

It was Quentin, of course. She didn't turn her head. She heard the scrape of a stool as he pulled it over and sat down. She couldn't stop him.

"Alice. We're going to go to the Neitherlands. We have a theory about what might be going on. We're going to try to find Ember and talk to Him."

"OK." She felt her tongue, the worm in her head, lightly kiss the roof of her mouth to make the *K*.

She didn't feel angry anymore. She wondered why she'd even bothered with all that anger, all that talking. Something had come over her, but now her rage was gone, a storm that had blown out to sea leaving behind a great peace. A flat strand swept smooth by the violence of the waves, dotted with sea wrack churned up from the depths. She just didn't care.

"I don't want to leave you here. I'd like you to come with us. I think you could help."

Very slightly, she shook her head. She closed her eyes. Sometimes when she closed her eyes she felt weightless again. The whiskey helped—it was better when she was drunk. And it gave her pleasure to poison this body.

"I don't think so."

Seven years ago he'd watched as she made a blue bonfire of her flesh. For seven long years her human self had slept, and she had roamed Fillory as a dream of rage and power. The dream was over now, Quentin had ended it, he'd woken her up and forced her back into her body. But he couldn't force her soul, her self. Did he actually hate her? That much? He said he loved her, once. That was both seven years ago and yesterday.

She wondered if she could burn again. Maybe she was like a spent match, to be struck only once, but she didn't think so. It would take time to get ready, to relearn the skills, but soon. She didn't mind if she died trying. Suicide was in everything she did now, and everything she thought. Suicide was her home: if she could find nothing else, then suicide would always have her.

And if it did work they would never catch her again. Never again.

"I'm going to touch your hand now." She felt him take her fingers; she left hers limp. It was the first time anyone had touched her since she'd come back, and it made her skin crawl. "You're going to get through this. It's not as bad as you think. I'm going to try to help you. But you have to try too."

"No," she whispered. "I don't."

Something happened in the silence that followed. Her eyes opened again. Something was pulling her back. It was something in the air, coming in through her nose and invading her mind. It was doing something to her. Magic? Not magic.

"What is that?" she said.

"What?"

"That smell."

"You know what it is," Quentin said. "Think."

For an instant she lowered her guard, and forgot to fight, and in that instant her body sat up and inhaled. Neurons were firing in her brain that hadn't fired for seven years. After eons of disuse, mental furniture was being uncovered, dusty drop cloths yanked back. Mental windows were being thrown open to let in the hot sun.

"Bacon," she said.

He had a tray with him. Now he picked up a plate and held it in front of her. It was good bacon, quarter-inch-thick strips, and it had warped and bubbled as he fried it; he'd let one end of it char a little because he knew she liked it burned. Had liked it.

Well, he'd done something with his seven years. He didn't used to be able to cook worth a damn.

She was tired, and she was famished—she wasn't, her mind wasn't, it was clear as a bell, but this body was hungry, this doll made of meat. It was weak, and it reached out and picked up the food and put it in her mouth. The meat took over and ate the other meat, and God it was fucking unbelievable, salty and fatty and smoky. When she was done she licked her thumbs and wiped her greasy hands on the sheets. It revolted her, she revolted herself, but there was so much pleasure in it. She was trying to reject her body like a bad organ transplant but she could feel herself trapped in its sticky embrace. It was trying to adhere to her, trying to become her, and Quentin was helping it. He was on its side.

"I hope," she said, "that you don't think you're going to keep me here with bacon."

"Not just bacon."

He handed her a plate with fresh slices of mango on it, intensely orange, like little arcs carved off a tiny sweet sun. She fell on them like an animal. She *was* an animal.

No, she was not. She was pure and beautiful and blue.

"Why did you do it?" she asked with her mouth full. "Why did you do this to me?"

"Because this is who you are. Because you're human. You're a person, you're not a demon."

"Prove it."

"I am proving it."

She looked at him, really looked for the first time since she'd been back. He had a narrow, symmetrical face, rendered interesting by a slightly too-large nose and an expressive, too-wide mouth. He never knew it, which had saved him from developing one of those pretty-boy personalities, but objectively he'd always been handsome. And he still was.

But he was different now too. He didn't stutter or duck her gaze the way he used to. He was right, he had changed.

"You could've got oysters," she said.

"You hate oysters."

"Do I?"

"You used to say they were like cold snot."

"I can't remember. What else do I like?"

"Hot baths. Fresh socks. Really big sneezes. That feeling when you successfully flip a pancake. And this."

He gave her a square of chocolate—good chocolate—and when she tasted it she actually shed tears. Jesus, she was losing all control. All control. Was the flesh going to win? It was getting harder to disentangle herself from it. The triumphant, righteous niffin in her shrieked defiance. She thought of flying, of plunging into the earth and flying again, of burning things, making them hurt the way she hurt, showing them how glorious the pain was. She shuddered.

"Why did you come here?" he said.

"To kill you." She said it without hesitating, because it was true.

"No. You came here so I could save you."

She laughed—yes, that sick wicked niffin laugh, she still had it. She loved it. But she couldn't let the food alone either. They were forcing her, making her give it up.

"I'm going to make my new body fat," she said. "I'm going to eat until it is morbidly obese and I die."

"You can if you want to. Here."

A noise. What was it? Her body seethed with pleasure at it. He had opened a cold, sweating bottle of champagne and was pouring some into a wineglass.

"This is hardly fair," she said.

"I never said it was."

"You want me to drink champagne out of a wineglass? You've gone downhill, Quentin Coldwater." Where were these words coming from?

"I've adjusted my priorities."

When she had drunk it, sitting up in bed, taking quick little sips like a child taking her medicine, she burped loudly.

"That might be my favorite part," she said. "Is this all you have?"

"That's all I have."

"No, it's not," she said.

Abruptly, awkwardly, like an inexperienced schoolgirl, she kissed him. She did it roughly and hard, without knowing she was going to do it. She leaned forward and mashed her lips against his, felt a tooth grind into her lip, tasted blood. As she did something warmed and melted between her legs. She shoved her tongue into his mouth, let him taste the champagne. The dike that kept her mind separate from her body was leaking in a hundred places. Somewhere far away her glass smashed on the floor.

She wanted him. She was remembering things—afternoons upstairs at the Cottage, in the stifling heat. He was lean and strong, stronger than he used to be, and she wanted him.

"Show me, Quentin." She ordered him. "Show me what bodies are for."

She was unbuttoning his shirt, but clumsily. She'd forgotten how. He trapped her hands.

"No," he said. "Not yet. Too soon."

"Too soon?" She grabbed the front of his shirt and kissed him again. His stubble scraped her. She smelled him; it wasn't like bacon, but it was still good. "You do this to me and then you tell me it's too soon?"

He was trying to get up! The little shit! Anger came so easily, still, with all those lovely anger-words too. Rage combined with the pleasure but it couldn't dispel it.

"Hang on. Alice. This isn't how it works."

"Then show me how it works." She got up too, advancing on him. She felt like an animal—a predator. She wanted to pin him and devour him. "Does my body disgust you as much as it disgusts me? Too bad. You brought me back, you show me it was worth it."

She was wearing one of his shirts, and it was big enough that she could pull it over her head in one angry swipe and drop it on the floor, leaving her naked except for a pair of underpants. Alice kissed him again, pushed herself against him, felt the electric roughness of his shirt on her breasts. He stumbled back until his head knocked against the door. With her hand she found his crotch and massaged it. Yes, that's how it went. He used to like this.

He still did. He was getting hard under her hand.

"Isn't this why you brought me back? So you could fuck me like you used to?"

Even she didn't believe that, but it was the cruelest, bitterest thing she could think of. She wanted to do violence to him, the kind of violence he'd done to her, but he didn't waver.

"I didn't bring you back for me."

And then he did kiss her. Not hard, but gently and firmly. That was it, you could do it that way too. He wrapped his arms around her, fitting her body against his, her head beneath his chin, and just held her. Memories inundated her, human memories. The night they walked out from Brakebills in the snow, and he'd put his arm around her shoulders. The day in Antarctica when they were foxes and he chased her the way she'd wanted him to do when they were human. The way he looked at her as if there was nothing else in the world for him but her. As if he loved her as much as she hated herself. He was looking at her that way now.

Suddenly she felt desperate to connect with him again. She'd been alone for so long. She needed this. Along with so many other things, she'd forgotten what it was like to need.

She put her hand up under his shirt, felt his smooth skin. Something strange had happened to his shoulder. She rested her head flat against his chest.

"It hurt, Quentin," she said. "It hurt so much when I died."

"I know. But this is going to feel good."

Afterward they lay next to each other on the bed. It had worked, for now, her body had gotten what it wanted. Not once but twice, which if she remembered correctly had been rather a rarity in the old days. But then again Quentin had had some practice since then. Poppy, why had she watched him with Poppy? It had seemed so funny at the time, but now it hurt her. She wished she could forget it.

She scooched away from him. She wanted to go away again. She let herself fall into herself, falling and falling, pulling away, into the inner darkness, dreaming of flying. She withdrew inside her body like a timorous crab inside an enormous whelk. She had felt so human before, so her old self, but she was losing it, and she let it go. She had thought for a moment that it was simple, but she was remembering that it wasn't.

He sat up and started putting his clothes on.

"I have to go," he said. "To the Neitherlands. To find Ember. Come with me."

She shook her head. She wanted him gone. It was so much easier this way. He was gathering up her clothes too.

"Alice." She didn't react. She would sleep now. "Alice. I want you to know that I mean it in the kindest possible way when I say that you are being the most unbelievable pussy."

He took her hand again and they vanished, both of them together.

CHAPTER 28

They were going to all go together, and from a tactical perspective Plum thought it would have been a better idea, but Eliot was getting impatient, and then there were the noises. From upstairs. Quentin and Alice. Plum and Eliot exchanged looks and nodded; no words were needed. It was probably a good development for all involved, on balance, but seriously: they were not going to hang around and listen to that.

Eliot made a big show about how interdimensional travel was really no big whoop to him anymore, but Plum was not going to let him ruin it for her. This was radical magic, world-expanding stuff, and even under the present grimmish circumstances she was a complete nerd for that shit. She could hardly wait. He held out his hand, in a foppish kind of a gesture, and she took it, and he put his other hand in his pocket and—*oh*.

Clear cold water. They were floating in it, floating upward. In spite of herself she laughed with pleasure and as a result almost choked on magic water. They rose up toward light, points of it, glittery and diffuse above them but getting more focused all the time, and then their heads broke the surface.

It wasn't what she was expecting, not based on what she'd heard. They were inside somewhere, in a vast room lit by two chandeliers, treading water in what looked more like an indoor swimming pool than a fountain.

"What the hell?" Eliot said. He seemed if anything more surprised than she was.

The pool was sunk level with a marble floor. Water trickled into it
from the open mouth of an angry stone face at one end; at the other end
steps led up and out like a Roman bath, blue water graduating stair by
stair up to clear. They stroked over to them in sync.

"This isn't right," Eliot said. "This isn't the Neitherlands, I don't
think. We've been hijacked. Button-jacked."

Magic water streamed out of their clothes as they climbed out, leaving them instantly dry. Awesome. The walls of the room were covered
in bookshelves.

"Who puts a fountain in the middle of a library?" Plum said. "It can't
be good for the books."

"No. It can't."

It was a library, maybe the grandest one Plum had ever seen. She would
have known it was a library with her eyes shut: the hush of it was enough,
like a velvet nest in which she'd been carefully nestled, and the smell, the
heavy spicy aroma of slowly, imperceptibly decomposing leather and paper, of hundreds of tons of dry ink. Every square foot of the walls was
bookshelves, and every foot of every shelf was full. Creamy spines, leather
spines, knobby and ribbed spines, jacketed and bare, gilded and plain,
blank spines and spines crammed with text and ornament. Some were as
thin as magazines, some were wider than they were tall.

She ran her fingers along them, one after the other, as if they were
the long back of some giant, friendly vertebrate that she was petting. In
three or four places a book had been taken down and the one next to it
was left slightly aslant, leaning its head against its fellow, as if in silent
mourning for its absent neighbor.

Even the beams and buttresses had been fitted with shelves—rows
and arches and fans of books. In the corners of the room, up near the
ceiling, there were little book-sized doors like cat doors. As she watched
one of them swung open with a squeak and a book came through, floating in midair, sailed the length of the room, and left through a cat door
on the other side.

"I take it back," Eliot said. "I think this must be one of the libraries
of the Neitherlands. I've never been inside one."

"I thought normal people weren't supposed to be allowed in them."

"You're not."

The voice came from a doorway behind them. It belonged to an odd-looking man: thirtyish, shaved head, his face round and doughy as an unbaked biscuit. He had a goatee that was maybe growing into something that was more than a goatee, which made him look like an angry barista at an indie coffee shop whose dreams of becoming a successful screenwriter were dwindling by the hour. He wore what looked like a monk's robe, and sandals, but the oddest thing about him was his hands. They were magical constructs of some kind, golden and translucent, and they gave off their own warm honey-colored light. He held them clasped in front of him.

"Penny," Eliot said. It wasn't so much a greeting as a statement of fact.

"The rest of your party should be arriving momentarily."

Sure enough, up popped Quentin and Alice, her sputtering and blowing and apparently furious, big surprise. She favored Quentin with a disdainful look, then swam breaststroke over to the steps, at which point it became apparent that she was completely naked. What, did they roll over onto the button halfway through?

Best not to think about it. Alice didn't seem at all self-conscious. Quentin followed and handed her clothes, which she put on clumsily.

"Hi, Penny," Quentin said. "Good to see you. Did you just kidnap us?"

"That was my question," Eliot said.

"I diverted you. All the ways of the Neitherlands are now mine to command. You are here as my special guests."

Plum was getting the impression they all knew each other already.

"Isn't the water bad for the books?" Plum said.

"We have taken precautions. Shelf space is a precious resource here. Nothing is wasted."

"That's great, Penny," Quentin said, "but we're actually in kind of a hurry. Important business. Really time-sensitive."

"I require your presence. I will explain."

"Well, thanks," Quentin said. "But, you know, be quick. Nice hands."

"Thank you. I made them myself."

The dime dropped: the people who'd jumped them in Connecticut had had golden hands too, exactly the same. Maybe it was a coincidence, maybe there had been a sale, but Plum doubted it. In which case she had a bone to pick with this Penny, maybe several bones.

"This is our friend Plum," Quentin said. "Plum, this is Penny. And you remember Eliot. And Alice."

"Hi," Plum said. Alice said nothing.

"Pleased to meet you." Plum was a little bit relieved that he didn't try to shake her hand. "It's good to have you back with us, Alice."

While saying nothing about it Penny somehow managed to convey that he and Alice had once slept together.

"Penny," Eliot said, "you should know that we really—"

"Walk with me."

Penny turned and strode into the next room without waiting to see if they were going to follow him.

"Who is this guy?" Plum whispered to Quentin.

"We went to college together."

They followed him. The next room was if anything even grander: a vaulted hall, also full of books but with soaring high windows that were dark and flecked with light rain. Through the lower panes Plum got her first look at the Neitherlands, a gray warren of broad squares and narrow alleys and Italianate palaces. It was night.

Penny walked with his magic hands clasped behind his back.

"The past year has been good to me," he said—the gracious tour guide. "My work defending the Neitherlands and safeguarding the flow of magic brought me to the attention of my superiors in the order—we take care of the Neitherlands, Plum, in case they haven't told you. At the same time we suffered significant losses of personnel, which created gaps in the leadership. I was advanced rapidly.

"The promotion was gratifying, of course, but the challenges have been non-trivial. The Neitherlands was changed irreversibly in the late catastrophe. Much of the old magic no longer works, or works differently. Things grow here now. There is *time* here."

He said it irritably, like they had a case of bed bugs.

"You cannot imagine the inconvenience of it. But the upshot was

that I was awarded the position of Librarian. It is one of the most pres-
tigious titles a member of my order can hold."

"Congratulations," Quentin said. "I've always wondered though,
what happened to the dragons? The last time I saw them they were getting ready to fight the gods."

"The dragons succeeded. If they hadn't, you would not have lived to
play your part in the crisis. Fighting the old gods, even distracting them,
is of course a chancy business. There's an art to it: they don't really coun-
terattack so much as just delete you from reality. But some of the dragons survived. They will repopulate, if they can remember how. I believe
it has been several millennia since any of them had sex. We in the order
have been assisting them with the research."

Plum guessed it stood to reason that out of all these billions of books
at least one of them had to be dragon porn.

They left the great hall and entered a low labyrinth. Even there the
walls were books, even the ceiling; they hung spine-down somehow,
over their heads, like bats in a cave. Every once in a while large swaths
of books shifted themselves over, grudgingly, like sleepers in a crowded
bed, to make room for some new addition further down the line. This
Penny guy was a bit of a pill, but she had to admit she was loving his
library. Loving. If anything Quentin had undersold this place.

It made her wonder if they'd undersold Fillory too. She felt herself
very close to Fillory now, just one fountain away, closer than she'd ever
been. When she was kicked out of Brakebills Plum thought her life had
gone straight off the rails, right into the muddy and unsanitary ditch by
the side of the tracks, and maybe it had—like Quentin said, there's no
one to tell you what would have happened, after the fact. But it had also
brought her here, to Fillory's very threshold. She wanted to see it. It was
time.

Plum spotted a narrow, olive-green volume with silver type on its
spine dangling above her. It was so tempting, like ripe fruit . . .

"Ah ah ah!"

Penny practically slapped her hand away. It was a measure of how out
of her depth she felt that she actually blushed. But Penny was off and
away again.

"I've already instituted some improvements that have been very well received. I don't know if you've noticed . . . ?"

He pointed up at one of the cat doors, through which books were entering and exiting at irregular intervals.

"Yes, very nice," Eliot said.

"Some of your best work," Quentin chimed in.

Plum was picking up a significant frenemy vibe off the Quentin-Penny dynamic.

"They've been adopted by several other libraries."

"Good for cats, too," Plum said. "Though they'd have to be flying cats."

"No animals, domestic or otherwise, are allowed in the building," Penny said, without humor.

"We really have to go," Eliot said. "Really."

"I've set aside a special room here for problem formats."

Curious in spite of herself, Plum poked her head in through the open door. It was the weirdest bibliographical menagerie she'd ever seen. Books so tall and yet so narrow that they looked like yardsticks; she supposed they must be illustrated guides to snakes, or arrows, or maybe yardsticks. One book was kept in a glass terrarium—a librarium?—the better to contain the words that kept crawling out of it like ants. One lay slightly open on a table, but only slightly, so you could see that its pages emitted an intolerably bright radiance; a welding mask lay next to it. One book appeared to be all spine along all of its edges. It was unopenable, its pages sealed inside it.

"Honestly, you wonder who publishes these things." Penny shook his head, and they kept walking.

It was a little like touring a chocolate factory, except with books, and starring Penny as a wonky Willy Wonka. Other adepts wearing robes that were similar to Penny's but not as nice bustled by them, nodding deferentially to him as they passed. Some of them had the golden hands too. Hm. She would wait for the right moment.

"There are catacombs underneath the library," Penny said. "That's another special collection: it's all the novels people meant to write but didn't."

"Ooh!" Eliot brightened up. "Can I go see mine? I'll be honest with you, I'm pretty sure it's going to be amazing."

"You're welcome to try. I spent far too much time looking for mine. You can't find anything down there!" He sounded exasperated. "But here's something people always want to see."

This room had only one bookcase in it, on the back wall, but that proved to be deceptive because apparently it was infinitely extendable: Penny took hold of one of the shelves and gave it a sideways shove, and it zipped along like a conveyor belt at amazing speed, frictionlessly, while the shelves above and below it stayed still. It reminded Plum a little of the motorized racks at a dry cleaners. Then Penny stopped it and pushed up on it, only lightly, just a touch, and the whole business began scrolling upward, shelf after shelf after shelf, as if it went on and on beyond the room in all directions, for unknown leagues.

"What is this?" Plum asked.

"These are everybody's books. Or rather, the books of everybody."

"I don't understand."

"Hang on, I'm looking for ours." They spun by, thousands and thousands of them, until Penny stopped the bookcase with one hand. "These are the books of our lives. Everybody has one. See, here we are. All together, as it happens, one book for each of us."

"You must be joking," Quentin said quietly.

Not that Penny ever joked, as far as Plum could tell.

"Not at all. Here is Plum's."

He put a finger on one spine. The book had, appropriately enough, a plum-colored dust jacket.

"Mine."

Penny's was tall and thin and bound in smooth pale leather, with his name clearly etched in black up the spine in a no-nonsense sans-serif font. It looked like a vintage technical manual.

"They're next to each other?" Plum said. "Please tell me that doesn't mean we get married."

"I don't know what it means. Nobody knows much about these things."

"Your middle name is seriously Schroeder?" Eliot said, like that was the surprising thing here.

"You're not going to tell me there's one of these for every person who ever lived," Quentin said.

"Only people who are alive have them. They come and go as people are born and die; this shelf goes on for miles in all directions, it must jut into some separate subdimension. I don't know where they go when you die. Remaindered, I suppose."

He tittered at his own joke.

"What's in them?"

"About what you'd expect. The story of your life, start to finish. Who you are and what you did and what you're going to do. Eliot's is in two volumes. Here's yours."

Penny put his hand on a squat navy blue book, as chunky as an unabridged thesaurus, with Quentin's name stamped on it in gold.

Quentin hesitated.

"I know," Penny said, more quietly. "Not as tempting as you'd think, is it? I've never opened mine. There are those in the order who have looked, and I've seen their faces."

Plum slid her volume off the shelf and held it cradled in her hand like a baby. The urge to read it was almost overpowering. Almost, but not quite.

"You spend your whole life trying to understand yourself, what your story is about," Penny said, "and then suddenly it's all there. All the answers, spelled out in black and white. Some of them are indexed even. Look at Quentin's, it's alphabetized." It was true: there were little half-moons cut into the pages, labeled A–B, C–D and so on, in a diagonal ladder down the side.

Slowly, reluctantly, Quentin handed his book back to Penny.

"I guess I'm supposed to be writing it," he said. "Not reading it."

Penny reshelved it—a little cavalierly, Plum thought. Plum replaced hers with appropriate care. You can't unread a book. She was dying to look, but she supposed that if she lived her life properly then by the time it was over she'd know what was in it. That was sort of the whole point, wasn't it? To understand your own story? Reading the book now would just be cheating. And what kind of jackass cheats at life?

"Hang on," Eliot said, "this raises a lot of questions. Does this mean we don't have free will? And if you burn somebody's book do they die?"

"Keep moving!" Penny shooed them out into the hall. "There's a lot to see! I thought you were in a hurry."

He hustled them along as far as a plain unmarked door, which he opened. It was the first room they'd seen that was completely empty of books. There was nothing on the walls, not even a picture. It had no windows either, only a desk with a leather chair behind it. In fact it was rather gloomy.

"Let me guess," Plum said. "Invisible books. Or no, microscopic. Like they're in the air, and we're breathing them."

"This is my office."

Penny sat down at the desk, facing them, and steepled his eerily luminescent fingers.

"The system notified me as soon as you entered the Neitherlands. There's a reason I brought you here."

"You have literally three minutes," Eliot said. He was practiccally fidgeting with impatience.

"You have something of mine," Penny said. "Quentin."

"I do?"

"A page. From one of my books."

"Oh."

Everybody looked at Quentin. Plum hadn't thought of that, but she guessed it made sense. Probably technically Quentin had stolen that page from the Neitherlands. But even so Penny was being kind of scoldy about it.

"Fair enough." Quentin extracted it from his coat pocket. "I took good care of it for you, I promise."

The page, with what seemed to Plum like a certain lack of sentimentality, slipped out of Quentin's hand of its own volition and through the air and onto Penny's desk like a toddler rushing to embrace its parent.

"Thank you."

Instantly a door opened and a robed woman entered, eyes on the floor as if to avoid gazing directly at Penny's magnificence. She took the page, bearing it in both hands as gingerly as if it were a limb in urgent need of reattaching. Which Plum supposed in some sense it was.

Penny leaned over and pulled up one of the floor tiles next to his chair, which turned out not to be a tile at all but the cover of a large book. It was embedded in the floor. Plum looked around: they were standing on books, big, dusty, thickly bound tomes fitted together like flagstones. Penny leafed through the tissue-thin pages, which contained columns of minute numbers, nodded, and then let the cover fall closed with a thump.

"Now," he said, "there is the matter of the fine."

"A fine?" Quentin said. "You mean like a late fee?"

"I do. You will be detained here for one year to work in the stacks until your debt is repaid."

Oh my God, what an ass!

"Don't be an ass," Plum said.

"You're not going to detain me," Quentin said. "Penny, Fillory is dying. We might be able to save it, but it can't wait. We have to go."

"There are thousands of worlds. They live and they die. But knowledge is power, Quentin, and wisdom is eternal." He actually talked like that. "You took some of ours."

"I gave it back."

"But you had the use of it for a year. A page from the *Arcana arcanorum,* in the hand of the Zwei Vögel scribe herself. Think what we could have done with it in that time."

"Almost certainly nothing. You have like a dillion books here, probably nobody would have even looked at it."

Penny stood up and walked around from behind the desk, raising his hands. His fingers—hey, those were spellcasting positions!

"The books must be balanced, Quentin. You always did have trouble accepting that. We will also have to remove from your mind the memory of what you read—"

He was going into Quentin's head now? No. Plum took a step back and raised her hands too. Everybody did; in one second they went from a loose clump of people with complicated feelings about one another to a single defensive phalanx. Quentin moved the fastest: he held up a hand and a tight, blinding shaft of light shone out of his palm, straight into Penny's face.

But the light didn't reach his face. With one weird magic hand Penny stopped the beam—his hand seemed to eat the light. With the other he grasped the beam like it was a solid thing and bent it 90 degrees downward so that it shone harmlessly at the floor. It stayed there. Too late Eliot weighed in with some kind of electric bolts, but those golden hands plucked them out of the air, one-two-three-four-five, in sequence and with inhuman quickness and accuracy. It was like a stage magician's bullet catch.

Plum was frantically weaving a shield in front of Quentin. She was still weak on this kind of magic, nobody at Brakebills taught it, but Quentin had showed her a thing or two, and she was nothing if not a quick study. But she already knew it wasn't going to be ready in time.

"I've waited a long time for this," Penny said.

"Then this is going to be kind of an anticlimax," Alice said, and she punched him in the face.

Boom! Oh my God. It was beautiful, just like in a movie: straight from the shoulder, feet planted, hips rolled, follow-through, the works. Penny never saw it coming. Do people really do things like that?

People like Alice did, apparently. Penny didn't fall down, but he bent over double, clutching his face with both hands.

"Ahhhhhh!"

He said it quietly but with real feeling.

"We're done," Alice said. "Let's go."

Quentin looked at Alice with an expression Plum had never seen on him before. Love, she guessed it was. It was as bright as that beam he'd shot out of his hand.

"Penny," Quentin said, "I don't know what you would have done with that page, but I'll tell you what I did with it: I made Alice human again. In case you were wondering how that happened. You're a great magician, you always have been, and I'm sure you're a pretty great librarian too. Magic and books: there aren't many things more important than that. But there are one or two. We saved Alice, and now we're going to save Fillory. Please don't get in our way, that's all I ask."

Penny was bent over, working his jaw, both hands pressed to his cheek. He raised his face at them blearily as they filed out, Alice in the lead. She was studying the knuckles of her right hand.

"For a second there," she said, "I saw the point of being alive."

"I'm glad you are," Quentin said. "You're pretty good at it."

"Can we get out of here now?" Eliot said.

But Plum had a thought.

"Hang on," she said. "Somewhere in this building there must be everything there is to know about Fillory, don't you think? Maybe before we go we should do a little research."

Penny came running up behind them, with a reddening scuff-mark on his cheekbone but otherwise steady on his feet. Plum would say this for him: he was impervious to embarrassment.

"Don't say anything," Eliot said, before Penny could speak. "Just listen. We need information. You have it. Where are the books about Fillory?"

"There's a whole room of them!" Plum deplored physical violence on principle, but it did seem to have a remarkably positive effect on Penny. "Large one. Come on, it's in the other wing!"

They never would have found it on their own; even with Penny leading the way it took ten minutes to walk there, up and down stairs and through a maze of passages. On the way Penny explained about his hands: they were a form of spectral prosthetic, quite groundbreaking in their own way, the theory was very elegant but the concepts were likely beyond what most of them, except for Alice, were capable of understanding. His fingertips could move at several times human speed, and they had a number of extra senses, including the ability to feel magnetic fields and refract light and gauge temperature to within a hundredth of a degree.

He had something of a cult of personality going among the sub-librarians, Penny went on, and a number of them had arranged for their own hands to be—painlessly, hygienically—removed and replaced with magical prostheses to match his. Plum was finally on the point of asking him about Connecticut when they arrived at a room that could have been a ballroom at Versailles, an immense expansive space with windows along one wall and the wall opposite paneled in books, two stories high, traversed by one spindly rolling ladder.

Penny was back to playing the host. It was a role he obviously enjoyed.

"Stand back against the windows. That way you'll get the full effect."

They did, and they did. Taken as a whole the spines of the Fillory books formed a faint, ghostly outline which even Plum recognized as a map of Fillory itself, the size of the entire wall. Each book did its part; the blues were the ocean, and the pale greens and browns were the land. Up close Plum never would have seen it, but now looking at them all together she couldn't see anything else.

"Beautiful," Quentin said.

"So can we look at the books?" Plum asked.

It was a measure of how much the power had shifted since Alice punched him that Penny pursed his lips with distaste but then nodded, reluctantly.

"Just . . . don't reshelve them. Please. Leave it to the professionals."

It was hard to know where to begin. Eliot didn't even move.

"Penny," he said, "you're the expert on the Neitherlands. What happens when a world ends?"

"Pretty much what you'd expect. The land dies. Over time the world disintegrates and ceases to exist."

"What happens here? I mean, what happens to the fountain?"

"Oh, it dries up. Falls into disrepair. It's a mysterious process, but consistent with the integrity of the Neitherlands as a whole, so we allow it to happen."

"Here's what I'm wondering: could the tail wag the dog, so to speak? What if you repaired the fountain? Rebuilt it or replumbed it or what have you? Would that bring a dead world back to life?"

Penny thought for a minute, his lips moving silently. He walked the length of the ballroom and then back to where the rest of them stood.

"It's not as stupid as it sounds," he said, "but no. You couldn't bring it back that way. You could wag the tail, but the dog would still be dead."

Eliot nodded sadly.

"That was my last idea. I didn't really expect it to work." The fire had gone out of him. "Look, this is going to take forever. Let's just go straight to the fountain."

"I need to do something first," Plum said. "Watch this: a magic trick."

She'd seen it almost as soon as they walked in, she was just waiting for her moment. Plum walked right up to the enormous wall of books, feeling very small with the ranks of them towering above her. There was one narrow gap, a thin space where a single volume was missing. She took her great-grandfather's memoir out of her bag.

Penny's face went slack when he saw it.

"The Door in the Page," he said, in a childlike voice. "It's the Holy Grail of Fillory books. The last and rarest one. I've been hunting it for so long."

She went to slide it in, paused, reflected, turned it the other way up, then shelved it. It fit perfectly, not just the size but the pattern: the spine was the perfect shade of a pale green, with a band of light blue near the top to fill in the last bit of the Lower Slosh, and a sliver of the Burnt River to go with it. It was so satisfying, like finishing an enormous jigsaw puzzle, that her fingers tingled, and she involuntarily let out a breath.

She was playing her part in the Chatwin story now. No more lingering in the wings, she was onstage, in the thick of it. She'd done what she could: she had brought Rupert home, or as close as he would ever get.

"Hey—Penny, is it?" Plum said. "That ought to pay for Quentin's library fines, don't you think? Or Alice could just punch you again, it's all good."

But Penny's attention was completely occupied by his new acquisition. He went trotting up to it—half running across the shiny ballroom floor—and slid it gingerly out again, touching only the upper edges of its pages in order to spare the spine. He let it fall open and sniffed the paper.

"How did you get this?"

"Stole it."

"We tried to steal it too."

"I know," Plum said. "From us. Next time try harder."

The failure didn't appear to sting Penny. He looked like a little boy with a new puppy. It was weird: he was obviously an asshole, but he wasn't a sociopath. He had feelings—in fact from the way he held the book it looked like he had an enormous capacity for love. He just wasn't very good at loving people, apart from himself.

Only Eliot looked grave.

"I just thought of something," he said. "That was the last book. The wall's full. The map is finished. That must mean the story's over, Fillory's history has been written. The apocalypse must have already come."

"You don't know that," Quentin said.

"Yes, I do," Eliot snapped. "And don't try to make me feel better."

Could it be true? The idea made its way through Plum in a cold ripple. All this time, all her life really, she'd been thinking about Fillory, dithering about it, hiding from it. Fillory and the Chatwins and the fatal longings they represented had been her dark side, and she'd tried to pretend they didn't exist. She'd wanted to have one side only, like a Möbius strip. A Möbius person.

But that was a mistake. She was starting to suspect that facing up to the nightmare of the past is what gives you the power to build your future. She was ready to face it, thought perhaps she might even quite like to face it, that there might be not just danger but joy and love in facing it—and just like that she'd lost it forever. She should have done what she'd told Quentin to do with Alice (totally correctly by the way): she should have met it head-on and made her peace with it when she could. Now she'd never have the chance. The books in front of her looked subtly different now. They'd gone from being about the present to being about the past.

Or had they? Maybe they had. But maybe that was giving up too easily. Fillory didn't feel dead to her, that was the thing. She could still sense it out there, just the other side of the thin partition that stood between this reality and the next. If she pressed her ear to it she could still hear Fillory singing to her, however faintly.

"The wall isn't actually full, you know." She cleared her throat—it was dusty in this damn library. "Not necessarily. You could run another row of books under there, along the floor."

She pointed. There was still space under the lowermost shelf.

"You certainly could not," Penny said.

"Well, you actually could, if you wanted to."

Fillory! she thought. We're coming! Just hold on a little longer! It was as if just by convincing Penny she could keep Fillory alive.

"I think you're looking at this too literally," Eliot said.

"Maybe you're not looking at it literally enough," Alice said, startling everybody, possibly including herself. "Those two walls are empty. And there's space between the windows too."

"It would be very irregular." Penny folded his arms, his gilded hands glowing with indignation. "But more to the point it makes no sense. The map is complete. There is no more Fillory."

"That's not completely true," Quentin said. "There's a whole bunch of outlying islands. Like Outer Island would be over there"—he pointed—"if you wrapped it around the corner of the room."

"And Benedict Island, I suppose," Eliot said, reluctantly picking up the thread. "That's way the hell over there. And who knows what there is on the other side, the west side."

"There's a whole other continent," said Quentin.

Plum couldn't tell if they were arguing for the sake of arguing or if she had a real point, but Penny was looking around the room uncertainly, as if the walls were crawling with insects. She even felt a little bad for him.

But not so bad that she shut up. Never let it be said Plum was without a plan. She wouldn't let Fillory be dead. It wasn't getting off that easily. No more hiding. The two halves of her life would become one.

"You could do the night sky!" she said. "The stars! You could have a bunch of navy books with silver dots on them. You could do that thing where you hang them from the ceiling!" She favored Penny with her most winning beam. "You love that thing!"

Penny was not a man much used to being beamed at. It had an effect.

"It's not complete," he said, half to himself. "It's not nearly complete. We're going to need more books, a lot more. Quentin, you have to save Fillory."

"That's what I keep saying," Quentin said. "And I think I've figured out how. I think I finally know how to fix everything."

CHAPTER 29

H istorically speaking," Alice said, "when people have said that they've almost always been wrong."

Quentin loved having Alice alive again. It was absolutely the greatest thing ever. Whether or not she loved him, whether or not she could stand the sight of him, the world, any world, was just so much better with her in it.

"What are you going to do?" Eliot said.

"Something stupid. Penny, where's the Fillory fountain from here?"

It had come over him slowly, but he'd been pretty sure for a while now. It was something Alice said. He'd been thinking about Fillory, trying to picture its dying agonies, what it would look like—but of course he knew what a dying Fillory would look like. Alice had told them. Alice had seen Fillory's beginning, and the end of the world that came before it. The dead ocean, the dead land, the dying god. Even if he wasn't completely sure how to do it, he knew what to do.

Of course it was also true what Alice said about people who thought they could fix everything, and it was quite possible that he was about to get himself killed for nothing, but he was going to try, and now was the time. It was six Neitherlandish blocks from the library to the Fillory fountain and they took it at a run. The Neitherlandish moon, which was small and strangely squarish, like an old-fashioned TV screen, was low in the sky ahead of them. As he ran Quentin felt that he was at the heart of a vast cosmic drama, as if the universe had chosen very briefly to turn around just him. Everything was happening at once but very slowly, as if time were both speeding up and slowing down at the same time. He noticed little details: the outlines of things, the texture of the stones, glimpses of water in canals, shadows in windows. Everything depended on his doing this right.

The Fillory fountain was in the shape of the titan Atlas struggling under the weight of a globe, which was a bit of poetic license since Fillory wasn't a globe at all, it was flat. Quentin had planned to hurdle the rim without breaking stride and hope Fillory's security was completely shot by now, but instead he pulled up short, because as he got closer to the fountain he saw that someone was getting out of it.

It was Janet, and she had Josh and Poppy right behind her. Janet and Poppy pushed themselves briskly up and over the side, as if they'd just completed Olympic dives; Josh threw an arm and then a leg over and sort of rolled out onto the pavement. Their clothes dried instantly, but their faces stayed shocked and haggard.

"It's over," Janet said. "Fillory's dead."

The words glanced harmlessly off Quentin's mind. It wouldn't let them in.

"Quentin, we just watched it," Josh said. "It was horrible."

The others straggled up behind him, in the darkness of the square. It was the first time in seven years that the five original Physical Kids—Eliot, Janet, Josh, Alice, Quentin—were in the same place at the same time, but the mood wasn't celebratory.

"What happened?" Eliot said. "What did you see?"

Josh and Janet were staring at Alice.

Janet grabbed her hand. Josh hugged her. Poppy, in the spirit of the moment, grabbed her other hand, even though they'd never actually met before.

"Oh my God," Janet said. "Oh my God, Alice."

"I know," Alice said gravely. "But just tell us."

"OK. OK." Janet didn't let go of her hand; it was like she needed a lifeline to hang on to. "The sun fell down. Everything started fighting everything else, even the trees. It was terrible. Then Julia came back from the Far Side and sent us back here."

"Shit." Eliot looked up at the night sky and shouted: "Shit!"

The city sent him back a faint echo.

"Where's Julia?" Quentin asked.

"She must have stayed behind."

Janet couldn't meet his eyes.

"So that's it?" Plum said. She looked as stricken as the rest of them did. Quentin stepped up to the fountain. If he was going to try, he'd better try.

"Quentin, stop," Janet said. "It's dead."

"In that case I'll view the body."

"There's nothing there."

"The fountain's still here. There has to be something left."

"No, there doesn't," Janet said. "And there isn't. Please, Quentin."

Even as she said it the statue of Atlas in the fountain began to move. It bent forward slowly and reached up to the enormous black marble globe it supported on one shoulder. It was preparing, at long last, to set its burden down.

"Hey!" Quentin said. "Not so fucking fast!"

If Fillory was going to be dead it was going to have to prove it to him personally, to his face. He side-vaulted over the rim into the water—it should have been cold, but it was hot and getting hotter. Probably in a few minutes it would start boiling away to nothing. Josh grabbed his arm, but Quentin shook him off. Atlas glared at him, but even though he was twice as tall as Quentin and made of stone he must have seen something truly murderous in Quentin's face because he straightened up a little and grudgingly shrugged the globe back into position.

Everybody was shouting at him.

"Don't be an idiot, Quentin!" Janet yelled. "For once!"

"Quentin, don't," Eliot said. "You don't have to."

"But I do."

Quentin fumbled awkwardly in his coat pocket for the button while trying to tread water at the same time. Somebody had his arm again, and he tried to jerk away, but at the same moment his finger touched the button and the bottom dropped out.

Once again he was free-falling down toward the magic land of Fillory. He never thought he'd see it again. It made him feel almost painfully tender—after all this, everything that had happened, Fillory was taking him back. The whole country was spread out below him, and he was inbound like a deorbiting space capsule.

He definitely never thought he'd see it like this. Far to the west he caught a smeary glimpse of a crash-landed sun like an egg yolk on a skillet, melting and burning in a steaming, boiling sea at the edge of the world. He had a close booming fly-by with a massive object which he only realized after it was gone was the moon itself, spinning low and off its axis. Fires blazed and dark armies surged across the surface of the world. Something colossal was slowly surmounting Fillory's rim, peering up over it with its enormous curious face: one of the great turtles that formed the foundation of the world, coming up at last to have a look at what it had been carrying on its back all these thousands of years. Fillory, his beautiful Fillory, was ruined and dying.

But it wasn't dead. Not quite. Not until there was nothing left.

Then he was down. The ground shook under his feet, and the air was full of rumbling and tearing and distant cries and the smell of smoke. Burning ash from somewhere whipped by on a hot wind.

His arm: someone still had hold of it. It was Alice.

"What are you doing?" he shouted over the noise.

"Being an idiot," she said.

She actually managed a slight smile, her first of the new era. He smiled too.

"Come on then. We have to find Ember."

The button had set them down outside the city gates of Whitespire. The wall around the city was half collapsed, and one half of the great gate hung askew. Some of the towers of the castle still stood, for now, but they were swaying. Quentin pointed to them; Alice nodded. There was no way they'd find Ember in all this unless He at least halfway wanted to be found, and if He wanted to be found at all that's where He'd be.

"I'll do shields, you do speed," Alice shouted.

They spent an intense minute casting on themselves and each other, then they held hands and ran through the gate together.

The streets were deserted. The town looked like it had been bombed, and the inhabitants were either dead or gone or huddled in their cellars. Quentin and Alice ran carelessly, bounding along with exaggerated magical strength. Sometimes they cut through ruins and leveled lots to save time; once a tremor sent a teetering wall of stone flopping down heavily right onto them, which would have killed them if Alice's spellwork hadn't been top-notch. Instead it just slammed them face down into the dust, and they shrugged off the heavy blocks and picked themselves up and caught their breath and ran on.

They didn't slow to a walk until they were passing under the portcullis and through the thick outer wall of Castle Whitespire; it was the first time he and Alice had been there together. They stepped out into the courtyard. It had been the longest of long shots—a dot in the shark, Eliot would have said—that Ember would be there waiting for them.

And He wasn't. But Umber was.

Quentin had never seen Him before, and until a week ago he'd thought Umber was dead, but it couldn't have been anybody else. He stood quite still, like a tame ram in a meadow, His head down as He cropped a stray weed pushing up between two paving stones, in the twilight of the dying world. He straightened up.

"I've been waiting for you," He said, between chews. "For ages. I made a bet with myself that you'd come, and now look. I've won."

Quentin hadn't planned for this, but he supposed one was as good as the other, for his purposes. But Umber seemed to know what Quentin was thinking.

"Well, come on. It's no good with just Me. You're going to need Us both."

Umber tossed His horned head at them, come-hither. Under any other circumstances Quentin would have hesitated, but on this day of all days His meaning was unmistakable. Quentin jogged over to Him and, as he'd imagined doing ten thousand times before, at least, he threw an arm and a leg over Umber's broad soft back and heaved himself up onto it. Alice climbed on behind him and put her arms around his waist. The instant Quentin had his fingers wound into Umber's cloudy gray wool the god surged forward under them and they were off.

Quentin had always wanted to do this—they all had—and now he knew why. After a few trotting steps to get up to speed Umber bunched all four legs together under Himself and leapt the castle wall, like the cow jumping over the moon. The rush and acceleration were beyond anything. He picked up speed as He bounded through the crumbled city and out of it, touching the ground ever more lightly and at wider intervals, trees and fields and hills and walls and rivers whipping past.

There was a strange fateful joy to it. The scene was catastrophic, his mission could not have been more dire, but Quentin Coldwater had come back to Fillory with Alice, and together they were riding a god.

"Hi ho!" Umber said. And Quentin answered Him:

"Hi ho!"

He still remembered the childish love he'd felt for the two rams, back before he'd known Fillory was real. It hadn't lasted: he'd met Ember in person, and He wasn't anything like as strong or as kind or as wise as Plover had made Him out to be. Then when Ember had thrown Quentin out of Fillory his disillusionment had tipped over into anger. But since then he'd learned a few things about acceptance, and his anger had cooled, even if the love hadn't quite returned. Now he saw the rams as They were: strange, inhuman, somewhat ridiculous beings, as limited by their godhead as They were empowered by it. But They were divine, and There was a majesty to Them that was undeniable.

Even as Quentin felt Umber's strength beneath him, Fillory was losing the last of its own strength. Its glorious greenery was withering away before their eyes. They passed men and animals bunched together in shivering packs, no longer even fighting, like the remnants of a party that had got out of control and been shut down and broken up by the police, leaving the celebrants suddenly sober and chagrined. Acres of trees lay knocked down and uprooted. Overhead the stars were beginning to fall, one by one, some in rapid arcs like meteors, others more slowly and gracefully, twirling and sparking and pinwheeling down.

Alice hugged him tight. A series of deep booming cracks sounded, like distant artillery fire, signaling that the land itself had begun to disintegrate. It was losing cohesion, losing even the strength to hold on to itself. Great crevasses opened in Fillory's surface, and widened into canyons, and in the depths of the deepest of them Quentin could see all the way down to the pale struggling dead of the Underworld, writhing in a mass like larvae inside a rotten log. Now Umber's great gallop found them hurdling enormous gaps in the land, which grew wider and wider until in places nothing connected the component shards of Fillory at all, and Quentin began to see stars between them. They were leaping from island to island in the dark of space, flying as much as jumping, soaring through the void.

He saw where they were heading. A single fragment of land lay dead ahead of them, an uprooted divot of enchanted turf with just a field and a pond and a tree, orphaned in the disaster, no longer linked to anything at all. On it, alone, stood Ember.

Umber touched down lightly and trotted away His excess speed. Quentin and Alice slid off. Quentin was just thankful that Alice was with him. She believed in him, or she once had anyway. That would make it easier to believe in himself during what was coming next.

Ember stood staring down at the pond, a round pool bristling with bullrushes around its edge, eyes locked with His reflection. His face was unreadable as ever, but there was something lonely about Him, something despairing and abandoned, as His world came apart around Him. For the first time Quentin felt a little sorry for the old ram.

"Ember," he said.

No answer.

"Ember, You know what You have to do. I think You've always known, since the beginning."

Quentin knew. He hadn't put it all together till those last moments in the library, but it had been coming to him, slowly, for much longer than that. He'd been thinking about parents and children and power and death. After his father died Quentin had gained a new kind of strength, and Mayakovsky, with his own kind of sacrifice, had given him a new strength too. That's what parents did for their children. Then Alice told him the story of how Fillory began. It began with death, the death of a god.

It was the oldest story there was, the deepest of all the deeper magicks. Fillory didn't have to die, it could be renewed and live again, but there was a price, and the price was holy blood. It was the same in all my-thologies: for a dying land to be reborn, its god must die for it. There was power in that divine paradox, the death of an immortal, enough power to restart the stopped heart of a world.

"It's time, Ember. The bird isn't coming. The spell is gone. This is the only way left."

The old ram blinked. He could hear Quentin.

"I'm not pretending it's easy, but You'll die anyway when Fillory dies. You know this. There must be only a few minutes left. Give Your own life now, before it's too late. While it still matters."

The truly sad thing was that Ember actually wanted to do it. Quentin saw that too: He had come here intending to drown Himself, the way the god before Him had, but He couldn't quite manage it. He was brave enough to want to, but not brave enough to do it. He was trying to find the courage, longing for the courage to come to Him, but it wouldn't, and while He waited for it, ashamed and alone and terrified, the whole cosmos was coming crashing down around Him.

Quentin wondered if he would have been brave enough. He would never know. But if Ember couldn't sacrifice himself, Quentin would have to do it for Him.

He took a step forward. He was a man proposing to kill a god. It was an impossibility, a contradiction in terms, but if it meant saving Fillory then there had to be a way. He held on to that knowledge tightly. If magic was for anything it was for this. He'd faced up to his dead father and Mayakovsky. He'd faced losing Fillory and losing Brakebills. He'd even faced Alice. He was circling back to all the things he'd fought and lost over the years, and one by one he was putting them to rest. Now it was time for him to face Ember.

He took another step and now Ember turned on him. The god's eyes were wild, blank with panic. His nostrils flared. Ember was out of His mind with fear. Quentin felt a surge of pity and even of love for the ridiculous old beast, but it didn't change what he had to do.

He'd hoped inspiration would come to him, but it didn't. It came to Alice instead.

"Your turn this time," she said, and then she did something strange: she bit the back of her left hand, scraping skin off the knuckles, and then touched Quentin's cheek with it.

It wasn't a spell Quentin knew, or would ever know—the technicalities were too much for him, and the raw power too, probably, but he'd seen Alice do it once before. As she chanted the words his arms burst with masses of muscle, and his skin thickened and toughened at the same time. He felt the special force that belonged to Alice's magic alone transforming him. His legs exploded with strength, he was rising upward on two pillars, and his neck lengthened and the base of his spine flowed out into a long sinuous tail. His head was stretching forward into a snout, and his flat grinding omnivore's teeth grew and sharpened until they interlocked with each other, the way teeth were always meant to do.

His nails sprouted into claws. His vertebrae threw up a ridge of spines—it was like his back being scratched only even better. He was made of power, and there was a furnace in his belly. He opened his mouth and roared a word, and the word was made of fire. He was a dragon, and he was ready. He was going to blast the immortal living shit out of Ember.

The fire bent and flowed around Ember's horns, but it scorched Him too—Quentin smelled the burning wool. Maybe as His world crumbled the god was losing some of His imperviousness. Well, bad luck. Quentin bounded forward, and Ember bolted, but it was all slow motion to Quentin's draconian reflexes. He pinned Ember to the ground with one massive taloned forefoot—none of your puny *T. rex* arms for this dragon—and tried to get his jaws around Ember's thick muscled neck while the god writhed frantically in his grip. Quentin's scales, he couldn't help but notice in passing, were the shiny metallic blue of a bitchin' muscle car.

He was a dragon, not a god, but he was huge and tough and strong, and this body was made for epic scrapping. Whereas Ember, for whatever divine reason, was a god with the body of an animal that occasionally took part in ritualized male dominance contests but spent most of its time grazing. Ember rolled and flipped Quentin over Him, Quentin lashing his tail crazily, hoping Alice was well clear. Then he was on top again.

"Enough!" Ember roared, and Quentin was blown back into the air. Spreading his wings—his wings!—like an angry angel Quentin checked his flight and power-dived back at the god, who dodged before Quentin could crush Him. They circled for a minute, pacing, the pond spouting steam whenever Quentin's overheated tail touched it, then he darted forward again and had Ember in his teeth. Lightning struck his back, once and then three, four, five times, jangling his nerves and blowing off half a dozen scales, and probably crippling his delicate bat-wings, but pain was something a dragon noted only in passing and then dismissed with contempt.

Any love or pity he might have felt for Ember was a human thing. There was no room in his dragon-heart for any such feelings. This was a job for a monster, and that's what he was now. Die, he thought. Die, you selfish bastard, you miserable coward, you old goat. Die and give us life.

Now he had a proper grip, and he held on and ground Ember between his molars like a cheap cigar, and the air bleated out of Him. He held on for Alice, for Eliot, for Julia, for Benedict, for his useless hopeless father, for everyone he'd ever loved or disappointed or betrayed. He held on out of pride and anger and hope and stubbornness, and he felt what was left of Fillory holding on too and waiting to see if it would be enough. Quentin blew white-hot fire between his teeth, and his saliva was toxic acid. The ram's ribs bent and groaned, and Quentin felt Him try to inflate His lungs, felt Him fail. He tasted burned skin, and he felt the skin tear.

Quentin held Him there, and when the ram had gone five minutes without a breath he spat Him out onto the ground. He'd done all a dragon could do.

Suddenly Quentin was human again, standing over the steaming, smoking body of the ram, flopped out on the grass like a sleeping dog the size of a bull. But it wasn't over. Ember's foreleg stirred. He was beaten, but some tenacious spark of life was refusing to leave His body. If Fillory was going to live Quentin would have to tear that spark out of Him and quench it.

This was what the knife was for, he realized, the one Asmodeus had gotten away with. Shit. Fate had practically shoved it into his damn hands, and he'd fumbled it away! He was in a fight with a god and he had no weapon.

Except that he did have one. Sometimes when you finally figure out what you have to do, you discover that you already have what you need. He'd always had it. Quentin felt around in his pocket, and his fingers found a thick round coin. Mayakovsky's last coin.

This was the last of his inheritance. He felt a twinge of sadness, just a twinge, at the knowledge that he would never make his land now. That would have been nice. But he felt no bitterness.

What Quentin did now he'd already done once, a long time ago, but then he'd done it in anger and confusion. Now he did it calmly, with a full sense of who he was and what he was doing. He still had some nickels in his pockets, the ones he'd brought back from the mirror-house. He went to one knee and made a little stack of them on a patch of bare ground, and on top of it he balanced the golden coin, goose-side up. Then he gripped the stack in his fist and it became the hilt of a burning silver sword, which he drew up out of the ground as if it had been embedded there all along, placed there for him centuries ago.

He held it up in front of him. The last time he'd held it had been on the day he arrived at Brakebills.

"It's good to see you again," he whispered.

Pale, almost transparent fire played along its length, surprisingly bright in the eerie half-darkness, as if the sword had been dipped in brandy and touched with a match. He adjusted his grip on the hilt. He tried to remember something, anything, from his fencing lessons with Bingle.

Ember's eye half opened, but He didn't stir. Maybe He couldn't. But if Quentin had had to put a name to what he saw in Ember's eye it would have been not fear, or rage, but relief. Quentin felt it too.

"I'm sorry," he said.

The sword cut almost all the way through Ember's thick neck in one stroke. The wound opened wide instantly, red and wet, the skin snapping back like taut rubber. The god's legs went stiff and sprang apart like a marionette with its strings pulled. Blood sprayed and then pumped from the stump.

Quentin felt Alice's hand on his shoulder. He took a shaky breath. It was done, Ember was dead. An age had ended; Quentin had ended it. It didn't feel like an exalted business—there was nothing grand about it. It hadn't felt noble and righteous, it felt rough and ugly and bloody and cruel. It was what was necessary, that was all. Quentin stepped back from the god's corpse.

Something big rocketed across the sky, and he looked up in time to spot a fat, stubby spacecraft already dwindling in the distance, an iron fireplug riding an inverted cone of blue flame. The dwarfs, if he had to guess. Always full of surprises. There were only three or four stars left, and even as he watched one of them lost its grip on the heavens and fell. Behind him a throat was delicately cleared, as if to alert an inattentive waiter.

"Everyone forgets about Me," Umber said. "As I said, you'll need to kill Us both. We were only ever really one god, between the two of Us."

He trotted over to Quentin, as meek as you like, sniffed fastidiously at His brother's corpse, and then stretched out His neck. He even waggled His shoulders a little, in anticipation, as if the operation were going to give Him pleasure. What a perverse creature. Quentin steadied himself and tried to think of all the good that Umber could have done but hadn't. Maybe the next god would do better. This time the sword stroked cleanly, all the way through.

The instant Umber died, Quentin exploded. He dropped the sword. He felt himself racing upward and outward—he was blowing out in all directions. His arms and legs stretched out—a hundred miles, a thousand. His view expanded to take in all of Fillory: he saw it hanging there in space in front of him like a shattered saucer. He was a phantasmal giant, a cosmic blue whale times a billion.

He wasn't disconcerted, but only because gods don't disconcert easily. The logic was clear to him, because the logic of everything was clear now. There was nothing that was not self-evident. A god could die, but a god's power did not, and without Ember and Umber to wield it their power had flowed into the one who sacrificed them. Therefore he, Quentin, was a god now, a living god, the god of Fillory. He was no longer Fillory's reader; he had become its author.

But what a broken world had been entrusted to Him! He shook His great head disapprovingly. Even now it continued to disintegrate before Him, its connective tissue weakening, its edges crumbling. This would never do. It must be mended. Mending was something Quentin understood well, and with the power that was in Him now there was nothing broken that He could not fix.

With a wave of His left hand He slowed the passage of time to a crawl, so that to everyone but Him the work of a millennium would pass in a fraction of a second. Then slowly, deliberately, and with inexhaustible patience, He began to gather up the pieces from where they hung and drifted in space. He collected the clods and clumps and grains of soil and stone that had been the flesh of Fillory, sorted them like the pieces of a jigsaw puzzle, and one by one fitted them together and knitted them back into a single whole, running His huge spectral fingertips along the seams until they vanished as if they had never been.

He worked with great care. The dirt of Fillory was marbled like a great side of beef, and He took pains to position its veins of ore so that they lined up just as they once had. He rethreaded Fillory's silver rivers and streams, or where it pleased Him He allowed them to find new paths, and He gently shepherded the shattered lakes and seas back into their basins. He swept up the air and the winds and heaped them up in invisible masses above Fillory so that the land could breathe again.

As He worked He rolled and sifted between His divine fingertips the remains of various objects He remembered from His human life. Odd little things, from long ago. The bones of the gentle bay He rode when He left the centaurs. The fragments of the Watcherwoman's shattered watch, which had been trodden into the earth over the years and dispersed and forgotten. The pistol Janet had brought into Fillory and then dropped on her way out of Ember's Tomb. The head of the arrow that killed Benedict. The last rotting remnants of the *Muntjac,* scattered in the shallows of the far Eastern Ocean.

Those animals and humans who had died in the apocalypse He allowed to rest where they were, but He moved among the survivors, healing them, rebuilding damaged organs, repairing and resewing skin and bones. He bade the great turtle return to its place in the tower of turtles that held up Fillory, and take up its burden again, and it did—it really wasn't suited for a more active lifestyle anyway. He rounded up the escaped dead and returned them to their gymnasium Hell and then, feeling divinely troubled by their plight, He bade them sleep, peacefully and forever. Their games were over for good.

He set the delicate green carpet of grass that covered Fillory to regrowing, and restored some of the trees, stepping them like the masts of ships, not all, but enough that they could reseed the forests. He spent a long time—years, maybe centuries—setting the seas to beating at the shore again, and nursing the water cycle into some kind of stable functioning state. He picked up the bodies of Ember and Umber with tender care and buried Them where They could decompose and enrich the soil around them. The ground above Them became green, and two enormous trees grew over Their graves, their branches spiraling curiously like rams' horns.

The moon He lovingly polished and set spinning again. One by one He rehung the stars like the crystals of a chandelier. He filled in the great crater that the sun had burned in the ocean floor, and He cooled the sea, and rebuilt and remortared the wall that ran around the edge of the world. He took the sun itself in His great cupped hands, pressing and molding it back into a sphere, feeling its fading heat. He blew on it till it burned white hot. Then He placed it back on its eternal track and set it going in its orbit again.

He rested. He looked at His work, watched it tick and turn like a great watch, here and there smoothing a rough edge or roughening a smooth one, slowing a torrent or urging on a tide, till all was in balance. When there was nothing else to mend He simply gazed at it, felt its atoms circulating and combining or simply shivering in place, and He subsided into a grand peace. Fillory lived again. It wasn't what it had been, yet, but it would be once it had healed, and that it could do without His help. He could have watched it forever.

But it was not for Him to do so. He had been given custody of this power, but He sensed that it didn't belong to Him. Wistfully, but not regretfully, He restored time to its customary rate of speed with a wave of His right hand. As His last act, a divine whim really, He retrieved the remains of the White Stag from the gullet of the giant snapping turtle of the Northern Marsh, fused its skeleton back together, reconstituted its organs and its skin, and restored it to life. He placed it on an island far out to sea to begin its wanderings again. The next age of Fillory would have a Questing Beast too.

Then He allowed the power to leave Him. As it did so He shrank and shrank, the tiny disk of Fillory rising up to meet him and then stretching out endlessly around him, until he stood on it again as just one more of its inhabitants.

He wasn't alone. When he was a god the particular names of Fillory's many inhabitants hadn't greatly concerned him, but now he was in the company of a woman and a demigoddess, and after a few seconds their names came back to him. They were Alice and Julia.

CHAPTER 30

Y ou let go of the power," Julia said.

Dawn was breaking over the raw, ragged, still-healing horizon, and he was losing it all already, everything but the faintest, most transparent memory of what it had meant to be a god. He savored the very last of it—the certainty, the power, that sense of total knowledge and well-being and control, forever and ever. It evaporated from his mind and was gone. It wasn't the kind of memory that a mortal brain could hang on to.

He was just Quentin again, nothing more. But he would always know that it had happened, that he'd known what it was like, both for a few seconds and, in the life of a god, a thousand years.

"I let it go," he said. "It wasn't mine."

Julia nodded thoughtfully.

"You're right, it wasn't yours. A more jealous god, or a more jealous man, might have tried to keep it, though I think the outcome would have been the same. Thank you for doing that, Quentin, for mending Fillory. I might have done it myself, but the fiddly stuff like coastlines always takes me ages. I don't have the knack for it. Also I thought you might enjoy it."

"Thank you. I did. Or I think I did." Already he wasn't crystal clear on what exactly he'd enjoyed.

She was recognizably her old self, still the Julia of Brooklyn, or directly descended from her, with her freckly face and her long black hair. But at the same time she was unmistakably divine: her height had been somewhat variable in the past, but at the moment she was seven feet tall. She wore a rather dramatic dress that wouldn't have looked out of place at a presidential inauguration, even though it was made of equal parts bark and green leaves.

"Walk with me," Julia said.

They walked, the three of them together. Fillory was Fillory again, though it was a wan and wasted Fillory, waking again piece by piece after its catastrophic illness. The meadow was still brown, the ground still dry and cracked. The new age was still in its first minutes.

Quentin was light-headed. He still had the blood of Ember and Umber on his shoes. It was hard to connect the brutal, bloody thing he'd just done with the renewal of Fillory. But this world was rudely, potently alive again, you could feel it.

"I have a question," Alice said. "Julia, why didn't you kill Ember yourself? I mean, it all worked out fine in the end, but you would have done a quicker job than we did."

"I might have. But there would have been no power in it. A demigod slaying a god . . . even if I could have managed it, those are not the terms of the ritual."

"Still, you seem more godly now than you did when I last saw you," Quentin said. "More divine. Am I wrong?"

"You're not wrong. I was made queen of the dryads. I'm a bit more than a demigod now—more of a three-quarters god. There ought to be a word for it."

Now and then Julia would brush a dead plant with her fingers, absent-mindedly, and it would straighten up and become green. When she pointed at a fallen tree its roots would come to life and grip the ground again, and it would pull itself up hastily as if it had been caught napping on the job. Quentin couldn't figure out how she decided which ones to revive. Maybe it was random; maybe some trees were more deserving than others.

"I'd like to do something for you, Quentin," she said. "On behalf of Fillory. You did us a great service today, and you've always served us well. Is there something here that you've never seen or done, that you've always wanted to?"

Quentin thought for a minute. He'd picked up the silver sword and was

carrying it, but a little awkwardly since for whatever reason he hadn't managed to summon a sheath to go with it, and he was leery of touching the
pale flames that licked along its blade. He stuck it in the ground and left it
there. Probably he'd be able to summon it again, if he ever needed it.

What did he want? It was a lovely gesture, but as far as he knew he'd
been everywhere in Fillory, or everywhere that was worth going. He
didn't feel especially interested in the dwarf tunnels, or the Fingerling
Islands, or in the tourist attractions of greater Loria.

But wait. There was one thing.

"Can you show me the Far Side of the World? Show us? Alice should
come too, if she wants."

"Of course."

"It's not like I haven't already been there," Alice said. "As a niffin."

"True," Quentin said. "I forgot. You should get a different reward."

"I'll save mine. This is for you. I'll stay here for a while."

So Julia took Quentin's hand, and they rose up together and flew west
out over the coast of Fillory, faster and faster, across the sea and then over
the wall at the rim of the world and down, head down, in a great curving
roller-coaster swoop. Soon Quentin became aware that his point of view
had changed, that without having turned around they were rising up
rather than diving down. Gravity had turned around. They surmounted
another wall and then they were looking out over the Far Side.

Julia paused, hovering. For him it would have been exhausting, but
for Julia flying was nothing, and as long as he was with her it was nothing
for him too. Her large hand encased his completely; the feeling reminded
Quentin of being a child. It was twilight on the Far Side; the sun had just
set there as it rose on Fillory. He couldn't see much, just hushed fields and
valleys. The difference was subtle, but even from this distance it was
quieter and more intense than Fillory—richer in whatever made Fillory
magical, more densely infused. There was an air of excited expectation.
Curious little motes of light sparkled in the dusk, like tiny glowing gnats.

"I can't show you everything," Julia said. "Not even I have those
permissions. But there's something in particular I think you might like."

When they moved the wind moved with them, so that the air around
them remained still as they flew. Down below there were dark rivers and

pale chalk roads. Quentin spotted what might have been an elaborate tree house in a forest, and a castle on an island in a moonlit lake.

"Are those fireflies?" he asked. "The lights?"

"No, the air is just kind of sparkly here. It's a thing. You don't notice it during the daytime."

Tiny lights were bobbing along in their wake, too, streaming out behind them, like the phosphorescent trail of a ship in a tropical sea. The sunset was in different colors from a terrestrial or even a Fillorian sunset: it ran more to greens and purples.

She set them down in the center of a grand, rambling garden. It must once have been laid out according to a precise design, like a French formal garden, all ruled lines and perfect curves and complex symmetries. But it had been left to go to seed, shrubs overflowing onto paths, vines winding themselves lasciviously through wrought iron, rose beds dying off into withered brown traceries, exquisite in their own way. It reminded him of nothing so much as the frozen community garden he'd wandered into long, long ago in Brooklyn, chasing the paper note that Jane Chatwin had given him, before he came out the other side and into Brakebills.

"I thought you'd like it. Of course it was different when it was new, but then when it started to get overrun everyone thought it looked better this way, and they let it go. But it's more than a garden, it's deep magic. Keep your eye on one spot and you'll see."

Quentin did, and he saw. Slowly, but far faster than they would have in nature, some of the plants were dying and reviving, crisping up before his eyes and bursting back into bloom, rising up and sinking down in slow motion, making tiny crackles and whispers as they did. It made him think of something, but he couldn't quite place it.

Julia could.

"Rupert mentions it in his memoir," she said. "We call it the Drowned Garden, though I don't know why. The plants aren't just plants, they're thoughts and feelings. A new thought happens and a new plant springs up. A feeling fades away and the plant dies. Some of the more common ones are always in bloom—fear, anger, happiness, love, envy. They're quite unruly, they grow like weeds. Certain basic mathematical ideas never go away either. But others are quite rare. Complex concepts, extreme or subtle emotions.

Awe and wonder are harder to find than they once were. Though there—I think those irises are a kind of awe. Once in a while you even see a new one."

The peace in the garden was inexpressibly calming. It made Quentin never want to leave, and at the same time he supposed that that feeling was itself manifested in vegetable form somewhere in the garden. He wondered where, and whether he'd know it if he saw it.

Julia stooped to one knee—an awesome sight, given the scale of her divine frame.

"Look. This one is very rare."

Quentin knelt down too, and a few of the sparkly motes gathered around them helpfully, for illumination. It was a humble little plant, fragile, a fledgling shrub with a few sprays of leaves—a Charlie Brown Christmas tree. As Quentin watched it wobbled, losing heart, and its leaves browned and spotted, but then it caught itself, filled out again and stiffened and even grew an inch. A couple of seedpods sprouted from its branches.

He recognized it. It was the plant he'd seen drawn on the page from the Neitherlands, and again in Rupert's spell. He'd given up on ever finding it, and now here it was, right in front of him. Julia must have known. All unexpectedly his eyes were full of hot tears, and he sniffled and wiped them away. It was ridiculous, crying over a plant—he hadn't cried when he killed Ember—but it was like seeing a loyal old friend he'd never even met before. He reached down and touched one leaf, gently.

"This is a feeling that you had, Quentin," she said. "Once, a very long time ago. A rare one. This is how you felt when you were eight years old, and you opened one of the Fillory books for the first time, and you felt awe and joy and hope and longing all at once. You felt them very strongly, Quentin. You dreamed of Fillory then, with a power and an innocence that not many people ever experience. That's where all this began for you. You wanted the world to be better than it was.

"Years later you went to Fillory, and the Fillory you found was a much more difficult, complicated place than you expected. The Fillory you dreamed of as a little boy wasn't real, but in some ways it was better and purer than the real one. That hopeful little boy you once were was a tremendous dreamer. He was clever, too, but if you ever had a special gift, it was that."

Quentin nodded—he couldn't quite talk yet. He felt full of love for that little boy he'd once been, innocent and naive, as yet unscuffed and unmarred by everything that was to come. He was such a ridiculous, vulnerable little person, with so many strenuous disappointments and wonders ahead of him. Quentin hadn't thought of him in years.

He wasn't that boy anymore, that boy was lost long ago. He'd become a man instead, one of those crude, weather-beaten, shopworn things, and he'd almost forgotten he'd ever been anything else—he'd had to forget, to survive growing up. But now he wished he could reassure that child and take care of him. He wished he could tell him that none of it was going to turn out anything like the way he hoped, but that everything was going to be all right anyway. It was hard to explain, but he would see.

"Someone must be feeling it now," Quentin said. "What I felt. That's why it's green."

Julia nodded. "Someone somewhere."

Though even now the plant shrank and dried and died again. Delicately, Julia pinched off one hard seedpod and straightened up.

"Here. Take this with you. I think you should have it."

It looked like a seedpod from any ordinary plant anywhere, brown and stiff and rattly, but it was unmistakably the one from the page. He'd have to find a way to show it to Hamish. He put it in his pocket. The plant didn't seem to mind. It would grow again, sooner or later.

"Thank you, Julia." Quentin dried his eyes and took a last look around. It was almost night. "I think I'm ready to go back now."

They found Alice where they'd left her, but she wasn't alone now. The others had come through while he was off on the Far Side—Eliot, Janet, Josh, Poppy—and they were standing around talking animatedly about plans to rebuild Castle Whitespire. Penny had stayed at his post in the Neitherlands, but Plum was there. She was off by herself, just looking around and trying to take it all in. She was seeing Fillory for the first time in her life. Quentin caught her eye, and she smiled, but he thought she probably wanted to be alone with it for a few minutes.

He remembered the first time he saw Fillory. He'd cried his eyes out in front of a clock tree. Not much chance of Plum doing that, but still: he'd give her some time.

"No more spinning," Janet said. "That's all I ask. The spinning thing was always bullshit. I don't know how the dwarfs sold them on that in the first place."

"I hear you," Eliot said. "I'm not arguing. We'll take it up with them when they get back. If they come back."

"But listen, what about the color?" Josh said. "Is that on the table? Because I gotta tell you, the white never did it for me. A bird took a crap on that thing, you could see it a mile away. I know Castle Blackspire was a house of unspeakable evil or whatever, but you have to admit it looked pretty badass."

"What about the name, though?" Poppy said. "We'd have to change that too."

"Ooh, good point," Josh said. "I guess we can't live in Castle Mauvespire or whatever. Or could we? Hi, Quentin!"

"Hi, guys. Don't let me interrupt."

They didn't. They kept talking, and he just listened. It was good seeing them all together in Fillory again, it made him happy, but there was a distance between him and them now too: a thin, almost undetectable gap, even between him and Eliot. They never would have admitted it—they would have hotly denied it if he said anything—but the truth was that he wasn't quite in the club anymore. He would always be part of Fillory, especially now that he'd held the entire world in his temporarily divine hands—it would always have his vast, invisible fingerprints on it, forever, like the paths of spiral labyrinths. But he knew his place too, and he was starting to think it wasn't here. He'd come back one day, or he hoped he would, but they were the kings and queens now.

He had a different role to play. Maybe he and Alice could be a club. He walked back to where she stood talking with Julia.

"It's too bad James never made it here," Quentin said. "He would have liked it. I sometimes wonder what happened to him."

"Hedge fund, Hoboken. He'll die in a skiing accident in Vail, age seventy-seven."

"Ah."

"Wait," Alice said. "But does that mean you know how we're going to die too?"

"Some people's deaths are harder to predict than others. James is easy. Yours I can't see. You're too complicated. Too many twists and turns left to come."

The first dawn was over, and the sun was up now, and Quentin had the distinct feeling it was getting to be time to go. He never thought he'd leave Fillory again, not of his own free will, but he understood now, with steadily increasing keenness, that he wasn't where he was supposed to be. Not yet. He had a bit farther to go.

"Julia," Quentin said. "Before I leave I should tell you: Plum and I ran into an old friend of yours. She called herself Asmodeus."

Quentin knew this might be hard for Julia to hear, but he thought she would want to know.

"Asmo," she said. "Yes. We were friends, back in Murs."

"When we found Rupert's suitcase, the one with the spell in it, there was a knife there too. She took it. She said it was a weapon for killing gods. She said to tell you she was going fox hunting."

"Oh, I know." Julia's great goddess's eyes had become distant. "I know all about it. Did you ever notice how Asmo always had a little more information than she was supposed to? That was me, keeping an eye on her. I didn't want to be too obvious, but I made sure she found what she needed."

"What about Reynard?" Quentin said. "Do you know if she caught him?"

"Caught him?" Now she half smiled, though her eyes remained at the same distance. "She gutted him like a furry red fish."

Quentin hoped that a three-quarters-goddess wasn't so lofty and divine that she couldn't enjoy some bloody and well-deserved revenge. He didn't think she was. He was enjoying it just by association.

Plum joined them. She was ready to talk now.

"This is kind of amazing." She still couldn't stop staring at every-thing; she held up her own hands and wiggled her fingers, as if she were looking at them underwater. "I mean, really amazing."

"Is it what you expected?"

"It is and it isn't," she said. "I mean, so far all I've seen is a whole lot of trees and grass. I haven't gotten to any of the exotic stuff, so it's not like it's that different from Earth. Except for you," she added, to Julia. "You're different."

"How do you feel?"

"Floaty, sort of. If that makes any sense. But in a good way. Like something incredibly interesting could possibly happen to me at literally any second."

"Do you want to stay?" Julia asked.

"I think so, if that's all right. For a while at least." Julia inspired a certain instinctive deference even in Plum. "I like it here. I feel whole."

"I'm sure they can put you up in Whitespire," Quentin said, "or whatever's left of it."

"Actually I thought I might pay a visit to my great-aunt Jane. It's way past time I got to know that side of the family, and I'm pretty sure I'm the only relative she's got left. I don't know, maybe she'll teach me how to make clock-trees. From what I hear about her I think we might get along."

Quentin thought she might be right. It was all beginning for Plum— he could almost see the plans forming in her head—but it reminded him again that for him things were ending. A cool breeze blew through the clearing. He wondered if Alice would come with him.

"I keep thinking about something," Alice said. "If Ember and Umber are dead, and Quentin's not the god of Fillory anymore, then it must be somebody else. But who? Is it you, Julia?"

"It's not me," Julia said.

Alice was right, the power must have gone somewhere, but Quentin didn't know where either. He'd felt it flow out of him, and he could tell that it knew where it was going, but it hadn't told him. If not Julia then who? Probably it was one of the talking animals, the way it had been before. The sloth, maybe. The others were listening—they wanted to know too.

"Fillory's always had a god," Quentin said. "It has to be someone."

"Does it?" Julia said. "When you were a god you mended Fillory, Quentin. You don't remember it, but you did. You did it well. Fillory's in tune now—it's perfectly balanced and calibrated. It could run on its own for a few millennia without any trouble at all. Maybe Fillory doesn't need a god right now. I think this age might just be a godless one."

A Fillory without a god. It was a radical notion. But he thought about it, and it didn't seem like a terrible one. They would be on their own this time—the kings, the queens, the people, the animals, the spirits, the monsters. They'd have to decide what was right and just and fair for themselves. There would still be magic and wonders and all the rest of it, but they would figure out what to do with them with nobody looking over their shoulders, no divine parent-figure meddling with them and helping or not according to his or her divine mood. There would be nobody to praise them and nobody to condemn them. They would have to do it all themselves.

The cold wind was blowing steadily now, and the temperature was dropping. Quentin hugged himself.

"Fillory will have you, though," Alice pointed out.

"Oh, I spend most of my time on the Far Side," Julia said. "I'll look in now and then. Fillory will have to make do with a part-time three-quarters god, but I have a feeling that will be enough. Things are different now. It's a new age."

"A new age."

It was very different. Very new. Fillory was a land reborn, and he'd been there, he'd assisted at the birth, but he wasn't going to see it grow up. He looked around: it was all really ending, the great love affair of his youth, and it was as if he were already gone, and he was seeing Fillory without him in it. Somewhere along the way he'd finally outgrown it, the way people always said he would. Long or short, great or terrible, Fillory's new age would happen without him. He belonged to the last age, the one he'd just ended with two strokes of a sword. This age would have its own heroes. Maybe Plum would be one of them.

Time to go, before he lost his composure in front of everybody. Eliot was staring up at the sky. It was covered over with a thick blanket of cloud.

"Oh, thank God," he said. "Or whatever the appropriate expression is now. Finally."

Out of a sky blank and pale as a clean sheet of paper, white snow began to fall. The flakes settled on the warm ground and melted there, like a cool hand on the forehead of a feverish child. The long summer was over at last.

CHAPTER 31

A week later Quentin and Alice stood together in the fourth-floor workroom of Plum's townhouse in Manhattan. A door to somewhere else stood in front of them. They felt neither comfortable nor uncomfortable with each other, or maybe they felt both at once. They both knew each other and they didn't. They were old lovers, and they were practically strangers.

It was just them now. Everybody else had stayed behind in Fillory.

"Are you sure you didn't want to stay too?" Alice said, frowning at him doubtfully. "I mean, obviously you're not a king anymore, but I'm sure you could have. Eliot would have loved it, and there's no Ember and Umber to kick you out anymore, and they never would anyway. Not after everything that happened."

"Really. I'm sure. This feels right."

She shook her head.

"I still don't get it. Back in the day you were the biggest Fillory weenie around."

"That is true. I was a huge Fillory weenie."

"I have this awful feeling," Alice said, "that you left for me. And/or that you left because you're pissed that you're not a king anymore."

"I'm really not pissed about it. At all. It wasn't that." He was a bit surprised himself at how untempted he'd been. "Fillory is who I used to be, but I'm somebody different now."

"I admit that you might possibly not be deluding yourself about that. Though it does beg the question, who the hell are you?"

"I could ask you the same question."

She considered that.

"Maybe the answer's in there," she said.

Alice indicated the door. It wasn't a grand or even particularly unusual-looking door, though it was handsome enough: tall and narrow, made of weathered wood painted a pale green. It was the kind of thing you'd find leaning up against the back wall of a vintage furniture store.

"Well," she said, "if we fuck up our lives completely we can always go crawling back to Eliot."

"Right," Quentin said. "We'll always have that."

She narrowed her eyes at him.

"You do know we're not going out anymore, right?"

"I do know that."

"I don't want you to have the wrong idea."

"I really don't have any ideas at all. Right or wrong."

That last part wasn't strictly true. He had a lot of ideas, of both kinds, most of them about Alice. But he could keep them to himself for a little longer.

As soon as he was back in New York Quentin had thrown himself right back into the process of making a new land. He knew right away that he was going to try it again. He'd thought that particular dream was gone forever, after he used the last of Mayakovsky's coins, but now that he had the seedpod from the Far Side it seemed worth a try at least. He didn't have Rupert's book anymore, or the page either, but he was pretty sure he knew them by heart; at this point he doubted he could forget them if he tried.

And he had Alice to help him. She seemed content to stay in the townhouse for now, and even seven years out of practice she was a better magician than he'd ever been, or ever would be. She kibitzed.

Whatever came out of it, it was good for him and Alice to have a project to do together. It took some of the pressure off. It was a chance to get to know each other again, and for that matter for Alice to get to know herself again. She still had a lot of healing to do, and they needed something to talk about that wasn't of life-or-death importance, some-

thing to bicker over, something concrete to focus on other than their
own bruised, confused feelings.

Maybe nothing would come of it, but Quentin thought it was worth
finding out, and he thought it wasn't impossible that Alice thought so
too. It was pretty clear to him now that if she'd ever loved him, back
then, it wasn't just for the person he was, it was for the person that he
might one day become. Maybe that's who he was now.

When they finished casting the spell, and the dust and smoke cleared,
there was a brand-new door on the far wall of the room. They studied it
for another minute. There was no hurry.

"The door knocker," she said. "Nice touch. Was that you?"

Quentin looked closer. He was going to have to get new glasses, his
eyes were getting even worse. But sure enough: it was in the shape of a
blue whale's tail.

"Remind me to tell you about that sometime."

The whale seemed like a good sign. He walked up to the door and
opened it. Cool white sunlight spilled through. It wasn't another ghost
house; this world had a proper outdoors. His first impression was of
cool, sweet air and a dark vegetable green.

The curse was lifted. They really had made a land, alive and brand
new. A bird called. He stepped through.

"Atmosphere's breathable," he said.

"Dork."

She joined him.

"So this is your secret garden," Alice said.

The weather wasn't much: a trifle brisk and with clouds moving in.
They were looking down an orderly corridor of trees, fruit trees: there
really was an orchard this time. What they could see of the sky contained
three moons of various sizes, like stray marbles: one white, one pale pink,
and a tiny bluish one.

"You are going to have some freak-show tides," Alice said.

"If there's even an ocean," he said. "And I wish you'd say 'we' and not
'you.' We made this together, you know."

"It's your land, Quentin. It came out of your head. But I like it here.
Looks like Scotland, sort of."

"Want an apple? Or whatever these are?" They were hard and round and red anyway.

"I really don't. Feels like I'd be eating your fingernail or something."

They strolled through the orchard and stepped out into open country. Quentin's land was an uneven land, covered with grassy humps and hillocks like ocean swells. They passed a copse of thin trees that resembled aspens, but with their trunks woven together more like banyan trees. The clouds were curious shapes, not cumulus and cirrus, new varietals of cloud that didn't occur on Earth. Something shot through the air overhead with a fast whirring sound, leaving a fleeting impression of gray feathers, but they turned their heads too late to catch it.

"Interesting," Quentin said.

For no particular reason there was a rainbow low above the horizon. Alice pointed it out.

"Nice art direction. Bit of a cliché, but nice."

"Like I'm sure your magic land is totally original."

Alice booted a pebble.

"You'll have to think of some clever secret way kids can find their way in here," she said.

"That should be fun."

"Don't make it too easy, though."

"No, not too easy. And not for a while." He took her hand; she didn't take it back. "I want us to have it to ourselves for a bit."

Their cheeks were turning red, and they had to stop and warm each other up with spells to keep going. Then they resumed tramping along, over short bristly grass, through sprays of tiny phosphorescent wildflowers that shut up frantically when they got too near, like sea anemones. It was a big country, bigger than Quentin expected: there were mountains in the distance, and soon they were skirting a sizable forest. When Quentin kicked up a clod of grass the soil underneath was smooth and rich as black butter.

Something tickled his breastbone, and he reached inside his jacket. His old Fillorian pocket watch: it was ticking. He thought it would never run again. It must like it here.

"Hang on, I want to do something."

He'd always half expected that the watch would turn out to have some sort of amazing magical power—turning back time, maybe, or slowing it, or freezing it, or something. It certainly looked magical enough. But if it had any powers at all he'd never found them. Funny how some things you're sure will pay off never do.

Slipping it off its chain, he approached a tree on the edge of the forest, this world's answer to a beech tree, and placed the watch against its trunk and pressed. After a moment's hesitation the tree accepted it: the watch sank into the smooth gray bark as if it were warm clay and stuck there, embedded, still ticking. He left it there. A homemade clock-tree. Maybe it would breed more.

Quentin recognized this land and yet at the same time he didn't. Could this be home? He didn't see any reason why not. But it was a strange, wild country. It was no utopia. It wasn't a tame land.

He'd come a long way to get here. He was very far from the bitter, angry teenager he'd been in Brooklyn, before this all started, and thank God for that. But the funny thing was that after all this time he still didn't think that that miserable teenager had been wrong. He didn't disagree with him—he still felt solidarity with him on the major points. The world was fucking awful. It was a wretched, desolate place, a desert of meaninglessness, a heartless wasteland, where horrific things happened all the time for no reason and nothing good lasted for long.

He'd been right about the world, but he was wrong about himself. The world was a desert, but he was a magician, and to be a magician was to be a secret spring—a moving oasis. He wasn't desolate, and he wasn't empty. He was full of emotion, full of feelings, bursting with them, and when it came down to it that's what being a magician was. They weren't ordinary feelings—they weren't the tame, domesticated kind. Magic was wild feelings, the kind that escaped out of you and into the world and changed things. There was a lot of skill to it, and a lot of learning, and a lot of work, but that was where the power began: the power to enchant the world.

They walked and walked, and they kept waiting for the land to end (how? A bottomless cliff? A sea? A brick wall?) but it went back and back and back. It was a lot more than a hundred acres. Some weather was coming on: they could see it advancing down the valley, clouds trailing smudgy gray rain.

"I didn't realize there would be so much of it," Quentin said.

"How deep do you think it goes?"

"I have absolutely no idea."

They passed a tree stump that must have been ten yards across. They climbed over a fence (built by who?) using a stile. Wind rumpled the grass and pushed at the trees; the leaves seemed to turn pale when the wind blew, until Quentin realized they just flipped over in the breeze, showing their white undersides.

He caught the deep thump of hooves, and a rustling and snapping in the trees. Something big was coming. Alice heard it too.

"What the hell is that?" she said.

He didn't know. Some monster that had escaped out of his unconscious, into this pristine new land? He hoped they weren't going to have to fight, he'd had enough of that for now. It was coming at them through the forest, and he could see disturbances in the canopy as whatever it was bulled its way closer. He looked back: they'd never make it back to the door in time. He couldn't even see it anymore.

Out of the woods, leaves spraying and branches springing back in its wake, burst an enormous equine beast. It was a horse the size of a house. It came trotting up to them and stopped a few feet away, breath steaming, as if it were awaiting their pleasure. Quentin's head was just about level with its massive, balding knees.

It was unquestionably a horse, a chocolate-colored horse, complete with a black mane and glossy, watery brown eyes as big as bowling balls. But it appeared to be covered in something softer than horsehair—it looked like it was part horse, part sofa. In fact—

"Is that velveteen?" Alice touched the thing's shin lightly.

"You know what?" Quentin said. "I think this must be the Cozy Horse."

"Has to be!" Alice's face lit up, and she laughed.

In all his time in Fillory he'd never once seen it. No one had, and Quentin had started to think it didn't exist, whatever Rupert said. It was easily the silliest single inhabitant of Fillory, a total nursery fantasy, but as it turned out it was extremely real. Uncomfortably real, even, to the point where it was currently blotting out the sky above them in an intimidating manner.

"But what's it doing here? Why isn't it in Fillory?"

The Cozy Horse regarded them dumbly. It wasn't going to tell. It flared its nostrils and gazed off over their heads in that supremely unconcerned way horses have. Quentin was pleased that it was here: he'd made a land, and the Cozy Horse's presence seemed like a stamp of approval.

"I have a theory about this place," Alice said. "Are you ready? I'm starting to think this land isn't an island after all, Quentin. I think it must go all the way through. You meant to make an island, but you also made a bridge. A bridge connecting Fillory and Earth. This big fellow must have come across it to welcome us."

She couldn't reach its muzzle so she patted its broad shin instead. Its coat looked worn in places, like that of a well-loved toy, and from below you could see it had a big stitched seam running along its tummy.

Alice smiled at him, and he noticed it again—that slight difference.

"Were your eyes always that blue?"

"I know," she said, "I saw it too. Do you think it's possible that you didn't put me all the way back? I've been wondering if I've still got a little niffin left in me after all. Just a touch. Just enough to make it interesting."

The Cozy Horse snorted at them, impatiently now, and tossed its massive head as if to say: Enough with the chit-chat, I've got places to be. Are you in or are you out?

"I always wanted to ride it," Alice said. "Where shall we go? To Fillory?"

"I don't think so. One day. But not yet. Let's go further."

"Let's."

"I never pictured it this big," Quentin said.

"Me neither. How the hell are we even going to get up there?"

He looked up at the Cozy Horse. It was the strangest thing, but he was looking forward to everything so much, he could hardly stand it. He never would have believed it. He never thought he would.

"You know what?" He took Alice's hand. "Let's fly."

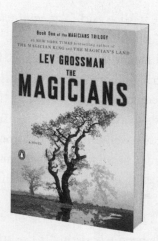 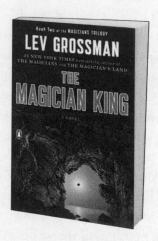